How to
Change your life

Rosie Milne lives in Hong Kong.
This is her first novel.

How to Change your life

ROSIE MILNE

A Pan
Original

First published 2002 by Pan Books
an imprint of Pan Macmillan Ltd
Pan Macmillan, 20 New Wharf Road, London N1 9RR
Basingstoke and Oxford
Associated companies throughout the world
www.panmacmillan.com

ISBN 0 330 48907 0

1 3 5 7 9 8 6 4 2

A CIP catalogue record for this book is available from
the British Library.

Typeset by Intype London Ltd
Printed and bound in Great Britain by
Mackays of Chatham plc, Chatham, Kent

In memory of JG

and for JP

PROLOGUE

Ginny was kneeling by her triangular, glass-topped coffee table, contemplating the scattering of books and papers which lay across it, and gnawing on her nails. After a moment she removed her hand from her mouth and reached for her fags. These were on the floor, next to a cafetière designed for one. She lit up. As soon as she sensed nicotine leaching into her bloodstream she leant across the table to pick up the list she'd compiled months back, before the fog of yearning she'd been living in for years had solidified into a strategy – Project Pregnancy, or Project P, for short. She knew this list by heart, but she re-read it anyway:

> *Cat? – Cat smell, fleas, dead birds.*
>
> *Dog? – Dog smell, fleas, walks.*
>
> *Other pet? – Boring.*
>
> *Man? – Fuck off, A.*

'A' stood for Adam. Ginny wrinkled her nose. She needed a steadying breath before she could carry on reading.

> *Woman? – Not a lesbian.*
>
> *Baby?*

This last item made Ginny laugh, and the noise echoed slightly in her cavernous sitting room. Here, the wooden floor was uncarpeted and the big windows were hung with metallic blinds. It was spring and the windows were open today, to let in air mostly laden with petrol fumes, but also hinting at apple blossom, newly mown grass and hope. The sounds filtering up from the street were of sirens and horns, but Ginny heard lambs bleating, chicks cheeping, calves mooing. Spring. The season when a young woman's fancy turns to reproduction.

'Baby,' Ginny said aloud, and the smile she permitted herself was secretive and intimate. It lingered on her face as she tossed the sheet of paper back onto the table – she didn't bother to read what was on the reverse, a second list she remembered just as well as the first:

Sperm bank? – Too bureaucratic/difficult.

Personal ad? – Too dangerous. Don't want to be murdered.

Old friend/lover? – Fuck off, A.

*Adoption? Here? Third World? – Too bureaucratic/
Can you do it if you're single?*

Stealing/kidnap? – Might be caught.

Some man?

Ginny's knees were getting stiff, so she shuffled backwards and levered herself up onto her sofa, a seductive looking thing, all brushed aluminium curves and smooth black leather, but very uncomfortable. Next, she reached for the cafetière, and her mug. The coffee had stewed, it was strong and black and bitter. Her eyes widened slightly at the first jolt of caffeine. Some Man. He was the only item on this morning's agenda. Ginny had already worked out a highly specific set of requirements which he must meet, and somewhere on the table was her summary:

Tall.

Good-looking.

Healthy.

Married.

A father.

'Tall' and 'good-looking' had been easy. So had 'healthy'. And Ginny had tried to convince herself health was linked to marriage. She had a pathological fear of pathogens, a morbid horror of morbidity, a virulent objection to viruses. But Project P demanded dirt – grimy, unprotected sex. There was no way she could ensure Some Man was germ free. Nevertheless she'd argued that, taken as a group, married men would *probably* be less risky on the HIV-syphilis-herpes scale than unmarried ones, because they were *probably* usually faithful to their wives, who were *probably* usually faithful to them. She wasn't happy about risking her life to three *probablies*, and recognized that, considered as a prophylactic, marriage was not as foolproof as a condom, indeed, a married Some Man, would, of necessity, be an unfaithful man. So it was lucky, really, that the benefits of marriage were not solely health related. A married man, she'd told herself, would have too much at stake, too much to lose, to get in deep with her, thus saving all sorts of complexities in the long term.

So much for the first four entries on Ginny's list. 'A father' was there because she'd read all about falling sperm counts; there were two or three alarming press cuttings amongst her Project P papers. The bogey of deformed or immobile sperm had convinced her that Some Man must have a relevant track record. Of course, that a man had already fathered children didn't guarantee he could do it again: who could doubt a father was more likely to have had the snip than a non-father? Ginny had briefly considered the feasibility of asking Some Man straight up, 'Have you had the snip?', but introducing the subject of birth control would carry its own dangers. She could just imagine the conversation.

> *Have you had the snip?*
>
> *No. Should we use a condom?*
>
> *NO.*
>
> *Oh. So are you on the pill?*
>
> *Yes.*
>
> *So why did you ask if I'd had the snip?*

It was impossible, but, perhaps, not as impossible as finding Some Man in the first place. Although she had two much younger half-sisters, Ginny thought of herself as an only child – there were no siblings to introduce her to Mr Right. Most of her friends had been Adam's friends, and she'd cut herself off from them when he'd gone. There was no workplace in which she could carry out a surgical snatch and grab raid. Thus for the past two or three months she'd been trusting to luck, and was averaging a one-night stand every three weeks. The sex simply wasn't regular enough, and the men were all so unsuitable. Take last night: she'd gone into the Eagle for a rum and Coke and come out with a guy who was short, fat and pimpled. Also wheezy. On the other hand he'd worn a wedding ring and mentioned an adult daughter living in Birmingham. But he'd been more inebriated than she'd realized. When he'd apologized and mumbled this had never happened to him before she'd not bothered to try to dissuade him from leaving. Despite her contempt, he'd taught her something: in the matter of finding Some Man, it was more than time to give fate a helpful nudge.

Ginny put down her coffee, and stretched across to the table, this time for a pad of lined paper and a pen. As she did so, she knocked a book to the floor – *Getting Pregnant* by Dr L.L.O. Case, obstetrician, gynaecologist. Ginny didn't just fret about diminishing sperm counts, but also about her own fecundity. She was thirty-two. Not old, but old enough not to take her ovaries and other pelvic innards for granted. She'd bought *Getting Pregnant* because the blurb promised it contained strategies for increasing her chances of conception, but when she'd tried to read it, she'd found it infuriating.

Chapter 1. Emotional Fitness. Are You Emotionally Ready for a Baby? *Shit, yes*, she'd thought and skipped to chapter two. Chapter 2. Physical Fitness. Are You Physically Ready for a Baby?

Ginny hadn't wanted a lecture on giving up caffeine and smoking, so she'd slammed the book shut before getting to Dr Case's useful advice on tracking ovulation, which was contained in chapter three.

Getting Pregnant made a soft thud as it hit the floor. Ginny didn't pick it up, but gave the cover an envious glance. It showed a heavily pregnant woman walking along a deserted beach. One day, Ginny would be that woman, but not until she'd found Some Man. By now, the pad of paper was on her lap. She picked up her pen and wrote, PLACES TO MEET SOME MAN, in big letters across the top. This not only helped focus her thoughts, but also made the paper seem less dauntingly blank.

Church or something? she wrote after she'd been staring at the expanse of white for some time. Religion had never been her strong point, and she'd gone off it entirely after Adam had left her. He'd not gone for any reason she could understand, like for another woman, but to join a Buddhist community. He'd held her hand and told her he hoped one day to become a monk, either in this life, or in some subsequent reincarnation. He hoped one day, one life, or lack of life, to annihilate his self, to become pure absence, to flow into a universal consciousness. Or something. He'd tried to explain it all to Ginny, but she'd just looked at him with uncomprehending anguish, and wrung her hands.

Evening classes? she wrote next. New hobby? But she had no inclination to take up flower arranging, or Spanish, or anything much, really. Too female, she wrote, too dull.

Voluntary work? Ginny pictured herself serving soup to the homeless, but the homeless stank. Then she imagined herself reading to an old person, but old people also stank. Too female, she wrote again. Too demanding.

A job? Ginny had never had a career, instead picking up occasional work in the hazy world where media meets performing arts meets design – many of the men inhabiting this world were gay, and those that weren't were nobody's idea of potentially excellent gene pools. What job could she do? And where did people work? Factories? Offices? Schools or hospitals? She didn't think there were any factories in London. Schools were full of moaning teachers and violent kids. Hospitals were crawling with the sick. So it would have to be an office. But at least getting into one should be a breeze, even she knew offices were stuffed with temps.

Ginny did a double take. Temping? For her purposes it was a brilliant idea. She sat up straighter on the sofa, and plotted. She would sign up with an agency and the agency would send her all over the place. On each assignment she'd look out for Some Man. When she found him she'd engineer regular injections of the life-giving fix she required. Once pregnant, she'd dump him, and her stooge would never suspect a thing. It would never occur to him he was to become a father (again). There'd be no mess, she'd just fail to show up at the office one morning, and that would be that. Temps came and went. Nobody but Some Man would notice she'd gone, and he, being married, would never bother to try to trace her.

But how to find a temping agency? Easy peasy lemon squeezy. Ginny stood up and went through to the tiny kitchen, which opened off her sitting room. She hunted around until she found the *Yellow Pages*, laid it flat on the breakfast bar, flipped to the right page and let her fingers do the walking. An outfit called Office Angels had placed a display ad. Ginny grinned. She rather fancied herself as an angel.

1

Seraph was feeling far from heavenly when her office door surged open.

'Hi, Seraph,' said Benedicta. 'You were supposed to give me the cover copy for *How to Change Your Life* three days ago. Where is it?'

Seraph picked up a cheap ballpoint pen, and rolled it between her fingers.

'I'm just doing it.'

Benedicta glanced at Seraph's blank computer screen.

'Good. Then I'll expect it by five.'

Seraph and Benedicta both worked for a publishing house which Seraph, but not Benedicta, referred to as 'Bladder and Scrotum'. Benedicta, the marketing director, was thin, blonde, and socially confident. At the glamorous parties she attended she had never once been heard to mention she worked on books other than novels by celebrity authors. Seraph suspected as much. She was the self-help and lifestyle editor.

When Benedicta was on the warpath, the consequences of failing to obey her were far more enervating than jumping to it. After she'd gone Seraph waited until the air stopped vibrating, then yanked her keyboard over, and started tapping. As she tapped she kept her eyes on her screen, watching words flash up in time to the rhythm of her fingers: 'Do you want to change your life?' Yes, please! She paused to consider all the things she'd change if she could. A new body would be nice, one which curved rather than bulged. And a new brain to go in it, a brain which managed to be analytic yet poetic, rather than just plain chaotic. A new brain might bring with it a new set of memories, but would a new set of memories count towards changing your *life*, or would that count as changing *you*? Seraph sighed. Her job constantly tempted her to waste time. If you said it quickly enough *self-help* sounded so cosy, promising that sorting out your self would be just like sorting out your taxes. But what, after all, was the self? And how could it be helped? Seraph had no idea. Did anyone? Perhaps it was the mysteriousness of the self, coupled with the fact that her own life lacked style, which had caused her to re-christen her list hypochondria and astrology.

Seraph shook her head in an attempt to free it of metaphysics, and told herself to focus on the job in hand. She got back to writing the copy:

> Do you want to change your life? This book will show you how. Comprehensive and authoritative it offers step-by-step practical advice on regaining control over your life by:
>
> > transforming your relationships
> >
> > empowering your career choices
> >
> > creating wealth and managing your money
> >
> > living with a sense of well being – emotional, spiritual, sexual and physical.
>
> Here, at last, you will find a structured programme empowering

you to generate and manage the changes required to let you live your life to its full potential. Packed with inspiring real-life case studies, questions and answers and trouble-shooting information, reading this book will be your first step towards making all your dreams come true.

Cassandra Jones trained in psychodynamics at the Oran Institute in Cincinnati, and now lives in North London where she runs a personal coaching clinic. She lectures all over the world, and has helped hundreds of women overcome obstacles to self-fulfillment.

Seraph had not yet read *How to Change Your Life* – the script was buried somewhere in her overflowing in-tray – yet she was pleased with her work. In three paragraphs she'd managed to weave in a 'transforming', an 'empowering' and a 'full potential'. She'd also managed to use both 'comprehensive and authoritative' and 'practical step-by-step', phrases which always pleased Eddie. Since Eddie owned Bladder, Seraph spent a fair amount of time trying to please him, or, more realistically, trying to avoid annoying him. It was stretching things a little to say that Cassie lectured all over the world, but she was Welsh, had spent ten years in the States, and now lived in London. No doubt she had spoken, in public, in all three places.

Seraph clicked the PRINT button on her screen and sat back to wait for her printer to spew forth. Nothing happened. She clicked PRINT again, to no avail. She got up and stared at her printer. She jiggled the paper in the tray. A green light was winking by a button on the control panel, so she pressed it, but still the printer remained idle. All her strategies were now used up, and suddenly she felt desolate. Inanimate things were forever springing these surprises on her, and she sat down, hard, at a loss what to do.

Above Seraph's desk were several shelves warping under jumbles of books and rejected manuscripts, dead plants, dirty coffee mugs and other accumulated rubbish. After a few moments she reached up and pulled down a paperback at random – *Essential Astral Projection*, from Compass Press, a leading publisher of mind, body and spirit titles. Seraph habitually engaged in 'me too' publishing, which meant she waited to see which of the books published by her competitors made the bestseller charts, then published something very similar. As a result, most of her titles were behind the times by about a year – a fate bound to befall *Astral Projection in Half an Hour*, which Seraph had only just commissioned. She flicked through Compass Press' offering, which was illustrated with a few schematic line-drawings of spheres and cubes, pyramids and cones. She closed her eyes and tried to imagine herself as a shimmering sphere of pure consciousness. But she couldn't do it, and instead began to fret about the Bladder title. *Half an Hour* had been a compromise, Eddie had wanted *Astral Projection in Ten Minutes*, but Seraph hadn't thought anyone would buy that. She'd wanted *Astral Projection in an Hour*, but Eddie had thought an hour was too long.

Following the prompting of some mysterious law, Seraph's printer at last began to sputter, breaking her reverie. She tossed *Essential Astral Projection* across her office, onto a heap of similarly discarded books lying beneath her window. There was a pigeon on her window sill. Blast!

Seraph's sliver of office was on the ground floor of what had once been an elegant London town house, before it became a publishing house, and her window looked over what had once been an elegant square, before it became an urban pocket-park plagued by drunks, pigeons, office workers and traffic. It was almost November, and the trees were leafless, their branches forming stark, architectural patterns against a flat grey sky. There were relatively few pedestrians about on this cold, windy day, but the narrow road in front of Seraph's office was, as always, congested with cars, taxis and motorbike dispatch riders. Pigeons were everywhere. Seraph detested pigeons. Now she fantasized about feeding poisoned grain to the one on her window sill, and watching it keel over with a terminal squawk.

Perhaps the pigeon guessed her thoughts, for it flew off, and Seraph became aware that her printer had fallen silent, its job done. She pulled out her copy and quickly scanned it. *At last,* in paragraph two, was perhaps a little over the top, since nobody was waiting with baited breath for the publication of Cassie's book, but she decided to let it stand, and made only one or two minor corrections. Then she scrawled a quick note across the top: 'What about a fully opened sunflower as the cover illustration?' The fully opened sunflower was one of the vaguest, and hence most useful, of her small stock of standard cover-illustration suggestions, others being: a small child eating an apple; a doctor examining an elderly patient; a heavily pregnant woman walking along a beach; lovers entwined in soft focus; and a selection of aromatherapy bottles.

At last. How to change your life, at last. Seraph was thirty-eight, over halfway through her journey and not the person she'd set out to be. But who was that person? She could scarcely remember. An angelic being, for sure – blazing, incandescent, made of fire and light. As it was, she felt like a tub of cheap margarine. With a sense of inevitability, she reached over to her in-tray and dug around until she found Cassie's script for *How to Change Your Life*. The top sheet was blank, except for the title and a dedication: 'This book is for Natasha Crewe.' Seraph knew Natasha, slightly. She owned Hecate, a bookshop on the Charing Cross Road which specialized in women's wisdom and spirituality. Seraph briefly wondered about the relationship between book-seller and author, then turned to the contents list:

> *Part 1 – Bodily health.*
>
> *Part 2 – Sex and relationships.*
>
> *Part 3 – Of work and wealth.*
>
> *Part 4 – Self-image.*

Bodily health. Seraph knew she was letting herself down. She ate badly, although she was vigilant about forcing fish, vegetables and brown rice on her children. She never exercised, and was a good few pounds overweight. She drank too much. She was addicted to caffeine, which interfered with her sleep, even when the children didn't.

Sex and relationships. Go together like a horse and carriage. But for her and Nick the horse and carriage seemed to have become uncoupled. Seraph really didn't want to think about that just at the moment.

Work and wealth. Nick dealt with their wealth – he hid the bills. And her position at Bladder was roughly equivalent to that of an amoeba.

Self-image. The Seraph in Seraph's head was eternally twenty and eternally thin. Her breasts did not dangle. Her stomach did not flop. Her conversation was witty. Men and women alike found her alluring . . .

The phone rang. Seraph was grateful for the interruption.

'Hello. This is Iris Basham,' said a quavery voice Seraph had never heard before, but which instantly reminded her of lavender water, talcum powder and blue rinses. A few moments later she'd learned that Iris was a newly retired beauty therapist, with an idea for a book.

'Unwanted bodily hair,' enthused Iris. 'It's the great neglected subject. The great unmentionable. Unwanted facial hair, hairy arms, over abundant pubic hair—'

'Yes,' cut in Seraph, 'I get the point.'

'Don't think it's just women. You'd be surprised how many men came to me with hairy backs. Ears. Noses.'

'Mm-hmm.'

'Nowadays there's a really wide variety of depilatory techniques. It's no longer just a matter of creams, plucking, waxing or even electrolysis. Lasers are having amazing results –'

'I'm sure–'

'–on all types of skin. And so many people take foreign holidays. Good depilatory habits are essential for the swimwear season, don't you think?'

'Errr . . .'

'I could supply all the necessary photographs. I have a wonderful series of the Brazilian butt wax.'

'Lovely, 'said Seraph, 'but I think our sales team might have some qualms.'

'They could be convinced. There's nothing like it on the market.'

Seraph didn't like to point out there was a good reason for that, so she kept silent.

Iris waited a beat before speaking again. 'My provisional title is *Hair Today, Gone Tomorrow*. What d'you think?'

Seraph swallowed. 'Why don't you send me an outline of your ideas?' Naturally she only suggested this because she couldn't say piss off, and she regretted her circumspection even before Iris promised to pop something in the post without delay.

Despite focusing her attention on women with moustaches, Iris had succeeded in lifting Seraph's mood. There were worse things than being an editor. She was not, after all, a bikini-line waxer. Nor a colonic-irrigation operative. Nor a chiropodist. She was, after all, only thirty-eight. Roughly half her life was still to come, God willing. She was healthy. She had three awe-inspiring children, Tom, Daisy, and Luke. Snapshots of them were tacked all around her office: Tom playing with his grandfather's golf clubs; Tom giving Daisy a bottle; Daisy in her ballet tutu, wearing such a wistful expression it made Seraph want to cry; Tom and Daisy peering into a bundle of blankets which contained Luke. Tom, Daisy and Luke. God, how she loved them. And, oh God, how they'd rampaged through her life. Not that they'd got away with it without a fight. She still had her career. Okay, she'd never now be prime minister, she'd never discover a cure for cancer, but at least she wasn't a stay-at-home mum.

For a few seconds Seraph felt more cheerful than she had all morning, but then she remembered how much she paid Kate. Seraph's life would collapse without a nanny, and Kate, a competent Aussie with a diploma in childcare, was worth every penny, but she directly swallowed a huge proportion of Seraph's salary, and indirectly swallowed a bit more, because she lived-in from Monday to Friday and Seraph and Nick paid most of her living expenses. 'Of work and wealth'. Indeed. Seraph let her eye fall once more on the manuscript lying on her desk. It was about the size and thickness of a telephone directory, although far less tidy, and it seemed to pulse. Lub-dub, it went. Lub-dub, lub-dub, expanding and contracting with the rhythm of her heart. Time to start reading.

Seraph decided now was not the time to stop letting herself down, and riffled through Part 1, bodily health, until she found the introduction to Part 2, sex and relationships.

Introduction: Keep Talking – the power of communication

Good relationships depend on good communication. Communication is hard work. It involves both talking and listening. You must:

— let your partner know what you are thinking and feeling, and make sure you are understood
— listen attentively to your partner and let him or her know you have heard what he or she is saying

Communication is not:

— talking to your partner when he or she is not listening
— nodding when you have not heard what he or she is saying
— second guessing what your partner wants to say, or cutting him or her off in mid-sentence

Before you sit down for a serious discussion with your partner, you must identify your aims – what do you need, or want, from the discussion? You cannot expect your partner to read your mind. You have to know what you need in order to get it. If you don't know what you need, and don't ask for it, how is your partner supposed to know? Your needs are important, you deserve to be heard and your partner deserves to be given the chance to hear you. This means you must wait to tell him or her about what you need until you can have his or her undivided attention, for as long as you think the discussion will take. Choose a time when you are both in good moods, and well rested.

If all this seems very hard, remember that communication is all about courage. It takes courage to identify your emotions, fears and ambitions and explain them in a way your partner can understand. It takes courage to persuade your partner to do the same. It takes courage for you and your partner to listen to each other and respect each other's opinions and feelings.

Personally Seraph was all for silence. When she and Nick were newly in love, and they'd both still thought of him as a poet, there had, of course, been a brief, ecstatic tumble of words. Yadda, yadda, yadda, all night long. Well, perhaps not all night long, but certainly for hours on end: 'Omigod! So he's your all-time favourite author too!' And, 'Omigod! You'll never believe it, but I also happen to think that's the greatest film ever made.' And, 'Sure I vote labour.' And, 'God, I love that band.'

And there was the other stuff too. Emotions, fears, and ambitions. Yeah, they'd done all that. But since those early days Seraph and Nick hadn't gone in for talking. Perhaps it was significant that they'd first met in a library, where talking was officially discouraged, and the loudest noise was supposed to be that of dry pages rustling. This had been towards the end of their final year at university, where Nick had been reading English, and Seraph had been muddling through a degree in politics and economics. The day she and Nick first made eye contact across the ranks of shelves, Seraph was supposed to have been reading up on rational decision theory, whatever that was, but instead she'd whiled away an afternoon in reciprocated longing. Just before closing time, Nick had finally taken his courage in both hands and come striding down the aisle between his table and hers. He'd looked to her like some sort of Celtic prince, caught in a time warp, a long, bony man with a long face and long black hair. He'd walked with a graceful ease, and she'd thought he should have been wearing a kilt, and come striding out of swirling mists, sea drenched and wind whipped. In fact he was wearing ripped blue jeans, a white T-shirt, and grubby sneakers. When he'd drawn level with her he hadn't introduced himself, or made any sort of small talk, but had launched straight into 'To His Coy Mistress', by Andrew Marvell. 'Had we but world enough, and time, This coyness, Lady, were no crime.' By the time he'd finished, Seraph was lost.

Then, of course, had come the slight embarrassment of telling him her name. Charles and Meredith, her solidly earth-bound parents, were not given to romantic flights of fancy, but Meredith hadn't conceived until she was nearly forty, ancient by the standards of her generation, and when her much longed for child was a daughter, she'd been adamant that she must be named Seraphina. Seraph had always hated it, and, as an adolescent, had once gone so far as to make a stab at re-inventing herself as a Tracey, but nobody had been able to get used to the new identity, including herself.

'Wow!' Seraph had said when Nick had finished quoting Marvell.

Nick had raised one dark eyebrow. 'Hi,' he'd said. 'I'm Nick.'

'And I'm Seraph.'

'Seraph?'

'Short for Seraphina.'

Nick had laughed. 'Seraph and Nick . . . Old Nick. The angel and the devil.'

Seraph hadn't known what to say to that, so she'd kept silent. Nick had given her a lopsided smile.

'Now you have to come for a drink. We're fated.'

Neither of them had actually believed in fate, but so what? Nick had quickly decided his private name for Seraph would be Angel, although she'd never been able to bring herself to call him Devil. A few days after they'd met he presented her with 'On An Angel Laughing'. It was the first time anyone had ever written her a poem, and she'd been thrilled to think of herself as a muse. She'd thought all Nick's poems were luminous – but then, what did she know? Not as much as the literary editors of the struggling magazines to which he submitted his poems, and by whom they were invariably rejected. If she'd not been besotted with their author, she would have admitted this was not surprising, since Nick's pieces mostly read like pop songs, with pretensions. As it was, she berated the literary editors as fools, and lovingly tacked pages torn from Nick's spiral-bound notebook to the wall above her bed.

Twenty years on, give or take, Seraph shifted uneasily in her seat, and tried to remember when it was, precisely, that Nick had stopped calling her Angel. She sat quite still for a moment or two, with a glazed expression in her eyes, then she gave a start and made a conscious effort to bring her attention back to the script in front of her. She decided to give herself a break and skip the rest of Cassie's stuff on communication, so flipped over a few more pages, until her eye was caught by an interesting headline.

Rediscover Each Other

She let her eye travel down from this heading to the text beneath. The sex life of even the most committed couple has its ups and downs.

Ups and downs? Did Cassie intend a double entendre? Seraph reached for a pen, but her editing style was non-interventionist, and she decided to let it go.

> The sex life of even the most committed couple has its ups and downs. If you have been living together for a few years, you may start thinking of your bed simply as a place to sleep. You may both be relaxed about this. As relationships develop sex takes its place amongst other concerns, such as raising a family and progressing a career.

Yup! Thought Seraph.

> Problems arise only if one or both of you is unhappy that sex has slipped down the agenda. If this is an issue for you, remember that your partner cannot guess how you feel. You need to persuade him, or her, to put aside some time so you can talk about sex, and your attitudes towards it. It may help to know that very many couples experience mismatches of sexual desire. Once the problem is acknowledged, you can confront it together, and begin the process of rediscovering each other. This means looking at each other afresh as sexual beings.
>
> A first step might be to plan an evening which would allow each of you to see the other as a sexy date, as when you first met. It is very important that couples have fun together.

Fun? Seraph pursed her lips. Between three children and two careers, it was scarcely surprising she and Nick never had the time, or the energy, for fun.

Choose an activity which you both enjoy, and which will give you a topic of fresh, stimulating conversation for the next few days. Perhaps you could take in a movie, or try out a new restaurant, or go bowling.

Bowling? Seraph had never in her life been bowling, nor did she ever intend to give it a try. But, if not bowling, what? She couldn't think of an alternative. To her dating meant parties – writhing couples snogging in the dope-scented dark, while music pummelled the less fortunate, who were compelled to dance. That's how things had been before she met Nick, and stopped dating in favour of flopping in front of the telly with a bottle of red wine. Seraph didn't want to remember what it felt like to be one half of a snogging couple, so she carried on reading.

You may prefer to create your own fun and stimulation at home!

Seraph crossed out the exclamation mark.

Do not be afraid to book a time which you both agree to devote to sex. If possible, set up your bedroom earlier in the day. Make sure you have clean bed linen, and, if the weather is chilly, turn up the heating. If you enjoy background music, prepare a selection of your favourite tapes or CDs. Perhaps burn some incense. When the time comes, you and your partner can take a bath or a shower together, and can then give each other sensual massages. Aromatherapy oils have psychotherapeutic effects, which can be used to enhance your pleasure.

There then followed step-by-step instructions on massage techniques, and a chart summarizing the psychotherapeutic effects of aromatherapy oils. Seraph gave all this a cursory glance.

After your massage, you can let your imagination run riot!

This time Seraph crossed out 'you can', and left the exclamation mark.

If you need inspiration, any of the suggestions below could help put spice back into a love that has begun to lose its savour, although the list is not exhaustive.

Here it comes, thought Seraph. She had published numerous sex books, lumped together in her mind as one book, *The Handbag Guide to Sex*, and it was an unbreakable rule of the genre that each one contain a version of the list Cassie was about to present. Of course, Seraph had nothing against illuminating dark places but these lists always made her feel inadequate.

Be tactful and sensitive when introducing the idea of these activities to your partner. Nobody wants to be told they are boring in bed.

True, thought Seraph.

Never force your partner to try something about which he or she is reluctant, but remember that there is no such thing as perversion.

Seraph inserted 'between consenting adults'. Now the text read, 'but remember that between consenting adults there is no such thing as perversion.' Was this true? The question was beyond her, but as a sop to the possibility that it was false, she indicated that 'between consenting adults' should be inset in bold, then carried on reading.

> Human sexuality is about choice. As gourmets we all make choices from the sexual buffet laid out before us. Enjoy!

Bladder usually laid on a buffet at its sales meetings. Seraph thought of the food on offer. Ritz crackers spread with cream cheese, vol-au-vents filled with concentrated, tinned mushroom soup, sausage rolls containing dog food. Missionary position catering. She returned to the text.

> *Videos and magazines.* Why not watch a sexy video together, or look through a magazine? You will probably find the visual stimulation arousing, and may pick up some good ideas which you can incorporate into your own love life.

> *Fantasy.* Try sharing your fantasies with one another. It might not be wise to admit to having fantasies involving sex with someone other than your partner. (Indeed, thought Seraph.) But used sensibly fantasy can greatly enhance your love life. Do remember that some fantasies, especially of violence, humiliation or degradation, remain exciting only if they are restricted to the realm of the imagination.

> *Lingerie.* Lace or silk lingerie can be very arousing, for men and women alike, especially stockings and suspender belts. Choose underwear in one of the colours of the body, of flushed flesh, of pubic hair: red, pink, beige, cream or black.

> *New positions and places.* You don't need to be a contortionist to try out a few new positions now and then, perhaps using furniture, such as sofas and chairs, as props. If you always make love in the bedroom, try varying your routine and moving to the kitchen, or stairs.

Fetishes. Boots and shoes, leather and rubber, nappies and dummies. You name it, somebody is turned on by it.

Sex toys. A wide variety is available. Any sex shop will provide a sample of what is on offer, toys do not begin and end with ribbed condoms and vibrators.

Think oral, think anal. (But not at the same time, thought Seraph, getting out her pen to separate the two items on the list.) You may be shy about oral sex, but if you are prepared to experiment, you may find you both like it. The same is true of anal sex.

Bondage and S&M. These must be kept within safe limits, but between consenting adults (good, thought Seraph) everything from wearing a blindfold to lashing with a cat o'nine tails can act as a stimulus to pleasure.

If you require greater detail, there is a wealth of specialist sex education books and videos available. The internet is also a good source of information, products and contacts. Your family doctor will be willing to discuss sexual difficulties, if you think you need professional help.

Quite apart from arousing the usual feelings of inadequacy, Cassie's list caused Seraph to wonder – who wouldn't? – about the sex life of its author. Cassie was seriously fat, and Seraph found it difficult to imagine her indulging in any of the activities she'd recommended. On the other hand, her comment about the colour of lingerie was possibly revealing. Cassie's first book had been *Rainbow Power: A Guide to Using Colour for Emotional Healing.* Bladder had published it in black and white, and it hadn't sold. But no doubt its author knew more than most about the colours of seduction. Seraph herself would have been happy to wear lingerie in any shade, if only Nick would still buy it for her, as he often had in the pre-children days, but she felt ambiguous about some of the other suggestions. Her own fantasy was of crisp white sheets on a bed made by somebody else. She liked the missionary position, if not its catering equivalent. The thought of herself lashed to her bed, wearing high heels and a nurse's uniform was ridiculous. In any case, suppose you did ratchet up your sex life like this, how would you ever ratchet it back down again on the nights all you wanted was a cuddle? Or sex as a soporific?

Sex as a soporific? Seraph drew a sharp breath. Had things between her and Nick fallen so far that the best she could hope for from sex was that it would help her to sleep? Not a question she wanted to answer. But how could it have happened? She remembered their early days together, when bed had been a place of astonishment. Now it was a place of peripheral pleasure. Bubbles in the bath. Or worse, an aspect of household management – clean the lint from the tumble dryer, fuck the husband. And come to think of it, how long was it since they'd last fucked? At least a fortnight. Seraph tried to tell herself it was silly to hanker after passion and lust. But then it was silly to hanker after a cheeseburger when about to bite into a wholewheat sandwich filled with alfalfa, avocado, raw mushrooms and grated carrot. She'd go for the burger, every time.

And Nick, what would he go for? Seraph had never been much of a home cook, so it was fortunate, in a way, that Nick was a junk-food man. He'd choose the burger, with onion rings, fries and extra ketchup. He already had. No he hadn't. Yes he had . . .

Oh God! It was starting again, the endless, pointless, internal debate. Was or wasn't Nick having an affair? Seraph had been suspicious for weeks now, but had managed to suppress her suspicions until Amy had forced her to confront them more or less directly. Amy was Eddie's PA, and one of Seraph's closest friends. Whenever they could the two of them skipped the office for Café Beso, the coffee shop favoured by all the Bladder staff.

Café Beso was teeny-tiny. The frontage was entirely taken up by a plate-glass window and a glass swing door, each decorated with enormous red lipstick kisses. Inside, the air was warm, steamy and coffee scented. The walls were hung with posters and photos of people kissing. There was no room for tables, but counters ran along the side walls, and stools were tucked beneath them. The back wall was dominated by another, wider counter, this one heaped with cakes and pastries. Usually, a shifting population of baristas worked the hissing coffee machine, but for the past few months Café Beso had been ruled by Avi and Hadar, a cheerful young Israeli couple – he dark, wiry and angular, she more rounded, with honey-coloured hair and skin. Avi and Hadar were working their way around the world – Seraph often wished she could join them.

The day Amy had forced Seraph to confront her suspicions about Nick, the two women had been perched at one of Café Beso's counters, drinking foamy *caffè con leche*, and sharing a slice of *torta espresso à la español*.

'Have you heard of Fran Wheeler?' Seraph had asked.

Amy shook her head.

'She writes for a whole raft of magazines. She did a piece in *Nova!* about how to tell if your partner's having an affair.'

'Oh, yes?' Amy wasn't listening, she was contemplating the slice of cake – a wedge of coffee truffle mousse, on a base of crushed nuts, its top and outer edge coated in thick, glossy chocolate and studded with chocolate-covered espresso beans. 'This is a work of art,' she said. 'It's almost a pity to eat it.'

'Rubbish!' Seraph plunged her fork into the mousse. 'Anyway, she got a huge response.'

'Who did?'

'Fran.' Seraph spoke through a mouthful of torta. 'To her piece about how to tell when your partner's having an affair.'

'Has your partner's daily routine suddenly changed? That kind of thing?'

'I don't know. I didn't read it.'

Amy scooped up a forkful of torta. 'Has he suddenly become more affectionate than usual? Or started showering you with gifts? Or experimenting with new techniques in—'

'Why do you assume it's the man?' Seraph snapped, too quickly, and too hotly. She felt herself blushing, and fixed her gaze on her coffee.

Amy gave her a long look, put her fork in her mouth and silently sucked at the coffee chocolate goo.

'*Nova!*'s a woman's magazine,' she said at last.

'True.'

'So, what's your point?'

'The point is she got such a great response she now wants to do a book.'

'That wasn't what I meant.'

'What did you mean?'

Amy sniffed.

'Have you got any evidence?'

Seraph continued to stare at the frothy surface of her *caffè con leche*, it was in a tall paper cup, just as she liked it.

'Not as such.'

Amy waited a second before she spoke.

'But?'

'It's just he looks at me strangely when he thinks my attention's elsewhere, and looks away when he realizes it isn't . . . I'm always having to repeat myself two or even three times before he notices I'm talking . . . I've smelled things on him . . .'

'Smelled things?'

'Vanilla, and something animal, sharp, but earthy. And he's been getting home late too often recently.'

Amy had poked at the torta with her fork.

'It's probably nothing,' she'd said, although she'd thought the vanilla sounded bad. 'Why don't you ask him?'

Just ask him, Seraph now told herself, as she sat at her desk, with her hands lightly resting on a list of sex tips. Just ask him a simple yes–no question. But she might not like his answer, and, anyway, her pride wouldn't stand it. Yes–no questions begged for evasion, and she wouldn't be evaded. If she wanted answers, she'd have to use methods more subtle than speech. But what methods? She chewed her pen, and re-read Cassie's list. Pornography. Lingerie. Fetishes. Sex toys. Oral and anal . . . Sex as a research tool? Why not? But not *only* a research tool. If she and Nick were to survive as a couple they certainly needed shaking up. Of course, if Nick were having an affair, that would shake them up. In all the wrong kinds of way. She meant they needed shaking up in a positive way, like cocktail ingredients being shaken together to make a drink more delicious than the sum of its parts.

Seraph checked herself. This was toying with the idea of

following Cassie Jones' sex advice. Was that sensible? A thirty-eight-year-old editor of self-help books contemplating following the advice in a self-help book was not unlike a thirty-eight-year-old single woman contemplating placing an ad in a lonely hearts column. The same desperation. The same sense of now or never. Seraph wondered how desperate she really was. What was she prepared to stake for her marriage?

Just as Seraph posed this question, her door swung open, and Amy came in. Since their discussion in Café Beso, Amy had been treating Seraph with solicitousness, but now she didn't notice her friend looked strung-out.

'Guess what?' she said, gloomily. Her voice was attractive, deep and raspy, much more arresting than her looks, which were pretty, but in a dull way.

'What?'

'I just saw Jude sloping off with Benedicta.'

Jude was the Bladder fiction editor, and he crackled with sex. He had carnal eyes, a lazy smile and hands which, both Amy and Seraph had secretly decided, were sure to be slow.

'Benedicta?' asked Seraph.

'Mm . . . have you heard anything about Lucian and this French woman?'

Lucian was Benedicta's consort, and one of Bladder's star novelists.

'French woman?'

'Yeah,' said Amy. 'Some sculptress.'

'I haven't heard a thing.'

'I've had it from two separate sources.'

'So you think Benedicta's making a play for Jude in case she gets given the push?'

'Of course. Insurance.'

Seraph imagined Jude's long, supple fingers sweeping a stray strand of hair from Benedicta's cheek, and her stomach gave a jealous lurch.

'Well, well,' she said.

'Mm,' said Amy. 'Just what I think. So how about a Beso?'

'I think we'd better,' replied Seraph, and she reached for her coat.

2

Seraph tipped half a mug of lukewarm instant coffee down her kitchen sink, then swung around so that she was facing into the room.

'Anyone seen the car keys?' she asked her children, who ignored her. 'Tom? Have you?'

Tom was sitting at the battered pine table, where he'd cleared a small space in the clutter of junk mail and unpaid bills. His coloured pencils and a half-completed drawing of an intergalactic battle lay before him.

'And this is the Tunungian death ship closing in on us,' he muttered. 'We'll launch the atomic spheres in ten quadsecs. Ten. Nine. Eight . . .!'

Seraph prepared herself to say something sharp, but was distracted by Luke who had toddled over from the toy box in the corner, and now held up a piece of Lego for her inspection.

'Keys,' he said.

'Thanks, love.' Seraph reached down to take the Lego. Once he'd relinquished it, Luke clamped his arms around her knees.

'Story,' he pleaded.

'Go away,' replied Seraph.

'Story. Story.'

'Tom, be a love and read Luke a story.'

'The Tunungians have raised their proton shield, but we've

scored a bull's eye on their fourth-dimension propulsion unit. Now there's no escape through . . .'

'Tom, did you hear me?'

'Sorry, Mum. I'm busy.'

'Tom!' Seraph thought about insisting he did her bidding, but decided she hadn't the energy for a fight, and glanced over to her daughter. 'Daisy? Would you read to Luke?'

Daisy was circling the room in a peculiar sideways gallop. She was wearing a frilly, pink tutu over her dress, and waving a silver spangled wand.

'*Chaussée, chaussée,*' she chanted, tunelessly. '*Chaussée, chaussée.* We do *chaussée* in ballet today.'

Tom stuck out a foot. Daisy fell, then jumped up and started using her wand to beat her brother about the head. Seraph sighed, theatrically, and bent to scoop Luke into her arms.

'I'm going to find Dad,' she said to Tom and Daisy, 'so sort it out yourselves.'

Nick was in the dining room, which doubled as both his and Seraph's home office. Even when the room was unoccupied it was easy to tell which was his end of the table, and which Seraph's, from the literature scattered around – unread copies of *Marketing Week* and *Consumer Pharmaceuticals Monthly* versus unread copies of *Publishing News* and the *Bookseller.* Nick had his laptop set up, but he wasn't working. Seraph had recently begun to develop a list aimed at the men's health market, and Nick was now engrossed in *V is for Viagra: How the Love Drug Can Improve Your Sex Life.* Riveting. He was sheepish about his enjoyment of the books Seraph brought home – and she teased him rotten –

but he liked their kick-ass attitude: how to, why not?, don't sweat!, don't worry! He liked all the promises. Read this and you too can become a millionaire/a five times a night stud/attractive/a genius/brave. Go on! There's still time! The upbeat message was irresistible to a man who'd long since sensed all his options shutting down: you can't do what you want with your life, it won't pay the bills; you can't screw who you want to screw, you're married; you can't do anything much, you're a dad, and the baby needs its nappy changed. Mid-life gloom. Common enough. And Nick had gone for a common enough remedy. Love drug? Adultery was an over-the-counter pill. Ginny, a temp from his office, was Nick's mid-life crisis.

When Seraph came into the dining room, carrying Luke, her husband gave a guilty start and snapped shut *V is For Viagra*. Seraph glanced at the cover – a bright orange V against an acid-green background.

'You're the wrong demographic,' she said. 'Right sex, wrong age – much too young . . . and I thought you were working.'

'I am.' Nick nodded at his screen. 'The German budget.'

Before he'd given up writing poetry, Nick would have argued all marketing was shit. But no longer. He'd recently been appointed to an important job – director of the European sales and marketing division of Fletcher & Mellor, an American owned multi-national manufacturing household cleaning products, such as toilet cleaner, laundry powder and washing-up liquid. Outside its walls the company was known as F&M. Its employees, of course, referred to it as S&M. Nick's own version of bondage required a lot of travel, and he had a trip to Frankfurt coming up the following week.

'Wish I were going,' said Seraph.

'No, you don't. Frankfurt's such a dreary city.'

Seraph scowled. It was a nagging source of discontent that this year Eddie had refused to send her to the highly prestigious Frankfurt book fair, on grounds of cost cutting. Nick saw his wife's face and sighed. He still thought Seraph beautiful, but the scowl was becoming her habitual expression. Or else she looked at him as if he were something moldy she'd found in the fridge. Whatever had happened to eyes sharp with invitation, or limpid with adoration?

'Down!' commanded Luke, who was bored with confinement. Seraph did as she was told. Luke ran in a wobbling curve to his daddy, and held out his arms. Nick also did as he was told, and lifted the tiny tyrant onto his knee. When Seraph had told him she was pregnant for the third time, Nick had hit the roof. Back then it had seemed to him they were already drowning under nappies and broken nights and car seats and tantrums and bottles and all the other crap that went with young children. Of course he'd come round. Now he slipped an arm around his son's small body and dropped a kiss onto the top of his head.

'Love you,' he said.

Seraph watched him, dispassionately.

'Have you got the car keys?' she asked.

'No. Why? Are you going somewhere?'

'I told you, I'm going out.'

'Did you?'

'Yes. I told you at lunch.'

'I forgot.'

'How convenient.'

'Sorry. But do you have to go out right now? This minute? I'm in the middle of revising sales expectations.'

Seraph shrugged.

'Surely that can wait? It could wait for Viagra.'

'But I'm leaving on Monday.'

'So? There's tomorrow. I want to go out.'

'What's so urgent? Where are you going?'

'Shopping . . . Brent Cross.'

Nick did a double take.

'You hate Brent Cross.'

This was true. Seraph regarded malls as hell, when she had both the time and the cash to go shopping, which was not often these days, she preferred to mosey round chic boutiques, or thrill to the thrift-shop chase. But Brent Cross's awfulness had its uses – there was no chance of running into anyone she knew among the grim mums roaming its even grimmer caverns.

'Yes, but I have to get some stuff.'

Luke, whose pudgy fingers were still smeared with the remains of the fish and potatoes he'd had for lunch, chose this moment to reach up and tweak Nick's nose. Nick laughed and lowered his son to the floor, then told him to run back into the kitchen and wash his hands. For once Luke did as he was asked. Nick and Seraph both watched him go.

'What stuff?' asked Nick, after this distraction.

'Stuff. Christmas presents. I've not done any Christmas shopping yet.'

'Christmas? It's ages away . . . Go in the week, after work. It'll be quieter.'

'Not at this time of year.'

Nick turned back to his laptop, and hit a couple of keys.

'Maybe,' he said, 'but can't you take the children with you? Or one of them, at least? Daisy would love to go.'

'For God's sake, Nick. I'll only be an hour. You can cope with them for an hour.'

'But—'

'I'm going, Nick.'

Nick found the car keys in the pocket of the jacket he'd worn the previous day. The car was a perk of his new job, and far sleeker than anything he and Seraph could otherwise have afforded. For Seraph the novelty of driving it had not yet worn off, and she enjoyed being in it, on her own.

She arrived quickly at Brent Cross, where, despite the greyness of the winter day, she put on a pair of sunglasses, in case her confidence that she wouldn't bump into anyone she knew proved ill-founded. The mall was heaving, and she had to battle her way through the crowds, until she reached her destination, the Inside Story. The Inside Story was a chain specializing in lingerie, and this was the flagship. The place was done up to suggest some focus group's idea of the boudoir, mostly in shades of pink and green. The carpet was deep, the fittings were faux mahogany and gilt, and incidental lighting was provided by plastic, wall mounted candles, with flickering, electric flames. What was it Cassie had said? 'Lace or silk lingerie can be very arousing, for men and women alike, especially stockings and suspender belts.' Willy-nilly, Seraph seemed to have answered the question of what she'd stake for her marriage. She'd stake herself.

The Saturday afternoon chaos on the floor of The Inside Story came under the cool, uncaring eyes of ranks of angels. These angels were everywhere, they stared down from posters six feet high, heavenly creatures adorned with feathered wings and golden halos. Each beautiful, emaciated model was naked but for some example of the Inside Story's product. Seraph shoved back her sunglasses, so they rested on top of her head, and stood and looked up at one of them for a long, long time – a gorgeous, pouting blonde, reclining against a fluffy ivory cloud, wearing knickers and a push-up bra in turquoise lace. Her hair was cropped very short, and Seraph could imagine how smooth it would feel under a man's caress. She touched her own hair, which was shoulder length and lifeless, with terrible split ends. Knackered, really – it did little to invite Nick to run his fingers through it. Or Jude . . .

Jude? Seraph winced slightly at the unbidden thought of him and tried to concentrate on the turquoise, gift-wrapped *angel* . . . would Nick resurrect his private name for her tonight?

Meanwhile a couple of miles away in her minimalist flat, Ginny was hoping for the ordinary miracle. She was perched on the very edge of her body-defying sofa, gazing intently at a sealed box she held in her hand. It contained a TrueBlue one-minute pregnancy test. The blurb promised this test would be simple and accurate, and that she could take it at any time of the day. Ginny hesitated a moment longer, then slid the box out of its cellophane condom, which she dropped to the floor. Inside the box she found: a leaflet called 'Pregnant or not? Next steps.' which she put on her coffee table; two small, pen-shaped foil-wrapped packages, which she placed on the sofa beside her; and an illustrated set of instructions, which she began to read:

> When you are ready to begin testing, open the foil wrapper, remove the test stick, and take-off the cap. With the tip pointing downwards, hold the absorbent sampler in your urine stream for 5 seconds only.

Ginny checked the diagram of the test stick to find the absorbent sampler.

> Still keeping the tip pointing downwards, remove the absorbent sampler from your urine stream and replace the cap. The result can be read after 1 minute. A blue line will appear in the ROUND window to show that the test has worked and is ready to read.
>
> **Reading the results.**
>
> *Pregnant* – if there is a blue line in the SQUARE window, as shown in picture 4, you are PREGNANT.
>
> *Not pregnant* – if there is no blue line in the SQUARE window, as shown in picture 5, you are NOT PREGNANT.

Ginny found the round and square windows on the diagram, and carefully studied pictures four and five. She sat frowning at the instruction sheet for a few moments, then dropped it besides the discarded cellophane. Her fags were on the coffee table. Only after she'd smoked a cigarette right down did she feel able to rip open one of the pen-shaped foil wrappers. She fumbled to remove the test stick, then stood up and made her way towards the bathroom.

Back at The Inside Story, Seraph was thinking that buying your own lingerie was nearly as bad as going to the fish 'n' chip shop 'n' buying chips for one. She remembered the distant past: Nick's hands holding out some nest of softly rustling tissue paper, and Nick's eyes devouring her as she teasingly drew out a sliver of silk or lace designed with teasing in mind. And hiding and revealing. And slipping and sliding. 'Lace or silk lingerie can be very arousing.' Uh huh. But at the Inside Story slivers of lace and silk didn't nestle seductively in nests of tissue paper, they flaunted themselves from every rack and table top. She briefly considered that even bunking off to W. H. Smith to do a bit of bookshop research would be more exciting, but then rallied herself, and started working the shelves.

While Seraph was browsing the lace selection, the ultra selection and the ultra-lace selection, Ginny was gripping the easy-to-hold handle of her TrueBlue test stick, and peeing onto its absorbent sampler. As Seraph was comparing push-up bras, low-cut bras, no-seam bras, and strapless bras, Ginny was biting her nails and watching the second hand on her watch tick round a minute . . . 57, 58, 59, 60 . . . Ginny blinked, rubbed her eyes, and blinked again. There was a thin blue line in the *square* window. At the very moment Seraph was ruling out baby dolls, the world stopped for Ginny. When it started up again she found herself crooning an ancient, wordless song to an oblivious mass of jelly-like cells inside her.

Seraph was overwhelmed. It wasn't just a matter of bras, there were also knickers – French knickers, thong knickers, G-strings and V-strings. Baby dolls were not the only impossibilities, she couldn't wear frills, or anything calling itself a teddy. She had nobody to advise her on the relative merits of bustiers, bodices and basques. How would she ever choose? She was about to despair when she remembered Cassie's rainbow theory. 'Choose underwear in one of the colours of the body, of flushed flesh, of pubic hair: red, pink, beige, cream or black.' The colours of the body. Right. It wasn't much to go on, but it was a start. A brownish-purple bra caught her attention, and she plucked it from its table. Was the colour hinting at pubic hair? Or was it hinting at a bruise? A black eye? The pleasures of violence? She put the bra down, quickly, and looked for something red. Red, the colour of blood. She'd be willing to bet that Jude would go for a woman in red lingerie, red's promise of danger, its dash, its daring, would suit his temperament . . . Seraph gasped, and only just stopped herself from stamping her foot. Fuck Jude! Nick would like red too. Just as once she'd loved to wear it herself, as outer wear – skirts and shirts, tops and trousers, dresses and jackets. But she'd never yet owned any red *lingerie*. Now she picked up a narrow lace suspender belt in a quivering scarlet, but couldn't help picturing her stomach quivering over the top. In any case, this red, like every other she could see, was electric, neon, inorganic. She replaced the suspender belt, and decided, on balance, it would be safest to stick to black. Black, the colour of dilated pupils, the colour of sin, the colour universally acknowledged to be most slimming.

Ginny's mood was streaked with the colours of dawn, golds and yellows, pinks and oranges, silvers and lavenders. She'd returned to her sofa and was reading 'Pregnant or Not? Next Steps'. It was divided into four sections: 'Pregnant and Pleased'; 'Pregnant and Worried'; 'Not Pregnant and Pleased'; 'Not Pregnant and Worried'. 'Pregnant and Pleased' advised her to make an appointment with her doctor or a midwife as soon as possible, and to be sure to discuss caffeine, cigarettes, drugs, alcohol and exercise with him or her. The authors had even provided the number of a counselling service for smokers wanting to quit. Ginny wrinkled her nose and dropped the leaflet – just another piece of paper to litter the floor. Then she lit a celebratory fag, and took a deep, deep drag.

After she left Brent Cross, Seraph drove to a parade of shops she didn't often frequent, but where there was a video rental place she knew Nick visited on those rare occasions he brought home a little something in the way of adult entertainment. 'Why not watch a sexy video together?' Why not indeed? 'You will probably find the visual stimulation arousing, and may pick up some good ideas which you can incorporate into your own love life.' One can but hope, thought Seraph, once again jamming on her sunglasses.

The video shop was small and stank of stale fast food. Sex was in an alcove behind costume dramas, where another woman was already browsing, forcing Seraph to pretend to be interested in them too. The shop was badly lit, and she could scarcely see anything through her dark lenses, but she gamely ran her finger along the rows of titles as if she were looking for something in particular, *Pride and Prejudice*, say, or *A Room With a View*. Eventually the other woman made her selection and went off to pay. As soon as she was unobserved, Seraph slid into the adult section. It was very cramped, and two men were in there already. One scurried out as soon as he registered that a woman had turned up, and the other shuffled uneasily. Seraph was very careful not to bump into him. She grabbed at a box and gave it a quick and pointless glance – she couldn't see the cover clearly in the gloom. But so what? The commissioning editor probably shared her own lackadaisical attitude towards covers. Anyway, as a genre, porn had always struck her as gynaecological, rather than erotic. Pornography as a debunker of myths and mysteries? Well, yes. Precisely. She really didn't care what she'd watch tonight, and Nick certainly wouldn't care either. So there was no point in spending ages choosing. As far as she could tell, this cover showed a montage of men being given blow jobs by big-haired women. A typical oral fixation. It would do.

Later that day Ginny was lounging on her bed, which had a headboard fashioned, like her sofa, from brushed aluminium. The room was dark, and she was feeling heavy limbed and languorous.

Meanwhile Seraph was feeling frazzled after a particularly traumatic kiddy bedtime, and hoping against hope that Tom, Daisy and Luke, who were all, finally, asleep, would stay that way, or, at least, stay in their beds. Her new lingerie was in her chest of drawers and the video she'd rented was hidden beneath the layers of tissues, semi-unwrapped cough sweets, inch-long crayons, stray pieces of Lego, bank statements and credit-card slips which silted up her bag. As always, she and Nick were eating in the kitchen, but tonight she'd tidied the table, and jollied it up with pretty yellow candles, and some asters she'd bought at the florist's next to the video shop. She'd like to have rustled up lobster and champagne, but was instead relying on the aphrodisiac qualities of a bottle of cheap Chardonnay and two pre-prepared chicken Kievs from the freezer.

After she and Nick had finished dinner, Seraph reached into her bag, which was hanging on the back of her chair, pulled out the video, and silently slid it across the table, face up. This was the first time she'd seen the cover in full light, but it didn't worry her unduly that all the featured women were squeezed into tight-fitting PVC or leather. Nick glanced at the box, and swallowed.

'What's that?' he asked.

'I thought you might fancy an early night.'

'An early night?'

'Mm-hmm.'

'Fine.' Nick spoke with an unmistakable lack of enthusiasm, which he instantly regretted. 'Great,' he added.

Seraph thought Nick's reaction was a setback, but she'd gone to a lot of trouble this afternoon and wasn't about to be discouraged.

'Why don't you set it up,' she said, 'while I go and get changed.'

'Changed?'

'Yes. I've bought myself some lingerie.'

For the split second before he got his face in order Nick looked horrified. Seraph's resolve wobbled.

'But I don't have to put it on.'

'No,' said Nick, who now felt mean and churlish. 'No, you go on up.'

Nick made his way into the sitting room, where they kept their only telly. As he knelt down to load the video he wondered what on earth had got into Seraph. Was it something to do with the menopause? He'd only the haziest understanding of the menopause, but perhaps Seraph was in the right age range? If so, anything could happen. Whatever the explanation, he wished she'd warned him she'd consecrated tonight to sex – he'd had a long week at work, and he was shattered. And that was quite apart from other considerations. Nick banged in the video, and rammed the thought of Ginny out of his mind.

Seraph was standing in her bedroom, stark naked, holding up her new black basque. The Inside Story had had no changing rooms, so she hadn't yet tried it on. Now she had a struggle to compress herself into it. It hooked up the back, so she had to put it on back-to-front, close the hooks, then yank the whole carapace of scratchy nylon lace round her body till the breast cups were actually over her breasts. Pulling on her seamed stockings wasn't much easier. The basque came complete with suspenders, but the fasteners were stiff and she had trouble clipping them to her stocking tops. In addition, the plastic bones digging into her ribcage were so tight she found it difficult to bend. But eventually she was more or less dressed. Or undressed.

Lying on her bed, Ginny was also aware of fabric against flesh. She reached down to the waistband of her black jeans and quite needlessly undid the stud above the zipper, then she let her hand flutter to her completely flat belly, and come to rest over her navel. She once again began to croon her wordless mother-song. But there was a problem – the song had no proper, special focus.

However new and miniscule her baby might be, Ginny knew it needed a name to confirm its individual existence. She wished she'd already bought herself a baby name book, without one she'd be restricted to testing out the better known options.

'Isabelle,' she whispered into the dark. 'Jocelyn. Daniella.' She paused for a moment, then began again. 'James. George. Harry.'

Of course she didn't know her baby's sex, and she began to see the point of the gender-free foetus names pregnant women sometimes used. She tried a couple in her mind. Bug? Sprog? Bump? All frightful. Bunny? Bunnikins? Sweetie?

'Sweetie,' she breathed tentatively, and then, with greater emphasis she repeated the name. 'Sweetie. Sweetie.'

The blob of jelly that was Sweetie made no reply, so Ginny supplied one herself.

'Mummy,' she whispered. 'Mummy. Mummy.'

Unfortunately the word conjured up images and memories of her own mother. Ginny's mood was broken and she sat up, and scowled. Her mother was the last person she wanted to think about just now. Or ever.

As Sweetie was being named, Seraph was dabbing on scent. The finishing touch. Now she smelled richly spicy, she was as ready as she would ever be, so she turned to assess herself in the full-length mirror hanging on the wall to one side of her wardrobe. The basque did what she required of it, which was to pull in her tummy, emphasize the curve of her waist, and thrust up her tits, but she thought she looked only half dressed, in the wrong sort of way. Incomplete. But what would have completed her outfit? Stilettos? Tassels? A feather boa? She took a deep breath.

'You're beautiful,' she reassured her image.

'You're lying,' her image replied.

'You look nice,' said Nick as Seraph paused in the doorway of the sitting room. He was lying back against the cushions at one end of their mustard-coloured sofa, a hideous piece of furniture but comfortable and sturdy. He'd not removed any clothes, but his flies were undone, and much more than bulging. His hand was doing what any male hand would do, under the circumstances.

'Nice?' queried Seraph.

'Nice. I like it.'

Seraph grunted. She was looking for more than *nice*. If there was another woman, then she surely got more than *nice*. So the lingerie wasn't an unequivocal success, what about the porn? From where she was standing, Seraph had a clear view of her husband, but none at all of the telly, because it was obscured in an alcove on the far side of the fireplace.

'Is it good?' she asked, taking a step into the room and nodding in the general direction of the telly. Nick smirked.

'It's very interesting,' he said. 'Educational.'

Seraph shot him a puzzled look. She moved across the room and slid onto the sofa next to him, then she turned her full attention to the video. Nick laughed at her expression.

'I thought it was deliberate,' he said. 'What with me working at S&M and all.'

'No,' said Seraph. 'I thought it'd be blow jobs.'

On the screen a woman who was not young, and not pretty, was slowly picking her way round the furniture in a small sitting room. She sported jet-black hair cut in a severe bob, dark glasses, pancake make-up, and an intense, humourless expression. She wore a peaked cap, a studded collar, a tight, low-cut biker's jacket, and thigh-length high-heeled boots. Her gear was all of shiny black PVC. In one hand she held a riding crop, in the other a dog lead. The dog lead was attached to a plump and elderly man, who was crawling on all fours at her feet. He too wore a studded leather collar and sported a self-absorbed expression, but his make-up was more lightly applied than the woman's – a mere suggestion of lipstick, rouge and eye shadow. Apart from the collar he was dressed as Mrs Mop, in a blue nylon overall, with an orange turban on his head. He was using a little dustpan and brush to sweep the dingy carpet ahead of his mistress's tread, while she regularly flicked at his back with her crop, and exhorted him, in a rich Brummie accent, to, 'Clean, clean, you pathetic little man, you worthless piece of shit.'

Seraph had no idea what to think. It seemed hard to believe that *cleaning* could be mentioned in the same breath as sex, but then she remembered all those saucy French maids with their feather dusters. Well, well . . . 'Fetishes. Boots and shoes, leather and rubber, nappies and dummies. You name it, somebody is turned on by it.' Quite, Cassie, quite.

'Not what you expected?' asked Nick, who was still looking amused.

'No. I'm really sorry. I—'

'Don't be.'

Nick leaned over and pulled her closer to him. He placed her hand where his had been, Seraph glanced down, but her husband's flesh – even this flesh – was not as compelling as the action on the screen, and she turned her eyes to the telly in time to see the mistress give a sharp tug on her dog lead.

'Stay!'

Obediently Mrs Mop halted in the tiny clear patch of floor at the centre of the room. The Brummie dominatrix took two or three steps to a cabinet which opened to reveal a television above some small drawers. She opened the top drawer, and pulled out an improbably large molded-plastic penis, and a selection of straps, then slotted the penis into the straps, before beginning the complicated process of slotting herself into the straps, too.

'What's she doing?' asked Seraph.

'Um . . .' lied Nick.

Mrs Mop was still kneeling patiently on the floor, his forehead on the carpet, his bum in the air. He'd hitched his overall up around his waist, exposing his naked buttocks, flabby and fish-belly white. Think oral, think anal? Seraph remembered herself separating the two items on Cassie's list. But surely this hadn't been what Cassie had had in mind? She gasped and lunged for the remote.

'My God!' she said.

Nick felt further aroused by the thought of what he might have been about to see, had Seraph not intervened – and shamed by his arousal.

'Well, love,' he said after a long silence, 'you live and learn.' Then there was another long and awkward silence, before they both burst out laughing.

Still lying on top of her bed, Ginny was by now drifting into sleep, dreaming plump, contented, half-awake dreams of herself nursing the naked, fat-limbed Sweetie. She knew nothing of breast feeding – the latching-on, the rock-hard breasts, the inconvenient leaks – so there was nothing to disturb the pretty picture of Sweetie, drunk on milk, turning wide blue eyes upon her, and giving her an adoring, and adorable, toothless smile.

Nick's head, too, was filled with visions. His body was fucking Seraph, but his mind was being entertained with images of Ginny playing the role of Mrs Mop's mistress, while he himself took the role of Mrs Mop – minus the silly costume. He and Ginny were acting out the video scenes Seraph had refused to allow him to see, and he was enjoying himself hugely. So was Seraph, who'd abandoned Nick and was fucking Jude. Jude with his long, piano-player's fingers. He was playing Chopin. All those trills. So hard, so tricky, so divine.

3

At roughly the time the virtual Jude was fucking Seraph, the real one was trying to ignore the fact that Benedicta's breasts were only millimetres from his face – she was leaning across him as she dished out platefuls of something which looked like boiled sea slug. Though Jude didn't find Benedicta's brand of brusque sexiness appealing, and her breasts were modestly, if tightly, clad in black crushed velvet, he was still unnerved – not least because Lucian was his friend, as well as one of his star authors.

Lucian had spent most of the evening holding forth about the novel he was writing. It had the working title *Candy,* and his starting point had been an idea about a celebrity being charged with rape. By now he had two hundred pages meandering round fame and responsibility. Two hundred pages is a lot of talking, but the sight of his girlfriend's breasts grazing his editor's cheeks shut him up. He'd drunk quite a bit, and the table was lit only by candles, but the flush spreading across his face was not alcohol induced, and was quite pronounced, even in the gloom. Benedicta smirked, and, for a moment, she leaned even closer into Jude.

Jude didn't recognize her heavy, musky scent, but whatever it was, it was suffocating at such close quarters. He sneezed, and to both his and Lucian's relief Benedicta straightened up.

'Chicken,' she announced. 'Thai green curry.'

She was a confident cook, chucking in the coriander and the lemongrass with wild abandon. Jude and Lucian both looked at her curry. Then each glanced up, and met the other's eye. Lucian's expression changed from hostility to a sort of resigned weariness.

'I like Thai,' said Jude, neutrally.

'Yeah,' said Lucian, in a tone which clearly implied that if Jude liked Thai he was about to be disappointed. Each man took a tentative forkful. Benedicta watched them, closely.

'Is it hot enough?' she asked.

Jude had bitten straight through an almost raw chilli. He sputtered and grabbed for his beer as tears began to course down his cheeks. Now Lucian was the one smirking.

'It's fine,' he said to Benedicta, then he returned to *Candy*. 'Of course it's not just this business of everyone being famous for fifteen minutes,' he said, with a waft of his fork, 'it's this whole notion of celebrity – fame, tabloid recognition – as a model for selfhood, which interests me.'

He looked expectantly at Jude, who put his beer down, and grunted. Jude wouldn't normally have let the fact that his mouth was on fire stop him from contributing, but tonight he just wasn't in the mood for stretching conversation. He was too rattled by Benedicta's behaviour. He twitched as she slid onto the bench next to him, and pressed her thigh against his.

'If, indeed, you allow the notion of a model of selfhood,' she said, provocatively tilting her chin in Lucian's direction, 'since we're all post-modernists now.' Benedicta had a degree in cultural studies, and was very proud of it.

'Balls!' said Lucian, much more fiercely than necessary. 'I'm talking post-post-modernism here.'

Jude shifted his position uneasily and took a second forkful of chicken-slug. Benedicta made sure she had Lucian's full attention, then she too shifted her position, so that she was all but sitting in Jude's lap, and he could feel the warmth and pressure of her body hard against his. Lucian glared at them both. Jude stood up.

'I need a leak,' he said.

The bathroom was cold, damp and grimy. Jude slammed the door, leaned back against it and dropped his head into his hands. He'd heard rumours about Lucian and an up-and-coming young French sculptress, but he'd dismissed them as idle gossip. Now he wasn't so sure. He didn't believe for a moment that Benedicta's performance had anything to do with lust for him. If she'd wanted him, Lucian was the last person she'd have let in on the fact. In any case, he was only an editor, Lucian was a critically acclaimed novelist, and Benedicta was a crashing snob. Nothing about this evening added up, unless she'd decided he'd make a cheap pawn in some war raging between herself and Lucian. Which she clearly had. Jude felt furious with her. He began to speculate about why she'd chosen him, and became angrier still – the only reason he could think of was that he was unencumbered by a partner whose own jealousy might de-rail her careful scheming. Single and expendable.

Who wouldn't be cross?

It was all made worse because Jude was still disorientated by being single – he hadn't yet got used to the idea. Temper led him to kick the side of the bath, and so forcefully that the whole panel wobbled. He was surprised by this kick and told himself to calm down. After he'd taken a few deep breaths he managed a rueful shrug – the horrors of this evening served him right, they were a punishment for arrogance. As recently as a year ago he wouldn't have thought it possible he could ever lack for a girlfriend, but that was before he'd met Shee-Chee . . . and before she'd left him bereft, as he'd known all along, that she was bound to do.

However hard he tried, it was difficult for Jude to maintain this air of detachment, either from his loss of Shee-Chee, or from his predicament tonight. He became morose as he reflected that Benedicta must think he was even sadder than he actually was. She must think he'd been single for the whole of the past year, whereas, in fact, it was only a few weeks since Shee-Chee had told him it was over. At first he and Shee-Chee had kept their affair secret out of professional scrupulousness, or delicacy – she was another of his novelists, and they didn't want to attract gossip. Then Jude had thought he wanted to show her off, to walk into a party with this prize on his arm. But Shee-Chee hadn't wanted to be shown off, and secrecy soon wove itself into their relationship as surely as lazy sex on Sunday mornings. To his surprise Jude hadn't minded. He'd become a miser, hoarding Shee-Chee to himself, like gold.

Shee-Chee. Jude hated the way his thoughts always circled back to her, but he was powerless to stop them. He kicked the bath a second time, although not as hard as before, then sat down on its edge and stared down into it. The bath was very grubby. It was ringed by a brownish-grey tidemark, and the plug was clogged with hair. Jude was not fussy about cleanliness, and his own bathroom was distinctly grotty, but there was something about Lucian's and Benedicta's effluvia which filled him with despair

But would he have felt any differently if the bath had been clean? No. Shee-Chee didn't love him. Even if every bath in the world had been bleached and Ajaxed to a gleaming white, he wouldn't have cared. Plus Benedicta was using him. He'd had it with women. Absolutely had it . . . except there was no way he could survive on a diet of porn and handjobs. Jude plucked a lightly mildewed flannel from behind the bath taps, and began rolling it between his palms. As he did so, he hatched a plan.

Jude was bruised. He'd taken a battering. What he needed to do now, or so he told himself, was to lower the bar. Since he'd always had his pick of women, he'd always picked ones who'd made other men's eyes widen with jealousy. He thought back over some of his pre Shee-Chee exes: Alexandra, all legs and blonde hair; Carlotta, the Italian heiress, pure sex; Camilla, perfect skin and huge blue eyes; Lucy, a body which more than compensated for her borderline personality disorder; Beattie of the bee-stung lips. These goddesses were all very well, but they could afford to be stroppy and demanding. What Jude thought he wanted now was a doormat. A woman who'd blush to look at him. A woman who'd gaze at him with adoration, simply because he'd said hello. A dull woman, with not much going for her, desperate to please and terrified of loss. He'd scarcely noticed such women before, but he was sure there must be plenty around, it shouldn't be too hard to find the one for him. Shee-Chee had taught him a lesson about feudalism, but still, he'd fuck his doormat like any feudal lord pulling rank to pull the wenches, and as soon as he felt better – up to starting on his near equals once again – he'd drop her. He knew full well this was a despicable strategy, but he didn't care. Women, or rather one pitiless bitch, had ripped his liver out and slung it to the hungry beasts. He felt fully entitled to revenge.

Jude felt sexy and strong as he replaced the flannel and wiped his hands on his trousers. He stood up and stretched, luxuriously. Lucian and Benedicta must be wondering what had happened to him. He'd take his piss, then it would be time to get back to them – to *Candy*, power struggles, chicken-slug and post-post-modern ideas about the self.

4

The instant Ginny discovered she was pregnant she named her baby, loosened her clothes, and started indulging herself with bizarre and fattening food, but one thing she didn't do was quit her job. S&M had been the third or fourth company she'd reconnoitered, courtesy of Office Angels. She'd started there in July, spotted what she wanted, and begun screwing it in August. A summer of love. A fruitful summer. But now winter lay upon the land it was time for Ginny to call it quits, both at S&M, and with Nick. At least such had been her plan.

Not quitting was going quite against the spirit of Project P, but Ginny felt placid, calm and slow-moving; effects, she thought, of the hormones sloshing around inside her. Quitting work was far too active a thing to do in this passive state. Of course, hanging on left her with the problem of what to do about Nick. Facing Sweetie's father and telling him it was over wasn't just active, it was radioactive – so she didn't face him, instead she stopped returning his emails and voice messages, stopped bumping into him by the vending machine in the lobby, stopped talking to him at all, if she could avoid it. Nick wasn't slow on the uptake, and, as she'd anticipated, he didn't kick up much of a fuss when he got dumped.

That didn't mean he wasn't regretful. And not just at the end of the affair. As at the end, so at the beginning – right from the start he'd been overflowing with the sorrow of loss. Seraph's books had helpfully explained how regret made men his age vulnerable – that mid-life gloom again, the galling thought of all the women they hadn't fucked, the daring sex they hadn't had. Nick had nodded his head as he'd read, and looked for an explanation of why regret continued to badger him as the liaison progressed. There wasn't one, but still, he'd asked the questions. Why hadn't this thing shattered him? Why hadn't it rearranged the very atoms of his being? Or, if that was a bit much to hope for, why hadn't it at least been good enough to banish guilt?

Not that he needed to think about that one too long. In truth, it was a no-brainer. Nick loved Seraph, and didn't love Ginny. Seraph might more often look at him with fridge eyes than bed eyes, but she was the one with the power to hurt him, his only love, his home, his own. Whereas he'd treated Ginny as a means. Which was wrong, and he knew it, even if he wasn't sure what his ends had been – apart from the obvious. One woman betrayed, one woman abused. There was no dilemma. He should have ended it. 'I should end it,' he'd told himself a thousand times a day. But he'd always managed to ignore himself, so when Ginny took the initiative he was grateful to have the inconvenient voice in his head silenced. And was also even more grateful that he'd no longer have to deceive Seraph.

Nick had found the constant fear of discovery exhausting. Almost as exhausting as the sex which made it necessary. And that sex had not only been regretful, it had been confusing. He'd quickly discovered adulterous sex meant three in the bed, and three in the bed was one more than he could handle. He'd never have predicted this lack of decadence in himself, in the past he'd frequently imagined delectable three-in-the-bed scenarios. But reality was different. Ginny wouldn't take him back to her place, and his was ruled out, so they'd done their trysting in a hotel which let rooms by the hour. Every time they'd gone there he'd been welcomed by Seraph's apparition sprawled naked across the grubby mattress, holding out its arms to him. He'd tried to ignore his wife as he'd fucked his mistress, but Seraph wouldn't be ignored. He'd caressed Ginny's breasts, while Seraph had hissed at their smallness. Ginny had groaned into his neck, while Seraph had spat poison in his ear. And when he was at home, fucking the flesh and blood Seraph, he'd felt Ginny's shadow slide between himself and his wife. And strangely, for a shadow, Ginny's had had a texture. His naked skin had rubbed against her nothingness, and been ground down as if by sandpaper.

No wonder he was relieved his affair was over. Relieved and complacent. Excluding Sweetie, complacency was the one thing he and Ginny still shared. Both felt quite sure their secrets were safe. Nick thought he and Ginny had been completely discreet – that nobody knew of their affair except the two of them, meaning there was no way Seraph could ever find out he'd been unfaithful. And Ginny was confident the secret of her pregnancy was secure. Nick had accepted their liaison was over, he suspected nothing, and she'd summon up the energy to quit S&M long before people noticed her belly and her breasts beginning to swell. So, neither of them worried about exposure. Why should they?

Margaret. That's why. Margaret was the long-time deputy head of UK sales at S&M. She loathed and deplored Nick. Before he'd been promoted, he'd been the head of UK sales, and when he got shunted up the corporate ladder, she'd assumed she would succeed him. But Nick had looked to an outside hire to fill his old job, and Margaret had been fobbed off with a small pay rise. She also loathed and deplored Ginny, or Virginia, as she was known in the office. For Margaret, it had been a *coup de foudre*: hate at first sight. She disliked everything about Virginia from her air of freedom and fearlessness, to her inability to make a cup of instant coffee without leaving flecks of non-dairy creamer floating on the top.

Everybody in sales and marketing knew about their boss's affair with the temp, it was all anyone could talk about in the office kitchen. For weeks Margaret had bided her time, waiting until she could most effectively use Nick's appalling lapse against him. Now she judged the time for action had arrived. For Margaret had a hunch that Virginia might, just might, be pregnant. It was only a slim chance, a slim hope – but slim or not, Margaret couldn't pass it up, and her bitter heart was gloating. She hummed to herself as she marched past Jean's desk. Jean was Nick's PA, and she sat just outside his office, a guardian dragon in a hand-knitted cardie. She'd always been suspicious of Margaret, and now she raised an arm in protest.

'I think he's busy.'

'I won't be a moment,' replied Margaret, who was carrying a bulky, spiral-bound document as cover for her mission. She smiled at Jean and put out her hand to push open Nick's door. Her own desk was in the open-plan area and it irritated her that Nick had an office – his door only added to her sense of grievance. The S&M building had a centralized air-conditioning and heating system, controlled by computer. Studies had shown that office doors obstructed the efficient circulation of cooled or heated air, pushing up energy costs. Thus they were few in number, only the most senior managers could boast of them. Like his company car, Nick's office door was a perk of the job, and he usually kept it shut. Margaret now pushed it open, without knocking.

'Here comes the shorty and the fatty,' she called as she entered.

Nick looked up from his computer screen, and sighed. Margaret habitually introduced herself like this, and he wished she wouldn't.

'Hi, Margaret,' he said. 'What's up?'

'You wanted my thoughts on price pressures on laundry powders in the Scottish market,' replied Margaret, stepping into the room and proffering her document.

'Thanks,' said Nick. 'You can put it over there.' He nodded towards a small, circular meeting table, on the far side of his office, then turned back to his computer. Margaret didn't move.

'You're looking very trim at the moment,' she said. 'Have you been *exercising*?'

'No,' said Nick, his attention on the screen, which displayed French sales figures.

Margaret patted her tummy. 'I've put on a bit recently. And have you noticed how Virginia's really piling on the pounds?'

Nick glanced up. 'What? Ginny?' He immediately realized he should have said Virginia.

Margaret gave him a smug look. Nick tried to cover his confusion by tapping at his keyboard, and accidentally deleted Parisian sales projections for Gone!, a stain remover. He reassured himself that Margaret knew nothing.

'Yes. *Ginny*,' said Margaret. 'I reckon she's put on at least half a stone.'

'Oh.' Nick clicked UNDO EDIT, to no avail.

'And she's eating strangely. She used to eat a slice of cake for lunch, but yesterday I watched her sit and eat a whole jar of gherkins.'

Nick half rose from his chair. 'If you don't mind, I'm snowed under with preparations for the management committee meeting . . .'

'I know,' said Margaret, who wasn't on the management committee. She was discouraged that Nick had reacted so calmly to her hints about diet and weight, perhaps her guess had been wrong? On the other hand, perhaps he hadn't really heard her? It was time to change strategy.

'And she's been coming in *late*,' she said.

'Late?'

'Yes. *Late every morning* this week.'

'Perhaps the tube? But we can't have that. Not in a temp. Have you warned her about it?' Nick hoped he sounded brisk and managerial.

'Oh, yes.'

'Good. I'll make sure I have a word too.'

The director of the European sales and marketing division having a word with a temp about her lateness? Margaret glanced down at her hands, and smiled.

'And she was throwing up in the loo the other morning,' she said.

'Virginia was?'

'Yes. I caught her at it.'

Although Nick was unnerved by the fact that Margaret insisted on talking about Ginny, he thought nothing of her statement, except that her choice of words was a little strange.

'Poor thing,' he said. 'It was probably food poisoning.'

'That's what she said.'

'There you go, then. Now, please, I really must . . .' Nick was standing by now, and he flapped his arms.

Margaret felt deflated.

'Throwing up,' she said, wistfully. 'In the morning.'

Nick's eyes widened. He took a sharp breath and gulped, making his Adam's apple bob. *Bingo!* thought Margaret, and her eyes glittered.

'Did she mention that to you?' she asked, flashing him a saccharine smile. *If* Virginia were pregnant, and hadn't even got round to mentioning it to Nick, then that was a better scenario than she'd dared to imagine even in her wildest dreams.

Nick felt giddy, and wanted to sit down, but didn't.

'Why should she?' he managed to say, after a beat or two.

Margaret just looked at him. 'Better get back to work. I'm starting on price pressures in the East Midlands today. Any thoughts?' Without waiting for a reply she wheeled round and left Nick's office. She didn't close his door.

Nick stood behind his sleek, cherry wood desk, and watched Margaret's retreating back disappear down the corridor to the right of the kitchen. So she knew about him and Ginny. Fuck! And what else did she know? Or had concluded? On what evidence? He wanted to punch something, and was grateful for the privacy of his office – the relative privacy. The inner wall separating him from the open-plan area was glass, so he could keep an eye on his staff. And they could keep an eye on him. His predecessor had installed floor-to-ceiling venetian blinds for the times he'd been forced to implement restructuring policies – S&M-ese for wholesale sackings – but Nick had never yet lowered them. Now he crossed his office and tugged the cord which sent them clattering to the floor. Jean saw what he'd done and was filled with dread. *Not again*, she thought, *please not again*.

Once he was safe from prying eyes, Nick began to pace. Ten

paces this way, ten paces that. This way and that way. Backwards and forwards. To and fro, like a poor, traumatized bear in a zoo. After a few minutes of this he threw himself into his swivel chair and tried to slump, but the chair was ergonomically designed to support his back, neck and shoulders, so was not easy to slump in. Thus he was sitting up unnaturally straight as he reached for his phone and tapped in the first two digits of Ginny's four-digit extension. But before he hit the third digit he changed his mind and replaced the receiver. He wanted to talk. He needed to talk. But who to? Not Ginny. Seraph was out of the question. That only left his brother, Pete. And there could scarcely be anyone more appropriate. All through Nick's life, Pete had led the way. Toy guns and war games. Booze and fags. Rock music and drugs. Girls and cars. Marriage and kids. And now adultery and . . .?

Pete was Nick's elder by two years, and an architect with his own practice in Bristol. Their mother, who'd been claimed by breast cancer a few years back, had brought her boys up more or less alone, while their father sailed in and out of their lives, according to the dictates of the navy. Eventually he'd sailed off for good, to run a bar in Perth, where he'd set himself up with an Aussie woman who really was called Sheila. With no father on the scene Nick and Pete had been thrown together, forced to rely on each other, two against the world. They'd remained close as adults. So close that Nick hadn't even asked permission when he'd plundered events from Pete's life for his first and only novel, *Acting Up.* And Pete hadn't minded, even though the character who'd been clothed in bits of his history was a berk.

Acting Up was a coming-of-age story about a sixteen-year-old who wanted three things: to be an actor, to lose his virginity, and to get drunk every night – so he spent a summer volunteering as a stagehand at his local repertory theatre, just as Pete had done when he was sixteen. Nick had written it in his twenties, after he'd given up on poetry. If he couldn't be a poet, he'd thought he might as well try to become a novelist. But he hadn't been able to find an agent, let alone a publisher. He'd dealt with rejection by turning his hand to scripts for television mini-series, a compromise within a compromise, since he'd have liked to have attempted screenplays for the movies – but North London was a long way from Hollywood. Despite the distance, he couldn't quite rid his scripts of a big-screen cinematic feel, which was perhaps why none of them had been optioned. He'd written three and a half over the years, their spacing, and the amount of time he could devote to them, largely determined by the number and newness of the babies in the house. His first script, *The Animals Came In Two By Two*, was an enviro-techno-thriller; number two, *Bang, Bang, Boom*, a financial-techno-thriller; and number three, *God, Guns and Gasoline*, a scathing criticism of American culture, or, more precisely, of the culture of Topeka, Kansas, where S&M had their global headquarters. Nick had spent six child-free months there, being trained to speak S&M-ese during the days, and writing his script in the evenings. He'd judged it the best thing he'd done in years, so when it became clear it would never be bought by Channel 4, or any other channel, he'd become very despondent. Poet. Novelist. TV script writer. The end of the progression. What lower form of writing was there left to try? He'd thought about journalism, but by this time his financial commitments were daunting, and his career was taking off, so he'd told himself he just couldn't be bothered and he'd even stopped writing for a while, but about a year ago he'd begun again. His work-in-progress, *Antidote,* was a medico-techno-thriller. Not that he'd got very far with it.

Antidote was about an outbreak of Ebola fever in Kensington, and part of the reason it was stalled was that Nick knew nothing about medicine and had no time to do research. He often wished he could ask Fiona for help. Fiona, a GP, had been Pete's first wife, a cool, poised, self-confident woman. If Nick had felt able to consult her she could certainly have told him what happened to the body when every capillary began to bleed. But Nick didn't feel able to ask, for Fiona was no longer his sister-in-law, but his ex-sister-in-law.

Fiona's and Pete's divorce had been as clichéd as they come. When their children, Lachlan and Catriona had been three and five, Pete had hired a new secretary, Donna – twelve years his junior, small-boned, like a bird, a bottle-blonde, with big eyes and big tits. He was anything but embarrassed by her obviousness, and didn't notice how ghastly she was, until it was too late.

'I'm pregnant,' she'd told him, one day. They'd had a row about abortion, then he'd tried to end the relationship, but Donna wouldn't be done for. She'd gone to Fiona.

'I'm pregnant,' she'd told her, along with much else besides. After a bit of argy-bargy, Fiona had chucked Pete out. He hadn't wanted to leave Bristol, because of the children, and it had seemed to him he'd nowhere to go but Donna's, nobody to turn to but her. As soon as he was safely in her armlock, he'd started longing for what he'd lost. But that was tough shit. For the sake of his and Donna's daughter, Bianca, he'd agreed to re-marriage as soon as the divorce came through. He'd lived more-or-less unhappily ever since, but there was nothing he could do about it – how could he walk away from his new life and his new wife, given what he'd sacrificed for them?

When the phone rang in Pete's studio, he was sitting at his drawing board, working on a commission to convert a derelict dockside warehouse into offices. The ground floor of the warehouse was entirely taken up with truck-loading bays, and Pete was experimenting with different solutions to the problem of converting them into a suitably impressive entrance and reception area.

'Pete, it's me,' said Nick. The brothers spoke frequently, although nowadays they saw each other only a few times a year. The distance between London and Bristol had increased since Pete's divorce, Seraph and Fiona had been extraordinarily close, but Seraph and Donna did not get on.

'Hi,' said Pete, absently.

'She's pregnant.'

Pete jerked his head back.

'What? Again? You two are like rabbits.'

'Not Seraph.'

'No? Then who?'

'Ginny.'

'Who's Ginny?'

'This woman I know.'

'You're phoning to tell me a woman you know is pregnant?'

'Yes.'

Pete began to doodle on one corner of his drawing. He drew

a pattern of interlocking triangles of different sizes, and types: isosceles, right-angled, long and thin, squat and splayed.

'How well do you know her?'

'Not very well.'

'You're phoning to tell me a woman you don't know very well is pregnant?'

'Yes.'

'How long have you not known her very well?'

'Not long. A couple of months.'

Pete added a triangle to his pattern.

'You fucking idiot,' he said.

'I know,' said Nick. 'But the point is, what do you think I should do?'

'Fuck knows . . . she planned it, didn't she?' Just like Donna.

'Dunno.'

Pete grunted.

'I suppose it's irrelevant now. When did she tell you?'

'She didn't.'

'Then how do you know?'

'Margaret told me.'

'Who's Margaret?'

'She works for me.' Nick hesitated. 'So does Ginny.'

'So Ginny told Margaret, who told you?'

'I don't think so. Margaret caught her throwing up in the loo. In the morning.'

Pete's hand froze over an incomplete obtuse angled triangle.

'Is that it? Is that what Margaret told you – that she caught Ginny throwing up in the loo in the morning?'

'Yes.'

Pete sighed.

'Nick, you really are a fucking idiot . . . It was probably food poisoning.'

'That's what I said. I said it was probably food poisoning.'

'Or a bug.'

'Could have been,' agreed Nick, eagerly.

'Right.'

'So d'you think I should ask?'

'Ask?'

'Ask Ginny if she's pregnant?'

'No!' advised Pete, firmly. 'Let sleeping dogs lie.'

'Like mum always said.'

'Yeah.' Both brothers were silent for a moment, hearing their mother's voice trotting out the homespun wisdom. Both of them were thinking *and look where it got her.*

Pete cleared his throat.

'How do things stand now between you and Gin—'

'Over.'

'Completely?'

'Yes.'

'That's good. And Seraph knows—'

'Absolutely nothing.'

'Well, everything's okay, then. You've nothing to worry about.'

'You think?'

'I do.'

'So . . .?'

'So nothing. It was probably food poisoning. Or a bug. Forget it. Just forget it.'

After Nick hung up he swivelled round in his chair so he could stare out of his exterior window. His office was on the seventeenth floor of a sixties' tower block, which was itself on a motorway access road in West London. The windows onto the outside world were permanently sealed and on this side of the building they looked out over a flyover. Today Nick's view was obscured by fog, but, even if it had been clear, traffic couldn't have held his interest. He stood up and resumed pacing, then he decided he needed a few lungfuls of exhaust fumes to help clear his head. As he left his office, Jean saw his face, and shuddered, but Nick didn't notice.

'I've got some business on the twentieth floor.' He told her. Human resources was on the twentieth floor, that's why he'd chosen it. Going up to HR was like going into a swamp, you could sink without trace up there. Jean clasped her hands.

'It's restructuring, isn't it?' she said, with anguish.

Nick frowned in puzzlement.

'What?'

Jean looked meaningfully at his lowered blinds, and Nick cottoned on.

'No,' he said. 'No, no. Please don't worry. It's not that. Not at all.'

Jean didn't believe him.

'Then what?'

'HR. Just HR stuff. Temps and such.'

'Temps?' Jean was responsible for hiring temps. She glanced in the general direction of Ginny's desk, at the far side of the open-plan area.

Nick realized that whatever his mental state, this was no time for carelessness.

'And such,' he said. There was silence for a minute.

'Right,' said Jean, relief making her a little cocky. 'If anyone asks, I'll say you'll be half an hour.'

Outside, Nick was freezing without his coat. He seemed to swim through the fog to the kiosk in the lobby of the next building, where he bought himself a cup of coffee and a Kit-Kat. But the coffee had been left to stew too long in its glass jug and proved undrinkable. There were no litter bins along the motorway access road, so Nick guiltily dropped the almost full Styrofoam cup in the gutter. After two circuits of the dreary, treeless block he sat down on a low concrete wall by a parking lot, and unwrapped his Kit-Kat. He took a bite, and tried to think. Ginny was pregnant. Or she'd had food poisoning. Or a bug. Or something. But suppose she was pregnant. Then what? Then Pete was right. He should forget it. If Ginny were pregnant, *if* she were, then it was up to her to tell him. If she chose not to, no doubt she had her reasons. Although the only reason Nick could think of was that he wasn't the father, which was as unnerving as the thought that he was. His mind flooded with images of Ginny's body bucking beneath men who weren't him, men who were much more inventive, acrobatic lovers than he would ever be. The Kit-Kat fell out of his hand, unnoticed. Several minutes later he stood up, and began to shuffle back to S&M, walking like an old man.

'Forget it,' he muttered to any urban ghosts who happened to be lurking in the fog, 'let sleeping dogs lie.' But the ghosts brushed at his words with their foggy fingers and scattered them the instant they were formed.

Jean started as Nick passed her on the way into his office.

'Are you okay?' she asked, thinking they were all going to lose their jobs after all.

'I'm fine.'

'Sure?' On the other hand, perhaps he was ill? He looked it.

'Yes.'

'There's something going round. Tony's had it.' Tony ran direct mail.

'I wondered where he'd got to.'

'A stomach bug—'

'A *stomach* bug?'

Jean was taken aback.

'Yes. He was in bed two days, sickness, a fever . . .'

Nick laughed, and Jean looked at him strangely.

'He's in today, though,' she said. 'He wants to see you, actually.'

Once inside his office Nick immediately raised the blinds, in case anyone else other than Jean thought he was using them to signal a restructuring. So Ginny *had* had a bug! What an idiot he'd been to panic! He sat in his chair and placed the palms of both hands flat on his desk.

'Just forget it,' he said again, more robustly than before, 'Let sleeping dogs lie.' Then he took a deep breath and swivelled sideways, intending to focus, as he should, on the French sales figures. His screen saver was running – a shifting mosaic of S&M products, and he reached out his hand to hit the space bar, which would bring the figures back onto the screen. But his hand had other ideas. He watched in fascination as it veered, in slow motion, towards the phone, and stabbed at four buttons.

'Ginny?' he heard himself saying a second or two later. 'Can you pop into my office for a moment?'

'Why?' Ginny asked, in a truculent tone.

Nick hadn't anticipated the question, and flailed around for a pretext.

'Our corporate image,' he said. 'I need to see what you've done on the cross-cultural comparison of major customers.'

'D'you mean the press clippings?'

'Yes. The press clippings. Can you bring them through, please.'

A while back Jean had handed Ginny a huge, disorderly pile of adverts and cuttings from the European press, and asked her to sort them by country. Ginny had done Portugal, but that was it. She now picked up the Portuguese folder, and scooped the rest of the cuttings into a loose bundle, then headed off to see Nick. She guessed what this summons was about, of course. It had been bad luck Margaret catching her in the loo like that, and she'd been caustic about the gherkins. But Margaret knew nothing, all the old cow had to go on was malice. *Don't worry, Sweetie, Mama can handle this. She just has to stare him down, is all.*

Outside the sealed environment of S&M the fog had condensed to drizzle. As Ginny crossed Nick's office, she watched flattened rivulets of water running down the window behind his head. Nick breathed in her sweet, vanilla smell – was it the soap she used? the shampoo? – and kept his eyes on his desk.

'Hi,' he said, to his blotter. He was acutely conscious of the watchful, inquisitive world behind his inner glass wall. Under the real or imagined gaze of his sales and marketing staff, he felt as if he were vanishing, slowly, like the Cheshire cat. Ginny ignored his greeting, adding to his sense that he was fading to nothing.

'Here,' she said, and tossed the folder and her cuttings onto Nick's desk. A page from *El Pais* fluttered to rest next to a framed photo of Tom, Daisy and Luke playing on the beach.

'Thanks.'

Ginny grunted and turned to go.

'No! Sit down!'

'Why?'

'Just sit down.'

Ginny hesitated, but sat. It was the first time they'd been alone together since she'd found out she was pregnant.

Nick no longer desired Ginny. Not at all. It was incomprehensible to him how he ever had. He fiddled with his tie and risked a glance at her face, then dropped his eyes. Now they were level with her breasts – the breasts of a possibly pregnant woman. He pictured Seraph's breasts. Each time she'd been pregnant they'd swollen to cartoon proportions, quite nice, really, at least when he'd managed to block out her grotesque belly, but once the babies had been born they'd been revoltingly milk-engorged for months. Pregnancy. He must be subtle. He must approach the subject with tact and humility.

'Are you pregnant?' he blurted.

The question throbbed between them. Ginny took a deep breath. *Serenity, Sweetie*, she inwardly hummed, but outwardly she remained silent. Nick stood up, crossed his office and yanked at the cord to lower the blinds. But as they began to fall he caught Jean's eye – she didn't look anxious now, but curious. He changed his mind and raised the blinds as high as they would go.

'So you are' he said.

Ginny had given no thought to what she'd do if, contrary to her plans, Some Man found out she was pregnant. The logical thing, the sensible thing, would be to lie now, to laugh and say, 'Do I look pregnant?' Or to say, 'Don't be ridiculous, you know I was rigorous about the pill,' or to say, 'Shit no, the last thing I want is a baby.'

'Yes,' she said, and immediately cursed her honesty. To excuse it she did some on the hoof theorizing: pregnancy *horror*mones must have a chemical structure similar to truth drugs. Not that it was something she'd seen discussed in *Getting Pregnant*, or, indeed, in Dr Case's sequel, *The Pregnancy Handbook*.

'You said you were on the pill!' Even to his own ears Nick sounded like one of the children, Tom or Daisy, whining, 'It's not fair.' But it *wasn't* fair, she *had* said she was on the pill. He'd taken condoms along, the first time, and even got them out, but she'd said, 'No need, I'm on the pill,' and tossed the whole box on the floor. He'd had qualms, of course, he knew the mantra: sex is great, but not worth dying for. But what was death when faced with naked flesh?

'I was,' Ginny said now, 'but something must have gone wrong.'

Nick made a harsh, guttural sound. It wasn't simply that he didn't believe her, it was also that the memory of anger was making him angry. 'Something must have gone wrong,' was almost exactly what Seraph had said when she'd told him that, despite taking her pill religiously every morning, they were headed for Jamieson baby number three.

'And?' he now asked Ginny, after a brief silence.

'And what?'

Nick thought of all the ands which followed from the fact that Ginny was pregnant. And. And. And. He swallowed his pride and picked one.

'And am I the father?'

Again, it was open to Ginny to lie, she could have said *no*.

'Yes.'

'Sure?'

'Positive.'

Nick thought about that for a moment.

'And what do you plan to do about it?'

'What do you mean?'

'Do you want to, you know . . . keep it?'

They both thought of posters put out by pro-life organizations, posters showing the profiles of semi-transparent fish caught in nets of blood vessels. Nick imagined little lips puckered around a shrimp-like thumb, sucking, sucking. Ginny saw a huge unblinking eye, judging her. The interior monologue directed at Sweetie was momentarily suspended, for what could she say? Nothing. Neither to her baby, nor to herself, nor to Nick, so she remained silent, but stood up, ready to leave. Nick stood too, they faced each other across the abyss of his desk.

Just at that moment Nick's door swung open, and Tony stuck his head in. Tony was gay, and was engaged in a long-running war with Margaret, who claimed, to anyone who'd listen, that his campness drove her to distraction. Their battleground was the office kitchen, and their artillery was gossip. Advance in any given skirmish depended on access to information, retreat swiftly followed if none was to be had. Tony nodded to Ginny, who briefly considered shoving past him and out of Nick's office, but some part of her wanted to deny him any pleasure in the scene he was witnessing.

'Hi,' she said.

Nick reached for Ginny's Portuguese folder, flipped it open, and ostentatiously began to shuffle the contents.

'Feeling better?' he asked.

Tony rolled his eyes.

'It was terrible. A temperature of a hundred and three, the shakes, the shits. But I'm over it now, and I need a word.' True, but it didn't explain why his eyes were shining.

'I'm a bit tied up at the moment,' replied Nick, wafting a press cutting.

'Shall I come back in ten? It's about the FabricFresh campaign.'

FabricFresh was a new product. It was a spray which removed lingering odours of cigarette or dog from curtains and soft furnishings.

'I'm free after lunch,' said Nick. 'How about two thirty?'

Tony looked disappointed.

'Okay, two thirty,' he said, and then, with visible reluctance, he backed out of Nick's office. At least he shut the door.

Nick dropped the Portuguese folder and looked at Ginny.

'Don't fly off the handle,' he said. 'I've only got your interests at heart.'

Ginny grunted.

'It's true.' Nick ran his hands through his hair. 'Have you thought things through? Have you thought what your life's going to be like? Have you thought of all the freedoms you'll lose? All the things you'll no longer be able to do? All the friends you'll never see?'

Ginny just stared at him.

'All the new fears? All the new worries? All these things going on and on for years and years and years?'

All the new fears. Ginny's stomach lurched. Both *Getting Pregnant* and *The Pregnancy Handbook* had helpfully explained that once a foetus's heartbeat had been detected the risk of miscarriage fell to 2 per cent, where it remained throughout pregnancy. But for all she knew Sweetie had no heartbeat yet, and even if it did, if it fell into the unlucky 2 per cent it would be 100 per cent dead. She took a step backwards.

'I don't have to listen to this,' she said, and turned towards the door.

Nick's face hardened.

'So I suppose it'll have to be a paternity test,' he said, to her back.

Ginny swung around.

'What?'

'You heard me.'

'A paternity test? Why?'

'I'll be fucked if I'm going to pay for someone else's bastard.'

Ginny laughed.

'Think you're a rock star?' she taunted him.

Nick was spared the need to respond when his door once again swung open. He instantly whipped up the Portuguese folder.

'Here comes the shorty and the fatty,' announced Margaret, who'd been thrilled to see Ginny enter Nick's office, and enraged to see Tony leaving it. 'I'm making coffee and wondered if either of you wanted a cup?'

Ginny saw her chance.

'Thanks,' she said, 'make sure the creamer's fully dissolved.' Margaret glared at her.

'Not for me,' said Nick, brandishing the file.

'Ah,' said Margaret with a knowing smile. 'The press clippings.'

'Yes,' said Nick. 'The press clippings.' His voice was much harsher than even he had expected. A dismissive voice. Margaret looked delighted, although she had no option but to retreat. As usual she left the door open. This time Nick broke one of his self-imposed rules and called to her to shut it, which she did, with yet another knowing smile.

'I don't want your money,' said Ginny, as soon as Margaret was gone. This was true. Unbeknown to Nick she was very rich.

Nick held the folder against his chest, as if it were a shield.

'Then what?' he asked. 'What do you want from me?'

'Nothing. Zero. Zilch. Zip.'

'I don't believe you.'

Ginny shrugged.

'You were the one who wanted to know if I was pregnant, I wasn't going to tell you.'

'But you did, and you are . . .'

The two of them locked eyes.

'Yes,' said Ginny 'And I want to bring this child up on my own.'

Nick snorted.

'I do. I can't say it any more clearly . . . You know there never was anything between us . . .'

There wasn't? thought Nick. *Okay I never loved her, but it wasn't supposed to be mutual.*

'Too right,' he said, emphatically.

'So now let's just forget about each other. And you can forget about the baby, as well. Go back to your wife.'

'Back? I never—'

'You know what I mean. Buy her some earrings or something . . .'

'What?'

Nick reacted as if Ginny had suggested treating his favourite, the Ebola virus, with Aspirin. But she was remembering how when things got bleak, her mother, Audrey, always sought solace in her jewellery box – her chocolate box. Ginny carried around a picture of her salivating as she ran her fingers over emeralds and sapphires, luscious as truffles. There was one blood-red ruby in particular, as large as a quail's egg, set with creamy pearls the size of peas. This ornament formed the centrepiece of a choker, its purpose was to draw a man's gaze to the hollow of a woman's throat. And to bring a gleam to that woman's eyes. It had been one of Audrey's last gifts from her husband, Ginny's father Marcus, he'd handed it over a few months before the bitter divorce. Ginny, who never wore jewellery, or make-up either, now thought of this stone as blood-red blood money, but she'd often seen her mother stroking it, as if it were a living thing, caressing it with her eyes, and cooing.

'Earrings,' she repeated, with a shrug. 'Or whatever. Anyway, the point is you should forget all about me. And the child.' *You and me, Sweetie. You and me.*

Like Cold War superpowers with finely balanced arsenals, Margaret and Tony had declared a wary, temporary truce, and both were hovering in the kitchen, watching Nick's door. When Ginny emerged they developed a keen interest in washing-up. She waggled her fingers at them as she sasshayed down the corridor and Nick, still stationed behind his desk, couldn't help admiring her boldness. He felt far from bold, and sat down, heavily. His chair swivelled slightly with his weight, and he found himself staring at his screen saver, at images of washing powders and pan scourers, toilet cleaners and bleaches twirling in a meaningless dance. Pete had assumed she'd planned it. And had she? It was a pointless question, since he'd now be too proud to ask. 'You know there never was anything between us.' Did that imply he'd been nothing but a sperm factory? Perhaps. 'I want to bring this child up on my own.' Supporting evidence. 'And you can forget about the baby.' Also consistent with his new view of things. 'Buy your wife some earrings.'

Seraph! Oh God! Nick had thought he'd got away with it. But perhaps he hadn't? He conjured up Seraph's face, and groaned aloud at the idea of what it might look like if she ever discovered he'd made another woman pregnant. And what she'd do if he tried to placate her with *earrings*. He was gripped by a powerful longing to call her, just to check there was nothing strange about her voice, no hint she'd magically overheard any of his conversations this morning. He lifted the receiver from the phone, but then it hit him that if he rang Seraph now he might give himself away, so, for the second time that morning, he keyed in the Bristol code.

There were six loading bays across the west frontage of the warehouse Pete was converting. He was toying with putting revolving doors in the two central ones, flanked by wide swing doors. But what about the porch, or awning? An upscale office block must have some sort of cover over the entrance, somewhere for taxis to pull in, on wet days. When the phone rang, he answered a little distractedly.

'Hello?'

'It's me again. She is pregnant.'

That got Pete's attention.

'This Ginny woman?'

'Yes.'

'How d'you know?'

'I asked.'

There was a long pause.

'You jerk! What did you do that for? I told you to forget it.'

'Yes. But I found I couldn't just let sleeping dogs lie.'

'Why not? I would've, if I'd been given the choice, which you know I wasn't . . . .And now what?'

'What d'you mean?'

'Well, for starters does she want to keep it?'

'Yes, she does.'

'Can you talk her out of it?'

'I tried. I don't think I can.'

'No,' said Pete, remembering Donna. 'It *is* hard, but are you sure you're the father?'

Nick swallowed.

'She says I am. I did suggest a paternity test, but she said did I think I was a rock star.'

'You suggested a paternity test? So you're not sure you're the father?'

'I'm pretty sure.'

'Yeah?' Pete sneered 'And what are her demands? Does she want you to leave Seraph, set up home with her, that kind of thing?' The Donna kind of thing.

'No.'

'No? So what about money?'

'She says she doesn't want my money.'

'Right,' said Pete, meaning *wrong*. 'So what does she want?'

'Nothing. Zero. Zilch. Zip. That's what she said.'

'But she didn't mean it.'

'She seemed to.'

'No chance. It's some sort of negotiating tactic.'

'I don't think so. She didn't want me to know she was pregnant. It was me who asked.'

'Like I told you not to.'

'Don't rub it in . . . she said she wanted to bring this child up on her own.'

'Wow!' Pete managed to inject implacable scepticism into this single syllable.

Nick said nothing.

'But it really is over between you?' Pete was speaking more sympathetically than he had been before.

'Yes.'

'And you really think she's prepared to walk away?'

'I do. She seems to want to.'

'She'll let you forget the whole episode? Including the baby?'

'I think so.'

'And Seraph doesn't know a thing?'

'No . . . Ginny said I should buy her earrings.'

'Earrings?' Pete laughed. 'I never tried it with Fiona, but it's worked with Donna once or twice. After the rows, the peace offerings.'

Nick made a piteous sound.

'Not a peace offering,' he said, 'a bribe.'

'But Seraph's completely in the dark, so you don't need to bribe her. And you could still get away with it.'

'I suppose.'

'There's no suppose. It's like I said before. Forget it, you lucky sod. Walk away and just forget it.'

'Right,' said Nick. 'Just forget it.'

5

'*What?*' said Seraph, who could scarcely believe she'd heard right. '*Jude's* asked you out?'

'Yes,' replied Amy, who was far too pleased with herself to notice Seraph's face.

Both women were in Seraph's office. Amy was leaning against the battered filing cabinet. Seraph was sitting at her desk, feeling her innards shrivel with envy. She wished she could convince herself the shrivelling was caused solely by anxiety on Amy's behalf – and, in truth, she *was* anxious about her friend, who was surely headed for pain. Jude was out of Amy's league. Seraph glanced appraisingly from the other woman's ordinarily pretty face to her clothes. Spots and flounces were this season's instant fashion, or, as worn by Amy, this season's instant disaster. Today she looked like an inverted toadstool. Her fawn shirt formed the stalk, the cap was her flouncy red skirt, which was spotted with white.

'So where are you going for this date?'

'I don't know yet. I'm letting him sort it out.'

'Is that wise? You might end up at a Polish art film shot in black and white in someone's garage.'

'Yeah.' Amy laughed, then paused for a moment. 'So how about a Beso?'

Seraph glanced down at the pile of unopened post on her desk. The top envelope was embellished with a little gold label giving Iris Basham's name and address. What a choice! Depilatory techniques, or gritting her teeth and pretending to be happy for Amy.

'Look at this,' she said, sweeping her hand over the desk in a vague fashion. 'I'm completely snowed under right now.'

Amy gave her a hurt look.

'That's *quite* okay,' she said. 'I'll ask Disha.' Disha, pronounced Deesha, was Bladder's pretty young receptionist. She never said no to gossip.

Seraph shoved Iris's envelope to the bottom of the pile.

'Good idea,' she said, keeping her face lowered, so there was no chance of meeting Amy's eye.

The sushi bar was sleek and smart. As soon as Amy walked in Jude regretted choosing it. Like everyone else he was dressed in black – black jeans, black linen shirt – but Amy's dress was horribly patterned and horribly fussy. On the other hand she had a pretty face, and a good figure. And when she greeted him the expression in her eyes was all that he'd hoped for. But her hair! Christ! Amy's hair was mouse brown and fell to her shoulders in ragged, shaggy layers. Jude couldn't help comparing it to Shee-Chee's, which was a smooth, blue-black curtain falling to her waist. She'd had a way of scooping it up in a loose ponytail, lifting it off her neck, and then letting it drop back with a heavy, sighing, swish. Jude had loved to brush Shee-Chee's hair, and to wash it, too.

Amy had never made much of a ritual of washing her hair, nor had she ever eaten sushi.

'You order,' she said.

Jude didn't demur, and she watched him study the menu for a moment, then give it a showy flourish.

'I don't suppose you want eel, or squid, or sea urchin?'

Amy shook her head.

'So how about salmon, tuna, sea bass, bluefish and a Californian roll?'

'Sounds fine to me.' It was a lie, Amy didn't like fish. What she really wanted was to bite down into the mousse and goo of *torta espresso à la español*, and there was a slice slouching right there on the chair opposite her. She didn't know it, but Jude had Lebanese blood in him, and his skin looked as if it should smell and taste of coffee. He had chocolate-brown hair and brooding chocolate eyes under heavy brows. He didn't wear his clothes, they coated him, like sauce. Amy wanted to dip her finger in, and lick.

After the business of ordering, conversation was stilted.

'What're you working on at the moment?' asked Jude, in desperation.

'Boring shit,' replied Amy. 'Admin. Contracts stuff for Gill.' Gill was the Bladder dictionaries and reference editor. 'And you?'

'*Bamboo.*'

'The new one from Shee-Chee Chen?'

'Yeah.' Jude was working on half a dozen titles, but he'd known if he mentioned *Bamboo*, he'd get to say Shee-Chee's name, or to hear it.

Amy's bookshelves were packed with Seraph's self-help titles. She didn't like to admit she hadn't even got around to reading Shee-Chee's first novel, *China Fun,* but she knew it was set in

Hong Kong, London, and Beijing, and followed three women, mother, daughter and grandmother, on July 1, 1997, the day Hong Kong ceased to be a colonial outpost of Britain, and passed back to Chinese control. It had been published to rapturous reviews, and disappointing sales.

'Any good?' she asked now, of *Bamboo*.

Jude made a choking sound, and flung his arms wide.

'Oh, God!' he said. 'She can do it all. Characterization, description, plot. The lot. The action really sweeps along, but she manages to explore her characters at so many levels.' He started ticking them off, on his fingers. 'In quotidian matrices of passion, desire and family conflict; in political matrices – I mean the sense of belonging to an alienated, and alien community; in spiritual matrices of the search for meaning in an indifferent universe . . . And her English is dazzling – it's hard to believe she grew up speaking Cantonese.'

Amy waited a beat before replying.

'My brother's been to Hong Kong.'

Jude frowned.

'*Bamboo's* set in London, New York and Singapore, actually.'

There was a difficult pause. Jude took a swig of his Asahi beer, and Amy stared at her red lacquered chopsticks – she couldn't use chopsticks, and they filled her with dread.

'I'm reading one of Seraph's,' she trilled, when the silence between them had stretched beyond acceptable limits. '*He Said, She Said: A Guide to Clearer Communication Between the Sexes.*'

Sushi was not as bad as Amy had expected. She copied Jude and mostly ate with her fingers. The chunks of firm fish on their beds of sticky rice were delicious, and she liked the wasabi. Once they'd both finished Jude ordered a couple more beers, and took out his fags – Gauloises.

'Want one?' he asked, holding out the crushed packet.

Amy gave him a mock frown, which she intended to be playful, but which came out as prissy.

'No thanks.'

Jude shrugged and lit up. He doubted that later on she'd refuse to kiss him on the grounds that he'd taste like an ashtray, but he'd rather risk it than forego a smoke. He inhaled, deeply, eager for the first nicotine hit.

'It'll stain your teeth,' said Amy, and they both looked slightly startled.

'What?'

'Sorry.' Amy felt herself blushing. 'I don't know where that came from. It just popped into my head.'

'Right,' said Jude, and took another long drag.

Amy had given herself a jolt, and for a moment Jude's face jumped and wavered, as if she were watching him on the telly, and something had gone wrong with the reception. 'You don't want to smoke, it'll stain your teeth.' That's what Dave always said to people who lit up in his presence. Dave was Amy's ex, and he was a dentist. If whoever it was he was talking to laughed at the prospect of stained teeth, he gave them a lecture on cancer of the tongue. Amy had always felt uncomfortable when he'd started his spiel, it was one of the reasons she'd left him.

'Will you marry me?' he'd asked, and she'd astounded them both by saying no.

'Why not?' he'd said, and she hadn't been able to provide him, or herself, with an adequate answer. She'd told herself 'Because you tick people off about smoking' just wouldn't cut it. Nor would, 'Because your parents are narrow-minded, racist, homophobes and I can't stand any more Sunday lunches with them.' Nor would, 'Because you're a dentist, and you live in Hitchin.' But all those things were true, and she'd thought they mattered.

'Is there someone else?' he'd asked.

'No. There's no one else.'

'Is it sex?'

Amy had thought about saying yes. The necessity of faking it every night was a reason they'd both have understood, but it wasn't a true one. Now, as she sat opposite Jude of the carnal eyes, lazy smile and hands which were sure to be slow, Amy was chagrined to notice that the unbidden thought of Dave had set up an equally unbidden vibration in her squashy parts. Her liver and spleen, her intestines and kidneys were all humming to the old, familiar frequency.

'It's not sex,' she'd said to Dave.

'Then what?'

'I'm afraid of commitment,' she'd replied. It was her self-help books talking through her; she'd been a medium of their message.

'Commitment?'

'Yes.'

'You're afraid of marriage?' Dave had looked incredulous. 'Okay. We don't need to marry. We can stay as we are.'

Amy had heard some stranger speak.

'I'm not afraid of marriage.'

So that was that. Goodbye to being a dentist's wife in Hitchin. And Amy was happy about her decision. Really. The vibration in her internal organs was nothing. She tightened her abdominal muscles to quell it, and Jude came back into focus. He seemed not to have noticed she'd tuned out for a moment, and was drawing deeply on his cigarette. Amy watched the way his lips pursed around the slim white cylinder. She watched his whole chest rise as he inhaled. She became a smoke molecule, sliding over his slightly yellowed teeth, slipping across his moist, pink tongue, slithering down his long, long throat into the spongy, wet darkness of his lungs. She watched his chest sink again, as he exhaled, and she was tumbling and swirling in one of the two blue-grey streams pouring from his nostrils. Chest up, chest down. Smoke in, smoke out. Up. Down. In. Out. Amy went with the rhythm, and forgot Dave.

Jude first kissed Amy on the street, as they made their way to Leicester Square, where she could catch the Northern line south, to Clapham, and he could catch it north, to Belsize Park – or they could both catch it in the same direction, as the case might be. He was casual about this first, very public kiss, nothing heavy, nothing face splitting, just half-parted lips and a tentative tongue. Very sexy. For an instant Amy, unused to kissing smokers, recoiled at his gutter taste, but then, beneath the nicotine, she caught a trace of *torta espresso à la español*, and she stretched her mouth, hungrily.

'So,' said Jude, when they broke for air, 'd'you . . . uh . . . want to come back to . . . uh . . . my place for . . . uh . . . coffee?' It was a clumsy invitation, because he wasn't used to offering them. Usually he and the woman just looked at each other and headed to bed.

'For coffee?'

In reply, Jude simply gave Amy his crooked smile. He was quite sure that tonight Shee-Chee's ghost would have some competition for his attention.

Amy swallowed. Of course she wanted coffee – but one of Seraph's books had contained a maxim she'd taken to heart: 'Never take coffee with a man until at least the third date.' Except it hadn't said *coffee*. 'Leave him begging for more, and he's yours for life.'

'I never have coffee in the evenings,' she said, primly. 'If I did I wouldn't sleep.'

Jude raised one mobile eyebrow.

Amy blushed, and swallowed harder. She reminded herself that making a man wait wasn't just a strategy she'd got out of a book, there was her self-respect to consider. Her self-esteem.

'That wasn't what I meant,' she said. 'What's the rush? I like to take things slowly.'

Now it was Jude's turn to swallow. The doormat was rejecting him! He gave a tiny, petulant shrug.

'It's your call.'

'Yes.'

The third date rule didn't let Amy down. Jude looked at her with greater interest than he'd shown all evening. *Right,* he thought, *in two minutes you're going to be regretting this.* Then he kissed her again, this time the way he'd kissed Alexandra, Carlotta, Camilla, Lucy and Beattie, but not Shee-Chee. With Shee-Chee his mouth had dissolved. With Amy, now, it simply became a cavern. He too had his maxims. *Leave them begging for more,* he thought, *and next time you try they're putty in your hands.*

6

Nick had had a tormented few days culminating in a miserable weekend, by the end of which he knew for certain he couldn't relinquish all claim to Ginny's baby. His baby. It was impossible. But on the other hand, he couldn't tell Seraph about it either, she'd never tolerate a love child. Or, for that matter, a not-love child. From the silence of its mother's womb, Sweetie disturbed its father's nights as surely as any yelling newborn, and at work first thing on Monday morning, Nick felt groggy and thick headed from sleep deprivation. He sat behind his desk, took a long slug of black coffee, then picked up the phone and punched in Pete's number.

'Hi, Pete. It's me.'

Pete was opening his post. He had a busy day ahead. His morning would be spent on-site at the semi-derelict warehouse, and he'd arranged a meeting with his structural engineers for the afternoon.

'I'm not a bloody agony aunt,' he said by way of greeting – but his tone was not unkind.

Nick rocked forward in his ergonomically designed chair.

'Pete,' he implored, 'you have to see it's my baby, too.'

Pete grunted, but said nothing.

'It's my baby too, Pete,' repeated Nick.

'So? What's your point?'

'I only want to get to know it a bit. It's not much to ask.'

'You're mad,' said Pete, without a second's hesitation. 'I thought you said she wanted to bring it up on her own?'

'I know, but—'

'Well then, if it's over between you and Ginny, why risk everything with Seraph?'

'I have to.'

'Crap! Ginny seems to have made it pretty clear you don't *have* to do anything.'

'I know. But—'

'You have the option of doing nothing.'

Nick leaned back and twisted the phone cord between his fingers.

'I don't,' he said, 'because of the smells.'

'Smells?' Pete was taken aback.

'The new-baby smells. You've smelled them. Spice and baking, warm and yeasty. Sour milk and cottage cheese. Blood.'

'Look, mate,' said Pete as patiently and yet as robustly as he could, 'you can't make any sensible decisions based on smells.'

'But when this baby's born, I'll be part of its smell.'

'Stinky nappies. Ammonia . . .'

'And I want to smell it.'

'Vomit . . .'

'And then there's the hole.'

'Hole?' Pete was running late for the warehouse, and was losing patience.

'Yeah. Say there's never any contact, then I'll always have this hole. A lost baby-shaped hole.'

'Look,' said Pete, 'you've been under a lot of stress lately. It's only natural—'

'And what if it spends its whole life yearning for its missing father? For me. Think of that, Pete! Think of us when dad did his bunk.'

Pete pursed his lips. He rarely let himself remember that rainy, grey summer. The fury and the longing, the leap of hope each time the phone had rung, or the post had arrived, and the devastation each time hope was crushed. He coughed, and scratched his shoulder.

'Madness,' he said, and then was silent a moment. 'What did you say you wanted to ask her?'

'She's not being reasonable, is she?' said Nick, quickly. 'She can't expect me to hand over a baby as if it were just another gift. Scent. Chocolates. Roses.'

'You gave her those things?'

'No. That's not what I meant . . . If I can just have some contact with our child. Some access.'

'Yes,' said Pete. 'But what about Seraph, and the kids?'

Nick picked up a pen in his free hand, and tapped it on the edge of his desk.

'Do you think I'd have to tell Seraph?'

'Not if you drop all this nonsense now.'

'But if I do ask Ginny? I mean ask her if she'll let me see the child. Would I have to tell Seraph then?'

'If you're lucky, Ginny'll carry on saying no.'

'But what if she says yes?'

Pete shrugged. 'D'you think you *could* keep a child secret? Visits? Payments?'

'Ginny doesn't want money.'

'So she says. And would you be so keen for contact if she did?'

'That's—' began Nick, angrily, but Pete drove straight through his objection.

'And what if Seraph found out six months down the line? Or two years? Or ten?'

Nick was cross, but he considered Pete's point for a moment. Were the effects of betrayal like interest on a credit-card debt? Did they accrue at a terrifying rate over time?

'So you think I should tell her?'

'No I don't. I think you should accept that Ginny wants you to have nothing to do with this kid, and be grateful for that. I think you should let her walk out of your life, like she wants, and not risk bouncing Seraph into walking out instead. The last thing you should do now is to ask for involvement with this baby.'

'But Seraph might understand.'

Pete made an incredulous sound.

'But she might,' pressed Nick. 'You know, if you were right and Ginny planned it . . .'

'What? "Onist, luv, it wasn't me, it woz 'er what done it!" ' Pete spoke with a cod London accent.

There was silence for a beat.

'Well, not exactly,' said Nick. 'But surely Seraph would understand?'

Pete grunted.

'Wanna bet on it?' he said.

Nick had no desire to bet on anything. Not for him the occasional flutter on the horses, the football pools, the arcade slot machines. He even thought playing the National Lottery was submitting to voluntary taxation. Yet almost as soon as he'd hung up on Pete he once more picked up his phone. He jabbed out Ginny's extension number very quickly, to minimize time for last-minute second thoughts.

'Ginny? Can I see you for a moment?'

'We have nothing to say to each other.'

This time Nick had already worked out his pretext for getting her into his office.

'I'm going to Rome on Wednesday,' he said. 'I need to see the Italian press clippings.'

'The press clippings? Again?'

'Yes.'

'I gave them to Jean.'

'All of them?'

'Portugal, Denmark and Holland.'

'I need Italy. Bring through what you've still got, if you would.'

Ginny immediately noticed Nick looked drawn and pale, but so what?

'Here you are,' she said, and once more chucked an untidy heap of cuttings onto his desk. 'The ones you want are somewhere in that lot.'

'I don't give a fuck about the press clippings,' said Nick.

'Not my problem.'

Nick ignored her.

'I've got something to ask you.'

'No,' she said. 'Whatever it is, no.'

Nick looked up, met her eye, and held it.

'I've been thinking,' he said. 'Last week I was shocked, stunned. I couldn't think . . .'

Ginny saw at once where this was going. *Don't worry, Sweetie, I'll see him off.*

'This baby's mine,' she said. *Mine.*

'Ginny, I can't just give it up like that.' Nick clicked his fingers. 'I can't.'

'You have no rights.'

Nick had no idea whether or not a lawyer would have agreed, but it sounded plausible. 'Rights?' he said. 'What have rights got to do with it?'

'Rights are rights,' replied Ginny. 'And what do you care? You asked me to have an abortion.'

'No I didn't.'

'Perhaps not in so many words. But still.'

'I was thinking of you. If you'd wanted to get rid of it, I would've supported you. But you want to keep it.'

'Yes. It's mine.' *Mine.*

'And mine too.'

'No. You wanted to get rid of it. It's mine.' *Mine.*

Nick was debating whether to tell Ginny how much he hadn't wanted a third child, and how much he now loved Luke, when his door swung open.

'Morning.' Tony stepped into the office, rubbing his hands together. He nodded at Nick's desk. 'Anything there on Fabric Fresh?'

They both looked at Ginny for an answer, but she just shrugged.

'Anyway,' said Tony, turning back to Nick, 'have you got a moment to go over postage costs for the upcoming mailshots?'

'Can't it wait?' said Nick, who hoped he didn't sound as though he were pleading.

Tony grinned.

'Shall I come back in ten?'

'Fine,' said Nick. 'See you in ten.'

Once Tony had gone, Ginny made to follow him.

'Not yet,' said Nick, keeping his eyes firmly on a stray cutting from *Le Figaro*. He wasn't fluent in French at the best of times, and now the headline might as well have been in Martian. 'You're sure I'm the father?'

'Yes.'

'And you truly want nothing from me?'

Ginny laughed.

'Just the baby.' *And I've got what I want, Sweetie!*

Nick twisted his wedding ring.

'What if I do too?'

'Do what?'

'What if I want the baby, too.'

'But you don't.' *He doesn't. I know it.*

'I'm its father, Ginny.'

'So?'

'What do you mean *so*?'

'What do you mean "you're it's father"?'

Nick spoke slowly, and loudly, as if to a foreigner. 'I mean, I'm its father. You're this child's mother and I'm its father. A child needs both its parents.'

'Not these days,' said Ginny.

What was that supposed to mean? In any case, thought Nick, these days weren't the issue. The issue was the future. In days to come would his child be able to think of him and think *so*?

He thought of a man whose face he might not recognize, living on a continent he'd never seen, with a woman he'd never met. Nick was pushing forty, and a father himself, but he'd like to punch that man. And then embrace him.

'I don't know' he began, tentatively 'you see my father—'

'Oh, *your* father.' Ginny cut in, and nothing about her tone betrayed she felt a shiver of sympathy for whatever it was she'd stopped him from saying.

One of Ginny's earliest memories was of asking her second or third nanny if her daddy lived at the office, a place she'd thought of as some sort of magical court, far nicer than home. Nanny had said, 'Of course not, silly,' but Ginny hadn't stopped wondering why she never saw him. Then, in her middle childhood, she began to notice the way her parents, Marcus and Audrey, flinched away from each other in doorways and on stairs. Not long afterwards the housekeeper more or less told her Marcus spent three or four nights a week in Pimlico, just down the road from her own home in Belgravia, in the arms of a woman called Belle. Ginny was shocked, but the shock had worn off by the time she and Audrey had found themselves banished to a flat in Hampstead, and herself encumbered with Belle as a wicked stepmother. Marcus had betrayed her. It was bad, but a much worse, and inevitable, betrayal was to follow. Two years later Belle produced a daughter, and another one three years after that. Melissa and Emily, the ugly half-sisters.

Nick was taken aback by the bitterness with which Ginny said, 'Oh, your father', and looked at her expectantly, but she said nothing, and he dropped his fledgling attempt to tell her his own tale of woe.

'Why?' he asked, instead.

'Why what?'

'Why're you so determined to exclude me?'

'Why're you so determined to muscle in?'

'It's not muscling in.'

'I think you're an irrelevance,' said Ginny. 'I just can't see the point.'

'Here comes the shorty and the fatty,' called Margaret from the door. Nick and Ginny both jumped, and his pallor became even more deathly.

'Hi Margaret,' he said. 'What can I do for you?'

'I wondered if I could do anything to help you prepare for Italy?' This was blatant, even by Margaret's standards. What could the deputy head of UK sales do to help her boss prepare for a trip to Rome?

'I think I can manage.'

'Yes,' said Margaret. 'I see you have Virginia to help you.'

'I like to do what I can,' said Ginny.

'We all know how indispensible you've become,' shot back Margaret, smiling so sweetly Ginny could feel the enamel dropping off her teeth.

'An irrelevance?' said Nick, the second he and Ginny were once more alone.

'Sure,' said Ginny. 'Apart from the obvious . . . in any case you're married.'

Nick rubbed a hand across his eyes.

'Yeah. I don't need reminding.'

'And you already have children.' The wife and children. According to Project P, these were the guarantors that Some Man would never allow himself to become messily embroiled in Ginny's life.

'So?' asked Some Man.

'So you can't be interested in my child.'

'Why not? It doesn't follow.' But Nick knew it might. Sort of.

'You should be grateful at getting clean away.'

'I am. I truly am. But . . .'

Ginny flicked her hands impatiently, as if she were brushing at a fly.

'I just don't want you,' she said. 'I just don't want you around in my life.'

Nick reached for the cutting from *Le Figaro*, and scrunched it up.

'You don't want me,' he said. 'Fine. You don't need me. Fine. You think you'll do better on your own. Fine. But what if our baby disagrees? What if it wants me? What if it wants a father?'

'It won't.' *You won't, Sweetie.*

'Please, Ginny. Think about what happens if our baby wants a father.'

After work that evening, Ginny let herself into her empty flat, and shivered – at this time of year the inadequate central heating barely managed to keep the place above freezing. She kept her coat on as she made herself a cup of coffee. Her answering machine was in the kitchen, and tonight the message light was blinking. After she'd set the kettle to boil, Ginny hit NEW MESSAGE, hoping her caller wouldn't be her mother, who phoned two or three times a week, for no reason whatsoever, as far as Ginny could see.

'Hi, Cookie.' Ginny pulled a face. Marcus insisted on using her childhood pet name, however often she asked him not to. 'No news and nothing much to say, but give me a ring when you've got a moment. Belle, Lissa and Ems say hi. They're all fine. Hope you are, too. Bye.'

Ginny scowled and ground her finger into the ERASE button. Then she thumped around the miniscule kitchen until the kettle had boiled. Still wearing her coat, she took her coffee through to the sitting room, and plonked herself down on the sofa. Her cigarettes and matches were lying on the coffee table, she lit up, and sucked hard on her fag, making the tip glow bright. No doubt at this very moment Marcus was sitting down to supper with Belle, Melissa and Emily. It pleased her to think of her half-sisters' unattractiveness. Their lumpen bodies, their fat, round faces – the features like currants lost in dough. And neither of them could string two words together. They must bore Marcus rigid. How he must long to be interested, entertained. Ginny grinned to herself, and tapped a caterpillar of ash into her ashtray. She tried, but failed, to imagine Marcus's face when she broke her news: 'Daddy, I've something to tell you.' Of course, he'd be bound to ask about the father, and Ginny had her answer all prepared. 'Some Man,' she'd say, in that tone she always used to Marcus when she wanted to forbid further questions. 'Just Some Man.' But whatever she planned to say to her dad, Ginny couldn't hide from herself that Some Man had a name. Nick. 'Think about what happens if our baby wants a father,' Nick had said.

Ginny took another drag of her fag, and faced the question – what if it did? 'Do you want a daddy, Sweetie?'

Sweetie declined to answer, and in the face of silence from her womb Ginny found herself imagining an adolescent's eyes, veiled and angry, hard with scorn: 'What about dad? Where is he, then? What did you do to him? What have you done with him?' Next thing she knew, she was sobbing. And also furious with herself. What was this nonsense? No doubt pregnancy *horror*mones, yet again. But the explanation didn't make her feel any better, for hormonally induced weeping was, after all, weeping.

'Stop it!' she commanded herself, aloud. 'Stop it! Stop it!' She drummed her fists on the sofa for added emphasis, then roughly wiped her nose and eyes on the sleeve of her coat. She was determined to tackle this emotional weakness in herself, before it escalated into full-blown hysteria. Perhaps one of her pregnancy books could tell her how?

The Pregnancy Handbook was lying open on Ginny's bedside table. She flopped down onto her bed and flipped through until she found a likely looking section.

The First Three Months: Your Emotions

We have already seen how during the first three months of pregnancy you will begin to notice a new you. So far we have concentrated on the physical changes taking place in your body. But change does not affect only your bra size and your waistline, emotional changes are also occurring.

Dead on, thought Ginny.

Some of these may be hormonal . . .

Right again.

. . . but remember that pregnancy is a time of transition. Your body, your life and your role are all changing. You are not yet a mother, but nor are you the same person you were before you became pregnant. Transition and its accompanying uncertainties can make pregnancy a time of intense emotional upheaval. You may be less able to hide or control your feelings, and your emotions may be more easily aroused than usual.

Sure, thought Ginny, but what do I do about it?

Pregnancy changes your life. It influences your decisions about everything: what you eat, what you do with your free time, who you see, how you spend your money. Your preoccupation with your pregnancy helps you to bond with your unborn baby, it is part of your emotional preparation for becoming a mother. Your partner, if you have one, may also . . .

Ginny skimmed through the next few paragraphs, about the way a pregnant woman's partner might be perplexed at how she'd suddenly become more dependent on him, and how he might resent her desire that he should learn about pregnancy, childbirth and baby care. 'He may feel your needs are taking the lead in the relationship, and wonder when his own will be fulfilled.' Ginny felt smug to be alone. After partners, Dr Case turned her attention to the equally hazardous topic of mothers.

During the early part of your pregnancy you may reflect on your relationship with your own mother when you were a child. This is partly because you realize you will soon be caring for a child yourself. As you begin to think about what kind of mother you would like to be it is natural that you should review the way your mother looked after you. Take anything from her parenting style which you admire and discard the rest. Pregnancy can be a time when you re-evaluate your relationship with your mother in very moving ways, but any negative feelings you experience about her are normal, they do not mean you will yourself be a bad mother.

Pregnancy as a time of emotional upheaval? Ginny had recently been crying, now she laughed – she'd always assumed the negative feelings she experienced in relation to her mother were entirely normal.

Ginny looked like her mother, but, in her mind, that was as far as the resemblance went. The template for the face, and the copy. She was not ungrateful for her nose and lips, and wished she'd inherited Audrey's violet eyes rather than her father's blue ones. There was no point in disputing Audrey had once been a great beauty – and beauty had its reasons. Ginny knew that, even if she herself hadn't figured out what those reasons were. But she was positive her mother had. The blood-red blood money. Ginny thought that Audrey thought that the purpose of beauty was acquisition. She lay on her bed and laughed to imagine her mother sorting through her jewellery box – checking off the sapphire bracelet, the emerald ring, the diamond earrings. Was it any wonder a woman in love with metal and stone had been unprepared to endure the drearier aspects of motherhood? If opals beckoned and gold called, why not leave the care of the daughter to the nanny? To a succession of nannies?

Not that Ginny had minded, very much. The nannies had let her get away with more or less anything, and her early years had been filled with a gleeful naughtiness no conscientious mother would allow. But her adolescence had been grim. When Audrey found herself exiled to Hampstead she'd got rid of all the staff – and it had been a terrible time for both mother and daughter. The first couple of years had been bearable, but then they'd hit a big problem: men. Ginny was suddenly surrounded by buzzing clouds of eager youths, and Audrey was equally suddenly unable to find anyone to give her the trinkets she'd begun to prize above kisses. Ginny cut a swathe through the spotty youths of NW3. Audrey sat at home and seethed. The rows were screaming. Ginny had finally had enough one stifling August day, when humidity leached from the air and lassitude leached into bodies, and the tiniest movement felt like swimming through honey.

'I'm so hot. *So* hot,' moaned Audrey, who'd been lying on a spindly chaise longue, flapping at her face with a fan.

Boys had given Ginny a taste for power. She'd risen from her own chair, and prepared her body for the full force of the coming explosion – legs and arms akimbo.

'I'm moving out,' she'd replied.

Despite Dr Case's confidence, Ginny couldn't begin to see how pregnancy might lead her to re-evaluate her relationship with her mother in very moving ways. *But don't worry Sweetie, I'll do better, I'll be better.* Anyway, she reminded herself, it wasn't thinking about mothers which had led her to turn to *The Pregnancy Handbook*. Weeping had been brought on by thoughts of fathers. Nick had asked, 'What if our child wants a father?' And she still hadn't answered his question.

Except Ginny suddenly knew that she had. She'd answered it ages back. What was her real motive in going to all the trouble of Project P, when she could have gone to a sperm bank? Had she really allowed herself to be put off by the thought of bureaucracy? And why had she not left S&M as soon as she was sure she was pregnant? Was it really because pregnancy hormones had made her passive? Why had she agreed to see Nick after Margaret had found her throwing up? She could have fobbed him off. Why had she admitted to him she was pregnant? Pregnancy hormones were not really truth drugs. Why had she not stormed out of his office when he'd mentioned abortion? Why had she bothered to listen to his pleas this morning when she really didn't have to? Why had she imagined an adolescent's eyes hard with scorn for the mother who'd deprived it of a father? Why? Why? Why?

Many whys, but only one answer. Ginny lounged on her bed and realized all her strategies and evasions arose from one simple fact – some part of her had known all along that she could never completely write off the possibility of paternal love for her child. All the time she'd been planning Project P she'd known this. She'd not admitted it to herself until now, but she'd known. Just as from the day she'd asked some nanny whose name she'd forgotten if it was true her daddy lived at the office, she'd known she wanted Marcus to forget about work and look at her instead. Really look at her. 'Watch me, daddy! Watch me!'

Ginny sat up and snapped shut *The Pregnancy Handbook*. She'd grant Nick's request for access to Sweetie. And she was glad he'd made it. *You'll get your daddy, Sweetie, just like all the other kids.* But could this mean she also wanted Nick for himself? For herself? Was it possible she'd deceived herself about that too? Ginny closed her eyes and imagined herself waddling down the street, seven or eight months pregnant, Nick protectively guiding her. She imagined them gazing into a cot where Sweetie lay a sleeping, and then kissing above the mobile which dangled there. The peachy scenarios left her cold. She imagined herself and Nick making love of a Saturday night, herself gazing up at the ceiling and willing him to get on with it . . . truly Nick was no use to her. For himself and for herself she only wanted Adam. *Oh, Adam, Adam . . .*

7

'Okay,' hissed Ginny. 'I agree.'

'What . . .?'

'I said I agree.'

'I h-h-heard . . . th-th-thanks Ginny.' Nick was in his office, and the hand holding the phone to his ear had just begun to sweat.

Ginny grunted. She was hunched low over her desk in the open-plan area, the eavesdropping area, the gossip cauldron, and she was speaking in little more than whispers. She didn't give a toss what people thought, but still.

'It means we've loads to talk about,' she said. 'All the details. But Tony and Margaret and Jean. I'd rather meet out of the office.'

Nick glanced at Jean, who was busily tapping at her computer.

'Yeah,' he said. 'Good idea.'

'So when's good for you?'

'Not today, and I'm in Rome tomorrow. I'll have to check my diary.'

'Fine. Give me a ring when you get back . . . I'd better give you my home number.'

As soon as she'd hung up on Nick, Ginny phoned Jean.

'Oh it's you,' said Jean. 'Good. I wanted to talk to you about some stuff for Tony.'

'No,' said Ginny. 'Not now . . . I'm phoning to tell you I've decided it's time for me to move on. I'm handing in my notice.'

Jean glanced at Nick, who was looking fixedly at a sheet of paper in his hands.

'Oh,' she said. 'That's a bit of a surprise. Any particular reason you want to go?'

'I'm a temp, remember? I've been here long enough. I don't want to become a fixture.'

The paper in Nick's hands had Ginny's home number scrawled across it. Not that Nick could see it, he was blind with panic. And he couldn't breathe properly. He needed calm, reassurance, a steadying voice. Where could he get it? Easy. Nick picked up the phone to call Pete, his rock.

'Pete,' he said when his brother answered. 'It's me.'

'You okay?' asked Pete, who couldn't miss the strain in his brother's voice.

'Well, I asked her—'

'Ginny?'

'Yes. I asked her if I could have some contact with the child.'

Pete was doing his accounts, there were receipts and invoices spread all over his desk – many covered with his trademark doodle of interlocking triangles. Now he speared a stray receipt with his pen.

'I knew you would. And? What did she say?'

'She said yes.'

Pete whistled.

'You're sure this is what you want?' *Be careful what you wish for . . .*

'I am. I think.'

'You *think*?'

'I mean I am.'

Pete was silent for a moment, then he switched tack. 'So what's it to be?' he asked. 'Alternate weekends. Annual holidays. Trips to the zoo and the park, that sort of thing?' He was thinking of his and Fiona's arrangements for Lachlan and Catriona.

Nick swallowed. 'I don't know about weekends and holidays,' he said. 'But trips, yes. Birthday presents. We haven't bashed out the details yet.'

Pete waited before responding. 'And what did Seraph say?'

'Nothing yet. Ginny's only just told me.'

'So,' said Pete, 'when will you tell her?'

'Seraph?'

'Of course Seraph!'

Nick sighed, heavily. 'Dunno. D'you really think I have to?'

'We've been over this. Yes.'

'But . . .'

'If you don't it's just disaster deferred.'

'But the disaster might never happen.'

'She'd be bound to find out. Say someone you knew saw you out with this kid? Or say it got sick, and you had to go to hospital in the middle of the night? Or say Seraph found a credit-card receipt for children's clothes she'd never seen? Or toys?'

'I'd be careful.'

'Say Ginny decided to spill the beans?'

'Why? She'd never do that.'

Pete made a dismissive sound. 'Donna did.'

'That was completely different. Completely.'

'Sure . . . but you never know with women.'

Nick said nothing.

'Tell her,' said Pete. 'Just tell her and keep your fingers crossed.'

'But I'm going to Rome tomorrow.'

'What's that got to do with anything?'

Nick fiddled with the phone cord.

'Dunno,' he said, then after a second, 'That earrings business . . . you said it worked with Donna?'

Pete shifted his position in his chair.

'Yeah,' he said. 'But it hardly compares . . . perhaps if you could run to the necklace and bracelet to go with the earrings?'

Both brothers were silent, wondering about the price-tag on forgiveness.

'Anyway,' said Nick, at last, 'what will I actually *say* to Seraph? If I tell her.'

'What actual words?'

'Mm.'

Pete leaned over and began to doodle triangles on his accountant's covering letter.

'Okay,' he said. 'Role play.'

'What?'

'Come on, role play. I'll be Seraph.'

Nick pictured his brother, tall and rangy, like himself, but with greyer hair, a beakier nose, and, he flattered himself, more wrinkles.

'You want me to pretend you're Seraph?' he said, doubtfully. 'You want me to pretend I'm breaking the news to her?'

'Mm-hmm.'

'Your voice is all wrong.'

'Detail.'

Nick swivelled in his chair, so he was facing the exterior window, and saw his anxious reflection hanging in space. He swivelled back again.

'Okay.' He paused. 'Seraph, darling—'

'Do you usually call her darling?'

'No.'

'Then don't. You'll put her on edge.'

'Seraph, love?'

'Too cosy. Start with Seraph, just Seraph, you can't go wrong with Seraph.'

'Okay. Seraph, you know I've always loved you truly and loyally. I still do.' He paused. 'Or how about this: Seraph, I love you. And I love the kids. You know that.'

'Don't mention the kids. Not just yet.'

'You're right. Keep the focus on Seraph.'

'Yes. The kids just complicate things.'

Nick didn't want to think about that.

'Seraph,' he said. 'I love you. But, I've something to tell you. It doesn't mean anything. Nothing at all. But . . . But what? I fucked another woman?'

'Too harsh.'

'I've been having an affair?'

'Too romantic.'

'I've committed adultery?'

'Too biblical.'

'I've been unfaithful?'

'It'll have to do.'

'Seraph, I've been unfaithful. Not for long, and not often. We only did it a few—'

'Do you think she'll care? Once is enough.'

'I suppose so.' Nick paused again and then took a deep breath. 'Okay,' he said, 'here goes. Seraph, I've got something to tell you. It doesn't mean anything. Nothing at all. But I've been unfaithful, and the thing is she's . . . she's . . . she's . . .'

'Pregnant.'

'Yes. Or should that be she's expecting a baby?'

'No, pregnant is better. Less coy.'

'Right. She's pregnant, but the thing is I love you, I need you, I want you.'

'Isn't that a pop song?'

Nick smiled, despite himself.

'Okay. She's pregnant, but the thing is . . . Please forgive me.'

'Good. But be a bit more pleading. Beg. Begging can't do any harm.'

'That's true. If I got her some, could I give her the earrings about now?'

Pete laughed. 'Whatever,' he said, 'but even begging might not work.' It hadn't for him.

'No guarantees,' said Nick, wistfully.

'Precisely.'

'I know that.'

The entire time he was driving home, Nick tried to decide whether it would be better to confess to Seraph tonight, before he went to Rome, and let her have a few days alone in which to get used to the idea of his betrayal – a cooling off period – or whether it would be better to wait to say something until after he got back, so she wasn't left to stew and work herself into a frenzy of solitary fury. Cooling or stewing? Which was more likely? Nick had no idea, and decided he'd let fate decide when he declared his sin.

The children were just finishing their tea in the kitchen and Kate, the Aussie nanny who took so much of Seraph's salary, was at a work surface, slicing fruit. Nick walked in and told himself to act naturally.

'Hi everyone,' he said, helping himself to a sausage Daisy had left on her plate. 'Where's mum?' He hoped it didn't sound like a loaded question.

'She phoned,' replied Kate. 'She said she'd be late.'

'Did she say why?'

'No.'

'Oh. Well.' *Reprieve,* thought Nick.

'Perhaps she's gone to get me my Black Hole Blaster,' said Tom, in a hopeful voice. The Black Hole Blaster was one of the weapons he'd put on his Christmas wish-list, even though he knew Seraph didn't approve of toy guns. Or real ones.

'Tom,' said Kate in a warning voice. 'It's Father Christmas who brings the presents.' She nodded in Luke's direction.

'And the elves help him,' added Daisy.

'That's right,' said Nick, dropping a quick kiss on the top of his daughter's head. 'But only children who've been good all year get anything at Christmas.'

'I've been very, very good,' said Daisy.

'Me too,' said Tom.

'Good,' said Luke. He was eating a peach yogurt and waved his spoon for emphasis.

'Or Mum might be getting the tree?' suggested Tom.

'*Tree?*' asked Nick, giving the impression he'd no idea what Tom was talking about. Daisy looked stricken.

'The *Christmas* tree, Daddy.'

'Oh, that tree,' said Nick. 'It's still a bit early, don't you think?'

'No,' chorused the children. Nick laughed.

'We'll all go and choose one together,' he promised, 'maybe on Sunday.' By which time, come what may, he'd have told Seraph. Oh, God!

'Tree!' squealed Luke, once again waving his spoon. Yogurt spattered all over Nick's jacket. Kate silently handed him some kitchen paper, before distributing bananas and slices of apple to the children. Luke dexterously peeled his banana, then squashed it down against his head, using both hands to mash it right into his hair. The older ones giggled, while Nick and Kate exchanged glances. Nick shrugged.

'Bath time soon,' he said.

'Good job,' said Kate.

'I'll do it tonight.' Nick turned to his children. 'Remember I'm off to Rome tomorrow? So I won't see you lot until Saturday.'

'L-L-L-L-Lazzio!' shouted Tom, punching the air, and trying to copy the tone of a football commentator.

Nick smiled and ruffled his hair.

'What are your plans for tonight?' he asked Kate. He hoped she had none. If she was in, he'd invite her to eat dinner with him and Seraph as she often did. With Kate around, it would be impossible for him to find the right moment to spill the beans, unless he waited until he and Seraph were preparing for bed, which, he thought, was a lousy time to tell your wife you'd been unfaithful. Let alone that your ex-mistress was pregnant.

'I'm meeting Sandra for a drink,' said Kate.

'Great,' said Nick, mournfully. Kate shot him a quizzical look, but said nothing.

A little later Seraph let herself in and heard a racket coming from the bathroom.

'I'm home,' she called, at the top of her lungs, but nobody answered. She shrugged out of her coat, and dumped it and her briefcase on the large, Edwardian coat stand she'd inherited when an aunt moved into sheltered housing, then she looped her bag over the newel post at the bottom of the stairs. The Jamiesons' house, at 17 Athens Road, was tall and narrow, sometimes it could seem like nothing but one long staircase. Kate had a studio downstairs in the basement, and from the ground floor there were two flights up to the bathroom, which occupied a half landing between the first floor, where Tom and Daisy had their rooms, and the top floor, where her own and Nick's bedroom was found, and Luke's, too.

Seraph climbed slowly upwards.

'Daisy,' she heard Nick shout, 'if you poke Luke one more time there'll be no sweets for a week.'

'But he kicked me,' whined Daisy.

There followed some ill defined yodels and grunts.

'Right. That's it. Out!'

'But, Dad–'

'Out, Daisy!'

'Hello everybody,' said Seraph, standing in the doorway. Luke and Daisy were in the bath, Nick was kneeling by the tub, his arms stretching towards Daisy, and Tom was standing by the loo, towelling himself dry. They all turned towards her, and fell silent.

'Wow!' said Nick a second later. 'Your hair!'

After work Seraph had gone to get her hair cut and coloured. Anything had seemed better than going home – Nick had been so snappy and moody for the last week or so, and she'd needed cheering up. She now touched her head, uncertainly.

'Do you like it? I've got to get used to it.'

'It's great,' said Nick.

Luke began to cry. 'Yukky,' he said. 'Yukky hair.'

'You look like a boy,' said Daisy.

'Thanks, you two,' said Seraph.

'I like it, mum,' said Tom. 'It suits you.'

Seraph smiled at him, then turned back to Nick.

'Want a hand?' She cherished a fantasy of the children's bath time as family quality time, filled with laughter and gentle splashing – this despite daily evidence to the contrary.

'Thanks,' said Nick.

As they so often had in the past, husband and wife set about the sweetly domestic task of washing the grime of the day off their children's velvet flesh.

Down at the Dog and Gun, Kate and Sandra were onto their second round. Sandra was also a nanny – her employers Nigel and Caroline, her charge two-year-old Zoe.

'I'm getting really pissed off with them,' Sandra was saying. 'They're at each other's throats all the time and it's exhausting. Plus Zoe behaves like the child from hell when she's heard them arguing.'

'I know,' said Kate, gloomily. 'It's been like *Nightmare On Elm*

Street round at mine recently. But you should think yourself lucky. At least you only have one of them to look after.'

'Yes, and how many times have I told you to find yourself a new job? An only child. A baby.'

'You're right. I probably should.'

'There's tons of work around. You'd have no problem getting something.'

'Yeah.' Kate sipped her beer, and decided to confide. 'But I might not need a new job, at least not in London. I'm thinking of telling Richard I'll move in with him, after all.' Richard was her boyfriend, and she spent her weekends with him, at his cottage near Sevenoaks.

'Kate! That's wonderful.'

'I'm not a hundred per cent sure.' Kate had met Richard, a solicitor, soon after she'd arrived in the UK, nearly two years ago. Within a few weeks he'd asked her to marry him. She'd laughed and said thanks very much, but she wasn't ready for the provinces and a garden just yet. But he'd carried on asking.

'So?' said Sandra. 'You'd only be moving in. You could always move out again.'

'Sure . . . it's just seeing him every day, eating breakfast with him every morning, sleeping with him every night . . . it has its disadvantages . . .'

'And its attractions,' Sandra couldn't wait for her boyfriend of eight years to propose.

'I know. I'm almost sure I'm ready. I probably will say something over Christmas.'

'His Christmas present?'

'Yeah. Plus socks and stuff.'

Tom, Daisy and Luke were all asleep. Downstairs, in the kitchen Seraph returned to the subject of her hair, which was now very short and very spiky, with platinum highlights. She was sitting at the table with a glass of wine, while Nick prepared their supper – he'd volunteered, which she'd thought suspicious.

'You don't think it makes me look like a dyke?' she asked.

Nick laughed.

'You think it does, don't you? It cost a fortune, I had it done at Ferrucci's. And I end up looking like a dyke.'

'Ferrucci's?'

'Marco Ferrucci's famous. He does actresses and such.'

'It looks fine,' said Nick. 'Supper's up.'

They were having sausage casserole. Nick's cooking was no better than Seraph's, and his casserole was sausage in tomato glop, garnished with bits of onion, pepper and mushroom.

'So how was your day?' Seraph asked, when they were both seated at the table, with their food in front of them.

'Oh . . . y'know. Yours?'

Seraph pulled a face, then they both lapsed into silence.

Nick decided this was it, and desperately tried to remember key points from his role playing with Pete. But his mind had gone blank. He dug his fork into a piece of red pepper, cleared his throat, then looked directly at Seraph, who was looking down, absorbed in pushing the sausage and tomato glop round her plate.

'Seraph,' he said. 'I love you.'

Seraph's head snapped up.

'I love you.' He repeated. 'But . . .'

'You love me *but*?'

Nick gulped, he'd hardly started and things were already going badly.

'We need to talk.' Those four terrifying little words weren't in Pete's script, but they'd have to do.

'We need to talk?' *So*, thought Seraph, *The confirmation. He was having an affair.*

'Yes. We need to talk.'

'No we don't.'

'What?'

'We don't. I know what you're going to say.'

'You do?'

'Yes.'

Upstairs, Luke began to cry, the sound amplified by the baby monitor they kept on top of the fridge-freezer. Seraph rose an inch from her chair, then sat down again.

'You're having an affair,' she said.

'An affair?'

'Yes. You're having an affair.'

'Well, not precisely . . . it's more that I've been unfaithful.'

Seraph snorted.

'Seraph, I beg of you . . . it meant nothing . . . I'll get you some earrings—'

'*Earrings?*'

'I didn't mean that . . . I only fucked her . . .'

'Oh shut up!' said Seraph, and stood up.

'But Seraph, it was meaningless. It's you I love, but . . . the thing is, she's . . . she's . . .' Perhaps Pete was wrong? Perhaps 'having a baby' was, after all, friendlier than 'pregnant'?

'Shut up! Not now. Now I'm going to see to Luke.' Seraph

took a couple of steps backwards, towards the door, Nick jumped up, too, and reached out an arm to grab her, but at the last moment he thought better of it. They faced each other across the chasm of their kitchen table, while their son wailed in the background.

'Darling . . .' said Nick.

'Don't darling me! I'd wondered, of course . . .'

'You had?'

'Of course. And I wanted to know. Really I did. But—'

'I'm so very . . .'

Seraph wheeled away from him.

'I don't care,' she said, to the door. 'Tom's sleeping bag's in the laundry cupboard. Tonight you can sleep on the sofa.'

Nick sat down and watched Seraph disappear into the hall. He knew he'd botched his confession – earrings, oh God! – but in an odd way he felt quite relieved. Seraph hadn't had hysterics, or grabbed a knife from the block by the sink and attacked him, or chucked him out. Under the circumstances, sleeping on the sofa was only to be expected. Although, of course, he hadn't told her everything – not even the most important things – and he briefly considered waiting half an hour, then going up to their room to try to re-open discussions: 'Baby, there's one more thing – a baby!' But he decided against. In any case, although he hadn't planned it, or run it past Pete, he thought that telling Seraph in drips might be quite a good strategy. Drip. I had an affair. Drip. She's pregnant. Drip, drip. I'm going to have a role in the child's up bringing. Drip, drip, drip. But you don't need to worry about any of that. We can put all this behind us and start again . . .

You'll be lucky, whispered a tiny voice at the back of his mind. Nick wriggled uncomfortably on his seat.

'So what would you do?' He said aloud, to the voice. But the voice had no answer.

Upstairs, Seraph found Luke sitting up in bed, crying. His nightlight was on, throwing the elongated shadows of books, bears and toy trucks all around his room. She plopped down beside him and reached over to stroke his hair. Luke's nights were filled with mysterious fears which he couldn't articulate.

'What is it, Luckie-boo?'

Luke stood up, leaned over and placed both hands on top of Seraph's head.

'Hair,' he said, through sniffs.

'Yes. It's going to stay like this now.'

Luke looked disappointed, but he sat down again, and stopped crying.

'Hole,' he said, after a moment. 'Luke fall in.' He used his feet to push back the duvet and pointed at a patch of sheet.

'Hole.'

'Oh yes,' said Seraph. 'But don't worry about that.' She looked around for something to use as a magic wand, and picked up a piece of Meccano, which had strayed in from Tom's room.

'See this?'

Luke nodded.

'This is my magic wand. Now listen carefully . . . Abracadabra, walamazoo, I shall make the hole disappear, psheww,' she spoke in a sing-song voice, and waved the piece of Meccano. 'Look! Magic! The hole's gone!'

They both stared down at the patch of sheet. Seraph thumped it, then so did Luke.

'Gone,' he said, gravely. 'Gone.'

'Yes, gone. And now it's time to go to sleep.'

When Seraph finally entered her bedroom, she flicked on the light, and crossed to shut the curtains in the big bay window, which looked out over her tatty garden, and her neighbours' gardens, mostly as tatty as her own. It was cold by the glass, and she shivered as she drew the curtains. When she turned back into the room her eye was caught by the tangle of cheap necklaces lying on her dressing table. She walked over and picked one up – a long strand of green glass beads. *Earrings!* What on earth had Nick been thinking of? But there was a slight glint in her eye as she let the beads slide through her fingers. She knew she wasn't immune to greed, or vanity or flattery. Perhaps if Nick were to agree to replace this imitation jade with the real thing, or with emeralds?

But what was this rapacious claptrap? Seraph dropped the necklace as if it were hot, and took a couple of steps to her bed, where she lay down, folded a flap of duvet around her body for warmth, and stared up at the ceiling. When she and Nick had first moved to this house she'd been pregnant with Tom, and they'd decorated their bedroom, and the nursery next door, in a fit of anticipatory nesting. Once Tom was born they'd run out of enthusiasm for colour charts, paint techniques and the rest, so most of the house was decorated in the same dirty cream the previous owners had chosen. But in here the ceiling was washed a pale aquamarine, the walls were ragged in many shades of blue and green, and the heavy curtains were patterned with seaweedy brown swirls on a fawn background. Seraph and Nick had chosen the colour scheme together, they'd thought it was calming, and that it was neither masculine nor feminine. But tonight it made Seraph feel submerged and watery, as if she were at the bottom of an ocean, staring up at the surface. Forget emeralds. There was no longer any room for doubt, her husband was an adulterer. Now she faced a night filled with mysterious fears she couldn't articulate. And who was there to walk in carrying a magic wand powerful enough to wave her fears away? Nobody. That's who.

8

Seraph was in her office getting ready for the weekly acquisitions meeting. The purpose of this was to determine which of the books and proposals sponsored by Bladder editors Eddie would actually agree to publish, and how little money he was willing to pay for them. The sums were always far lower than those expected by authors and their agents, except for sports books, which Eddie commissioned himself. This week Seraph had two proposals to take to the meeting. One, *You Lucky Stiff: A Man's Guide to Oral Sex*, was for her men's health list, the other, aimed more at women, was for an American anti-bloating diet. The diet's US publisher had sent her copies of several glowing reviews which she'd promptly lost. She was scrabbling for them among the piles of paper on her desk when Amy came in, and gasped.

'Seraph,' she said, 'your hair!'

Seraph stopped scrabbling and patted her head self-consciously.

'Do you like it?'

'It's great. But do you feel okay? You look a bit pale.'

Seraph looked worse than pale, she looked hollow-eyed and drained. Last night, alone in her bed, she'd not slept at all and this morning she had a thumping headache, plus her mouth felt as though it were full of feathers.

'I'm fine,' she said. 'It's probably just that I look deathly without my hair.'

'Rubbish,' said Amy. 'It's fab. And you've had it coloured, too!'

'Lightened a bit. Do you think it's too young for me?'

'No! It's taken years off you. Where did you go?'

'Ferrucci's.'

Amy pulled a face.

'That jerk!' Unlike Nick, Amy had heard of Marco Ferrucci, who was famous for two things, his passion for short hair, and his frank dislike for women over forty. He'd once tried to exclude them from his salon, but had run into legal problems and tabloid headlines. At the height of the fuss Seraph had approached him to write a guide to hair care, but a competitor had got in first, waving an open cheque book.

'Okay,' said Seraph. 'But whatever you think of him you have to say he's great with short hair, and I couldn't risk coming out looking as if I'd fallen into a food processor – although I'm a bit worried I look like a dyke.'

'Sure you do,' said Amy, whose face and tone belied her words. 'Did Marco do it himself?'

'No, one of his underlings. It was cheaper.'

Amy combed the fingers of one hand through her own shaggy hair.

'Much cheaper?'

'Quite a bit.'

'Jude said I should get mine cut.'

Seraph flinched slightly at Jude's name.

'He did?' she said, after a second.

'Yeah. At lunch yesterday. He said I have pretty hair, and that it might really suit me short and boyish.'

'He's right,' Seraph spoke without inflection. 'Why don't you take him up on it?'

Amy shrugged.

'Dave always said he really liked it like this.'

'Oh.' Seraph was startled.

Amy grimaced.

'But what he thought is neither here nor there – what's everyone said about yours?'

'Luke said it was yukky.'

'Luke's two. What about Nick?'

Seraph's face shut down, she turned away and once again started sifting through the papers on her desk.

'I've lost a whole slew of reviews,' she said.

Amy pursed her lips, remembering Seraph more or less telling her that Nick was having an affair.

'Seraph?' She began, concerned, but not wanting to pry.

'Gracious!' exclaimed Seraph briskly, glancing at her watch. 'We'd better get going. We're already late.'

Acquisitions meetings were held in the boardroom on the first floor. This had once been a grand, formal dining room and the ghost of luxury still hung about. The walls, now graced with photos of Bladder's more successful authors, were wood panelled. The high ceiling was ornamented with intricate, cobwebby, plaster moulding. Six tall windows gave a view of grey sky and scudding cloud above the busy square. A filthy crystal chandelier hung above an oval, rosewood table big enough to seat thirty. Once this table had glowed with a rich, satin sheen, but now it was matte and pock-marked with rings from carelessly placed coffee mugs. Unlike the table, the chairs had never seen better days. They'd always been cheap, mismatched, and uncomfortable.

By the time Seraph and Amy got to the meeting it was already in full swing. They slid as quietly as they could onto a couple of wobbly plastic chairs standing against the wall, just inside the door. Jude was speaking. He wafted a half-smoked Gauloise in one hand, and a sheaf of papers in the other. A mug of strong, black coffee sat before him on the table. To Jude this coffee mug was a sort of talisman. It had been produced as part of the sales campaign for *China Fun*, and was adorned with a grainy reproduction of Shee-Chee's face, so each time he took a sip of coffee, his lips grazed the top of her head.

Everybody noticed Seraph's hair, a few people flashed her smiles, or discreet thumbs-up, and she felt herself blushing. The distraction allowed Jude to meet Amy's eye and hold it a fraction too long, without anybody catching them, except Benedicta, who frowned. Jude had been talking about lyricism and an ever-present sense of the supernatural in *Heaven.com* a manuscript by a well-established author, Baz Whitney. Once Amy and Seraph were settled, he continued where he'd left off in the midst of a plot summary.

'Given his soul-hunger,' he said, 'the wanderer's surprising refusal of Melinda's steamed dumplings prepare the reader for his assertion that he is God, and that he is, in some sense, her. All in all a satisfying, elegiac exploration of identity and divinity, suffused with the numinous. I think we should publish.'

Eddie was anxious and distracted this morning – earlier he'd seen Bladder's latest sales figures, which were beyond abysmal – but nevertheless he nodded his agreement.

'Anyone got anything to add?' he asked.

Benedicta raised her hand.

'Lucian read it over the weekend,' she said. 'He and Baz go way back. He thinks Baz has such a strong sense of rhythm. So do I. Rhythm is god.'

Everyone looked at her.

'Quite,' said Eddie. 'Anybody else?'

'Heaven dot com?' queried Gill, the dictionaries and reference editor. 'Shouldn't that be gone dot com? I thought all that stuff was over?'

Jude looked pained. 'Baz doesn't intend his title to be taken literally,' he said.

Nobody responded to that.

'Okay,' said Eddie, 'we'll do it. Jude, you can see me later about the offer.'

He glanced around the room, and his eye settled on Seraph.

'What have you got for us?' he asked.

'*The Anti-bloating Diet* and *You Lucky Stiff: A Man's Guide to Oral Sex*.'

'Start with oral sex.'

'Surely there isn't a book in it? Sounds more like a health education leaflet.' This was Gill.

'Oh, I dunno,' replied Seraph. 'It's for the men's list.'

'An area we need to grow,' said Eddie.

Seraph nodded.

'It's by Bruno Faversham,' she continued. 'He's done a couple of books for Compass Press. This one's a guide showing how men can get great oral sex whenever they want.'

Seraph sensed Amy stiffen besides her.

'Not very politically correct,' demurred Gill.

'I agree,' said Benedicta. 'It sounds terrible.'

'But commercial,' said Seraph, firmly.

'Yes,' agreed Eddie. 'Go on.'

'Here are the chapter titles.' Seraph began to read from the contents list. 'Keep it Up, 2, 3, 4; The Big Gulp; Baby, Remember my Name – well, anyway, you get the picture. It's quite well written.' She turned a page, jabbed her finger down at random and started reading, 'The beauty of the blow job is you don't have to do any work. You can hang up the hip action, free your forearms and save your sweat for the soccer pitch. But—'

'Sounds fine,' said Eddie. 'What do you think Jude?'

'I think it would sell.'

Eddie grunted and turned to Edo, a deceptively ascetic-looking Polish lexicographer who worked for Gill.

'Edo?'

'If it's sensitively handled, I think it could be very stimu–interesting. The market surely needs a serious study of fellatio.'

'Okay, Seraph,' said Eddie. 'Go for it! Has he got an agent?'

'No.'

'Good.' Eddie began to run through a payment schedule for the author. It was miserly.

'But—' Seraph began to protest.

'He can like it, or lump it,' said Eddie. 'Now, do you mind if we leave your other one for next week? We've got a lot to get through.' Without waiting for Seraph to reply, he called on Gill to present the first of her five proposals.

─────

Half an hour later Amy and Seraph were back in Seraph's sliver of office. Seraph was sitting at her desk, lurching, while Amy was upright, but swaying. The lurching and swaying were caused by laughter, great whoops and swoops and whorls of it.

'What a load of balls!' shrieked Amy. 'Did you mean it as some sort of joke?'

'Of course not!' Seraph struggled to speak. 'Like I said, the men's market. It's in my five-year plan.'

'Oh yes, the five-year plan!'

'Okay. But Eddie thinks men are neglected when it comes to self-help.'

'Self-help!' Amy cackled like an old crone.

'You're being unfair,' objected Seraph, gasping, 'you know I'm supposed to publish a million books this year and he's a well-respected author.'

'A well-respected author,' mimicked Amy, then, in mid-sentence, she switched voices and began to mimic Edo instead, 'who'll produce a stimulating study of fellatio.' She was not a good mimic and her remark was not funny, but it acted as a catalyst to boost Seraph into truly hysterical laughter. She was quite unable to stop. Her whole body rolled and heaved with seismic convulsions. Tears poured down her face, which blushed a blotchy purple. After a while Amy became very quiet, and very still, watching her.

'It wasn't that funny,' she said.

Seraph laughed on, oblivious. Amy took a deep breath and shuffled forward a couple of steps. She knelt next to her friend, and awkwardly placed an arm across her shoulder.

'Seraph?' she said. 'Seraph, are you okay?'

She kept her arm in place, until Seraph's laughter began to die down, then she stood up and leant against the filing cabinet.

It took Seraph a few more minutes to get herself fully under control.

'I'm sorry,' she said, when she'd finally succeeded. 'I'm so sorry.' She would not meet Amy's eye.

'No need,' said Amy, who fixed her gaze on the floor. Just by her feet was a huge stack of page proofs for a medical encyclopedia. She hesitated a moment or two, then spoke again, 'What's up?' she said, keeping her eyes on the proofs. 'What is it, Seraph? Is everything okay? I mean between you and Nick? You really haven't seemed yourself recently.'

Seraph turned her head to stare out of the window. Her eyes stung, and a dull ache was developing beneath them. If she wasn't herself, then who was she? She watched a solid-looking woman make her way across the square, a sturdy woman. It was a cold, windy day and the woman was making slow progress, her coat flapped about her legs, and her scarf streamed behind her. Council workers had recently put up a Christmas tree, and she stood to admire it, or to listen to the band from the Salvation Army which was gathered around it, presumably playing carols, although no music penetrated Seraph's office. The tree listed alarmingly in the wind, it was decked with brightly coloured lights, and topped with a glittering gold star. To Seraph it looked tawdry and municipal, while the Salvation Army always made her feel guilty.

And right at this moment, so did Amy. Talk. That was what Seraph wanted to do now. She knew explaining her problems to someone would help clarify her thoughts and force her to name each of the emotions swirling around her brain, clogging it, like cloud. If she could only name her emotions, then perhaps she'd be able to tame them? Perhaps even be able to see what to do next? Or, short of that, she could at least ask her confidante for advice: 'Tell me what to do.' But, as she'd discovered as she lay tossing and turning the previous night, choosing a confidante wasn't easy. She couldn't burden her parents, they were both nearly eighty, and her father had a weak heart. Any hint of problems between Nick, whom they dearly loved, and their darling Seraphina, would send them plummeting into a tailspin of panic and anxiety. Georgina and Helen, her two closest friends from university, could be of no help either. Georgina and her husband were currently ripping each other to shreds in an acrimonious divorce, while Helen's husband's job had taken her off to Tokyo three years ago. The time difference, and the cost, made long, anguished telephone calls very difficult. In the depths of the night Seraph had even toyed with the idea of phoning her ex-sister-in-law, Fiona.

From the moment they'd met Seraph, an only child, and Fiona, who had three younger brothers, had treated each other like sisters. For many years they'd phoned each other every day, to laugh and moan and exchange gossip. Their personalities had complemented each other nicely. Practical Fiona was good for Seraph, who, while far from silly, could sometimes be a little dreamy. And Seraph was good for Fiona, she stopped her from becoming too down-to-earth and literal. Of course, Nick and Pete had always been a bond between the two women, so, in time, were their children. Fiona, the elder by three years, had been the first to succumb to her biological clock. She'd produced two children, a sensible number, two years apart, sensible spacing. Lachlan and Catriona. The boy, then the girl. So typical. Then that was it for her. No inconvenient third child for the proficient GP who ran a Well Women clinic every Thursday. By contrast

Seraph had been stunned to find herself pregnant with Luke, her accident, her mistake. Not that she'd been able to turn to Fiona for advice when she needed it, for by then Fiona and Pete were already divorced, and the two women had begun to drift apart. We're like sisters, they'd reassured each other, again and again through the happy years. But they were not actually sisters, whereas Nick was Pete's brother – his *actual* brother, not *like* his brother. When Fiona and Pete had been falling apart at the seams, Seraph had not held back from blame. She'd been outraged by Pete's behaviour, and had willingly given up her Saturdays to make round trips to Bristol, where she'd held Fiona's hand, brewed tea, soothed, bolstered, clucked and frowned. But once the dust had settled she'd known she'd have to reach an accommodation with Pete and Donna, for her husband's sake. There were family Christmasses to think about, outings, holidays. Pete was her children's uncle – and Bianca was their cousin. She couldn't ignore these facts, and it had been hard to keep up her friendship with Fiona. Both women had tried, but it was increasingly difficult to maintain their intimacy as their lives and families evolved along different paths. The year before Seraph found herself pregnant with Luke, Fiona had met Dominic, an anaesthetist at a Bristol hospital. He was as rumpled and blond as she was dark and smooth. Opposites attract and they hit it off immediately and married eighteen months later. Seraph went to the wedding, but afterwards contact between the two women dwindled to an annual exchange of Christmas cards, occasional phone calls, and whatever information Lachlan and Catriona saw fit to pass on. Seraph saw the children three or four times a year, and they always filled her in on what Fiona was up to, and, later, told their mother Seraph's news.

The star on top of the Christmas tree blurred slightly as Seraph continued to stare at it. However close she'd once been to Fiona, the hard truth was that she hadn't spoken to her ex-sister-in-law for nearly six months. Picking up the phone now would be assuming a relationship which was no longer there, and which Fiona showed no signs of wanting to revive. Amy, who was not prone to panic, was not in the midst of her own unhappiness and was not in Tokyo, should have been Seraph's ideal listener. Plus Seraph owed her an explanation for the scene she'd just witnessed. But to talk to Amy now? To ask advice of Amy now? Jude made it impossible – although Seraph wasn't quite sure why. It wasn't, she tried to convince herself, as if she'd ever had any *real* interest in him, she'd known all along he was monosodium glutamate – superficially tasty, but non-nutritious. He was a PotNoodle, while Nick was a bowl of home-made chicken soup – and Nick's confession had truthfully shoved Jude from her mind. Still, she felt constrained, and guiltily so.

'Don't,' she said, speaking to the window. 'Please. Just don't ask.'

'All right,' said Amy, after a long silence. 'But if you need me, just let me know.'

'Thanks.'

'That's okay.'

Both women fell silent, and after a moment or two Amy reached out her hand and rested it against Seraph's door.

'I'd better get back to work,' she said.

'Me too.'

'Mm-hmm. But you know where I am.'

'Yes.'

Amy opened the door.

137

'I'm going shopping in my lunch hour,' she said, over her shoulder. 'For clothes. Want to come?'

Seraph managed a wan smile.

'Are you suggesting retail therapy?'

'Absolutely.'

'I'd love to, but my hair cost a small fortune and the kids all need new shoes. Again.'

'Pleeeeease.'

Seraph looked at Amy's clothes. Today she was wearing a hairy, figure-hiding angora sweater in corpse yellow, over a style-forsaken A-line skirt.

'You want something for Saturday.' It was a statement, not a question. She knew Jude and Amy had another date fixed for Saturday night.

Amy grinned and nodded.

Seraph looked down at her hands, struggling with herself. She owed Amy, in all sorts of ways. The generous thing now would be to offer to help her find something to stop Jude in his tracks. Did she have it in her to do it?

'If I come,' she said, slowly, 'will you promise you won't let me spend anything?'

'Promise.'

'Okay. On that condition, I'll come.'

Precision was as busy and as artificially jolly as was to be expected in the run-up to the office-party season. The spray-on cheer was provided by loud canned carols, giant baubles suspended from the ceiling and an excess of glittery clothes – sequins were much on display. When Seraph and Amy arrived they separated. From habit Seraph crossed to the sale rack at the back of the shop, where she found a few pairs of bright scarlet Capri pants in a stretch cotton, left over from the summer. But she wasn't looking for Capri pants, she was looking for something to make Jude catch his breath. A rail of evening skirts beckoned, long swirl skirts in a gauzy, synthetic fabric with an iridescent shimmer. She chose one in a sea blue-green, folded it over her arm, and went to find Amy, who was browsing a rail of shirts.

'I'm glad you're back,' said Amy. 'What about this?' She held up a tan blouse with pearl buttons and a pussycat bow at the neck.

Seraph pulled a face and silently shook out the skirt, which rippled like water and looked as if it were shot through with fish scales. Amy fingered the fabric, longingly.

'I couldn't.'

'Why not?'

'It's not practical. It would need dry cleaning. And I've nothing to wear with it.'

'Fuck practical,' said Seraph. 'See those over there?' She nodded towards a shelf of lycra T-shirts. 'What about the apple green? Or if not, they've got it in lime.'

'Lime? It's a bit radical.'

'Rubbish. I'll fetch one for you.'

'Not lime. Apple green.'

Together they fetched an apple green T-shirt and Amy went to change. The skirt made a satisfying swish as she swung her hips, and the T-shirt had pretty, three-quarter length sleeves, and a low neckline which clung softly over her breasts.

'You look like a mermaid,' said Seraph, when Amy stepped out of the changing room.

'Yes?'

'Mm-hmm. And it really shows off your figure.'

'You think?'

'You're so lucky. I wish my waist was so tiny.'

After Amy had paid for the outfit she turned to Seraph with a smile.

'Your turn,' she said.

'You promised. Remember the kids' shoes.'

'Go on,' urged Amy. 'You might as well look, while we're here.'

'Well . . . there was this pair of Capri pants'

A couple of minutes later Seraph held them up for Amy's inspection.

'Um . . .' Amy thought they were a bit loud.

'What? Not my normal style?'

'Which is?' Amy wasn't being sarcastic, she was curious.

Today Seraph was dressed all in grey. Despite the season, it was hot inside Precision, and she'd undone her coat. Now she glanced down at a cardigan baggy from frequent washing, and a long, shapeless skirt. Her clothes looked defeated.

'Non-existent.' she said as she stroked the Capri pants. 'Do you think these are too young for me?'

Amy dodged the question.

'Look at the price!' she said.

'They are a bargain, aren't they?'

'Fantastic value for money.'

'You're right. I'll try them on.'

Once she got back to her office Seraph immediately began to regret her extravagance. She'd never wear the damn Capri pants, they were much too young for her, much too tight, and much too red. She used her foot to nudge the tell-tale Precision bag under her desk, right to the back, where it was out of sight, then attempted to settle down to some work. She phoned Bruno Faversham to give him the good news about *You Lucky Stiff*, and the bad news about the advance, but he was out and she had to leave a message on his answering machine. Then she dashed off an e-mail to the US publishers of *The Anti-bloating Diet*, who had been expecting a decision today. Once she'd dealt with those tasks, she took a deep breath and pulled Iris Basham's proposal for *Hair Today Gone Tomorrow* from her in-tray. The envelope was still unopened, and she weighed it in her hand. What was it Iris had said? 'Good depilatory habits are a must for the swimsuit season.' Seraph was no longer conscientious about bikini-line waxing and these days, when she appeared in a swimsuit, she had forests of pubic hair sprouting at the tops of her thighs. She sighed, put the envelope down again, and closed her eyes.

What she saw was a red dress, which was better than excess pubic hair, but still not good. Once upon a time she'd had a cotton sundress in much the same shade as the Capri pants. It had been clingy and slinky, with a scoop neck and spaghetti straps, and she'd liked to wear it with a big-brimmed straw hat, and enormous sunglasses. She'd thought the hat, the dress, and the glasses made her look like a movie star, and she'd been wearing them one summer afternoon as she and Nick had walked down Piccadilly on their way to a picnic in Green Park, not long after they'd met. The air had smelled of traffic fumes and garbage, and had been so hot it could have come straight off a radiator.

The humidity had been high, too, Seraph remembered a damp stickiness all over her skin, and in the fabric of her dress. Nick had been carrying the picnic hamper, and he'd suddenly dumped it on the ground, right there, in Piccadilly. He'd swung in front of her, forcing her to a jolting stop, and the sea of pedestrians had parted around them as if they were Eastern royalty, and untouchable. They'd stood face to face, his hands resting on her shoulders so he'd filled her field of vision. He'd leaned towards her, and she'd breathed in his scent of soap and toothpaste and sweat.

'All I ask is that you be faithful,' he'd said, and the world around Seraph had blurred and faded. She'd half closed her eyes, tilted back her head to expose her neck, and run her tongue over her lips.

'Faithful?' She'd replied. 'Oh no, not that. Never that. We all know sexual jealousy is irrational.'

She'd thought at the time she was being so sophisticated, so metropolitan. But, Seraph could now see, she'd just been parroting fag ends of sophisticated, metropolitan arguments she'd misheard while thinking about something else in her philosophy of politics lectures, or her classes on feminism. She'd thought at the time she was giving Nick the sort of come-on suitable to leaders of the intellectual avant garde – whatever that might be – when in fact it became immediately apparent that all she'd done was hurt him. He'd sulked for days, and even stopped writing her poems, for a while.

9

Disha was trying not to gawk.

'Joy,' breathed the woman she was trying not to gawk at, 'I'm Cassie Jones. I'm here to see Seraph Jamieson, but I'm a few minutes early.'

'Joy' was Cassie's habitual form of greeting, but Disha didn't know this. Since Cassie spoke with a strong Welsh accent, and her surname was Jones, Disha guessed it was a Welsh salutation. She was a broad-minded young woman, keen to respect other people's traditions – on her visits to Café Beso she always greeted Hadar and Avi with *shalom*.

'Joy,' she politely replied, and then picked up her phone.

'Hi, Seraph,' she said, in her East London accent. 'I've got a Cassie Jones out here. Says she's a bit early.'

'Oh God!' said Seraph, 'I'd completely forgotten. Give me a minute, can you?'

'No problem. Buzz me when you're ready.'

Disha turned to Cassie.

'She'll just be a moment. Please take a seat.'

Cassie jellied over to a sofa, and eased herself down.

'I like your nails,' she said, when the folds of her flesh had settled. Disha proudly glanced down, her nails were fabulous as any ancient maharanee's, long and curved and ornamented. Today they were frosted light blue, and embellished with leaf designs in silver. She also wore a silver bindi – her family was Hindu, but this was purely a fashion statement.

'Thanks,' she said. 'I do them myself. The colour's Icicle Ice. It's a peel-off varnish. No need for remover. The leaves are transfers.'

'Ah, yes,' said Cassie. 'Pale blue, for steely determination, and silver for a touch of lunar insight.'

Lunar insight?

'Oh, *Cassie Jones*,' said Disha, with heavy emphasis. 'Forgive me, I didn't at first recognize your name . . . *Rainbow Power*. I loved that book.'

Cassie beamed at her.

'Thank you.'

'And I understand the purple now.'

Rainbow Power explained that purple was a spiritually magnetic colour – the colour of intuition and healing. Cassie always draped herself in it from head to foot. Today she was wearing a plum-coloured trouser suit, over a lavender shirt. At her wrist she wore amethyst power beads, more amethysts dangled at her ears, and her own nails were done in Blackberry Ripple. The only exception to the all-pervading purple was a little amulet which hung around her neck on a leather thong. This amulet was the brownish-pink of rough, unpolished sandstone and came from Syria. Since it was about 4,000 years old, Cassie readily excused its colour on grounds of age, and holiness – it was carved into a small, squat figurine of a woman with an oval, geometric face, full spherical breasts, a rolling mound of stomach, and simply enormous buttocks. Disha, who thought the amulet was cool, couldn't help noticing the strong resemblance between its general shape, and Cassie's.

Cassie forgot to wish Seraph joy.

'Your hair!' she said as she oozed into her editor's office. 'It looks wonderful.'

Seraph was standing to greet her guest. She always took a moment to adjust to Cassie's bulk and style. Now she also felt disconcerted by memories of acting on Cassie's sex advice. How could she ever have mistaken such a whale for a sexual guru? Or was that being fattist and unimaginative?

'Thanks.'

'You've obviously been following my advice,' Cassie added, knowingly.

Seraph grunted, in a non-committal fashion. To her shame, she'd not glanced at How to Change Your Life since the day she'd written the blurb, but she did remember that Cassie had devoted a section to self-image. No doubt she'd included something on the power and significance of hair as a symbol of sexuality, confidence and assertiveness. Cassie's own hair was brown, and slightly coarse. She kept it long, and let it swing loose about her shoulders, in untidy, ratty strands.

'And I see you've been shopping too! You've been reading my chapter on the therapeutic properties of revising your wardrobe!'

Seraph grunted again. Yesterday she'd been so successful at shoving the Precision bag out of sight under her desk, that she'd quite forgotten to take it home. So today she'd pulled it out and left it in a prominent position by the window.

'Did I include enough practical advice on how to re-vamp your look on a limited budget?'

Seraph made a mental note to check this when she got around to reading the manuscript.

'Yes.' She hoped it was true.

'What did you buy?'

'Capri pants. Big mistake.'

'Why?'

'They're tight, and bright red.'

'They sound great. Red is such an animal colour. A sexual colour. Forceful and bold.'

'But a bit young for me.'

'Red?'

'Red Capri pants.'

'Nonsense!'

Seraph shrugged, ruefully. 'Can I get you a coffee?' she asked. 'Here, let me help with that chair.'

Seraph's office was too cramped to accommodate two chairs as permanent features. She quickly pulled over the picnic chair she kept folded against the wall for visitors, and unfolded it with a swift, well-practised motion. They both eyed it, wondering whether it would support Cassie's weight. Cassie sat down.

'Nothing to drink, thanks,' she said, and stayed very still for a moment. When it became clear the chair would not collapse, she plonked the plastic bag she had been carrying onto her knee, and began to search through it.

'Here,' she said, and pulled out a small brown-glass bottle with a dropper in the cap. She passed this to Seraph.

'Thanks.' Seraph sat down. 'What is it? A flower essence?'

'No. Lithosomatic liquor.'

'What?'

'I was at Hecate this morning. Natasha was doing an event on vibrational healing.'

Seraph remembered that Natasha was the dedicatee of *How to Change Your Life.*

'How was it?' she asked.

'Inspirational. And I got you that. Lithosomy's a new therapy Natasha's developing. She grinds up crystals and fixes the energy they release in alcohol. That one's amethyst and rose quartz, for quietness of spirit. I know editors are very busy people, so I thought you'd need it.' She fingered the amulet round her neck. 'You certainly look tired today, I hope you're not overdoing things?'

'Me? No.'

'You don't want to get burn-out.'

'No, I don't.'

Cassie gave her a searching look.

'I take tiger eye for creativity,' she said. 'The dose is two drops at night.'

'I'll have to ask Natasha to do a book on it.' Seraph unscrewed the bottle and filled the dropper. The liquid was the colour of meths. Gingerly she put a drop on her tongue. Wow! Perhaps it really was meths.

'The alcohol is quite strong.'

'Yes, Natasha brews it herself. You have to keep it in the dark, or the crystal energy will dissipate.'

There was a moment's silence. Seraph decided they'd had quite enough of Natasha . . . she didn't know that Cassie could never get enough of her.

'You were very kind to think of me,' she said, as she closed the bottle and put it on her desk. 'And now you want to talk about progress on *How to Change Your Life*?'

'Among other things.' Cassie also wanted to pitch Seraph her next book, *Ta Biblia*. This was a semi-completed sacred manifesto for the Daughters of Astarte, a new-age, neo-pagan, sub-neo-feminist cult she belonged to, and of which Natasha was the high priestess. When finished, *Ta Biblia* would be a book to guide and comfort believers, and convert the doubtful – part mythic herstory, part guide to conduct and part poetry. But first things first.

'So . . .?' said Seraph.

'Of course, you know how appreciative I am of everything you and your team have done for me,' Cassie began. 'I know you publishers are the experts, but I have a few constructive suggestions for your handling of *How to Change Your Life*.'

Seraph's heart sank even lower than it already was.

'Yes?'

'Yes. For a start I'm not sure I'm happy with the blurb. It's very good, and I value your contribution, but I don't think it quite conveys the way in which my book will help readers discover unexpected psychological realities in themselves, how it will help them achieve a rounded self-understanding and live in response to a new sense of purpose. So I've taken the liberty of re-writing it for you.'

'Fine. Thanks.' Seraph watched as Cassie once again searched in her bag. This time she pulled out a tatty sheet of paper and passed it over.

'I'll look at this closely later.'

Cassie smiled.

'You know, I like to think of *How to Change Your Life* as a breakthrough book. A reader is at place A in her life and she wants to be at place B. This book shows her how to make the breakthrough from A to B.'

'A breakthrough book?' Seraph considered the idea. 'That could be an interesting marketing hook. I'll mention it to Benedicta.'

Cassie looked thoughtful.

'I'll get to Benedicta in a moment,' she said. 'But first, let me hear your ideas for the cover.'

Seraph may not have read the script, but at least she had this off pat.

'I think a fully opened sunflower might be appropriate.'

'A fully opened sunflower?' Cassie was doubtful. 'Sunny and open. Those are the right messages, I suppose. And yellow's always inspirational. But I'd rather imagined a butterfly emerging from its chrysalis.'

'That might work. It's an idea.'

'Apart from the obvious symbolism I thought the brown of the chrysalis would contrast nicely with the colours of the butterfly.'

'I can certainly mention it to the designer.'

'Good.' Cassie clasped her hands. 'I don't mean to be difficult,' she began, 'but back to Benedicta. Nobody's been in touch with me about marketing or promotion.'

'Benedicta's been working on a plan.'

'But has she? She doesn't seem to be doing anything. I sent her a very full list of media contacts, and she didn't phone any of them to follow up on it.'

'I do apologize. She's rushed off her feet at the moment. But

I'll chase her. No doubt you'll be hearing something soon. We're hopeful of wide press coverage.'

'Yes. It should be perfect for the women's pages.'

'Local radio is sure to be interested.'

'Of course. I have many friends in local radio.' Cassie gave Seraph a shrewd look. 'I'll be disappointed if the marketing for this one is as casual as that for *Rainbow Power. How to Change Your Life* has taken a year of *my* life, but what's the point if nobody knows it's been published?'

Both women stared into their laps. Cassie leant down and dumped her carrier bag onto the floor.

'So,' she said, looking up and abruptly breaking the silence. 'Why did you get your hair cut?'

'What?' Seraph was startled.

'Why did you get your hair cut?'

'Oh. Y'know.'

'You must have had a reason.'

'Not really.'

'You must have wanted to send a new message to the world. But why? And what message?'

Seraph thought Cassie was being impertinent. But an editor saying 'What the fuck do you think gives you the right?' to an author was not an option. At least not for Seraph. Jude might have got away with it.

'I got fed up with the bother of long hair.'

'It wasn't long. It was shoulder length.'

Seraph shrugged and flapped her hands.

'And new red Capri pants,' continued Cassie, in an accusatory tone.

'New red Capri pants?'

'Yes. Red, as we said, a forceful colour, a symbol of movement, ambition and daring. Capri pants, suggestive of beaches, summer days and freedom.'

Seraph stared at Cassie.

'They were a bargain. And I don't like them.'

'So you say. But clearly you're grappling with the need for change in your life. The desire for change. Why should that be? Are you yourself seeking a new sense of purpose?'

Cassie had no argument: hair plus red trousers did not equal pain, but Seraph was exhausted, and logic had never been her strong point. She burst into tears.

Cassie pursed her lips, and once again fingered her amulet. Clearly *Ta Biblia* would have to wait for another day. She pulled a couple of crumpled lavender tissues from her sleeve, and held them out to Seraph, who was sobbing so hard she couldn't manage to take them. Cassie hauled herself up, took Seraph's hand, and closed her fingers tight around the tissues.

'They're quite clean,' she said.

After a few minutes Seraph was able to blow her nose and mop at her eyes.

'I do apologize,' she blustered. 'Ridiculous, unprofessional behaviour.'

'Don't be silly,' Cassie murmured soothingly. 'But what's wrong?'

'I'm under a lot of stress,' said Seraph, vaguely.

Cassie was not to be deterred.

'Here? Or at home?'

'Oh, y'know.'

'I don't unless you tell me. What kind of stress?'

Seraph wafted one hand.

'Marital stuff,' she mumbled.

Cassie looked down at her amethyst bracelet, and twisted the beads. Her diploma in psychodynamics had included six months of couples therapy.

'Infidelity?' she asked.

Seraph sniffed, and fresh tears threatened to over spill her eyes. Cassie raised one eyebrow.

'Are you sure?'

'He told me. A couple of nights ago.'

'Just like that? Out of the blue?'

'Sort of.'

So not totally unexpected, thought Cassie, but now wasn't the right moment to press the point. Couples therapists fell into two camps when it came to the question of whether it was wise for someone who was having an affair to confess to his or her spouse. Cassie herself thought it was impossible to generalize about whether lying was a greater betrayal than adultery, so much depended on what type of affair it was, and the underlying reason.

'Is it still going on?' she asked.

'I don't know. He said it was a mistake . . .' Nick hadn't actually used the word *mistake*. He'd said he loved Seraph, and his affair had been meaningless. In Seraph's mind, as in anybody's, these words had added up to error, mistake, deviation from life's proper path. Of course, he could have been lying.

'A mistake? So it's over?'

'My Capri pants were a mistake. It means nothing.'

Cassie let that pass.

'You absolutely have to find out if it's over,' she insisted.

'What's the point?'

'If it's over, your relationship could still have a good chance of survival.'

Seraph rubbed one hand across her forehead.

'I don't think I could ever forgive him, even if it's over.'

'That's natural. You only just found out.' Cassie leaned forward and placed a squidgy hand on Seraph's knee. 'What's your husband's name?'

'Nick.'

'Learning of Nick's infidelity must have been one of the worst moments in your life. It's much too soon to think about forgiveness, but just remember that if you can't eventually forgive him, you'll never be able to repair your marriage.'

'If I want to.'

'If you want to.' Cassie removed her hand from Seraph's knee and sat back in her chair. 'Why did he do it?'

'I don't give a shit.'

It was an axiom of psychodynamics that the injured party, on being informed that their spouse had been unfaithful, went through five clearly defined stages: denial, anger, bargaining, depression and acceptance. It was clear to Cassie that Seraph was in anger.

'Okay. Then why do you think he told you?'

Seraph gave her a blank stare, and shrugged.

'You see, he could have wanted . . .'

'I don't care what he wanted.'

'. . . to get your attention. It's drastic, but quite common. People have affairs to grab the attention of their spouses, because they see that something is lacking in their relationship, that something is seriously wrong, and they can think of no other way to—'

Seraph made a sound only just short of blowing a raspberry. There was a short silence.

'An affair can be an expression of frustration,' said Cassie, when she judged Seraph was ready to listen.

'Like a toddler throwing a tantrum? Come off it.'

'Just like a toddler. The toddler throws a tantrum because she can't communicate her needs.'

'I just don't see—'

'But you do see that an affair is a sign of deep, underlying problems in a relationship?'

Seraph turned to stare out of her window. The Christmas tree looked sadder than ever.

'Sure. But so what?'

'Do you have any idea what your own problems are?'

Seraph twisted her engagement ring – sapphires and diamonds set to resemble a flower. She'd never much liked it, but when Nick had presented it to her, she'd felt she couldn't very well complain.

'Not really,' she answered. Was it a lie? She wasn't sure.

'You said it came out of the blue,' said Cassie *'Sort of.'*

'I had a feeling something was going on.'

Cassie fiddled with her amulet.

'Who was it with? Did he tell you? Someone from work?'

'I've no idea who she was.'

'And you don't know for sure what he wants to do next, or what—'

'I haven't asked if he wants to walk out, if that's—'

Cassie held up her hand.

'Or what you want to do next. I know you're in shock, but

it's very important you start to think about what you want to do next.'

Seraph grunted. She was thinking that another woman's wants might have more influence on her life than her own. But she said nothing.

'There's no rush,' continued Cassie, 'but you must both think carefully about what you want. You must identify your needs as individuals, and as a couple.'

'Mm.'

'Figuring out what you each want is the first step to redefining your marriage.'

'I don't know if I want to redefine it.'

'If you don't, or if Nick doesn't, it will die.'

Seraph picked up the bottle of lithosomatic liquor and rolled it between her palms.

'I keep imagining Nick holding this other woman in his arms. I keep wondering if she's thinner than me, with firmer breasts.'

'Jealousy,' said Cassie soothingly. 'It's quite normal. It would be strange if you weren't jealous, if you felt apathy.'

'I suppose so. And I suppose it's true we couldn't keep jogging along the way we were.'

'That's right. If you want your marriage to survive the shock of adultery, you won't be able to fall back into the same old patterns. You'll need to start over.'

Seraph, who had flinched at the word *adultery*, was spared the need to reply when her door swung open. It was Eddie, fresh from an alarming meeting with the Bladder bankers. He was immune to emotional atmosphere, but couldn't help noticing Cassie.

'Oh,' he said to Seraph, 'I see you're busy.'

'We're just finishing up,' she replied. 'Do you know Cassie Jones?'

Eddie knew the name, but couldn't quite place it.

'Author of . . .'

'*Rainbow Power: A Guide to Using Colour for Emotional Healing.* And now *How to Change Your Life: A Practical Guide to Self-fulfillment,*' supplied Cassie.

Eddie slapped his forehead then leaned over to shake her hand.

'Of course,' he said, 'I keep meaning to paint my office silver-grey to attract financial success.'

'Grey?' questioned Cassie in astonishment. 'Not grey. *Green.* Green for financial success. Grey for analytical thinking skills.'

'Green,' said Eddie, who'd never read *Rainbow Power* and had guessed at silver-grey because yellow-gold seemed too obvious. 'I meant green, of course. But I could do with analytical thinking skills too.' He paused. 'And I can't wait for *How to Change Your Life.*'

'I'll be interested in your reaction, when you've read it.'

Eddie smiled and turned to Seraph. 'When you're finished, can you pop in to see me for a minute. It's about your budget.'

Seraph always did her budgets on the backs of envelopes.

'I'll be about twenty minutes,' she said.

As soon as Eddie left, Seraph and Cassie returned to their conversation, as if the interruption had never happened.

'So,' Seraph said, bitterly, 'everything will be fine, if only we can start over.'

'I didn't quite say that, but to give yourselves a chance you need to make changes.'

'Easy to say.'

'I know . . . change starts with speech.'

'Communication?'

Cassie couldn't quite read Seraph's tone, but recognized it as hostile.

'Yes,' she agreed, 'you must talk to him. You don't need me to tell you that.'

'We need to talk,' repeated Seraph, in the same bitter tone she'd used a moment earlier.

'Mm-hmm. You need to talk. And each of you must listen to what the other has to say.' Cassie paused, it was her firm belief that very few couples could move on from the crisis of infidelity, either together, or apart, without support from a professional. 'And when you begin to talk, I want you to promise me something.'

'What?'

'I want you to promise to call and let me know how things are progressing. Don't forget I run a personal coaching clinic. Helping people find a way through crises and problems is what I'm best at. I could help you and Nick.'

'You do marriage guidance?'

'Couples therapy is a big part of my work. You and Nick need an unbiased, neutral third party to help you understand what went wrong in your relationship, and to focus you, in constructive ways, on coming up with solutions.'

'Solutions!'

'I know. But if you both want to repair your relationship, and you're both willing to make a commitment to the time and hard work that would take, then I could help your marriage survive.'

'Yes. And if not . . .'

'And if you decide that's not what you want, I can help you work towards a good divorce.'

Seraph flinched again, this time at the word divorce.

'We have children.'

Cassie nodded, she had noticed the snapshots around Seraph's office. 'I can help there, too. Family therapy.'

Seraph stopped rolling the bottle of lithosomatic liquor between her palms and put it back on her desk. Rose quartz and amethyst. Therapy. Where was the difference?

'Thanks Cassie,' she said. 'I'll remember that.'

'You promise you'll call?'

'I promise I'll call.'

10

It was not unusual for Seraph to work at home on Fridays during term-time. With Tom and Daisy at school, and Luke out and about with Kate, home was the best place for uninterrupted reading – no phones ringing off the hook, no e-mails, no colleagues coming in to make demands, no memos to respond to asap. And there were other advantages – chocolate biscuits, a constant supply of decent coffee, music, if she wanted it. Cassie's visit had increased Seraph's considerable guilt about still not having read *How to Change Your Life*, so the previous night she'd lugged it home, along with a newly delivered script from her tame obstetrician and gynaecologist, Dr L.L.O. Case. Livia's new one was *Baby Manual: A Guide For Expectant Fathers*. Seraph was cautiously optimistic about it since Livia's two earlier titles, *Getting Pregnant* and *The Pregnancy Handbook* had both sold well. *Baby Manual* was modelled on car maintenance manuals, and would be advertised as part of the fledgling men's health list, as well as in the pregnancy and childcare section of the Bladder catalogue. Of course, Seraph knew there was no chance men would actually buy anything written by an obstetrician and gynaecologist, but she hoped their partners would force Livia's book upon them.

Quite apart from chocolate biscuits and coffee, working at home allowed Seraph to take Tom and Daisy to school before settling into her own day. Both children attended St Bernard's:

school colours, claret and grey; school motto, Only my best is good enough for me; school song, dreary; school emblem, a cute St Bernard's dog. When Tom had been coming up to four his parents had spent hours discussing the pros and cons of private education. They were ideologically and financially in favour of the state, but in the end they'd decided that bankrupting themselves and abandoning their principles was better than entrusting Tom to the vagaries of their local primary. This was inner London, after all, and, in contrast to what was on offer for free, St Bernard's set an entrance test, required a uniform, and expected pupils to complete homework every night. It also threw kids out if they failed to keep up with their peers. Culling. Not nice. Of course the Jamiesons could have moved out and found a cosy little village school in the Home Counties. Seraph had always felt ambivalent about London, she knew you had to accommodate yourself to the city if you wanted to make it with the brightest and the best, but it was such a cut-throat place. London red in tooth and claw. So she'd been keen to make schooling the excuse to flee. But Nick wouldn't hear of it.

'London *is* England,' he'd argued, 'there's nowhere else worth bothering about.'

'That's so narrow-minded,' she'd replied. 'It's almost provincial.'

Nick had laughed.

'Provincial?' he'd said. 'Try Stoke-On-Trent! Stockton-on-Tees! Stourbridge!'

When Seraph arrived home from the school run Kate was just bundling Luke into his coat, she was taking him to play with

Zoe, so she could gossip with Sandra. Relations between Seraph and Kate had been strained for the past few days, and they exchanged only the most cursory chit-chat. As soon as Kate and Luke had left, Seraph made herself a coffee, and dug out an unopened packet of chocolate biscuits she'd hidden in the larder. She carried her booty through to the dining room, where evidence of Nick was unavoidable. He'd left consumer leaflets and briefing documents scattered all over his end of the table. And his smell hung about, his soapy, salty, masculine smell. For the millionth time since Tuesday, Seraph's inner eye saw him making love to a woman younger, prettier and thinner than her, with a better body and no face. Cassie might have been right in dismissing this jealousy as normal, but to Seraph it felt pathological. She stomped to her end of the table, which was its usual mess, banged down her coffee and the biscuits, then shoved aside enough papers to clear a manuscript-sized space. Cassie's *How to Change Your Life*, and Livia's *Baby Manual* were lying next to each other on a small side table, inherited from the same aunt who'd given her the coat stand in the hall. The phone was on this table, too – cordless, with an integral answering machine. Seraph picked it up, and wondered whether to check in with the office, but decided not to bother. She replaced the phone and dithered between the two manuscripts. Guilt told her to read Cassie, commercial sense told her to read Livia. Guilt won. She picked up the script, took it to the big table, and settled down to read.

Part 1. *Bodily Health*

Cassie opened with a discussion of diet, nutrition and exercise, which Seraph read while chain-eating her chocolate biscuits, then moved rapidly into a plea for women to have regular cervical smears, followed by step-by-step instructions for undertaking monthly breast examinations. Seraph had watched her mother-in-law die of breast cancer, and was prepared to be more conscientious than usual in checking that the presentation of this text was logical and unambiguous. She thought the best way would be to work through the instructions herself. Step 1 was to strip to the waist and stand in front of a mirror with the arms hanging loose. This was clearly impractical for an editor in the middle of her work, however conscientious she might be feeling. Steps 2–7 were all about checking the appearance of the breasts in the mirror, so Seraph skipped straight to step 8, which told women to lie flat on their backs, with a folded towel behind the shoulder blade on the side of the breast being examined. After that the instructions became more feasible. Use the right hand for the left breast and the left hand for the right. Seraph could do that, she reached her right hand up under her jersey, and caressed her left breast, through the fabric of her bra.

> Feel only with the flat of the fingers, do not pinch the breast tissue between the fingers and the thumb, as this way it will always feel lumpy.

So far so good.

> Work round each breast systematically, checking each of the four quadrants, and the tail of the breast which points up to the armpit. Feel carefully for lumps in the armpit.

Seraph did as she was told, and found a lump. Her body jolted, as if she'd plugged herself into the mains. For a moment her mother-in-law's eyes burned into hers. But she quickly remembered she had two breasts. She reached up with her left hand, and determined that her right breast had an exactly similar lump. Was it possible symmetrical lumps could be malignant? Seraph thought not, and guessed she'd been scared by a bump in her rib cage. Just as she was breathing a huge sigh of relief, the phone rang. Seraph decided to screen the call first.

'Hi, Seraph,' said Amy's voice, broadcast by the answering machine. 'It's me. Pick up the phone if you're there.'

Seraph picked up the phone.

'It's me, not the machine.'

'Good! What's up?' It was only a couple of days since Amy had seen Seraph hysterical, and they both knew this question was not as meaningless as it seemed. But Seraph chose to ignore any undercurrents.

'Nothing. I was just examining my breasts.'

'Oh.' Amy didn't seem surprised. 'Find anything?'

'No.'

'Good.'

'Yes. Do you check yours?'

'No.'

'You should.' Seraph waited a moment. 'So what's going on?'

'Not much, I'm just knocking out a memo about stationery expenses . . .'

'Stationery expenses?'

'Yeah. Eddie thinks we spend way too much, especially on envelopes and spiral-bound notebooks. He wants everyone to cut down on usage . . . but guess what?'

'What?'

'I've done it! Where you led, I've followed! I've had my hair cut!'

'You have?'

'Yeah – an impulse thing, last night.'

'Good for you! So? What's it like?'

Amy was sitting at her desk outside Eddie's office, now she held the phone away from her ear for a moment, and tossed her head experimentally, her hair swung with a satisfying swish.

'A bob. Quite short, it comes just below my ears. I had auburn lowlights put in as well.'

'Wow! Where did you go?'

'Ferrucci's.' Amy sounded slightly defensive.

Seraph laughed.

'I won't say anything.'

'Gee, thanks.'

'And how's it gone down?'

'We-e-ll, Jude said it was sleek and sexy, showed off my eyes and made my nose look pert.'

Seraph was silent. Amy's nose was snub. By no stretch of the imagination could it be called pert.

'Seraph?' asked Amy. 'Are you still there?'

'Sorry. Yes, I'm still here.'

'You okay? You sound a bit chesty.'

Seraph wheezed theatrically, and made incipient pneumonia an excust to hang up. Luckily Amy didn't press her on it, and Seraph determined to get back to her reading. But after cervical smears and breast examination, Cassie turned her attention to sexually transmitted diseases. Aids.

Fuck!

When Seraph and Nick had been at university herpes was a fear, and there had been vague rumours of a disease in the States, killing off immigrant Haitian drug addicts, but nonetheless anyone who felt like it had fallen into bed with anyone else, and since all the women were on the pill, nobody used condoms. Nearly twenty years on, Seraph realized, with a shock, that she must have fossilized in her youthful mind set, for it had not yet occurred to her to worry whether or not Nick had taken sensible precautions, perhaps because she'd never believed that latex could be a sensible precaution against anything very much. And if she had fossilized, why not Nick? Had he heeded all the warnings? And what about his co-sexee? Had she insisted on a condom for her own safety? Or was she a virus on two legs, seeking to replicate? A wave of nausea swept over her. Then something else hit her. She'd been assuming this was Nick's first affair. But suppose it wasn't? Suppose he'd had hundreds? And suppose he'd never once, in all this long history of adultery, bothered to use a condom?

For the second time that morning the grave yawned before Seraph, but now she truly felt she was on the brink, the cusp, of toppling in. She stood up and walked two or three times round the dining-room table – her tread was unsteady and she felt as if her body no longer belonged to her. She needed a shot of something, and the only substance available was caffeine, so she went into the kitchen to make herself another cup of coffee. By the time she'd made it and drunk it she felt calmer, able to reassure herself this really was Nick's first affair – if he'd been playing around before, she'd have been suspicious before, her Nick radar would have picked up other-women blips. And he wasn't stupid, he probably had used a condom. Even if he hadn't, the chance that she'd contracted HIV from him was remote. She tried to remember infection rates she'd seen quoted in the papers. Whatever they were, it was statistically unlikely that Nick had picked up the virus. It was unlikely she was herself infected. And even if they'd both been unlucky, there were all these new wonder drugs keeping death-row inmates alive for years and years. Aids was a chronic disease now, not a killer. One way or another, it was unlikely her children would be orphans before they hit their teens. But Seraph didn't want low probability. She wanted certainty, and its lack made her furious with Nick.

Seraph clattered everything clatterable as she made herself yet another coffee. Once it was ready, she returned to the dining room, and eyed the phone. Her desire to talk was an itch, and yesterday's chat with Cassie, a professional acquaintance who happened to be a professional caregiver, had done nothing to soothe it. She needed to talk to a friend, someone who really cared. But who? Once again she ran through her list of potential listeners. It hadn't grown. Amy? Jude had said her nose was pert. Her mother? Seraph wasn't held back solely by concerns for her parents' health, she knew that running to mummy would be an invasion of her's and Nick's marital privacy. Of course, *if* she left Nick she wouldn't be able to keep the secret for ever, but in the meantime Charles and Meredith need know nothing. Her university friends weren't genuine options. Georgina was so crazed with hatred for her ex she couldn't see straight, and it was coming up for midnight in Tokyo, so Lizzie wouldn't thank her for a call. That left . . . nobody. Unless she phoned Fiona, the woman who'd first been her sister through marriage, and then become a stranger through divorce.

But could a sister ever become a stranger? Seraph sipped her coffee and argued that in times of crisis people often rebuilt old alliances they'd let decay. And Fiona certainly knew all about surviving marital meltdown. She'd conquered it, vanquished it, come out victorious with her hair, her nails and her self all in place. Seraph stopped dithering and picked up the phone. She couldn't remember Fiona's work number offhand, so she pulled open the drawer in the side table and sorted through a selection of menus from home-delivery pizza places and the like, until she found her address book. She flipped through to the Ms – not the Js or anything else. When she and Nick had married, she'd taken his surname, not without qualms, but Fiona had kept her maiden name, McDonald, through both marriages.

'Sorry,' said the harassed sounding receptionist when Seraph got through, 'but Dr McDonald's out today. Can I take a message?'

'No,' said Seraph. 'It's okay. I'll try her at home.'

Fiona was in her kitchen, she'd just got back from doing her big weekly shop at Cooper's and the functional white counters were covered with overflowing grocery bags. Their untidiness affronted her, and she was deftly stowing her purchases in their allocated storage spaces. She liked her kitchen to be clean, and clear of junk. Dominic often joked that he needn't bother going into the hospital, since this room could easily double as an operating theatre. Fiona didn't mind his jibes, she'd have sterilized the place, if she could.

'Seraph,' she said in her well-modulated Edinburgh voice, 'what a lovely surprise.' She tucked the cordless phone under her chin, and continued to place dairy items in the fridge.

'Yes. I thought I'd give you a call. I tried work first.' Seraph eyed Cassie's script, which lay on the table in front of her, the pages she'd already read were lying face down on the left, pages she had yet to read were face up, on the right. The script looked like an open, unbound book, except the back of every page was blank. She picked up her blue biro, the expanse of white paper lying to her left was too inviting to resist, and she started to draw a wide, loose spiral across it – on the other side was the text on Aids which had set off her panic.

'I'm down to four days a week,' replied Fiona. 'Domestic chores today – It's been too long, hasn't it? When was it we last spoke?'

'I can't remember. Ages ago. Easter, probably.'

'Yes. Just before we went to France.'

'That's right. How was it?'

'It seems so long ago I can scarcely remember.'

'I know what it's like. This year's flown.'

'Hasn't it just.'

'Yes. Terrifying.' Seraph paused. 'How're the kids?'

'Flourishing. Lachlan loves his new school, he's captain of the first-year football team, and he's doing well academically. They've started him on German, as well as French. Catriona's going to be Gabriel in her school's nativity play, so she's really excited about that. I've got to make her costume.'

'A couple of old sheets and a coat-hanger halo wrapped with tinsel?'

'Something like that. And Ingrid's dazed by this boy she's met. She's ecstatic, although Dominic's a bit iffy.' Ingrid was Dominic's daughter by his first marriage, she was fifteen.

'Why? What's wrong with the boy?'

'Animal rights, cropped orange hair and a nose stud.'

'Sounds great.'

Fiona laughed.

'Wait until it's Daisy. How is she? And the others?'

'Fine. Tom's into soccer too. He and Daisy are both in the end of term celebration, but it's about a Christmas pudding, not a nativity play. Daisy's a raisin and Tom's the sixpence. Luke's fine, chattering away.'

'And Nick?'

Seraph paused, and began a second spiral, as wide and as loose as the first.

'That's why I'm phoning.'

Fiona plucked a wedge of Edam cheese from her shopping bags. She took her time about putting it in the fridge, then she turned her back on the groceries, and sat down at her white Formica kitchen table.

'Ahhh.' She sighed. It was a long, intimate, complicitous *ahhh*, almost the sound a lover might breathe on being reunited with his or her beloved after a long, even acrimonious, separation.

'Yes,' replied Seraph.

'What is it?'

'Another woman.'

'Oh dear.'

'Mm. I thought you might have some suggestions.'

'I'll do my best. What's the score?'

'I don't really know. All I know is he's been having an affair.'

'No details?'

'No. I didn't give myself time to ask, and anyway, what's the point? – He said it was a mistake—'

'A mistake?'

'Mm – he said he'd give me earrings.'

'*Earrings?*'

'Yeah.'

'God! Perhaps a couple of diamond tiaras might do it.'

Seraph remembered her calculation as to the effect of an emerald necklace.

'My thoughts exactly.' Both women had been speaking ironically, but both now paused to wonder if they really could be bought off with baubles.

'You think he meant it?' asked Fiona, breaking the silence.

'That he'd buy me earrings?'

'No. That it was a mistake.'

'I haven't a clue.'

'But it's over?'

'I don't know . . . I didn't ask.'

'What did you ask?'

'Nothing. He's in Rome, by the way, until tomorrow.'

'Lucky him. You need to talk to him.'

Seraph stabbed her pen down onto the centre of the spiral she'd just drawn, with such force she made a small hole in the paper.

'So everybody is determined to remind me.' She spoke more sharply than she'd intended.

'Sorry.' Fiona waited a moment before continuing. 'So how're you coping?'

Seraph started another spiral.

'I want to kill him. I mean literally kill him. Strangle him, or pay someone else to.'

'I don't blame you. I considered poisoning Pete, a doctor has the means.'

'Don't you take some oath?'

'And I could slip you a little something, if you're serious . . .'

'I might take you up on that.'

Neither woman was laughing.

'At least Nick's – you know – flooze. She isn't pregnant. Not like Donna. You don't have to deal with all that,' said Fiona.

'No, thank God. Although I realized this morning I'd got the whole Aids thing to think about.'

'There is that.'

'Do you think I should be worried?' Seraph knew she'd jumped in too quickly.

'The test is cheap, quick and accurate – anyway, however bad this woman is, she can't be as bad as Donna.'

Seraph didn't like the way Fiona had avoided her question, but daren't press her on it.

'Yeah,' she quipped instead, 'if anyone deserves poisoning . . .'

Now they did laugh.

'Enough!' said Fiona. 'She did me a favour, really, although it didn't feel like it at the time. I should thank her, someday.'

'I can't imagine ever thanking Nick's – what did you call her? Flooze?'

'Flooze. But we're getting off the point.'

'What point?'

'How you feel about him, and how you feel about your marriage.'

'Yeah,' said Seraph. 'But what about how *she* feels? And how *he* feels about *me*?'

'That too.' Acknowledged Fiona.

'Maybe he doesn't know how he feels about anything at the moment – I certainly don't.'

'Sure. So give yourself some time. Don't make any decisions until you've got some perspective on all this. Don't do anything until you're sure it's what you want to do.'

'Let things settle? See how things turn out?'

'Mm. There's no rush. Assuming he was sincere when he said it was a mistake.'

'Assuming . . .'

'You need to find out.'

'I know.'

'But assuming, then now you're the one in control.'

'Meaning?'

'You're the one with choices.'

'Whether or not to blow my family apart?' said Seraph. 'Some choice!'

'That's not what you said to me, when I faced the same decision.'

'Yes . . . but still.'

Fiona had noticed a tiny smear of tomato ketchup on her table, and now rubbed at it with her finger.

'D'you know how long it was going on?' she asked.

'No, and I'm not sure it matters.'

'Oh, I think it does.' Donna and Pete had been seeing each other for exactly a year when Donna got pregnant. From May to May, the whole calendar violated. 'I might have been more forgiving if Pete had only been at it for a few weeks.'

'Might have been?'

'Okay. And might not.'

They were both silent, thinking about how things might, or then again, might not, have been.

'I'm scared,' said Seraph, after a moment. 'Scared I'll do something for the wrong reasons. I mean stay for the wrong reasons. That only fear will keep me in the marriage.'

'Fear of being alone?'

'Sure. I never have been. Never. Home. Boyfriends. Nick.'

Fiona sucked in her breath.

'I was scared too,' she said, 'but it wasn't so bad. Not good. But not unbearable.'

'I'm thirty-eight.'

'I was thirty-nine when I married Dominic.'

'So?'

'So don't be afraid.'

'And then there's the children . . .'

'Yes. Think of the kids.' Fiona's tone was ironic.

'Well, you can't ignore them.'

'Children are adaptable. Look at my two. They're fine. Absolutely fine.'

Seraph grunted. Her pen twirled across the back of Cassie's page. She knew Fiona spoke truly, yet still she thought, *you would say that wouldn't you?*

'Look,' said Fiona, 'when did you say Nick got home?'

'Tomorrow.'

'What time?'

'I think about lunchtime.'

'Any point in my driving up first thing? I could, the kids will be with Pete.'

'Thanks,' said Seraph, 'that's really kind . . .'

'You did it for me.'

'Sure. But there's really no need. Anyway my three would swarm all over us and there wouldn't be enough time before Nick got home – I'll talk to him tomorrow and take it from there.'

Fiona cleared her throat, wondering whether to spell out she'd divorced Pete, not Seraph. But she decided it was unnecessary.

'Phone again,' she urged, instead, 'phone again and let me know how things stand.'

After she'd said goodbye, Seraph picked up the page she'd covered with doodles, and held it to the light. It looked as if an Ancient Briton had got at it, and covered it with woad designs. Cassie, whose script she'd decorated, would probably have seen something significant in these spirals and swirls. *How to Change Your Life*. There was a good joke. From left and right the shadows of a million women crowded in on Seraph. On the left drooped those who'd got too old, or too fat. Babes who'd become mothers, and found themselves replaced. On the right marched the babes who were still babes. The replacers . . . . . . Had it never occurred to Cassie that other people could change your life more quickly and more profoundly than you ever could yourself?

But this was self-pity. Seraph stopped musing and tried to get back to work. She had just about finished Cassie's text on bodily health, and rapidly arrived at part two, sex and relationships. It was lucky she'd already read most of this, because today she really wasn't in the mood. So she skipped to part three, work and wealth. Cassie had kicked off with a quiz. Readers were asked to answer a long list of multiple-choice questions on their attitudes to: teamwork versus individualism; innovation versus implementation; adventure versus stability; aggression versus pacification; rationality versus intuition; and introversion versus extroversion. The scores determined which of six colour groups readers belonged to – red, orange, purple, yellow, blue or green. Cassie suggested ten jobs suitable for each colour personality. Seraph quickly whizzed down the questions, totted up her score, and came out a green. According to Cassie this meant she was a lousy team player (true, thought Seraph), preferred implementing other people's plans to coming up with her own (false, thought Seraph, much peeved), preferred stability over adventure (she didn't know, as she never had any adventures), avoided aggression at all costs (naturally), depended on intuition to solve personal problems (who didn't?), and had a good balance between introversion and extroversion (???). The list of careers Cassie suggested for greens was: florist, horticulturist, caterer, carpenter, electrician, physiotherapist, dental assistant (assistant, thought Seraph, why not the dentist?), optician, aerobics instructor and theatrical make-up artist. So that was it, then, she was in the wrong job – editors were supposed to be orange.

And nannies were supposed to be purple, although this morning both Kate and Sandra were feeling a little blue. They were lounging on the floor in Zoe's bedroom-cum-playroom, nursing coffees, and keeping the vaguest of eyes on their charges, who were playing at opposite sides of the room from each other.

'She's like that all the time now,' said Sandra, referring to the fact that Zoe had only just calmed down after an epic tantrum. 'It was bound to happen. Caroline and Nigel had another row this morning.'

Kate eyed Zoe, thoughtfully. The little girl was now quietly transferring large wooden beads from one empty baby-wipes box to another.

'Could just be the terrible twos?' she suggested.

'No chance.'

'Then I suppose I'd better get ready for something similar . . . When I got in from the pub on Tuesday I found Nick preparing to sleep on the sofa.'

'Yes?' Sandra was sharply interested. 'Did he say anything?'

'No. And I didn't ask, but, then, who'd need to?'

'True. How's it been since?'

Kate shrugged.

'He's been away on business. He'd left for Heathrow by the time I started on Wednesday. But Seraph's been a cow all week. And this one's starting to play up.' She nodded at Luke, who was examining the wheels on a toy dumper truck. 'I hope he doesn't turn into monster baby.'

'A collapsing family,' said Sandra, gloomily, 'every nanny's nightmare.'

They were both silent for a moment. Kate was the first to speak.

'Roll on this evening,' she sighed, 'off to Sevenoaks.'

'To your true love. Will you say anything?'

'To Richard? About moving in?'

Sandra nodded.

'Maybe. Maybe not.'

'I wish I could be so . . . careless?'

'Not careless. Indecisive.'

'I'm not buying that. I'm sure you've made your mind up – Anyway, what're your plans for the weekend?'

Kate laughed, and leered.

Sandra grabbed a rag doll from a pile of Zoe's toys, and used it to hit her friend.

'I didn't mean that. I meant is it all country pubs and country walks?'

'Sure,' said Kate, 'and village fairs. There *is* a cinema, though, and a couple of semi-decent restaurants.' *Dull* she thought, but she was twenty-eight, thirty minus two, and way old enough to have stopped believing in Wham! Bam! Here I am! Richard might not live up to her idea of a dark prince, but he was there, and that was something. More serious than something: everything.

11

Ginny stood outside her father's house, and eyed the Christmas garland Belle had hung on the door. The dark, glossy green leaves, bright-red berries and tartan bow promised wealth within. When, as a child, Ginny had speculated that her father's office was a sort of magical court, she'd not been far wrong. The Coopers were a dynasty, and her father, Marcus, was its current king. In the nineteenth century, one Albert Cooper had owned a small grocery store in Leicester. When he died his son bought three more shops all in the same city, and then expanded into Nottingham. The next generation of Cooper men subdued Derby. Marcus's father built the tidy little business he'd inherited into the mighty Cooper's grocery chain, with links in every high street in Britain, the place where millions of women did their weekly shop. Marcus himself had taken Cooper's global, now there were outposts on every continent except Antarctica. Tins of beans and packets of soup paid for his comfortable house in Chelsea, Audrey's flat in Hampstead, and Ginny's pad in Notting Hill. Pickled cucumbers and Marmite had purchased Ginny's minimalist furniture. Salami and smoked salmon had given her the freedom to conceive a child without worrying for a moment about how she'd feed and clothe it.

Ginny stopped gazing at Belle's garland, and pressed the buzzer by the side of the door. There was scuffling inside, then Melissa opened up.

'Oh. It's you.'.

'Yes,' said Ginny, thinking Melissa was too fat for the tight-fitting, mock zebra-skin coat she wore.

Melissa looked like her father, and knew she was large and florid and jowly, but she was determined not to be intimidated by her half-sister. Her *old* half-sister. A has-been.

'Go on in,' she said. 'I'm off out – to see my boyfriend.' She watched Ginny's face, but was denied any kind of reaction. 'A singer,' she added, 'in a band – Deadwood.'

Ginny deliberately misunderstood.

'Your boyfriend's dead wood?' she asked, pretending surprise.

Melissa flushed.

'The band's Deadwood.'

'The *band's* dead wood?'

God, Melissa hated Ginny.

'You know I mean the band's *called* Deadwood,' she said, angrily, and then she shoved past Ginny, on her way to her rendezvous.

Ginny grinned and stepped over the threshold into her father's house, where she immediately gagged on the stench of incense – pregnancy had made her ultrasensitive to smell. She hoped she wasn't going to throw up, but decided that if she did, she'd aim for the very centre of the Persian rug at her feet, an expensive silk one, with a traditional peacock design. Everything in this house reflected Belle's faux Arabian-souk taste. The walls, floors and furnishings were a riot of jewel-like colours and intricate patterns, every surface was cluttered with fiddly artefacts in sandalwood, brass and enamel. Ginny didn't know how her father could stand it.

Belle was coming down the stairs, barefoot, and wearing one

of her trailing, hippy-chic skirts, her long hair was loose, like a young girl's, even though it was now more grey than black. She was a tall woman, almost six foot, and to Ginny, looking up at her, she seemed even taller, unnaturally tall, as if she'd been stretched, like elastic.

'Hi,' called Belle. 'I see Lissa let you in.' Her elongated face was gaunt and beautiful, but its expression was wary.

'Yes,' said Ginny. 'She did.' *Don't worry, Sweetie. This witch's powers are on the wane.*

Belle reached the Persian rug, and leaned over to air-kiss her stepdaughter once beside each cheek.

'So good to see you,' she purred. 'Daddy and Ems are cooking. Let's go.' She led the way to the large family kitchen, which was in the basement. Marcus and Emily were working side by side: Marcus, dicing red and green peppers; Emily, slicing mushrooms. A large bowl of chopped onions, a couple of heads of broccoli, a few celery sticks and a plateful of green string beans lay on the counter beside them. The smell of garlic hung about.

'Cookie!' Marcus called to Ginny, with a wide, but slightly nervous smile. Ginny stood in the doorway.

'Hi, Dad,' she said. 'Hi, Ems.'

Marcus put down his knife and leaned over to lift an opened bottle of wine from the top of the cabinet style fridge-freezer – the broken veins over his nose and cheeks were not solely the product of genetics, and he always reached for a bottle when confronted with his eldest daughter.

'Glass of this?' he asked.

'Please.'

Marcus took down three glasses from the cupboard above his

head, poured Ginny a generous glassful, and held it out. She crossed the room to take it, tolerated Marcus giving her a quick peck on the cheek, then lifted the wine to her lips, and swallowed.

'Château Beychevelle, 1982,' said Marcus.

'Oh,' said Ginny.

'Can I have some?' asked Emily, who was thirteen.

'Okay.' Marcus reached down another glass, and sloshed some wine into it.

Once everyone had a drink, he returned to chopping.

'We're doing stir-fried chicken with noodles,' he said. 'I've marinated the chicken with lime, ginger and coriander.'

'Oh. Good,' said Ginny.

'Totally awesome,' added Emily, although whether this was a comment on the wine she was drinking, or the food she would soon be eating, was unclear. Belle flashed her daughter an annoyed look.

Once the vegetables were prepared, dinner didn't take long to make. The four of them sat down to eat at the big, stripped-pine table which occupied one end of the room.

'Wine robust enough for the food?' asked Marcus.

'Sure,' replied Emily. All three adults ignored her, and the two women also ignored Marcus's question.

'Did Lissa tell you about her boyfriend?' Belle asked Ginny.

'Yes.'

'He's the lead singer for Deadwood. You heard of them?' This was Emily, she'd fixed her half-sister in her gaze.

'No.'

'He's like totally cool.'

'Mm.'

'You see her coat?'

'Yes.'

'Cool,' said Emily, again. 'Totally cool.'

Ginny grunted, Marcus laughed, and Belle looked pained.

'Ems,' she said. 'Please, not totally cool. You make yourself sound brain dead.'

She is brain dead, Sweetie.

'We asked her if she wanted to invite him over tonight,' said Marcus, after a short silence. 'But she didn't think he was up to it.'

Ginny's defences bristled.

'Up to what?'

Belle's heart lurched on her husband's behalf.

'Parents,' she said, crossly. 'She's sixteen. He's seventeen. At that age parents are just too much.'

Ginny looked directly at her father, and held his eye.

'I remember,' she said.

Belle wanted to slap her. Look Ginny, she wanted to say, you're too old to persist in blaming your parents and me for the mess you're making of your own life. She sighed, and pushed her noodles around her plate. With luck, Ginny would bugger off as soon as the meal was over, and let her and Marcus and the girls start their weekend for real. In Belle's opinion, there was nothing to choose between Audrey and Ginny – mother and daughter were equally arrogant, malicious and manipulative. Poor Marcus! No wonder he was knocking back the Château Beychevelle, 1982 as if it were soda. *In vino anaesthesia.* Belle took a long pull on her own wine, trusting it would soon start to blur the harder edges of her evening . . . but Marcus needed more than wine to dull the pain from the wounds he bore. He thought he'd fucked up with Ginny, and nothing Belle could say would persuade him Ginny would have turned out fucked up whatever he'd done, whatever sort of father he'd been. It was Ginny's destiny. It was her mother's genes. Belle thought Audrey was mad. Not mad as in dizzy and fun, but mad as in quite insane. Beautiful, and seductive, but mad. Audrey just didn't function like other people. Even today, in her fifties, she tried to act the little-girl-lost. Nearly twenty years ago, at the time of the divorce, Belle and Marcus had had to cope with eating disorders, wild mood swings, half-hearted suicide attempts, depressions, furious temper tantrums, and verbal and physical abuse. In the end they'd extricated them-selves from this psychological war of attrition, but at a terrible cost. Belle had succeeded in rescuing her beloved from one unbearable female, only to see him become enslaved to another. Not that she'd immediately seen the danger. She'd thought Ginny an unpleasant, sly and secretive little girl, nevertheless she'd supported her new husband in his attempts to win custody. They'd fought for Ginny with everything they'd had on Audrey, and still they'd lost. Predictably, Ginny had thought her father had abandoned her, and, equally predictably, she'd managed to persuade him to think the same way. Things were bad enough, even before the debacle when Ginny moved out of Audrey's – by which time Belle had two baby daughters of her own. Belle had put her foot down and point-blank refused to have Ginny living with her, as Marcus had wanted. She and Marcus had had huge rows about it, but in the end she'd won and he'd bought Ginny the flat, a beautiful flat, in a safe, smart area – not that it was good enough for his eldest daughter. Oh no! Ginny had cleverly plucked the strings of her father's guilt, and Belle had watched with increasing fury as her husband had become more and more frantic. He'd not only bankrolled Ginny's exist- ence, he'd showered her with love. Or attempted to. But, Belle thought, Ginny was as showerproof as a mackintosh. Loveproof. She'd tried pointing out that she was Marcus' wife, and that his fixation on making up for his imagined failures during Ginny's childhood and youth wasn't fair on her, or on her own two children, but it was no use: Ginny was Marcus's prodigal daughter, and he wanted her back. He wanted absolution – Ginny's forgiveness. In Belle's opinion, there was nothing to forgive.

Cooper's had gone global, and so had Marcus's cooking reper- toire. The Chinese-style stir-fried chicken was followed by American-style apple pie à la mode. Then came Columbian coffee. Once the cafetière was empty, Belle nodded towards Marcus and Ginny.

'Why don't you two go upstairs, while we clear up?'

Emily pulled a face.

'Oh, Mum . . .'

'Yes,' said Belle. 'I'm not doing it on my own.'

'We'll help too, won't we Cookie.' Marcus eagerly volun- teered.

'No,' said Belle, with a bright smile. 'We won't be long . . . then after you two have had a drink and a chat we can call Ginny a taxi.'

In the drawing room Ginny settled herself on an Indonesian daybed, heaped with cushions, while Marcus went to the drinks cupboard. 'Liqueur?'

'No, thanks.'

'Sure?'

'Mm-hmm.'

Marcus poured himself a large measure of Scotch, straight up, downed half, then topped up the measure. As he crossed the room to the daybed he could feel the whisky scorching his throat and gullet. He sat down next to his daughter and made as if to place one hand on her knee, but changed his mind at the last minute, and dropped it onto his own fleshy thigh, instead.

'So,' he said, 'how's things?'

'Good, thanks. And you?'

'Good.'

'Good.'

Marcus took a burning gulp of Scotch, and Ginny lifted a maroon silk cushion into her lap. It had a deep fringe, and she fiddled with this, to distract her fingers from fingery thoughts of cigarettes, Belle didn't allow smoking in the house.

Here goes, Sweetie.

'Dad,' she said, 'I came tonight because I wanted to tell you something.'

Marcus took another mouthful of Scotch, and the hand holding his glass was slightly unsteady.

'Yes?' he said, imagining all sorts of horrors.

Ginny stared down at the cushion. She had looked up both 'breaking the news' and 'telling people' in the index to *The Pregnancy Handbook*, but the only remotely relevant text she could find was 'How do I tell the children?' Well, she thought now, why not as simply as possible?

'I'm pregnant,' she said.

Ginny was more than satisfied with her father's reaction. He was electrified. After he'd put down his glass, he gave her a spontaneous hug. Usually he planned these demonstrations of affection, and usually Ginny flinched away, as she did now, but only very slightly, as if from habit.

'Cookie! That's wonderful.'

'Yes?' Ginny sounded uncertain.

'Wonderful!'

Marcus unwrapped his arms from Ginny, retrieved his glass and took yet another swig of alcohol.

'Who's the father?' It was a friendly, interested question, not a challenge.

'Oh,' said Ginny, 'just Some Man.'

'Some man?' Marcus remembered various men from Ginny's past. But he wasn't aware of anyone special since that jerk Adam had dumped her to go and live a life of celibacy in a Buddhist monastery somewhere in Sussex. 'Umm . . .'

'We had a brief fling. Now it's over.'

Marcus slowly sloshed his whisky around his glass.

'Over?'

'Mm-hmm.'

Marcus told himself not to ask.

'So. A single mother.'

'Yes.' *You and me, Sweetie, you and me.*

Now Marcus told himself not to make an inappropriate, old-fashioned comment.

'Great,' he forced himself to say. 'You'll be brilliant.'

I'll be amazing, Sweetie.

'I hope so . . . although I *have* said he can have a measure of involvement.'

'The father?'

'Yes.'

'Joint parenting?'

'Not quite.'

'So?'

'Access, and stuff.'

Marcus nodded to himself.

'That's good. Good for the child, and good for you.' He stared down at his whisky, wondering about the father of his grandchild. He would have liked to have seen this man's face appear on the wavering surface of the honey-brown liquid, but it didn't.

'Perhaps we'll meet . . .?'

'Perhaps.' *No chance, Sweetie.*

'I'd like that.'

'Mm.'

'How've you been feeling?'

'Fine. A bit sick, but fine.'

'Eating properly and all that stuff?'

'Yes.' Not counting cigarettes, caffeine and wine. 'A craving for gherkins.'

Marcus frowned.

'Have you seen a doctor?'

'No.'

'Don't you think you should?'

'What's the point before about week twelve? They don't actually *do* anything.' *Except lecture you about your lifestyle, Sweetie.*

'What about hospitals?'

'I haven't thought yet.'

'The Portland?'

'We'll see.'

Marcus considered his daughter's attitude distressingly casual, but he didn't like to argue.

'If you need any extra help – financial help.'

'No, I – you're already very generous. Thank you.' They were both taken by surprise by this, and both struggled not to show it. Ginny had never before thanked her father for his cash – or anything else. He held his breath, and she risked giving him a small smile. The pregnancy hormones, once again.

'Don't thank me,' said Marcus. 'Really, if you need any-thing . . .'

'Let's wait and see.'

'Sure. When's it due?'

'Not until the summer.'

Marcus laughed.

'A summer baby! The best time of the year for getting up in the night.'

'Getting up in the night? I hadn't thought of that.'

Marcus laughed harder.

'You will!' he said. 'Sleep deprivation! Of course, we always had maternity nurses, but even so, it's torture. Not so bad in summer, though. With Ems I used to quite look forward to the two of us sitting by an opened window in the nursery, warm air washing over us in the middle of the night. We could smell the garden, earth and grass and honeysuckle, and the sounds of London were her lullaby. No wonder she was such a good baby.'

Ginny was astonished.

'You got up for Ems?'

'For all of you. Sometimes. Like I said, we had nurses, and I couldn't let myself get too exhausted, because of work. But I was a dab hand with the bottle. You and Lissa being winter babies, nights weren't so nice. Cold.'

Ginny tugged at the fringe on the cushion she was holding. The thought of her father giving her a bottle was confusing. And she didn't much like the idea of sleep deprivation, with or without a maternity nurse.

'I'll probably breast feed,' she said unenthusiastically. 'At least for a bit. The books all say the first few days are the most important for antibodies and whatnot.'

Marcus smiled, and watched her fingers for a moment or two – they were now plaiting the cushion's fringe.

'Belle and the girls will be so excited.'

Ginny coughed.

'They will. They all love babies . . .'

'Pah!'

Marcus's joy at Ginny's news tarnished, a little. Women wars. He could understand the loathing with which Audrey regarded Belle, but not why Belle detested Audrey. And the mutual hostility between his first daughter and his second family baffled him. He'd once loved Audrey, and craved her, too. In her presence he'd been unable to resist touching. In her absence he'd been unable to resist pining. Then, quite suddenly, loving and craving had been switched off. And they hadn't been switched on again until he'd met Belle. But why should that leave *all* his women at each other's throats? Leaving aside Audrey, whom he pitied, what was there to stop love blossoming between the other four?

'Give them another chance, Cookie. Especially now. It's the perfect time.'

'Dad, please don't call me Cookie.'

Marcus sighed, and took a swallow of whisky.

'Well I'm thrilled. Thrilled. And thrilled for you.'

'Thanks.'

'You clever girl.'

'It wasn't so hard.' No need to let her father in on the complicated details of Project P.

'Think of it! Me, a grandfather!'

Ginny met her father's eye.

'Old man,' she teased.

Usually Marcus didn't like to be reminded of his age, but now he laughed with pleasure at his daughter's playful tone. Once again he leaned over to place a hand on her knee, which projected under the cushion she was holding. This time he didn't change his mind. Ginny stopped fiddling with the cushion's fringe, and let her own hand slide over his. They sat like that in silence – until Marcus felt Audrey's eyes upon him. They were there in the room, floating about, outsized, eerie and focused on his soul.

Audrey was the only woman Marcus had ever met who'd had truly violet eyes. He'd seen those disks of purple flash and hint and flaunt every expression, every emotion. He'd seen them blank, and been able to interpret their blankness. He'd looked in – really looked in. There was no question in his mind that their ghostly presence was now commanding. 'We were young together,' they seemed to say, 'we loved each other. You owe me.' Marcus felt no temptation to deny it. 'I know I do,' he whispered in his head. The required payment was obvious. Ginny. So be it. He'd try to deliver Ginny to her mother, at whatever personal cost. After all, he guessed from being her father that being Ginny's mother was an unenviable thing to be. Not that Audrey made it easy on herself, or on her daughter either. Marcus could recognize covetous, selfish love when he saw it. But covetous, selfish love was still love, and better than nothing. At least to the lover, if not to the beloved. And Audrey had never re-married. She had no other children. Who was there for her to love, but her wayward, disappointing child? Marcus knew what he was risking, but felt compelled to speak.

'What about your mother?'

At the mention of her mother, Ginny withdrew her hand from Marcus's, as he'd guessed she would. She leaned away from him, against the arm of the daybed.

'What about her?'

Marcus's hand felt cold now it was no longer covered by his daughter's.

'Have you told her yet?'

Ginny scowled. Pregnancy hormones might have softened her up to risk the first few steps towards reconciliation with her father, but even *horror*mones were powerless in the face of her mother – that woman was still way beyond her emotional pale.

'No.'

Marcus squeezed his daughter's knee, very slightly.

'She'll be delighted.'

Ginny grunted.

'She will.' Marcus took a deep breath, 'When will you tell her?'

Ginny brushed aside his hand, and stood up.

'When I'm ready,' she said. 'I'll tell her when I'm good and ready.'

12

Nick was supposed to have arrived back from Rome at midday on Saturday, but when his plane had been hurtling down the runway it had come to a juddering stop just before it should have begun to soar. The captain had announced he'd detected a problem with one of the cabin doors, necessitating a return to the gate. This news was met with silence, as each passenger imagined the door blowing out at 30,000 feet and him- or herself being sucked into oblivion. But by the time they'd all been sitting at the gate for an hour, forbidden from disembarking by airline and customs regulations, the passengers had begun to rediscover their voices, and there were many bad tempered exchanges with the cabin crew. The plane eventually took off three hours late. The flight was bumpy, and the landing even bumpier. Nick still felt queasy when he climbed into a taxi at Heathrow for the ride home. He felt even worse when he allowed himself to contemplate what Seraph might have in store for him.

When he finally made it to Athens Road the children were just finishing their tea, macaroni cheese, with cauliflower – Seraph had realized too late that washed-out macaroni cheese and pasty-coloured cauliflower would look like sick and wallpaper paste.

'For goodness sake you lot,' she was saying, as Nick entered the kitchen 'If you don't eat up . . .'

'Hi, all.' Nick dumped his bags on the floor, and gave a general wave.

'Hi, daddy,' said Daisy, jumping up and running over to give him a kiss, but she changed her mind when she got close, and held her nose instead.

'Pheew! You smell!'

'Sorry! Plane air.'

'*Hola*, stinky,' said Tom.

'Dada. Me. Me,' yelled Luke, who banged his fork on the table with each me.

'*Hola*'s Spanish, Tom, not Italian,' snapped Seraph, then she turned and glared at Nick. 'So where've you been?'

Nick spread his hands in a gesture of helplessness or supplication.

'I couldn't phone. There were technical problems with the flight.' He thought technical problems sounded scary, dangerous, the words might prompt Seraph to consider that he could have been killed this afternoon. 'It was bumpy all the way and a fucking awful landing.'

'Language.' Reproved Seraph, with a glance at the children, then she turned her back on him, to do some bad-tempered pan scouring at the sink.

'Sorry.' Nick scuffed one shoe against the other for a moment. 'Perhaps I'll just go upstairs, unpack my bags and grab a quick shower?'

'Do what you like,' muttered Seraph, scrubbing fiercely.

Tom, Daisy, and Luke all fell silent. Three pairs of saucer eyes tracked from one parent to the other, and back.

The children's bedtime was more than usually stressful that night. Nick took Tom and Daisy, both of whom were playing up, and Seraph took Luke, who was feeling weepy and clingy, and wouldn't let her leave him until he was fast asleep. By the time she got downstairs Nick was waiting for her in the kitchen, a half-drunk bottle of beer in his hand.

'Did you hear the screams?' he asked. 'Tom broke that wand thing of Daisy's.'

Seraph ignored him, so he took a slug of beer, scratched his shoulder, and began again.

'I was going to cook, but there doesn't seem to be anything to eat.'

'Look again. There's plenty.'

'Oh.' Nick remained where he was, sitting at the table. 'Shall we order from Namaste?' he asked, when the silence became unbearable. Namaste was their local Indian, and it offered home delivery.

'Whatever.'

'Okay, where's the phone?'

'In the dining room, where it always is.'

In the dining room Nick noticed that Seraph had left a manuscript lying on the big table, and another on the side table by the phone, but he was far too anxious to indulge his fascination for the no-worries school of thought. He didn't give either title page a glance, but simply found Namaste's menu and set about ordering.

'I got you chicken jalfreze and some dhal,' he said, when he returned to the kitchen five minutes later.

Seraph shrugged. She'd poured herself a glass of red wine, and was nursing it at the kitchen table. Nick crossed the room to sit opposite her, and picked up his beer. He rolled the bottle between his palms. Time to make a stab at self-justification.

'Um . . .' he began.

Seraph scowled and reached across the table to push aside a vase of dead lilies.

'That's better,' said Nick, with false brightness. 'We can see each other now.'

'For God's sake,' said Seraph, and Nick's jaunty smile died. There was another long silence. This time Seraph broke it. 'So,' she said, 'we need to talk.'

'Yes,' agreed Nick. 'We do.'

Seraph took a gulp of her wine.

'Well, then,' she said. 'You've been having an affair.'

Nick ran one finger round the rim of his beer bottle.

'Do you remember once telling me that sexual jealousy was irrational?'

'I was twenty. Now I'm nearly forty. Ideas change.'

Nick took a pull of beer.

'Back then I thought you were wrong. But now I don't. It's true there's nothing possessive about love, that love and sex—'

'Shut up,' interrupted Seraph, 'just shut up.'

'But we both know there's more to fidelity than sex.'

Seraph leaned across the table and slapped him hard, once, across the cheek. Crack! Nick didn't even lean away from the blow, he just sat and took it.

'Why?' she asked.

'Why'd I do it?'

'Of course.'

'I told you – it was meaningless – a kind of madness. It wasn't me.'

'Who was it, then? Mickey Mouse?'

'It wasn't me. I was blind. I was acting in this kind of mist—'

Seraph banged her wine glass down on the table.

'You'll have to do better than that,' she said.

Nick looked at her.

'What do you mean?'

'I mean why did you really do it? What's wrong with our marriage?'

Nick looked down at his hands.

'Well come on,' said Seraph, 'it's not been much fun recently, has it?'

Nick shrugged.

'I dunno,' he said.

'You don't know? You don't know if our marriage has been fun?'

'I suppose it's true our world's been shrinking.'

'What?'

'Sometimes I feel like I'm living in a box. A coffin.'

'And you hoped sex with some – flooze – would show you how to smash your way out?'

Nick winced at Seraph's tone. The answer to her question was partly yes. But he didn't feel he could admit it, and in any case his hopes had been dashed, screwing Ginny hadn't shown him how to blast the coffin to smithereens, just reminded him the coffin was where he was headed.

'You know I love you—'

'Ha!'

'You know I do. I didn't love her. It was more . . .'

'A sex thing?' Seraph sneered.

She and Nick looked at each other.

'Our marriage,' said Nick. 'You have seemed a bit distant, lately.'

'Distant?'

'Withdrawn.'

'So it's my fault!'

'No. I didn't mean that. But things have changed, haven't they? Especially since Luke.'

Seraph's face hardened, and she thrust out her chin.

'I knew it!' she said, defiantly. 'Go on, blame a two-year-old.'

'I didn't mean—'

'Oh shut up! Who was she?'

'Just this woman from work.'

'Of course, I assumed it was an office *romance*.'

The word romance hung between them, as if in a little heart-shaped bubble.

'There was no romance,' he said. 'She's a temp. Her name's Ginny.'

'A temp? I should have known you couldn't even pull a proper secretary.'

Nick swallowed, but said nothing.

'And how long . . .?'

'Not long. No time. A few weeks was all – but the thing is . . .' In the outer world which housed Seraph, Nick's voice trailed off. But in his inner world it continued loud and strong: *The thing is it only took a single lunch hour to get her pregnant.*

'And you used a condom?'

Nick hung his head.

'My God! You didn't, did you?'

'Seraph—' *Seraph, I didn't use a condom, and she's pregnant.*

'You put us all at risk!'

'I'm sorry, I—'

'Its over, isn't it?'

'Yes,' said Nick, eagerly. 'It's completely over. I can promise you that. And Ginny's made it quite clear she's not remotely interested—'

'*Ginny's* made it quite clear?'

A look of horror flitted across Nick's face as he realized his mistake. It was quickly followed by a look of pleading.

'But of course what she thinks is irrelevant.'

'Right!'

'I'm not interested in her. Not at all. Only in you – Like I said, it's over, it's just . . .' *It's just she's pregnant, and I'm going to help her bring up the baby.*

Seraph made a dismissive sound.

'When I said *it's over*, I didn't mean your silly affair . . .'

'Not my . . .?'

'No. Us. We're over.'

Nick's beer bottle slipped out of his hand and fell to the floor, where it shattered with a crack as loud as Seraph's slap. Green shards fell across the red lino in a beautiful glinting arc, and the spilled beer spread into a foaming scented pool with the shape of a bird. Nick was aware of all this, but it was as if he were observing the scene from a great distance, or from the bottom of a swimming pool. He felt calm and detached, both from himself, and from his surroundings.

'No,' he said, at last, in a soothing, gentle voice. 'We're not.'

'Nick, if one out of two people says it's over, then it's over.'

'Seraph, you're angry.'

'Damn right I am!'

'You can't think now. Not yet. It's too soon.'

Seraph stood up.

'I've had four days to think. It's over. I could never trust you again. I could never forgive you.'

'Four days . . .'

'It's enough.'

'It's not. You don't know what you're saying. You haven't thought things through.'

'Don't patronize me!'

'Sorry. I didn't mean to . . . it's just I don't believe you.' Nick still spoke softly, reassuringly, as if to a frightened child, or an injured animal.

'You don't believe me?'

'You don't mean what you say. And what's more you know you don't.'

Seraph stared down at the mess on her kitchen floor. How dare Nick try to tell her what she meant? Nick interpreted her silence as hesitancy, and tried to press home his supposed advantage.

'And think of the kids,' he said. 'We couldn't do it to them.'

Seraph gave him a contemptuous look.

'You'd better clear up the glass,' she said, and started walking towards the door.

'Seraph . . .'

'The sleeping bag's still in the laundry cupboard. You'd better fetch it.' With that she quickened her pace and left the kitchen.

And think of the kids. On her way upstairs Seraph stopped to check on them. Tom's light was on and there was a scatter of opened books across the floor. He was hanging half off his bed, although fast asleep. He opened his eyes and mumbled something as she hauled him back onto the mattress and pulled his duvet up around his shoulders, but he didn't wake up. She kissed him and flipped off his light as she left his room. Next door Daisy was sleeping in her frilly pink ballet tutu, one hand clutching the spangly silver star Tom had snapped off her wand, the other flung out. She was flat on her back, snoring quietly, and so beautiful Seraph could scarcely bear to look at her. Daisy had never had a child's prettiness, but always a dark, solemn beauty which threatened to be merciless once she was older. The mother is beautiful, but the daughter more so. Yes indeed. Seraph kissed her and tiptoed out.

Luke was still as peaceful as when she'd left him, his breathing deep and even. He looked like a little convict in his striped pyjamas, and was cuddling Bagel, his floppy, furry dog. Seraph wanted to take her baby in her arms, undress him and lick his sweet, naked flesh from head to toe, but instead contented herself with stroking his soft, warm head. His hair was finer than cobweb, and his skin softer than moss. She leaned over and breathed in the scent of him. He smelled of the earth – and of her and Nick. No, Nick had said, we're not over. You can't think now. Not yet. It's too soon. You don't know what you're saying. You haven't thought things through. I don't believe you. You don't mean what you say – and what's more you know you don't. Seraph knew he was right, of course, and hated him for being right. Love and hate. Hate and love. Seraph and Nick. Nick and

Seraph. Light and dark. Dark and light. Yin and yang. Yang and yin. Marriage. Marriage. Marriage.

Downstairs Nick stayed frozen at the table for a few minutes after Seraph told him his marriage was over, then galvanized himself to fetch the dustpan and brush, and the mop. He still felt suffused with calm, and this ordinary household task, cleaning up the mess of glass and beer, was Valium. He was almost catatonic as he swept. Just as he was finishing he remembered the video Seraph had rented: 'Clean, clean you pathetic little man, you worthless piece of shit.' That woke him up, and when the doorbell rang he was stumbling about the kitchen, groaning aloud, with his head in his hands. The doorbell rang a second time, and Nick pulled himself together enough to go and answer it. The delivery man from Namaste had arrived. Nick took the bag of hot food through to the kitchen plonked it down on the table, and stared at it. What should he do about feeding Seraph? Should he call her? Or take her a tray, as if she were an invalid, or a prisoner? In the end he decided if she was hungry, she was perfectly capable of coming to fetch something, and, if not, she wouldn't welcome interruptions from him. He liked Indian food, and despite his mental turmoil, the spicy smells reminded him he was ravenous – he hadn't eaten anything since the shrink-wrapped sandwiches provided on the plane. He served himself a generous portion, then fetched another bottle of beer from the fridge and sat down to eat. The food worked its Eastern magic. By the time he'd finished eating he was feeling restored – optimistic, even confident. He'd been right. There was no way Seraph could have meant what she'd said, she'd just been letting off steam – which was quite understandable, under the circumstances. But they had nearly twenty years and three children behind them. Shared habits and rhythms. Little idiosyncrasies. Surely they could survive this mishap? Things were not so bad, thought Nick, now that he'd told Seraph about Ginny's baby. She'd heard the worst, there was nothing else. Tonight was their nadir. From now on they'd be on the up. Nick took a long pull on his beer, quite satisfied with his argument. Then it hit him.

Had he, in fact, told Seraph about Ginny's baby? He knew he'd meant to, could even remember framing the words. But thinking back over their conversation, it dawned on him that he hadn't actually spoken them aloud. Each time he'd tried, Seraph had cut him off. She still didn't know about the baby. She still didn't know the worst. The nadir was still ahead of them. Nick pounded his fists on the table, making everything on it jump, a few bits of paper, junk mail and bills fluttered unregarded to the floor, and the dead lilies shed most of their remaining petals. What should he do? Should he go upstairs right now, knock on his bedroom door and call out, 'Seraph, there's one more thing?' Use his baby there's a baby line? Or should he fall back on his ad hoc drip, drip strategy of confession? And was there any genuine choice? Not really. Going upstairs now was clearly impossible – emotionally impossible. Drip, drip was the only option – he'd have to tell Seraph about the baby tomorrow.

13

Amy felt apprehensive as she pushed through the door of the little French bistro she'd booked for tonight's date. She slipped out of her sensible jacket and handed it to the coat-check man, who swept his eyes over her with flattering greed. Seraph had joked she must treat her new clothes as weapons, and set them to stun – it was clear her first victim thought she'd gone nuclear. Although she strongly suspected Jude would be a better defended target than the coat-check man. She was late, and he was already here – she could see him sitting at a table tucked away towards the back of the restaurant, a book in one hand, a Gauloise in the other. So far he hadn't seen her. She swung her head, to check her newly bobbed hair still swished, took a steadying breath and headed towards him. Her mermaid skirt rippled and shimmered about her legs, and she caught quite a few men glancing at the way her lycra T-shirt clung to her tits. Jude kept reading until she was within a couple of yards of his table, then he came to the end of a chapter, snapped his book shut, glanced up and met her eye. Amy found his expression most gratifying.

'Hi,' she said.

'Hi,' he replied. 'You look amazing.'

Amy said nothing, but swung her hips a bit, so her skirt did its thing, then slid onto the empty chair facing Jude's. Jude took a long drag on his Gauloise, and raised one eyebrow at her. His eyebrows were heavy, but mobile. She wanted to lean across and run her tongue over them, but glanced down at the red and white checked tablecloth instead. There were already two menus and a bottle of red wine on the table. Jude leaned across to pour her a glass and she took a sip. Neither of them could think what to say next, but luckily Jude's book came to the rescue.

'Have you read this?' he asked, holding it up.

Amy read the title aloud from the cover.

'*Is This Book?*' She looked at Jude blankly. 'Is this book what?'

'Precisely,' said Jude.

'Oh.'

'*Ist Dieses Buch?* The translation's pretty smooth, given the density of Braumer's original. It's a bestseller in Germany.'

'I'm sure.'

'The first sentence is "This sentence is false." '

'Mm.'

'Yeah. If it's true, it's false, and if it's false it's true. The protagonist's a logician, you see.'

'Magician?'

'Logician.'

'Interesting.'

'Certainly is – Braumer's playing with genre. He mainly sticks to the rules of the detective story.'

'A detective? I thought you said a logician?'

'Yes, Otto, he's the detective. An amateur—'

'Like Miss Marple?'

'Agatha Christie?' queried Jude, looking thoughtful. 'True she was a wonderful storyteller, but in *Is This Book?* Otto's an amateur detective, but a professional logician. It's his boyfriend who gets murdered – or perhaps it's suicide? You see the real heart of the book is an investigation of self-identification. I-thoughts.'

'I-thoughts?' Amy had no idea what Jude was on about.

'Y' know, I am here now, and such.' Jude wafted his Gauloise in a vague fashion. 'What is it for a subject to identify himself self-consciously? How do I know where to draw the boundary between self and other? What happens when the switch gets thrown – hence the possible suicide. The boyfriend's a logician too. I forgot to mention that. It's a fucking amazing book.'

'Mm.' Amy knew she didn't give good book chat, and for a moment longed for Dave, who read legal thrillers, science fiction and novels about crazed submarine captains. Plus he never talked about what he'd read at dinner. He talked about his friends, his day, sport and the traffic.

'You should read it,' Jude urged her.

'I'd love to.'

'Bodily self-ascription is in there, too. How do I gain knowledge of my physical states and properties?'

'How indeed?'

Jude waited then blasted out one of his lazy, crooked smiles.

'How do I know I'm aroused?' he asked.

For God's sake! thought Amy.

'Who cares?' she snapped.

Jude's smile flickered and vanished. Amy picked up a menu.

'I can recommend the charcuterie,' she said.

The same book which had cautioned Amy never to sleep with a man until the third date, had also advised her never to sleep with one until she'd made a thorough investigation of his attitude to children, his bank balance and his past. Amy's own attitude to children was ambivalent, and she would never have stooped to being a kept woman, but as she nibbled on a piece of air-dried ham, she did consider pressing Jude on all the girlfriends he'd ever discarded. But she didn't know which would be worse – if he refused to tell her anything, or if he told her everything. If he told her everything, she'd have to reciprocate, and tell him about Dave – which she didn't want to do, so she kept silent.

After they'd eaten, Jude and Amy moved on from the bistro to a Soho drinking club where Jude had membership. It was in a tall, narrow building, dark and smoky. Jude found a red velvet bench, where they sat side by side, held a couple of inches apart by the force field pulsing between them. They downed two rounds of vodkas and tonics in near silence.

'Another?' asked Amy, who was thinking how much she liked beginnings, anticipation, the thrill of the unknown. Meanwhile Jude was thinking she might have held out once, but this was surely his lucky night. He reached across and drew the tip of one finger along her cheekbone.

'Fuck this,' he said. 'Let's go back to my place.'

Jude's place was in Belsize Square, it had been carved out of the attics of a large, white stucco house, which must once have been quite imposing. Amy felt disembodied as her two legs trudged her up the wide, shallow stairs to his plywood front door. Once inside she was hit by the smell of long neglected damp laundry, festering gym shoes, mould and stale cigarette smoke. Didn't he ever open a window? Dave, being a dentist, was scrupulous about hygiene. Amy squashed thoughts of Dave, and looked around

Jude's sitting room, which was as dirty as it smelt. She reminded herself she was not his wife, and tried neither to mind the squalor, nor to imagine how pleasant it would be to bring bleach and Ajax, flowers and cushions, to this miserable hole.

While they were stripping, Amy kept getting distracted by worries about the state of Jude's sheets . . . which turned out to be grubby. Even the taste of his skin – creamy chocolate swirled into smooth, rich coffee – couldn't quite stop her wondering what had made the stains. And Jude seemed distressingly content to lie back and let her feast on *mocca frappacino*, which she didn't mind, too much, until she realized she was about to taste something far less appetising. Jude realized the same thing, at the same instant.

'Stop!' he said. 'You're going to make me—'

Amy pulled her face back, and Jude scored a direct hit in her eye.

'It's all right,' said Amy half an hour later. 'It's fine. Really.' Her eye stung like crazy, and was watering profusely. She thought she might be allergic to his cum. Cum conjunctivitis. Great! And did cum-to-tears count as a risky exchange of bodily fluids? She glanced across to Jude's bedside table. They'd both unfussily accepted the need for a condom – they just hadn't got round to rolling it on – and it was still lying there, unopened, in its little foil packet.

Jude followed her gaze. The condom stabbed at him, an accusation and a challenge. He leaned up on one elbow, so he could look down on Amy's face, but quailed slightly at her expression and her eye. Far better to look at her breasts, which were small and firm, like Shee-Chee's, but where Shee-Chee's were a warm ochre, Amy's were startlingly white. He reached out his free hand to tweak one of her neat pink nipples.

'We could always . . .' he began.

'No thanks. I'm tired.' Did he think he was twiddling radio knobs?

Jude slid his hand lower. Amy trapped it with her own hand, and lifted it off her body.

'I'm tired.' And did he think she was some sort of mechanical doll? That a little bit of technically accomplished rubbing and pressing would sort everything out?

'Okay,' said Jude, then he leaned down and kissed her. Amy didn't feel she could shove him off, but as they snogged, she was already longing for daybreak. She'd leave just as soon as the tubes started running.

It was a chilly morning, and Amy walked fast up the long hill of Belsize Road, to the tube. As she walked she swung her arms for warmth, and wished her jacket was a long overcoat. Her legs were freezing under her mermaid skirt, and her black grosgrain pumps were not the most practical of footwear. Nevertheless, she had no intention of going home to change. There was simply no point in fighting any longer. She had no choice but to submit to the Dave vibration humming through her inside tubes, her liver, spleen, kidneys. Her large and small intestines. Her heart.

A couple of hours later Dave rolled over in bed, and groaned. Then he heard it again. Someone was determinedly ringing his doorbell. He hauled himself upright, and pulled on his dressing gown, then stumbled downstairs, preparing to deliver a bollocking: did no one respect the Sunday morning lie-in anymore? In a fury, he flung open his mock-Georgian front door. Fury was at once displaced by hope and longing. Amy stood on his doorstep. He said nothing, but looked her up and down. It was clear she'd come direct from another man's bed – why else the Saturday night vamp's skirt so early on Sunday morning? Her eye was red and swollen. She'd cut off the wild chestnut hair he'd loved so much, and replaced it with some ghastly auburn travesty.

'Hello,' she said, in the same sexy, sandpapery voice he'd never been able to refuse. 'Can I come in?'

By lunchtime Jude was sitting in his local, smoking and nursing a pint, trying to justify what had happened the previous night. Of course, not counting masturbation, which he didn't, he hadn't had a sexual encounter in ages, and even when sex had last been a regular feature in his life, Shee-Chee had always been very miserly about dishing out the blow-jobs. Under the circumstances it was quite inevitable that when Amy had so generously – not that he'd intended the still pristine condom just for show. He'd planned to soil it. Although, granted, lowering the bar meant sticking to doormats who'd uncomplainingly give head when he wanted it, and not expect anything much in return. The trouble was, Amy wasn't a doormat. But then nor was she a goddess. He really, truly had been doing her a favour, and they both – *both* – knew it. She'd never have made it into his bed if . . . If what?

If he hadn't been such a bastard. That's what. Jude sighed

and took a long drag on his cigarette. 'It'll stain your teeth.' Despite himself, Jude grinned, but his smile quickly faded. He'd behaved badly to women before, of course, and even felt bad about behaving badly. But this morning he felt *really* bad. Okay, there was the sexual humiliation to factor in, but that wasn't the whole story. In the past his cruelty had been casual, with Amy it had been calculated. He'd had a plan. Not that it had worked. Amy hadn't boosted his ego. Far from it. She hadn't helped him shove aside memories of Shee-Chee, and at least when Shee-Chee had gone he'd had the miniscule, the microscopic, the *electron*-microscopic satisfaction of knowing she'd been the one to do the dirty. He'd held the moral high ground. Now he'd lost even that.

14

Seraph had no intention of immediately telling Nick he'd been right to say she didn't know what she was saying when she'd said their marriage was over. Let him sweat. On Sunday morning her priority wasn't her husband, but her kids. They were still twitchy, and she wanted to give them a happy, distracting day – with or without Nick's help. In the afternoon she suggested a trip to Bookberries, their local bookshop, which had an excellent children's section. Her idea was met by groans. Gallingly, Nick's alternative got a red-hot reception.

'Christmas-tree time,' he announced. 'Remember?'

By three o'clock there was an enormous, soft-blue spruce swaying drunkenly in the corner of the Jamieson's sitting room, and of the five people busily hanging ornaments on its spreading branches, only two needed to pretend to be enjoying themselves. Not that there was anything unusual about that. Seraph's and Nick's history with Christmas trees was not joyous. Every year something or other sparked an exchange of words – the lights, the tinsel, real versus artificial. The very first year they'd been together, they'd had the standard furious row about whether to top off their silver fake fir with a fairy or a star. They'd solved the problem by leaving the tip bare, and attaching both a fairy and a star to the branches just beneath. They'd continued that tradition ever since, and it had worked well while they'd had only two children – Tom got to hang the star, Daisy the fairy. But with three kids they needed yet another topping-off ornament, so this year Seraph had bought a Father Christmas for Luke to hang. Soon, fairy, star and Father Christmas presided in tacky trinity over a riot of clashing colours, flashing lights and cheap baubles. The children went wild to see the result of their work, and could scarcely believe their ears when Seraph announced she had a post-tree-dressing treat lined up for them: cakes of the sort she never usually allowed in the house, industrially air-puffed sponges, covered with tooth-rotting frosting in chemistry-lab colours.

'Where'd you get these from then?' asked Tom, when he saw them.

'Coopers,' replied Seraph. 'I nipped in while the rest of you were paying for the tree.'

Once the additive addicts were settled round the kitchen table, Nick judged it politic to remove himself from their mother's sight for half an hour or so, and used paperwork generated by his Rome trip as an excuse to bolt to the sanctuary of the dining room. He dutifully set up his laptop, but found it impossible to concentrate on the revised management flow-chart he was supposed to be preparing for the Italian office, so he got up with the idea of wandering over to the window, to see what was going on in the road outside. As he drew level with the side table he saw the manuscript Seraph had left lying there. Unlike last night, he now read the title: *Baby Manual: A Guide for Expectant Fathers*. That stopped him in his tracks. He hadn't read a single word in preparation for the birth of any one of his first three children, they all, even Luke, pre-dated his penchant for Seraph's books. But, he now thought, wouldn't it be wonderful if the author of *Baby Manual* had included something for men in his position. Married men who'd impregnated women other than their wives, but who wanted to stay married. And to be proper fathers to *all* their children. He didn't hesitate to pick up the script, and take it back to the table, where he pushed aside his laptop, and started reading.

Of course there was nothing directly relevant to him, although an early paragraph was headed, Why Do You Feel as if You're About to Have a Breakdown?, and there was a brief discussion of how to fix things if you'd screwed up when your partner first told you the news – 'remember a bad start doesn't mean you'll be a bad father.' True, but how bad could a bad start be? Greeting the news by suggesting abortion seemed to be well beyond the scope of the book. But even though *Baby Manual* was irrelevant to Nick's needs, it was a lot more interesting than the revised management flow-chart. It was packed with snappy lists – ten lies men should tell their pregnant wives, (Do you still find me sexy? Yes. Do you mind that my breasts will sag after the birth? No. Is my ass sagging? No . . .) ten things the partners of pregnant women should never do (Agree she looks fat. Ogle a sexy woman in a clinging outfit. Admit to fearing that sex after childbirth won't be as good as before . . .) and so on and so forth. Nick was so engrossed in these lists he didn't hear Seraph come into the room until it was too late.

'I've given them their tea,' she said, 'and now it's . . . what're you reading?'

Nick looked up and met her eye. All the colour drained from

his face. She frowned and glanced down at the script on the table, for a moment, seeing the tidy pile of manuscript pages, it occurred to her that Nick might at last have finished *Antidote*, and printed it out. But then her eyes took in a heading: Ten Ways Pregnancy Can Wreck Your Sex Life – and What to do About Them. Seraph herself had suggested the list approach to Livia, and had told her to browse through laddish men's magazines for ideas. She looked back at Nick, and their eyes locked. All the colour drained out of her face, too. They were like a pair of ghouls staring into each other's soulless depths.

'Forgive me,' said Nick.

Seraph wheeled about, and left the room.

⬤

'I told you it's over,' said Seraph, later that evening when the children were in bed.

'You did,' replied Nick, 'but I didn't believe you, and I still don't.'

Once again they were sitting at the kitchen table. Seraph looked down at her hands, and twisted her engagement ring. She did know of women who, after a year or so of marriage, refused to wear engagement rings they'd never liked, or gone off. In the past she'd looked at such women askance, but perhaps they knew something she didn't?

'You'd almost persuaded me you might be right,' she said, 'that perhaps I hadn't meant what I'd said, but now . . .'

'It makes no difference.'

'That she's pregnant? Come off it!'

'You didn't mean what you'd said about us being over. So why should this change things? If you can forgive me for—'

'Who said anything about forgiveness?'

'But if you didn't mean what you said – if you can overlook – you know – the basic act. You can overlook—'

'The unintended side-effect?'

'I suppose—'

'Bullshit!' Seraph flung out her arm, and knocked over the vase of petal-free dead lily stalks, which luckily had no water in it. They both watched the vase topple, but neither reached out to pick it up.

'Are you certain it's yours?' asked Seraph.

'Fairly.'

'So as well as not using a condom, you didn't even think to ask if she was using contraception.'

'I did. She said she was.'

'So a mistake? Like Luke?' Seraph's tone was sarcastic.

'You're right.' Nick said. 'I think she planned it. At least I guess she did.'

'So what? That's no excuse.'

Nick had played his best card. If Ginny had used him without seeking his consent for the use she'd put him to, surely that absolved him of guilt? Apparently not.

'Perhaps not,' he conceded, in a panicky tone, 'but—'

'But nothing – I assume she wants to keep it,' Seraph knew teenage girls had abortions, but surely mistresses never did?

'Yes.'

'And yet still you say it's over between you.'

'Yes.'

'Oh, come on!'

'It's over. I told you. I never had strong feelings for her. Never, it was just . . . And it's the same for her.'

'But what if it wasn't?'

'Wasn't what?'

'The same for her? What if she were sobbing at your feet, begging you to leave me?'

Nick looked blank.

'She's not.'

Seraph was frustrated. She pulled a face, and shook her head before changing tack.

'But the child,' she began. Men did often did walk away from children, of course, but it never occurred to her Nick might have considered doing so. Not Nick, who knew what it was like to be abandoned by a father. Not Nick, who let his kids use him as their climbing frame, and who was forever telling them he loved them. Nor did she pause to consider that Ginny might not have wanted Nick's involvement. Why ever wouldn't she have done? Nick wasn't violent, or insane, or an abusive alcoholic, or anything.

'It can't be over if there's a child,' she continued. 'You can't pretend your life's not going to interweave with hers for the next twenty years.'

Nick looked at his wife with a mixture of dog-like devotion and respect.

'That's exactly it,' he said. 'And surely you, a mother, can understand?'

Seraph ignored that.

'Even if we stick to thinking just about money—'

'She's not interested in our money—'

'Ha!'

'It's true. Forget money.'

'We can't. Anyway, what about visits and—'

'Yes.' Nick jumped in. 'There'll have to be visits. Please Seraph, you know I couldn't live with the loss . . .'

Seraph's vision blurred, and she briefly closed her eyes.

'But you could live with the loss of me, and the kids.'

'Not at all.'

'Balls! You put our marriage at risk when you started screwing this woman. Our marriage, our lives and our children's lives – you knew you could lose me. Lose the family.'

Nick bit his lip, then spoke, plaintively.

'Please. You're not being fair.'

'Fair? Who are you to—'

'But listen—'

'So what do you imagine? You and me, living happily ever after, while you spend alternate Thursday evenings, or whatever it is, with some brat I never, *ever* want to meet?'

'We haven't—'

'You can be sure I never want to see it. *Never.*'

So much for maternal understanding, thought Nick.

'Seraph, please. All this misses the point.'

'Oh the point,' Seraph said tauntingly. 'So what's that then?'

'I love you. And you love me. That's the point.'

Seraph was silent for a long moment.

'Words, Nick. I don't know. I just don't know any more.' She looked directly across at her husband. 'I think we need to spend a few days apart.'

'We just have.' The panicky note in Nick's voice was stronger now.

'But I didn't know the half of it and I think . . .' she was going to say, you should move out for a week or so, but then she realized such an arrangement would leave her at home, looking after the kids whenever she wasn't at work. She didn't want to look after the kids. She wanted some time alone. 'I think I'm going to move out for a few days,' she said. 'I mean I know I am. Just a few days to think things through.'

'Seraph . . .'

'Perhaps just until Friday? That wouldn't be too tough on the children.' *Would it?*

'But . . .'

'Between school and Kate, they'll hardly notice I'm gone.'

'You know that's not true.'

Seraph did. She glared at Nick, and stood up.

'It's the best you're going to get,' she said, shortly.

'But . . .'

'So count yourself lucky.'

Nick bowed his head.

'I do, love. I do.'

15

When Margaret barged into his office, Nick was staring at a pile of his underlings' expense claims.

'Here comes the shorty and the fatty.'

Nick hadn't the energy to pretend to be polite.

'What is it?'

Margaret smiled.

'You look terrible,' she said. 'Did you pick something up in Rome? Or here? The dreaded lurgey?'

'I'm fine,' said Nick, impatiently. 'What can I do for you?'

'Actually, I came about Virginia. I just wanted to remind you this'll be her last week.'

'Jean's already done it.'

'She has?' Margaret paused. 'Anyway, no loss.'

'Temps come. Temps go.'

'They do. I expect Jean's already put in a call to the agency.'

'I expect so.'

When she left his office, Margaret didn't shut Nick's door. He watched her walk over to Jean and begin to say something. After a moment both women glanced in his direction, so he purposefully picked up an expense claim and held it in front of his face. It was from one of the reps, who'd claimed for pay-per-view TV in his room at a businessman's hotel, where he'd stayed for a trade fair. *A porn channel, no doubt*, thought Nick, who signed the form, but ringed the relevant amount and reached for a Post-it. Okay this time, he wrote, but no more claims for TV, please. PS what were you watching? Once he'd dealt with that, he glanced back to Jean's desk. Margaret had gone, and Jean was on the phone. He resumed his vacant staring, and watched in fascination as a rippling image of Ginny's face spread like liquid across his desk. Her glistening mouth opened wide.

'Wanna chat?' it asked.

Next thing Nick knew he was holding the phone, punching out Ginny's extension number. 'Could you come through for a minute?' he asked, a moment later.

'Oh, you're back,' said Ginny. 'I thought we'd agreed not to talk in the office?'

'Did we?'

'Yeah. You know. Margaret and that crew.' Ginny was once more hunched low over her desk, whispering.

'But that was about arrangements and such,' said Nick. 'Practicalities.'

'And this isn't?'

'No.'

'Surely it's not *work*?'

'No.'

'No?' Ginny was surprised, and beginning to be alarmed. 'Then what?'

'Can't you just come in and see me?'

Nick's tone gave his sadness away. Ginny couldn't guess at the cause, but she groaned inwardly. It wasn't that she felt hostile – but nor did she feel very much like becoming a shoulder for him to cry on. She'd never been much good at that sort of thing. There was a long silence.

'Okay,' she said, grudgingly. 'I'll be through in a moment.'

Nick hardly let her get into his office before he hit her with it.

'Seraph's walked out.'

'Oh,' said Ginny. She remembered Adam walking out, and a wave of nausea broke over her. Morning sickness. *The Pregnancy Handbook* dismissed it as a misnomer: 'You may find you feel most nauseous when your stomach is empty, especially in the morning after an entire night without food – that's where the misnomer "morning sickness" comes from.' Ginny needed a stomach-settling cigarette. She was wearing a long, loose cardigan with deep pockets, and she patted at these until she found her packet of fags, and her lighter. At least Nick was too distracted to scold her for smoking. When she lit up she stared him straight in the eye.

'Why?' she asked. *None of this has anything to do with us, Sweetie.*

'Why's Seraph walked out?'

'Yes.' *And why are you telling me? It's none of my business.*

Nick looked at her to see if she was making some sort of joke, but saw nothing in her face to suggest irony or sarcasm.

'I told her about you. And the baby,' he spoke incredulously.

'What?' Ginny was shocked.

'I told her you're pregnant.'

'Oh.' *Jesus!* 'I assumed you'd keep things secret.'

'The baby?'

'Both you and me, and the baby.'

'Well yes,' said Nick. 'You and me was one thing, but I didn't think secrecy would be possible in the long run, given what we've decided.'

Ginny took a long drag on her cigarette.

'Why not? You should have kept quiet.'

Nick felt his body temperature plummet. Had he been wrong to listen to Pete? Could he have pulled it off? Could he have fathered the result of his extra-marital affair, without telling his wife it existed, and hence without putting his marriage at risk? No. He loved Seraph too much. He loved her enough to risk telling her the truth.

'I couldn't have done,' he said, with as much firmness as he could muster. 'It would never have worked.'

Ginny made a little move. Since it hadn't occurred to her that Nick would let Seraph in on the secret of Sweetie's existence, she'd not thought to worry about relations between her child, and Nick's existing family – she'd assumed there wouldn't be any. But now . . .? Suppose Seraph returned to Nick, would she see herself as some sort of stepmother to Sweetie? A Belle? *No way, Sweetie, no way!* But it wasn't just Seraph. There was also the matter of brothers and a sister. An off-the-peg family. She glanced across at the framed photo of Tom, Daisy and Luke on Nick's desk.

'Your children . . .' she began, but she couldn't deal with the complexities of fraternal relationships just now. She hesitated and changed tack. 'Did she take the children?'

Nick shook his head.

'Not *yet*,' he said, with emphasis.

Ginny inhaled once more. *Your marriage is your problem, and your kids are your look out.*

'Well, I suppose it's always sad when a marriage breaks up,' she said, 'especially if there are children involved.'

Nick did a double take.

'I hope she's not gone for good. I hope she'll be back.'

'Yes?' *Why? She's only a wife, for God's sake.*

'Of course. I love her.'

'Well I expect it'll sort itself out.'

Nick clicked his fingers.

'Just like that,' he said. 'Easy.'

'I'm sure it'll work out if you want it to.'

'It's not just me, though, is it? At the moment Seraph doesn't seem too keen on the idea of reconciliation.'

Ginny shrugged, slightly.

'She'll come round.'

Nick shot her an angry glance.

'Is that it?' he said. 'Don't you have anything else to say?'

Ginny's eyes also hardened.

'You don't think it's my fault, do you?'

Nick kept silent, and glared at Ginny.

'It's not,' she said. 'No way. When a relationship collapses there are always pre-existing fault lines.'

Fault lines. Adam's words. And even as she spoke, Ginny felt an unexpected rush of pity for Nick. Very inconvenient. According to Project P she was not supposed to have pitied Some Man. But then, she hadn't slept with Some Man, she'd slept with this particular one. Sweetie's father was not Some Man, but Nick. Okay, so what? She owed him nothing. She'd already done far more for him than she'd ever planned, simply by agreeing to let him have access to Sweetie. And what exactly did Nick expect from her anyway? What did he expect her to do or say? What *could* she do or say?

'Did you tell her I want nothing from you?' she said, but more gently than she'd spoken before.

'Yes.'

'That I don't want to move in with you, or marry you, or anything?'

'She knows there was nothing between us.'

'And still isn't.'

'Except the child.'

Ginny took a drag of her fag, then slowly exhaled. She might not want to, but it was difficult not to think about Nick's life now that she'd agreed to maintaining some sort of contact with him for the next twenty years. It was too bad! Some Man would not have made her feel remorseful. Some Man was good-looking, tall and healthy, but nothing else. Nick was all these things, but he was also . . . nice. But niceness counted for nothing, she reminded herself. It wouldn't stop him becoming a millstone round her neck. Ginny sighed. Could she change her mind? Could she say, 'Actually I've been having second thoughts, and I don't want you to have any contact with my child, after all?' No, she couldn't. It wouldn't be fair on Sweetie, to whom she'd now promised a father. *And I'll always keep my promises, Sweetie.*

'Tell her how you feel,' she said, at last. 'Tell her what she means to you.'

'I've tried.'

'Say you'd do anything for her.' Ginny longed for her pre-pregnancy, hard-boiled self. She knew how to manage that self, but not this soppy new one – all this sloshing around in a sea of *horror*mones stuff was becoming a drag.

Nick looked at her.

'She knows I love her,' he said.

'Well tell her it was meaningless.'

'I did . . . I told her it was a kind of madness. That I was acting in a mist.'

'Oh.' Despite herself, Ginny was peeved. A mist. Cold and damp and gloomy. 'Well . . . whatever. Tell her again. Keep telling her until she hears.' She made a sweeping gesture with the hand which held her cigarette. They both watched the patterns the smoke left hanging in the air.

'Tut, tut! Smoking in the office are we?' It was Tony, who'd pushed open Nick's door, and now stood in the entrance with his hands on his hips, staring at Ginny with mock ferociousness.

Ginny took another drag.

'You're quite right, Tony,' said Nick. 'Put that out would you Gi—Virginia.'

'Oh, I think you could let her finish that one,' said Tony. 'It's not as if she's pregnant or anything.'

Nick showed admirable self-control, and forbore from jumping up and strangling Tony.

'You have a problem for me?' he asked, in an even tone.

'Yup,' said Tony, perkily, 'with the consumer leaflet for Fabric-Fresh. The printers—'

'E-mail me on it. I'm tied up right now.'

'Everyone wants to hear they're loved,' Ginny continued, the moment Tony had gone.

'You got it!' said Nick.

Ginny didn't like his tone.

'So just tell her,' she said, uncertainly.

'Is that it? Is that your advice?'

Ginny gave a small shrug.

'I think I already suggested jewellery?' she said, after a second or two.

Nick groaned.

'Earrings,' he said, hopelessly.

Ginny wrinkled her nose.

'Perhaps not earrings,' she said. 'Perhaps a necklace? Other than that I really don't know what to suggest.' *Okay, Sweetie, so mummy's not cut out to be an agony aunt.*

Nick grunted, and looked at her cigarette, and then, pointedly, at her stomach.

'Tony was right,' he said. 'You shouldn't be smoking.'

After Ginny left his office, Nick succeeded in slumping in his slump resistant chair. It was distressing to think the mother of his child could greet his pain with such a mixture of platitudes and incomprehension. Next time he'd risk turning down an invitation from a liquid face. Fortunately, he knew of a more reliable source of succor.

'Ah,' said Pete, 'I thought you must be back from Italy. How was it?' He was opening his post, and mulling over his strategy for a client meeting he had later that morning. The client was a successful local businessman who wanted a house. Pete hated doing houses, but they paid the bills.

'How was Rome?' asked Nick, stupidly.

'Sure,' said Pete, already fearing the worst.

'Okay.'

'And on the home front . . .?'

'I told Seraph.' Nick paused 'I told her everything.' He eyed the pile of expense forms on his desk, and wished he could rip them to shreds.

'Everything?'

'Yes.'

Pete grunted.

'So how'd she react?'

'She walked out.'

Pete slit an envelope and pulled out a flyer from a leading manufacturer of bricks, crumpled it up, and tossed it towards the bin, but it fell short.

'Ooops.'

'Yeah. Not great. I told her yesterday. She said we needed a few days apart – a few more days – to think things through. She slept at home last night, but after work she's going to take herself off.'

'Where?'

'Dunno.'

'To her parents?'

'Perhaps.'

'And what about the kids?'

'We haven't said anything . . . at least, I haven't.'

'I meant will she take them with her tonight?'

'No. She said they wouldn't miss her between Kate and school.'

'Good. So it's not a bunk, not if she's left the kids.'

'Mm.'

There was silence for a beat or two. Pete broke it. 'And how did she seem when you told her?' he asked. 'I mean, apart from walking out, how did she seem?'

'Seem? She had said our marriage was over. But I didn't

believe her and then she admitted she might not have meant it . . . then I told her about the baby. That was last night. Now she's left.'

She had said it was over . . . THEN I told her about the baby? Pete decided to let that pass.

'Right,' he said. 'And how are you coping?'

'Okay. I suppose.'

'I could make an excuse to visit London later in the week.'

'Thanks. I'm okay.'

'Well, let me know.'

'Sure.'

'She said just a few days apart?'

'Mm.'

'So when are you expecting her back? Did she say?'

'She said Friday.'

'And she fully understands it's over?'

'I think she thinks it can't be, because of the baby.'

'She's got a point. But she does know you're not screwing Ginny any more?'

'Yeah . . . Ginny thinks I should never have said anything. About any of it. About her, or the baby.' There was an accusatory note in Nick's voice. He'd temporarily forgotten his idea that love demanded truth. 'Perhaps I shouldn't have done. Perhaps I shouldn't have listened to you.'

Pete took a deep breath. Ginny thinks? So Nick had talked this over with her – surely the sort of on-going contact worrying Seraph? But it would be cruel to point that out to Nick right now. He crumpled another circular, this one from a firm of interior designers, tossed it to the bin, and once again missed.

'We've been over all that,' he said, 'I explained why I thought you had to tell her.' He paused for a long moment. 'Do you think I should have a word with Fiona?'

Nick was thrown.

'What? Why?'

'They were so close, for so long. She might be able to help – I mean, help Seraph.'

'Bollocks,' said Nick, forcefully. 'Fiona *left you*, remember. *Left you.*'

'Yeah,' said Pete. 'I know. It's just I thought – female bonding, or something. A support group.'

'No,' said Nick.

'But she's a doctor.'

'What's that got to do with it?'

'She's, you know – good at emotional messes,' she'd been much better than Pete at their own emotional mess.

'She's a bloody feminist,' said Nick, remembering Fiona's intelligent, appraising eyes. 'For God's sake leave her out of this.'

'Okay,' Pete spoke regretfully, not only for the chance of help which he believed Nick was foolishly passing up, but also for himself. He longed for any excuse to talk to his ex-wife about anything other than how they split the assets, and the children.

Later that day, towards midnight, Ginny was lying naked in her double bed, alone apart from Sweetie, and thinking back over her conversation with Nick. She'd not lied. She'd said, 'Everyone wants to hear they're loved'. Jesus, it was true. In her head Adam's voice breathed, 'Darling, you're the one', words he'd never actually breathed in her ear. Ginny sniffed and rolled over onto her stomach, so her tingling breasts were crushed into the mattress. They'd already swollen two cup sizes, and she didn't like them this big, they made her look and feel top-heavy. And it was surely not long now until her belly started swelling too? She supposed at first it would be romantic to be showing, but the romance would quickly balloon into the reality of being fat, and being fat would then whale up to the truly grotesque. And no doubt her ass would soon start to sag, and probably remain saggy for life. As for her vagina . . . were you allowed to ask for a C-section on the grounds that you still wanted a penis to be a tight fit, after childbirth? The Natural Childbirth Trust probably wouldn't approve, but then the NCT could take a running jump. All those flabby, unattractive mothers flashing their droopy tits at the slightest excuse. She'd never be one of those. Never.

Except she would. *Fucking Hell, Sweetie.*

Ginny rolled onto her back once more, and stared up at her ceiling. 'Everyone wants to hear they're loved.' And desired. Faced with the prospect of never again being a sex-object, Ginny submitted to an intense flashback to the days when she'd been precisely that. Or not precisely, but more or less. Nights with Adam. She smiled at the memories – but not for long. Adam had said he wanted to obliterate his self. Fair enough. But why couldn't he have stuck to sex to do it? Why all that crap about meditation and reincarnation? 'Our fault line', Adam had called it – meaning his beliefs, her attitude towards them. But he'd been wrong. It had been a bloody great *rift. Fault line. Rift. Two people adrift.* It sounded like the sort of meaningless song she'd croon to Sweetie. Not that it was meaningless. And not that Sweetie would get the meaning. Her baby was far too firmly anchored in her to understand what it meant to be unfastened from the world. Her baby could have no inkling of the way she herself had been cut loose. Or of how she'd cut others loose.

Ginny sat up and slapped her palms silently against the duvet. Guilt. She knew how to exploit other people's – as Belle, for one, had noticed – but to her, the actual feeling was unfamiliar, and unwelcome as toothache. She decided she'd better do something to get rid of it. The problem was: what? Was there any way she could help Nick heal the rift she'd helped to cause? She reached down and pulled the duvet over her knees, hugged it to her and picked at its edge with her fingers. She really was trying to cut down on fags, but it was hard, and her fingers needed something to do. After a moment or two she gave in to her craving and reached over for the opened packet lying on her bedside table. She lit up and inhaled. Smoking always helped her to think, and almost at once she came up with the beginnings of a plan.

How would it be if she were to approach Seraph directly? What if she were to explain her side of the story – elaborate the details of Project P? Any woman would understand her longing for a baby, and once Seraph knew how blatantly she'd used Nick (here Ginny blushed, unseen in the dark) she surely couldn't remain furious with him? She would surely see that none of this had been completely her husband's fault – that he really had been acting in a kind of mist. A clammy mist of Ginny's own devising. A web spun from her half truths. Her lies. Her deceits. 'It was me,' she imagined herself saying to Seraph, 'I'm the one to blame.' Seraph, a wife, would surely see the truth of her argument, and immediately go back to Nick. Bingo! No more guilt. She, Ginny, would be happy. Nick would be happy. Even bloody Seraph would be happy. *Sweetie, all will be well.*

16

Seraph was in the kitchen, wondering what, if anything, to say.

'Listen,' she began, as she poured Cornflakes for Tom, 'Mummy's going away for a few days.'

Tom, like Daisy, was in the St Bernard's uniform, and his attention was mostly on a model spacecraft he was dismantling.

'Why? Are you going on holiday?'

Seraph briefly grappled with her conscience.

'Yes – Should you be doing that? Will you be able to put it back together again?'

'Doesn't matter. I want the parts for a time machine. Can we come with you?'

'No. It's a holiday just for mummies.'

'What about daddies?' this was Daisy.

'No. Just mummies.'

'Daddy will stay here to look after us?' Daisy looked anxious.

'Yes.'

'So when will you be back?' asked Tom.

'Friday.'

'Sure?' Asked Daisy.

'Yes. Do you want Cornflakes, or Weetabix?'

'Nothing.'

'Don't be silly, Daisy. You need a good breakfast, or you'll be hungry at school. And watch it, you're about to spill your milk.'

Daisy's cup was dangling in her hand. She tightened her grip around the handle.

'Can I have Fruity-Os?'

Seraph disapproved of Fruity-Os, which were loaded with sugar and additives, but they made good bribe food, and Daisy knew there was a packet lurking at the back of the larder.

'Okay. Just this once.'

'Me too,' said Luke. Who was still in his convict's pyjamas and was shredding an unpaid phone bill he'd found on the table. Seraph took it from him.

'Okay,' she said.

'Where're you going for this holiday?' Tom called to her back as she delved into the larder.

'Not far. I'll be able to get home quickly if I have to, and I'll phone every evening.'

Seraph returned to the table and started tipping luridly coloured Fruity-Os into two bowls. She passed the first one to Daisy.

'Luke too,' said Luke.

'Yes Luke. Here it is.' Seraph pushed the second bowl in his direction.

'No. Holiday. Luke come too.'

'No Luke.'

'Why?'

'Because it's a holiday from us lot,' said Tom, bitterly.

'No Tom, that's not true,' said Seraph. Then Luke began to cry, and Daisy joined in.

Despite the wails, they all heard the front door slam and even Luke and Daisy turned their heads. A moment later Kate appeared in the kitchen doorway, carrying her overnight bag. Every Monday she got up in time to catch the 6.45 fast train to

London from Sevenoaks. She usually arrived at Athens Road by eight o'clock.

'Hi,' she said. 'Sorry I'm late, leaves on the line – what's up with you two?'

'Hi, Kate,' said Seraph, before her children could answer. 'Can I have a word in the sitting room a moment?'

Oh no thought Kate, who could more or less guess what was coming. It couldn't be worse timing. Over the weekend she had, a little hesitantly, told Richard she'd consent to move in with him – not to marry him, but to give him a fair trial while making up her mind on the M word. Richard had been elated, but he was still fearful of losing her, and he'd insisted she hand in her notice right away! No prevaricating! She'd promised, and this morning she'd planned on being the one to ask for those few words in the sitting room. But her boss had got in first. And now it looked as if she'd have to break her promise to Richard. Oh well, probably the first of many.

Seraph set off for work carrying the expandable canvas briefcase she always carried, and also an expandable canvas overnight bag she'd packed in a hurry. The briefcase contained her mobile, *How to Change Your Life*, *Baby Manual*, and a slew of memos from Benedicta which she knew she'd never read, but couldn't quite bring herself to throw away. The overnight bag contained a nightdress, a toiletries bag, underwear, tights, a skirt, three shirts, a cardigan and a jersey. She had no idea where she'd be unpacking it that night. When she sat down at her desk, finding somewhere to stay should have been her first priority, but she decided to read the *Mail* instead. It wasn't her usual choice but a headline she'd spotted in other people's papers as she'd jolted her way into work on the tube had prompted her to buy her own copy. Some report had just come out claiming that 81 per cent of working mothers wished they could stay at home with their children. As far as Seraph could tell, it was unscientific propaganda, relying on a ridiculously small sample including *pregnant* women, most of whom, she guessed, must be first-time mothers with no idea what they were letting themselves in for. But the fact that she didn't believe the figures didn't prevent something from tightening in her stomach, and refusing to loosen. She pulled over her phone, this was just the sort of claptrap she and Fiona had so often excoriated in the past, and she wanted her ex-sister-in-law's reassurance that her own opinions were sound. And, of course, she wanted to update her on the weekend's unhappy developments.

'Dr McDonald's with a patient,' said the receptionist at Fiona's surgery. She sounded even more harassed today than she had on Friday. 'Another flu case,' she added.

'Can I leave a message?'

'Let me get a pen.' Seraph heard rustling. 'Go on then.'

'Can you ask her to call Seraph.'

'Who?'

'Seraph.'

'As in Seraphim and cherubim?'

'Yes.'

'S-e-r-a-p-h?'

'Yes.'

'Okay, I'll tell her.'

After she'd hung up Seraph returned to the question of where she'd sleep that night. Should she call her parents in Guildford, and ask if she could stay for a few days? But she couldn't face the inevitable questions, flaps and panics, so she listened to her voicemail instead. There were three messages from agents, all chasing delayed payments. An author, who really needed a shrink not an editor, had called twice on Friday. The most recent message was from Iris Basham.

'I don't want to bother you,' she began, and Seraph smelled lavender water and talcum, 'I know you're busy, but I wonder if you've had a chance to look at my proposal for *Hair Today Gone Tomorrow*?' There was a tiny pause on the tape. 'And if so, do you like it?'

Seraph pulled a face. She wished potential authors could get it into their heads not to call her. What was the point? If she'd read *Hair Today*, and loved it, did Iris really think she'd have kept her enthusiasm to herself? She jabbed at the ERASE ALL MESSAGES button, then transferred her gaze to the untidy, sagging bookshelves just above her head and returned her attention to the accommodation problem: should she beg a bed off Amy for a night or two? She was still trying to decide when Amy herself came in, carrying a pile of books.

'These just came in from the printers,' she said, and dumped them on Seraph's desk.

'It's fabulous!' said Seraph.

'My hair?'

'Yes.'

'Look!' Amy swung her head. 'See how it swings?'

'Jude was right about how it transforms you.'

It cost Seraph dear to force that out, but Amy merely laughed and shrugged.

'You look tired,' she said.

'I am, a bit.'

Amy, by contrast, looked radiant, even her clothes couldn't make her look dowdy, though they tried – she was in a twin set and a pleated skirt whose colour put Seraph in mind of the creamed mushrooms on toast she sometimes gave the children for tea. Seraph thought she knew *exactly* why her friend looked so happy, and was only surprised Amy hadn't already started to pick up on her beloved's style by dressing in his favoured black. Bugger! If she begged a bed off Amy she'd find herself sharing the bathroom with Jude. She forced herself to smile.

'So, then, it went well.'

'What did?'

'Your date.'

'Date?'

'With Jude.' Seraph was distracted by her own worries, and positive she'd read the signals correctly. She wasn't particularly curious about Amy's obtuseness.

'Oh, that.' Amy blushed, slightly. 'Well, y' know . . .' She felt shy about discussing her weekend with Seraph, not because she'd slept with Jude – sort of – and it had been a disaster, but because she'd slept with Dave, and it hadn't. She wanted to hug her secret close for just a little longer, while she got used to the idea that she and Dave were an item once again.

'So? Spill the beans!'

Amy picked up one of the books she'd just dumped on Seraph's desk, and read the title out loud.

'*Happiness: Your Twelve Step Programme* . . . looks interesting.'

'Don't change the subject.'

'But who came up with the cover?'

'Marketing.' The cover showed a photo of a naked couple walking through a wood. They'd been photographed from the back, of course, and their bodies had been painted with flowers and leaves in luminous shades of yellow and red. Leaves also streamed from the woman's hair.

'What's the target market?' asked Amy. 'Nudist ecologists?'

Seraph laughed, but her laughter hid confusion. Amy didn't usually make fun of the books, and she was being uncharacteristically reticent about Jude. It must be love. What could be more powerful than the desire for gossip, except the desire to protect something precious from intrusion? Well, then, Seraph wouldn't pry. And perhaps it was for the best – right now exposure to Jude-induced joy would zap her as surely as a ray-gun.

'Okay . . .' she said, intending to change the subject. But she needn't have bothered because at that moment her phone began to ring. It was Fiona.

'Hang on a sec,' said Seraph, into the receiver, 'I've got somebody with me.' She turned to Amy, who waggled her fingers and backed out of the door, grateful to make such an easy escape.

'She's gone now.'

'I got your message.'

'Thanks for getting back to me.'

'So what's up?'

'She is pregnant after all.'

There was a long silence.

'The flooze?'

'Yes.'

'Oh dear.'

'Yes.'

'So now what?'

'Well, I've moved out for a few days.'

'You have? Where are you staying?'

'I don't know yet. I'm going to sort something out this morning.'

'D'you want to take a few days holiday? Come and stay with us?'

'That's kind. I've thought about holiday. But I was off for half term, and I don't want to work between Christmas and New Year, so it's impossible.'

'Couldn't you get some sort of compassionate leave?'

'Probably, but I'd have to tell my boss what's up, and I don't want to.'

'Oh. Well, I don't suppose it's practical to come and stay here and commute up each day?'

'No. But thanks for the offer.'

Seraph heard someone calling for Fiona in the background.

'Coming,' Fiona replied to this unseen person, and then she spoke to Seraph again.

'Look,' she said, 'I've got a crazy waiting room. I think we might be seeing the beginnings of a flu epidemic. Will you be able to call tonight, d'you think?'

'I'll try.'

'Good. The offer of a bed stands, if you change your mind about holiday.'

Seraph hung up and wondered whether she should ring round a few cheap hotels. Then she remembered Oliver's mum, Belinda. Oliver was Tom's best friend at school. Seraph and Belinda had struck up their own friendship, of sorts, based around discussion of the boys' eating and sleeping habits, the St Bernard's staff, soccer practice, the national curriculum as it related to private schools, and other mind-numbingly dull topics. But Belinda was more than just an acquaintance – she was also a single mother who'd carried off a three bedroomed house in a clean-break settlement. Who better to sympathize with Seraph's predicament? And she had room enough for a temporary guest. Seraph had just resolved to call, when, once again, her own phone started to ring.

'Joy,' breathed the deep, Welsh voice on the other end.

Seraph swallowed. She now regarded it as deeply unfortunate that Cassie had ambushed her last week. The only reason she'd allowed herself to cross the invisible, but powerful, line between the personal and the professional, was that she'd been in a low and weakened state. Naturally she'd intended to break her promise to phone and let the other woman know how she and Nick were getting on.

'Hi Cassie,' she said now, in a careful, neutral voice.

'Hi Seraph. How are you?' Cassie's voice was kind and concerned, or else it had a therapist's veneer of kindness and concern.

'Fine thanks. And you?'

'But *are* you fine? I phoned to find out.'

'I'm so sorry. I meant to ring, but I've been snowed under.'

'At work?'

'Yes.'

'Tell me about it.' Cassie paused 'Did you and Nick manage to talk?'

'No.' Seraph lied.

241

'No?'

'Well, not really.'

'Not really?'

'We only sort of talked.'

'Good for you! And?'

'Oh, you know . . .'

'What?'

'It wasn't great.'

'Which means?'

What the hell, thought Seraph.

'I've moved out for a few days.'

'Oh.'

'Yes.'

'Are you okay? Where are you staying?'

'I only moved out this morning.'

'But where to?'

'Umm . . .'

'You haven't got anywhere fixed yet?'

'Not exactly.'

'But that's ridiculous! Come and stay with me!'

'With you? That's so kind, but I couldn't possibly—'

'Why not?'

Just because, thought Seraph, feeling like a child being asked to give a reason for some piece of naughtiness. Because I'm an editor, you're an author, and I work on your books. Because last week you found me at a bad moment, and I blabbed when I shouldn't have done. Because Belinda will put me up.

'I couldn't possibly impose myself like that.'

'It wouldn't be an imposition. Don't you know I keep a spare room especially for troubled women?'

Seraph was taken aback.

'No, I didn't know that.' Was she a troubled woman?

'Yes, I keep a room for women needing the space and time to ground themselves, to find themselves, to re-evaluate and prioritize.'

'Oh.' And had she lost her self?

'We all do it – all of us trained at the Oran Institute. We each commit to creating a refuge for our clients. Male practitioners take in troubled men, and women take in women.'

'A network of refuges?'

'Yes. I've put up lots of women over the years.'

'I had no idea.'

'Well, there you are. Come and stay with me.'

'But I'm your editor!'

'So?'

'It just seems odd. I'd feel I was a bother.'

'Rubbish! This is no time for such silliness. Of course you must come. Let me give you directions to get . . .'

'But—'

'. . . the best thing would be if you took the tube to Golders Green, and I met you at the station.'

'But—'

'If you don't come to me, where will you stay tonight?'

Seraph was silent for a moment.

'You see!' said Cassie.

'Are you sure it's no trouble?'

'None at all.'

'Golders Green?' It was an easy commute into work, and close to home if, God forbid, there was an emergency with one of the children. And even though she'd surely be unable to avoid the subject of her and Nick, at least she wouldn't have to talk about the national curriculum.

'Yes. At the station. At six.'

'Well . . .'

'Good. See you at six.'

17

Cassie's house, a three-bedroomed semi dating from the 1930s on a side street off the busy Great North Way, was a testament to her beliefs in the power of colour. The pebble-dash exterior was painted a pale violet. The sitting room had once been two rooms, but she'd knocked them through on the advice of a Feng Shui consultant, and then decorated according to her own ideas, entirely in shades of brown. There were red-browns, yellow-browns, blue-browns, orange-browns, green-browns and purple-browns.

'Brown,' said Seraph when she walked in. 'The colour of transformation.' She was frantically trying to remember anything at all from *Rainbow Power* and wishing she'd thought to flick through a copy before leaving the office.

'Exactly,' said Cassie, who was resplendent in a purple caftan with gold embroidery. 'Brown draws us down to the underworld and reminds us of the transformative power of death.'

'Earth to earth?' Seraph ventured.

'Yes.' Cassie fingered the little figurine she wore around her neck 'Brown and green, the colours of the Earth Goddess. The heart of the earth. That's why brown speaks not only of transformation, but also of safety. It evokes the Earth Goddess's hidden crevices, caverns and passages. Of course the Earth Goddess is but one manifestation of the Great Mother.'

Seraph, to whom the brown in this room evoked shit, judged it safest to fall back on book design.

'It's like your idea for the cover for *How to Change Your Life*,' she said brightly 'The dead brown of the chrysalis nurtures the living colours of the butterfly.'

'That's it exactly.' Cassie beamed. 'You did speak to the designer?' she added.

'I did. She's promised me a rough design soon after Christmas.'

'That's marvellous,' said Cassie, who celebrated the winter solstice, not Christmas.

Cassie, never svelte, had eaten herself fat during her years in Cincinnati. More recently Natasha, who was stick-thin, had taught her to regard her coils and loops of blubber as homage to the similarly shaped Great Mother, and an affirmation of female potency. Excess flesh might be spiritually and politically desirable, but it had annoying practical implications. Cassie was so fat she had to pause and lean on the banisters every three or four steps as she showed Seraph upstairs. But eventually she made it, and led Seraph into the room she kept for troubled women. This was done up in pink, every shade of pink from the almost red found at the centre of a pink peony, to the almost white found along the petals' edges. Pink curtains, pink carpet, pink linen on the bed. Even the dream catcher hanging by the window was embellished with rose quartz and Flamingo feathers. Seraph felt as if she'd fallen down a giant's throat.

'Pink promotes quietness of spirit,' Cassie explained, and then left Seraph to settle in while she slowly eased herself back down the stairs.

Once she was alone Seraph fished out her mobile. Nick had left a message in her voice box. He'd probably still be in the office, but she decided not to call him back, instead she phoned home. Luke refused to speak to her and Tom came on the line only to say he couldn't talk because he was in the middle of a call to Mars on his space phone, which Seraph knew to be two paper cups tied together with green wool. But Daisy was enchanted with Seraph's description of her pink bedroom. Kate, who'd earlier had a long and anguished discussion with Richard, grumpily promised that the kids were fine and added that Nick had phoned to say he'd definitely be home by seven. Seraph felt semi-reassured. Next she phoned Fiona, but got Dominic, who sounded awkward and embarrassed.

'She's at the theatre,' he said. 'The RSC on tour with *Julius Caesar*. I think she'll be in around eleven thirty.'

'Can you tell her I'll call tomorrow evening.'

'Sure – I do hope everything's . . .I mean you're not . . .'

'Thanks. I'm fine. I'll talk to her tomorrow.'

After she'd hung up, Seraph quickly unpacked a few things before making her way back downstairs. Cassie was not in the sitting room, so Seraph pushed open the only other likely looking door and found herself in a kitchen of such vivid, headache-inducing orange that she had to close her eyes for a moment against the glare.

'What're you making,' she asked, when she opened them.

Cassie was standing at the stove, stirring the contents of a simmering pot.

'Tea. Vervain and hops. They'll relax you. Rosemary and thyme to stimulate thought. Raspberry leaves to purge you of negativity. I make it for all my women, it'll soon perk you up.'

'Oh.' What Seraph really longed for was a stiff vodka and tonic.

'It's nearly ready, but you mustn't drink it in here. You don't need orange, you need brown.'

Seraph inhaled slowly and thoughtfully. She was beginning to wish she'd phoned Belinda, after all. How bad could a solid dose of the national curriculum actually be?

Once they were in the sitting room Cassie waved Seraph into an armchair to one side of a long, low table decorated with a collection of rocks, stones and pebbles, and opposite an unlit gas fire of utilitarian design. Once Seraph was seated, Cassie lowered herself into a squishy sofa. The two women were now at right angles to each other. Cassie had planned this, she believed that conversation flowed most easily when the participants were at right angles. Seraph started to drink her tea. Cassie watched her. They were both silent. When Seraph had drunk all the tea, which was the colour of urine and tasted vile, she decided she was expected to say something. But what? She leaned forward and picked up a smooth, oval stone from the table in front of her. It was the colour of dried blood. No doubt there was some significance there, if only she could see it.

'Thank you for having me,' she said, at last.

Cassie made a quick, dismissive gesture with her hands.

'I'm here to help.'

Seraph clasped the stone tightly in her fist. Of course she'd known all along that disclosure would be the price for the pink room, and she supposed that in some cobwebby corner of her mind she must have hoped it would be, otherwise she'd be at Belinda's. Perhaps she secretly hoped personal coaches, especially those who chose to write on the subject, were granted insights denied to the rest of us?

'So, you want to know what happened between me and Nick,' she said.

The therapist in Cassie badly wanted to know what had happened, and also, quite genuinely, to help. But the author in her had another agenda. Cassie-the-author wanted to pitch *Ta Biblia*, and tonight would be a wonderful opportunity. There was nothing in the Oran Institute's code of practice to prevent it, and, Cassie told herself, taking advantage of Seraph in this way was not discreditable, but rather a sacred duty she owed to the Great Mother. Anyway, failure would disappoint Natasha, who'd first suggested *Ta Biblia,* and had contributed so much to it. Quite apart from these considerations Cassie was busy for the next couple of evenings and knew she might not get such a good chance again. However, she knew she must be circumspect.

'If you want to tell me.' She put on her listening expression.

'I suppose I do.'

'Then go ahead!'

'We did try to talk,' said Seraph, slowly, 'but it all went wrong. He said he loved me and he wanted us to stay together. I told him it was over. Although I didn't completely mean it and he didn't believe me.'

'That sounds like a good platform from which to begin the

process of re-building. He loves you. You're angry, naturally, but willing to think about forgiveness.'

'Forgiveness?'

'You admit you didn't mean it was over. And he's not willing to give up on the relationship without a fight. A promising start to re-creating your marriage.'

'Yes,' said Seraph. 'But there's more. After he told me he didn't believe it was over he went and told me his mistress was pregnant. They've split up, but – y'know – shared parenting.'

Cassie took a sharp breath and leaned back on the sofa.

'Oh,' she said. 'Well that complicates things.'

She'd heard many stories like this from her women in trouble. The injured party, the guilty party, the third party, the baby. Ordinary tales of this that and the other. She thought longingly of Natasha. True love in middle life was a wonderful thing.

'We both need food before we talk,' she said after a lengthy pause. 'Let's go into the kitchen and get something.'

Cassie's size made it hard for her to bustle, but in the kitchen she rallied herself to a bit of bustling and came up with a collection of salad vegetables. The two women began to prepare their dinner, working side by side on one of the orange worktops.

'This is very healthy,' said Seraph, casting a surreptitious glance at Cassie's buttocks. How did they get so huge if she ate like this?

'I'm vegan,' Cassie replied, and started grating a carrot. She didn't mention that she'd acquired veganism along with Natasha. In Cincinnati she'd slurped in the burgers and the sliders, sucked up the fries, and sloshed down the shakes – all with as much enthusiasm as the locals.

'Yes?' Seraph found herself craving bacon.

'Yes. I refuse to pollute myself by ingesting energy that's ever been sentient.'

Seraph reached for a cucumber and began to slice it. What was sentience? Didn't cucumbers grow towards light? Towards water? Wasn't that sentience? But pitying a cucumber was plainly mad, so she sliced more quickly and more viciously, until the knife slipped and she cut her finger. The cucumber's revenge. In retaliation she popped a slice into her mouth, and chewed, with relish. Her life might be a mess, but she could still show members of the vegetable kingdom what's what. And considered from some angles there wasn't all that much evolutionary distance between Nick and a cucumber. She laughed aloud at her infantile joke. Cassie shot her a questioning glance.

'Oh, y'know . . .' said Seraph, vaguely wafting her hand in front of her face. After that they worked in companionable silence until the salad was ready. They ate at the kitchen table. The salad was delicious, and there was plenty of good bread to go with it, but Cassie offered nothing to drink but water.

'I'm teetotal,' she explained. 'All artificial stimulants are poisons.'

Seraph decided that tomorrow she'd have to smuggle in some wine.

Once the meal was finished they returned to the sitting room, because Cassie again said they needed brown, not orange, and Seraph felt in no position to disagree. Cassie began to speak the minute they were settled.

'Seraph,' she said, 'do you mind if I speak to you of my religious beliefs?'

Seraph was startled, but what could she say?

'Religion,' Cassie went on. 'There's a time for psychodynamics, and there's a time for spirituality. Not that there's a hard and fast boundary between the two. They overlap, of course.'

'Of course.' Seraph thought this must be retribution for all those times she'd slammed the door on assorted Jehovah's Witnesses and Mormons.

'Yes. My spirituality informs my understanding of the human psyche – for what else, after all, is psychodynamics but the study of the human psyche in its natural setting? And my role as a healing counsellor continually alerts me to the glory and the marvellous incomprehensibility of the Great Mother.'

Seraph made a strangulated sound.

'Do you know who this is?' asked Cassie, in an apparent change of tack. She held up the little figurine she wore suspended round her neck. Seraph looked at it properly for the first time. She looked at the pinkish-brown carving with its oval, geometric face, full rounded breasts, mountainous stomach and outlandish, jutting buttocks.

'The Great Mother?'

'The Great Mother cannot be represented.'

'Oh.'

'But you're right, this is one of Her manifestations.'

'Oh,' said Seraph again. 'Then is it a pagan fertility goddess?'

'In a sense. She is indeed the goddess of fertility and fecundity.'

'And she's called . . .?'

'Astarte. This is a carving of Astarte, but it was made many centuries before she was named. It comes from what is now Syria, where almost four thousand years ago Astarte reigned supreme. Astarte, the ancient ruler of men. Astarte, the death in life goddess, She who dies and is reborn. The dark that gives birth to the light.' Cassie cupped the figurine in both hands and held it up, so that it was level with her eyes. 'Both virgin and courtesan, she governs procreation and destruction, love and cruelty, sensuality and vengeance. She is earth goddess, moon goddess, sea goddess.'

Cassie held her pose for a few seconds, before reverently lowering the figurine to its usual position between her melon breasts. There followed a long silence. At last Seraph, who was feeling very uneasy, could stand it no longer.

'The moon goddess,' she said, wildly. 'The moon. Symbol of female intuition.' Here she was drawing on a fragment from one of the better-selling titles on her list, *Moon Signs for Romantics*.

'Indeed,' replied Cassie, in a dreamy voice. 'The lunar, nocturnal and feminine preceding and succeeding the solar, active and masculine.'

'Mm.'

'And Her watery aspect too is symbolic of femininity, of our emotional, irrational natures. She is queen of all things moist.'

'Mm.'

'She is glorious, yet She is but a cloak. She is the cloak of dreams in which the earth is dressed. She is radiant, yet She is but a veil . . . and what does a veil do?'

It was not a rhetorical question. Cassie's tone had changed from dreamy to sharp, and she looked at Seraph, waiting for an answer.

'Hides a face?' Seraph's tone was hesitant. She wasn't sure whether she approved of veils. Somewhat reluctantly she'd worn one as a bride, but now she pictured Arab women swathed in heavy black, and merry widows hiding their flirtatious eyes.

'Precisely,' said Cassie. 'Astarte hides a greater queen behind the black veil of Her night sky, spangled as it is with all the stars.

She hides the Great Goddess who cannot be named, but whom we, Her adoring daughters, may invoke as the Great Mother.'

Seraph's concentration wandered. Surely Cassie had said Astarte was a manifestation of the Great Mother? Now she was saying Astarte was a veil hiding the Great Mother. Was this a contradiction? How could one thing manifest as a veil hiding itself? She wanted further details. But before she could frame a question, she realized Cassie had stopped talking about the divine, and was on to the human.

'As a daughter you have experienced your mother's love . . . '

Seraph, not in the happiest of moods, thought of greedy, needy mothers consuming their daughters, and of daughters struggling for years to escape their mothers' clutches.

'. . . and as a mother you offer your children love . . . '

True, but so what? Love flowed down the generations, no news there.

'Think of that love on a cosmic scale . . . '

Maternal love on a cosmic scale? What fuck-ups that would bring.

'What about . . .?' Began Seraph planning to quiz Cassie on her relationship with her own mother. In fact Cassie's mother had suffered a fatal heart attack when her daughter, Christine, was four. Cassie had never thought the name Christine was romantic or dramatic enough for her personality, and had adopted Cassandra as a sixteenth birthday present to herself. But stepping away from the name her mother had bestowed had not helped her step away from her dead mother's shadow. Now she waved a hand to cut off Seraph's interruption.

'Accept that love,' she said. 'Offer yourself to it. *Lose* your self in maternal love for all humanity, and thus *find* your self in redemption. Understand that Astarte is the Goddess of losing and finding.'

'Mm.' Seraph shifted her weight, unhappily.

Cassie glanced at her, then leant back on the sofa, closed her eyes and began to speak in the sing-song voice of someone uttering a prayer, or a creed.

'The Great Mother is a loving, creative force. She is on our side in our struggles against illness, ageing, death and pain. She knows and understands all things.

'She precedes all things, is present in all things and will endure beyond the end of time. She is to be dreaded by her enemies. She tempts her enemies to the way of darkness, of falsity, of not-being. To her children She offers the way of lightness, of truth, of being.

'To her children She offers rebirth and healing.'

Cassie kept her eyes closed for a few moments after she had finished speaking, engrossed in silent, slow-breathing meditative prayer. Meanwhile Seraph, wriggling with embarrassment, grew more and more uncomfortable. She coughed. Cassie opened her eyes, and looked directly at her.

'So, what do you think?'

'About what?'

'You and Nick. Your family. The Great Mother.'

Seraph hesitated.

'I'm not quite sure I fully understand the link.'

'Unity in duality,' said Cassie, who had become almost businesslike. 'Eternally dual yet eternally one, the Great Mother nurtures masculine and feminine alike. If male and female – in your case you and Nick – humbly and sincerely petition Her for guidance, She will not fail to provide it. For you and Nick that means you must each approach Her separately, and also jointly, as a couple. Prostrate yourselves before Her. Submit to Her will. Open yourselves up to Her divine, healing energy. Have the confidence to accept that life is a journey, and allow the Great Mother to inspire you to travel it well.'

Seraph looked down at the mud-coloured carpet. This was la-la land marriage guidance, and had no connection with her own life. It was impossible to imagine Nick prostrating himself before the queen of all things moist. She cleared her throat. 'I think Nick might have a hard time with that,' she said, with diffidence, for she didn't want to offend Cassie, who was clearly sincere. Plus she was one of Seraph's authors. And her hostess.

'Men often do,' replied Cassie. 'That's part of the dilemma for a woman in your position. You are at a crossroad. You have so many choices, so many possibilities for change—'

'Yes, change,' Seraph cut in, gloomily.

'There's no need to fear change. The cycles and phases which rule so much of a woman's life give her a natural understanding of this. Menstruation, pregnancy, the menopause. The female body tells its owner not to fear the unknown, to go with the future and embrace it.'

Seraph looked at her, astonished.

'Are you telling me to leave Nick?'

'Not at all. I would never *tell* you to do anything, I just facilitate choices. Freedom, self-sufficiency and personal growth are all positively charged values – but that doesn't mean you have to embrace them, and I would never *tell* you to.'

'Thanks,' said Seraph, a little tartly.

'You must do what's right for you. Leave, if you must, but also remember what I told you last week about the possibilities for saving your marriage, about how I could help you save it. You do remember that?'

'Of course. But saving my marriage clashes with not fearing change, going with the future, and embracing it.'

'No. Embracing the future applies whether you stay with Nick, or leave him. I'm just telling you today's the day, so seize it.'

'Right,'said Seraph, 'seize the day!'

'Yes. Seize the day!'

And why not? Cassie pounced on the chance to follow her own advice and introduce *Ta Biblia*.

'Of course,' she said, 'there are many ways to seize the day. I'm sure you've guessed what I want you to do?'

'Umm?'

Cassie paused, and once more caressed the figure of Astarte which hung around her plump neck.

'I want you to make today the day you offer yourself up to the Great Mother. Join me, and hundreds of women like me, in our movement, the Daughters of Astarte!'

Seraph was stunned into silence.

'Cassie—' she began, when she'd recovered her voice. She intended to say she was a committed Catholic, or a Jew, but Cassie cut in before she could.

'Very many of my troubled women choose Her path of light and truth and being.'

'I'm sure.'

'I hope to persuade you to do the same.'

Seraph looked at Cassie. She felt let down.

'So your pink room's got nothing to do with psychodynamics?' she said coldly. 'It's just a recruiting station for your cult?'

Cassie was used to hostility. She was fat. She dressed in purple. Barbed comments and sniggers often followed her down the street – and she told herself the mockers had meaningless bodies garbed in meaningless clothes. It was the same with her religion. She knew how easy it was to disbelieve – and the scoffers were ripe for conversion.

'Not cult,' she said evenly, 'religion. And I told you, everyone trained at the Oran Institute commits to keeping a spare room as a refuge for clients . . . Although I don't deny it comes in useful as I struggle to serve the Great Mother. It's one of those points at which my role as a healing counsellor and my spirituality connect. Converting people to the Great Mother's cause is a part of my life's work, and being able to offer a bed to potential converts helps sometimes.'

Seraph grunted.

'Service,' continued Cassie, 'just think of its psychic rewards.'

'I give to Oxfam,' said Seraph, harshly. 'That's where I get my psychic rewards.'

Cassie ignored her.

'And you are in such a privileged position,' she insisted. 'You, Seraph! Just think of your power to help spread the word—'

'Jesus!' Cut in Seraph. 'So that's it – I'd be a good catch.'

'What?' Cassie looked blank.

'The Great Mother wants me for my publishing contacts. For my rolodex.'

Cassie seemed to have missed Seraph's bitterness.

'Yes,' she said, serenely, 'my point exactly.'

'She doesn't want me for myself.'

'That's not what I meant . . .' Cassie hesitated and took a

deep breath. 'I'll be completely straight with you,' she said, 'I've been writing a book – one you don't know about yet – and it's nearly finished now. *Ta Biblia*. A call to arms for the Daughters of Astarte, but with an appeal far wider than our congregation. It lays out the principles and beliefs which guide the faithful, and the herstory and mythology surrounding ancient goddesses. I've tried to keep the style simple and accessible, and the text could easily be broken up by boxes, lists and questions and answers, just as in *Rainbow Power* and *How to Change Your Life.*'

Seraph was still cross, but relieved that the conversation could be said to have shifted from Cassie's stamping ground, religion, to her own, publishing. She cleared her throat, in preparation for interrupting. But Cassie had no intention of letting her speak.

'Many Daughters have submitted hymns for inclusion, I could let you see some, if you like. And there's detailed instruction on religious ritual, both day-to-day, and for the holy days. It's not at all dry, or academic, and so far I've keep it quite short. The movement really does need *Ta Biblia,* and in our male-dominated, overly technological world where reason, science and the secular hold sway over intuition, magic and the holy it would be bound to sell.'

'Yes,' said Seraph, 'I'm sure . . .' *I'm sure it would be an exhilarating book of boundless wisdom and beauty, which would make all the other books on my list seem tawdry by comparison. For that reason, I'd be unable to publish it.*

'Natasha would write a foreword – she's our High Priestess. Did you know that?'

'No.' Another one? *It's like* Invasion Of The Body Snatchers. Cassie smiled.

'The Great Mother has graciously given me the gift of communication,' she said, 'in order that I may better serve Her. She wants me to sing of Her love and vengeance, Her baleful sensuality, Her powers of protection and destruction. And She wants you to help me. That much is clear. That's why She brought you to me.'

Cassie sat back and crossed her arms. Her case was made. Seraph was furious.

'You think Nick's and my problems are part of the Great Mother's plan to get your book published?' she said hotly.

'Don't be miffed. You and Nick are certainly part of Her plan to spread knowledge of Her power and love. The personal and the sacred overlapping as they always do . . . you and me. Not just healing counsellor and troubled woman, but also author and editor. It fits. Don't you see?'

Seraph didn't, and had to bite her tongue to stop herself snapping out something she'd truly regret. But the Great Mother wasn't the only one with a veil. She might have bagged the night sky, spangled with all the stars, but Seraph had publishing.

'I think the book you describe might be served best by a small, specialist press,' she said.

'Oh no. What's the point of selling a few hundred copies to my friends? You've been sent to help me reach a wider readership, the masses, women in every corner of the land, and beyond Britain, too.'

'Yes, but—'

'Everyone's fed up with the sterility of modern society, and its speed and stresses. Computers. Cars. Satellites. Laser guns. Nothing's human any more.'

'Yes, but—'

'And when we're not raping Mother Earth we're choking Her to death. Is it any wonder we're being killed off by cancer and Aids? For millennia now the Great Mother's been biding her time, watching us hash things up, and waiting. She was here aeons before the Great God, who's had it all His own way for so long. But now His power is waning and it's time for Her to make a reappearance. It's time for Her to be acknowledged for what She is.'

There was a short silence.

'What about an anthology of women's wisdom?' suggested Seraph, at last. 'Or a sacred meditation for each day of the year? Perhaps, with special sections devoted to incantations for the pagan holidays?'

Cassie looked thoughtful.

'Funnily enough I'd thought of doing a companion to the pagan year.'

'Great! Get me a proposal and I'll certainly look at it.'

'But first it's my duty to finish *Ta Biblia*.'

'Oh.'

'You know I burn to help people, especially women. *Ta Biblia* would be one more way of helping women everywhere.'

Seraph leaned forward and shoved her hands between her knees. *You old fraud*, she thought, unfairly, since Cassie had spoken with conviction. The word *fraud* triggered a shimmer across her brain, and she remembered the way Cassie had used the sex tips in *How to Change Your Life* as a platform to urge lingerie and pornography on her readers. Anal and oral sex. Fetishes. S&M. More fraud. That stuff couldn't possibly be sanctioned by the Great Mother.

'Can I ask you something?' she said, coldly.

'Of course.'

'It's a bit of a change of subject.'

'That's okay.'

'In *How to Change Your Life* I remember you were in favour of lingerie, pornography, and such.'

'For couples who'd got stuck in a rut. To spice up their sex lives.'

'Why settle for plain vanilla when you could have double chocolate chip?'

'Yes.'

Right, thought Seraph, time to skewer the old bat.

'But surely the Great Mother wouldn't approve?'

Cassie neither blinked nor blushed.

'Why not?'

Seraph felt slightly flustered. Wasn't it obvious?

'Pornography treats women as a means to an end,' she began, hoping she could construct a coherent argument, 'as objects. Playthings.'

Cassie looked dismissive.

'Oh that old chestnut,' she said, with an off-hand wave. 'I told you, the Great Mother is a courtesan. She's a warrior queen who feeds on blood and demands the human heart as Her sacrifice. And She's always hungry and thirsty.'

'So?'

'Well, we must remember that four thousand years ago sacred prostitution was practised on Her altars. This—'

'Why?'

'Why what?'

'Why was prostitution practised on her altars?'

'Oh. In memory of Her sacred marriage to Tammuz, the shepherd god who was her husband, brother and son. He was killed by and reborn through Astarte.'

Seraph was lost.

'I thought it was Astarte who died and was reborn.'

'She was. That refers to Her descent into the underworld, from which none but Her return. Now I'm talking of Her husband. He died by Astarte's hand, and was reborn through Her too.'

'I'm not sure I follow.'

'I explain it all in *Ta Biblia*.' Cassie was beginning to feel irritated. 'The whole mythology. For now, just remember Astarte is the dark that gives birth to light, like I told you before. So, once a year in memory of death and rebirth . . .'

So, once a year in memory of Tammuz's death and rebirth a male representing him would be sacrificed after having sacred sex with a woman representing Astarte. The sublime and the horrific in unity. So you see, the Great Goddess has always used sex to get at men. Pornography can be a powerful weapon in a powerful woman's hands.'

Seraph got the punch line, it was, after all, another familiar old chestnut, but she thought Cassie's argument, if it could be called that, was as full of holes as her opposing one. Although she'd understood the phrase 'sex to get at men' well enough. What, it suddenly occurred to her to ask herself, had she really been doing on the night she'd tried to follow Cassie's sex advice and seduce her husband with cheap lingerie and cheaper porn? Gambling with herself? Perhaps not. Playing the spy eager for pillow secrets? Sure. But what else had she been playing? The courtesan? The warrior queen? Seraph liked the idea – that mix of high-octane sex appeal, cruelty and power. Sex as an act of – what? Not love, at any rate. Sex to get at men? Sex to get at Nick? It made sense. Perhaps Cassie wasn't such an old fraud after all.

18

When Seraph went to bed after her conversation with Cassie, she found the pink rays lapping over her body did not, as advertised, quieten her spirit. She tossed and turned, thinking up a different version of the future every time she changed position in bed. She rolled to her right: she'd stay with Nick. She rolled to her left: she'd leave him. Eventually pearly grey light began to show at the window in a long crack where the curtains failed to meet. Seraph sat up in bed to greet the dawn. And sat. And sat. Eventually she decided even reading Benedicta's memos would be better than this. Her briefcase was lying on the floor. Yesterday she'd left *How to Change Your Life* and *Baby Manual* in the office and replaced them with a thick stack of sales printouts, but, as ever, Benedicta's memos formed a thick silt against the briefcase's wall. She fished them out and returned to bed. By six she'd ploughed through them all. By 6.30 she was dressed. She sat some more. Nick usually left Athens Road at 7.15, and by 7.30 she judged it late enough to avoid the risk of his picking up the phone, so she reached for her mobile and punched in her home number. Kate answered, sounding flustered. She had the phone in the kitchen, and Seraph could hear the children yabbering in the background.

'How are they?' she asked.

'Fine.'

'Will Luke talk to me now?'

'Luke,' called Kate, 'do you want to talk to mummy?'

Seraph heard Luke shout *no* across the kitchen.

'No,' said Kate.

'Well give him a kiss. What about the others?'

'Tom? Daisy?' said Kate.

'Hi, Mum,' shouted Tom, at the top of his voice.

'Hear that?'

'Yes.'

Daisy came to the phone.

'Hello Mummy,' she said. 'Can I paint my bedroom pink?'

A technicolour version of the room she now sat in filled Seraph's mind. Roman blinds, swags and frills. A little girl's paradise.

'I'll think about it. Are you all okay?'

'Yes.'

'What are you going to do at school today?'

'Dunno. Kate's letting us have Fruity-Os for breakfast.'

'Right.'

'I'm going to go and eat them now. Bye!'

'Bye, love. Put Kate on again would you?'

Seraph finally hung up, then sat on her bed and fretted about Luke's refusal to speak to her. Was it normal for a two-year-old to indulge in emotional blackmail? Sometimes it felt as if her children were a trio of bats, or something – creatures with an intelligence alien to her own. She was still thinking about this as she made her way downstairs, where she found Cassie at the cooker, stirring a big saucepan of porridge. Cassie was in a voluminous lavender nightie which clashed horribly with the predominant orange.

'Want some?' she asked, waving her wooden spoon. 'I make

it with water, not milk, its very re-hydrating. Or how about a cup of wake-up tea? It's caffeine free.'

Seraph couldn't see the point of caffeine-free drinks.

'Thanks, but I'm running late. There's a coffee place near the office. I'll grab a cup on my way in.'

Cassie pursed her lips.

'You should make time for yourself in the morning. It's not healthy to dash about on an empty stomach.'

'I know. But I get by.'

Cassie shot Seraph a disapproving glance, but then smiled.

'I hope you feel you benefited from our talk last night? That you're gaining insight into your problems? And thanks for listening to my ideas for *Ta Biblia*.'

'That's okay.' Seraph spoke semi-sarcastically, but Cassie missed it.

'I'd like to think that tonight we could carry on where we left off yesterday, but unfortunately I'm busy this evening.'

Yes! thought Seraph, who'd resolved to phone Belinda when she got into the office, but now changed her mind.

'I'm lending support to Natasha,' Cassie continued, lingering over Natasha's name. The only disadvantage of the pink room was that when it was occupied Natasha could never stay. The Oran Institute's code of practice specified a troubled client should be insulated, as far as possible, from his or her therapist's private life. This was to protect the therapist as much as the client. 'She's lecturing on lithosomy at St James's on Piccadilly.' Cassie waved her spoon, and spattered porridge in a wide arc. 'It might be quite late when I get in. You've got your key, haven't you?' Seraph nodded. 'Help yourself to whatever you want, there's plenty of food about. I hate leaving you in the lurch like this, but I did promise Natasha.'

Seraph had a nothing kind of day. As soon as she arrived at Bladder, she went in search of Amy, to see if she wanted a Beso, but Amy was busy collating financial data for Eddie, and couldn't spare the time, so she went with Gill, instead. Afterwards she had lunch with a gossipy agent and didn't get back to the office until three, when she picked up a message from Fiona apologizing for missing her, and telling her to be sure to phone that evening. She again went to find Amy, who was still tied up and couldn't chat, then spent what remained of the afternoon wandering in and out of bookshops along the Charing Cross Road, doing bookshop research – she made sure to stop off at Hecate to wish Natasha good luck with her lecture. Before she knew it, five o'clock had come and gone.

Back in Golders Green, the emptiness of Cassie's house wrapped itself around Seraph like a comfort blanket. She'd picked up a bottle of Merlot from a twenty-four-hour deli, and now poured herself a glass. She took this, and her mobile, through to the sitting room, where she drew the heavy tan velvet curtains, and lit the gas fire. The first time she tried to phone home, the number was engaged – she didn't know it, but Sandra was in the middle of persuading Kate to perfidy.

'It's terrible the way they've dumped on you this week,' Sandra was saying. 'Richard's right. You should quit asap. You have to think of yourself, and him – not employers who don't give a monkey's about you.'

'I know, I know.' Kate sighed. 'But I owe it to them to delay, to get the timing right.'

Serpah got through on her second attempt, ten minutes later.

'Don't worry,' said Kate, 'they're all eating well and they seem fine.'

'Good. Any chance Luke'll speak to me?'

Luke still refused, but Daisy came on the line.

'Hello Mrs Poo-poo Head,' she said, then collapsed in a fit of giggles and quickly passed the phone to Tom.

'Hi, Mum,' said Tom. 'Guess what!'

'What?'

'Oliver put his blazer on the wrong way round before break. He pretended to be a lobster and we all laughed, but Mr Crittendon yelled at us.'

'Oh.'

'Can we watch a bit of telly after tea? Kate said we could if you said yes.' He sounded eager; the children weren't allowed telly on school nights.

'Okay. Ten minutes.'

Tom held the receiver away from his ear.

'Kate,' he yelled, 'Mum says we can watch telly.' Then he spoke to his mother again. 'Bye, then.'

'Bye, love. Remember ten minutes.'

'Sure. Bye.'

After she'd hung up on the kids, Seraph took a long glug of wine, then punched in Fiona's number, Dominic answered, but quickly passed the phone to his wife. Like Seraph, Fiona was lounging on her sofa, with a glass of wine. The wine was white, and the sofa was a smooth pale-green affair which, with the help of her cleaner, she managed to keep pristine despite the presence of two, and sometimes three, children in the house. Her sitting-room carpet was a pale green, too, and it was spotless.

'Hi,' said Fiona as, without spilling a drop, she shooed at her husband with her wine-bearing hand. 'Dominic's taking himself off to the study so we can talk,' she waited until he'd left the room. 'Sorry to miss you last night.'

'No problem. Dominic told me it was *Julius Caesar*. How was it?'

'Not great. I completely forgot about it when we spoke yesterday – and I still haven't got your number. Where are you?'

'Staying with an author. She keeps a spare room as a sort of bolt hole for women like me. She's being very kind. Have you got a pen?'

Seraph gave Fiona the number of her mobile, then they both knew it was time to get down to business.

'Okay,' said Fiona, 'so she's pregnant.'

'She is.'

'And where does that leave you?'

'Dunno.'

'He still claims it's over?'

'He does – but it can't be, can it?'

Fiona took a sip of wine.

'Looked at some ways, not really.' She paused. 'But he still says he wants to be with you?'

'Uh-huh. And actually, I believe him. I really do – but, since they'll be sharing the parenting . . .'

'Wouldn't she settle for the legal minimum in child support?'

'Nick wouldn't want that.'

Fiona grunted.

'The ties of blood and genes.'

'And his own father.'

It wasn't until she was pregnant with Lachlan that Pete had finally begun to admit to Fiona what the loss of his father had meant to him. She remembered his anguish now.

'Yes. I don't know what Pete would have done if I'd agreed to have him back and asked him to abandon Bianca.'

'But you didn't,' said Seraph.

'No . . . Anyway, you think that's what the flooze wants too? I mean, she wants Nick to be involved?'

Seraph wriggled to get more comfortable on Cassie's sofa.

'I assume so. Why wouldn't she?'

'She might not—'

'Might not what?'

'Oh, y'know . . .' Fiona's surgery served a poverty-stricken housing estate where men – even working men – were considered redundant by most of the women. At the other end of the social scale, one of her friends, a high-flying psychiatrist, was determined to raise her son without male interference. She didn't go into all this, but re-directed the subject. 'So how will they organize themselves, day to day?'

'I'm not sure, exactly.'

Fiona tucked her legs underneath her, and took a sip of wine.

'What does he expect? That you and he'll live happily ever

after and he'll just bunk off for the occasional Saturday to visit this other child?'

'Something like that.' Seraph paused, and bit her lip. 'I told him it was over.'

'No! Did you?'

'Yes.'

'Did you mean it?'

'Yes, when I said it, but I wasn't so sure half an hour later.'

'So it's not. Nothing's over until you're sure.'

'I know. But that was before he dropped this new bombshell.'

'You told him it was over *before* you knew about the baby?'

'Yes, but then still before he told me, I also half persuaded myself we could make everything work, that jealousy was irrational, and whatnot. That there's more to fidelity than sex. That's what Nick said – there's more to fidelity than sex. I slapped him, at the time. But still . . .'

'I hope you gave him a black eye! Anyway, then he told you about the baby?'

'Yes.'

'And he expects you to forgive him?'

'Or at least accept the situation.'

Fiona leant over and put her wine glass on a highly polished side table, then she swung her feet to the floor, and sat up straight.

'But supposing you do stay together, would he expect you to welcome the flooze's child into your home? Overnight visits, and such?'

'Tough, if he does. I've already told him I don't want to meet it. Ever.'

Fiona thought that whatever happened it would be almost impossible for Seraph *never* to meet Nick's fourth child.

'Of course you feel like that now,' she said soothingly. 'But surely, given time . . .?'

'No,' said Seraph. 'I won't soften.'

'Okay,' said Fiona, who didn't believe her, 'but what about your three? Would he want them to get to know it—'

'Over my dead body! I suppose they'll have to know it exists. Better they find out now, from us, than years down the line from – and when they're older they might want to get to know it, a bit, since it'll be related to them, but I wouldn't encourage brotherly – or sisterly – love.'

Again, Fiona had her doubts, both about the wisdom of preventing Tom, Daisy and Luke from meeting their half-sibling, and about the likely durability of Seraph's opposition to such a meeting.

'My children and Bianca get on reasonably well,' she said. 'Most of the time. Lachlan and Bianca do, anyway.'

'That's different. You left Pete. He married Donna.'

'God knows why.'

'True, but he did.'

'Because I cut off his options.'

'Yes – and if I chucked Nick out and he ended up living with her, or if he wanted to leave me and marry her, then I suppose I couldn't stop my three *visiting* Nick, so of course they'd get to know this other kid, but as it is – no way!'

Fiona noticed that despite her anger Seraph still seemed to be assuming she and Nick would stay together.

'But since you don't seem sure it's over,' she said tentatively. 'And I know I'm not blameless.'

'No. But there are degrees of blame.'

'Yeah.' Seraph took a sip of wine. 'Anyway,' she said, 'I'd be willing to bet the flooze wants the same as me. I mean on this particular issue – she surely wouldn't want me and my kids to get involved with her kid.'

'Have you asked?'

'No.'

Fiona sniffed and took a sip of wine.

'What about money?'

'That pisses me off,' said Seraph. 'Money which should by rights be going to mine, going to hers. Nick says she doesn't want our money, but I just don't believe it.'

'Seems unlikely if they're going to share responsibilities.'

'That's right,' said Seraph. 'In some ways it's all much easier to imagine how everything would work if Nick and I did split up, then it would simply be a case of a man on his own, with two families by different women.'

Fiona grunted.

'We get stuff like that in the surgery all the time.'

'Not just in your surgery. Everywhere.'

So now, thought Fiona, the assumption had shifted. Now the assumption was that Nick and Seraph were history.

'Okay, if you did split, d'you think he'd fight for custody of the children?'

'No. We'd shred each other and he wouldn't put them through it.'

'Pete was the same, he's a good father.'

'So's Nick. I'm not denying that.'

'A pity, in some ways. A worse one might've shrugged his

shoulders and walked away from the flooze's child. So, anyway, you'd get custody?'

'Mm.'

'What about housing, schooling? All that stuff.'

'Dunno. I expect Nick would let me have the house in a clean break settlement.'

'It worked well for us.' Fiona and her children had continued to live in the what had been the family home, until Fiona married Dominic, when both she and he sold their properties and bought a new place. A new start, in a new house.

'Mm. And if I stayed put, I don't see why Tom and Daisy shouldn't continue at St Bernard's. We should just about be able to afford it, depending what Nick was paying out . . . I'd certainly have to get rid of my nanny, though. Kate. You haven't met her, have you?'

'No. There are cheaper options – child minders, after school clubs, that sort of thing.'

'Yes. I'd manage.' Seraph took a deep breath and pursed her lips. 'I'm most worried about Daisy. I tell you, if it's a girl, she'll be jealous as hell. A boy might not be so bad, I suppose, but she's a real daddy's girl. Her daddy's *only* girl. That's another reason for the kids not to meet. It's one thing for Daisy to know she's got a rival, quite another to be forced to play with it.'

'Yeah,' said Fiona. 'Catriona was beside herself with resentment when Bianca was born – she's still prickly about it sometimes . . . but whatever happens it seems pretty clear your three won't find themselves confronted all at once with a new stepmother and a new half-sibling in their dad's new house.'

'There is that.' Seraph guessed how Fiona felt about the upsets in Lachlan's and Catriona's lives. 'But yours coped brilliantly. You said yourself, they're absolutely fine. And they get on with Bianca most of the time.'

'Except when Catriona doesn't.'

Seraph couldn't think of anything reassuring to say, so said nothing.

'So anyway,' said Fiona. 'What do you think you want to do?'

'God knows,' said Seraph. 'I do love him.'

'It's hard to let go.'

'It's not about letting go.'

'The inertia bred of familiarity, the habit.'

'It's not that, I don't think. I do love him. And I probably should stay, for the children.'

'We just agreed, children are adaptable.'

'I know.'

'We agreed you can't stay just for their sakes.'

'We did.' Seraph paused. 'It wouldn't be just for them. But it's like we said last week I don't want to stay out of fear – fear of never finding anything better. If I stay, I want it to be for the right reasons – and if I go, I want it to be for the right reasons too.'

'Not just a knee-jerk reaction?'

'Precisely. The author I'm staying with – she's out tonight—'

'You're on your own?' Fiona didn't like the idea of that.

'Yes. She's a counsellor. She pretty much told me to quit in the interests of freedom, self-sufficiency and personal growth. "Positively charged values", she called them.'

Fiona laughed, and then sighed.

'Poor you!' she said. 'I was certain there was no future for me and Pete almost from the moment he told me about Donna. But I remember, it's hell, all this swinging back and forth.'

'Sure is.'

'But there's no rush. You've plenty of time to think it all through.'

Plenty of time to think it all through. To Seraph it didn't feel like it. Perhaps it was the time of year. Christmas bearing down on her, and then the new year, with its ideal of new beginnings. Resolutions. Seraph never kept hers, she wasn't habitually resolute. So? It was time to act out of character. She needed resolution now, for she surely couldn't stay with Nick out of the reasons Fiona had tossed at her – habit, laziness and the inability to think things through properly. And if there was hard thinking to be done, the sooner the better. For a start she'd have to work out how much of her wanted to get at Nick, how much of the time, why, and what that meant for their future.

Seraph lay back on Cassie's nubbly brown sofa, and stared up at the light-dung coloured ceiling. All this brown put her in mind of being buried alive under a ton of soil – was that what Cassie had meant when she'd said brown suggested Mother Earth's hidden crevices and caverns? She turned her head, her eyes were now level with the stones decorating Cassie's coffee table. One of them caught her attention. It had a pleasing, roughly triangular shape, patterned in regular stripes of many shades of grey, and glittering with specs of mica. She reached over and picked it up. The stone was heavier than she'd expected, but cool. She touched it to the centre of her forehead, then removed her hand. The stone remained where she'd placed it, lying quite still between her eyes, like an overgrown version of one of Disha's bindis.

Seraph had published many books on Eastern beliefs, and these all claimed the centre of the forehead to be the site of an energy centre, a chakra, providing a kind of short cut to higher consciousness, whatever that was. Other books on her list explained that stones pulsed with a benign energy – the basis of Natasha's new art of lithosomy. Seraph was sceptical both about the existence of chakras, and the power of stones, but the cool surface of the mineral lump lying against her skin soothed and calmed her. She felt its weight as a gentle pressure, and closed her eyes, intending to think about Nick, her marriage and the children. But her thoughts wouldn't co-operate, and she found herself wondering whether her scepticism about stones and chakras was misplaced. Perhaps believing in these things, in the teeth of the evidence, demonstrated a kind of mental toughness she ought to try to cultivate? And if so, should she also be a little more respectful of Cassie's beliefs about a powerful and ancient goddess? But the goddess stuff was all so confusing. And what relevance had it to her own life? As she understood it, the Great Mother (or did she mean Astarte?) had had no family, unless it was what's-his-name, the mysterious shepherd god, whom, Cassie had said, was at once her husband, her son and her brother. How could that be? How could one man, or god, be both husband and son? Or both brother and son? Or both husband and brother? Seraph sighed. Incest. She didn't want to think about incest. She wanted to think about Nick, who was neither her son, nor her brother, but her legally wedded husband. How much fun for the Great Mother to ignore things as mundane as marriage certificates. And how much more fun to be able to exercise her magical powers. When the goddess got fed up with her son, presto, she could change him into her husband and, presumably, experience, or re-experience all the joys of early married life. And when she got fed up with her husband she could murder him, to resurrect him only when she felt like it. If she ever got round to feeling like it. How tidy Seraph's own life would be if she could only organize it like this. She'd certainly murder Nick now, if she knew it needn't be permanent.

Permanence was also much on the minds of Amy and Dave. They were in Hitchin, in his neat kitchen, winding down the longest, deepest discussion of either of their lives. It had been an intermittent discussion, with interruptions for food, sex, sleep and work, but its sporadic nature had only added to its force. As it approached its natural end, she was washing-up after supper, and he was drying. They were quite deliberately taking their time. After the kitchen would come the bedroom. Anticipation throbbed between them. Dave finished drying a plate and tossed down the teatowel.

'How're you getting on?'

Amy was scrubbing carbonara sauce off the bottom of a pan. 'Nearly done.'

Dave took a couple of steps towards her and wrapped his arms around her from behind. Amy laughed, but continued what she was doing. He nuzzled her neck.

'Stop it,' she said, without much conviction.

Dave continued to nuzzle, and slipped one hand under the waistband of the flouncy, red and white spotted skirt he liked so much – he called it her woodland-elf skirt. Amy shivered, so he slid his hand under the top of her tights, insinuated it beneath her knicker elastic, wriggled it downwards, spread his fingers.

'Sure?'

Amy let the pan clatter into the sink, and twisted round to face him, dislodging his arm. They looked at each other.

'So,' Dave said, after a long and very pregnant pause, 'have you reconsidered?'

After all their talking, there was only one question left to ask, only one answer left to give. Amy knew this was a proposal – and that silence was her best reply. She reached up and cupped her hands about his face, drew it down to her own, and kissed him.

19

Disha was on the phone. Ginny stood by the Bladder reception desk waiting for her to finish. She took in the other woman's jangly earrings, then became entranced by her nails. Disha saw where the visitor was looking, and held up her free hand for closer inspection.

'Flu?' she said into the phone. 'You poor babe.'

On the other end, Amy snuggled closer to Dave. He licked her ear, and she began to giggle, but turned it into a cough.

'It's just terrible,' she spluttered into the phone, 'I don't think I'll be able to drag myself out of bed today.'

'You stay put, and keep warm,' replied Disha. 'I'll tell Eddie. There's nothing much going on, anyway.' She hung up and raised her second hand, for Ginny's benefit.

'Mango Daze,' she said.

'What?'

'The colour. Mango Daze, d.a.z.e., not d.a.y.s. I thought a splash of the tropics might cheer everybody up in all this winter gloom. The palm trees are transfers. I do them myself.'

Ginny balled her fists to hide her own nails which were bitten and unvarnished.

'The bindi's fun, too,' she said, referring to the tiny golden sun in the middle of Disha's forehead.

Disha smiled – then remembered she was at work.

'Anyway, can I help you?'

'Yes,' said Ginny, 'I haven't got an appointment but I hope to see Seraph Jamieson. Can you tell her Ginny's in reception? I think she'll want to see me.'

Disha reached for the switchboard phone, and punched in Seraph's extension.

'I've got a Ginny out here says you'll want to see her. She's not got an appointment . . . Seraph? Are you there?'

'I'm here.'

'What? I can't here you.'

'I said, I'm here.'

'Good. Can you see her?'

'No. Tell her to fuck off.'

Disha turned back to Ginny.

'I'm afraid Seraph's tied up in meetings all morning. Can you come back later in the week?'

'I only want ten minutes of her time.'

Disha spoke into the receiver once more. 'She only wants ten minutes of your time.'

'No. I don't want to see her.'

'I'm afraid that won't be possible,' said Disha to Ginny. 'She's very busy this morning.'

To Disha's astonishment, Ginny leaned across the reception desk and took the phone from her.

'Look, Seraph,' she said, 'how bad can meeting me be? I just want to set the record straight. That's all. It won't take long, and I won't make a scene.'

Disha's jaw dropped. This was shaping up to be nearly as exciting as the time she'd had one of Jude's exes in reception, threatening suicide. Lucy had been her name.

Seraph caught a whiff of vanilla, it reeked of sex like any cheap scent. Meanwhile Ginny, with her pregnancy super-charged nose, thought Seraph's office reeked of mothballs. Perhaps the stench explained why she felt so sick? Or was it morning sickness? No, it was neither. *Keep calm, Sweetie. All we have to do is keep calm.*

'I'm bunking off work,' she said. 'It's my last week, and nobody'll miss me.'

Seraph, who hadn't stood up at Ginny's entrance, said nothing.

'Can I sit down?'

Seraph thought about saying no, but decided that risked giving Ginny the moral high ground, so she nodded towards the picnic chair leaning against the wall.

'Mind if I smoke?' asked Ginny, as soon as she was seated.

'Go ahead!' *Go ahead, stunt the runt! Poison it with alcohol! Help yourself to heroin and kill it off! Eat a Listeria sandwich, while you're at it.*

'You're probably thinking I shouldn't, because of the baby. I've cut right down from forty a day to ten or so.' Ginny attempted a smile. 'Got an ashtray?'

Seraph, who'd given up smoking when she came off the pill before conceiving Tom, shoved over the cracked coffee mug she kept for visitors' butts. Ginny took it, lit up and took a long drag. *Here we go, Sweetie.*

'I expect you're wondering why I'm here,' she began. 'It's for Nick.' This wasn't quite a lie. Assuaging her own guilt had the beneficial side effect of also helping Nick – and Seraph . . . who now laughed.

'To help him,' continued Ginny, nervously. 'I know you've moved out—'

'Of course I have.'

'Yes. But Nick loves you. He wants you back. He told me.'

'He should have thought of that before.'

Ginny wafted her cigarette, and long tongues of smoke licked about her head.

'Anyway,' she said, 'I've come to tell you my side of the story. I hope when you've heard it you'll be less angry with him.'

'I doubt it.'

'Be able to forgive him, even.'

'Save your breath. Nick's told me all I need to know.'

There was silence for a long moment. Ginny stared at the glowing red tip of her cigarette, and the ring of ash behind it. Seraph stared at *Eating for a Healthy Heart* the book she'd been reading before Ginny had interrupted her. It'd been sent by the American publishers of *The Anti-bloating Diet*. 'One in four of us will die of heart disease', began the blurb.

'I planned it,' said Ginny. 'The pregnancy, I mean.'

'Nick guessed. But what if you did?'

Ginny soldiered on. 'Did he tell you I finished things with him the moment I knew I was pregnant?'

Seraph shrugged.

'Who cares?'

'Did he tell you I didn't want him to find out about the baby?'

Seraph's eyes widened slightly, with surprise.

'What?' she said challengingly. 'You wanted to be an independent single mother?'

'Yes.'

Seraph remembered Fiona's hesitancy in the face of her own

conviction that, of course, Ginny must have wanted Nick to be involved in her child's upbringing.

'Free and self-sufficient?' *Positively charged values.*

'Yes.'

Seraph snorted.

'So what went wrong?'

'He didn't tell you how he found out?'

'No.'

'A colleague guessed – d'you know Margaret?'

'Margaret?' Seraph knew Margaret well enough.

'She's the one who guessed. She dropped hints to Nick and he cottoned on.'

'I don't care about any of this. All I care about is that you're pregnant.'

'Yes, but it's over between me and Nick – I mean it never was, really.'

'So what? Whatever you wanted at first, you and Nick are now bound together whether you like it or not.'

'I never wanted him for myself—'

'That's not my point. I said you're bound together whether you like it or not.'

Ash fell onto Ginny's skirt and she brushed it off. 'Look,' she said, 'now you know I used him . . . '

Seraph made a harsh sound. 'What? You made a grab for him, and got him?'

Ginny paused uncertainly. 'Well, yes,' she said, 'I suppose so . . .'

'And that's supposed to show me how I can forgive him?'

'It wasn't his fault.'

Seraph laughed again.

'Did you hold a gun to his head while he fucked you?'

'No but—' *What's wrong with the woman, Sweetie, why won't she play ball?*

'Oh, shut up.' Seraph turned to stare out of her window. It was a grey day, damp and drizzly. The gaudy lights on the municipal Christmas tree were blinking on and off, on and off, a fuse must be loose somewhere. Traffic was gridlocked. She could hear blaring horns and just in front of her office a taxi driver was yelling at a motorcyclist who'd clipped his mirror. She turned back, to face Ginny.

'So how will it work?'

'How will what work?'

'Joint parenting. Shared responsibilities.'

Ginny was silent – how would it work? She and Nick had yet to get down to the nitty-gritty.

'I thought so.' Seraph leaned in towards Ginny, who shrank away. 'I never want to see your child,' she said. 'You should know that. If Nick and I stay together, I wouldn't let him bring it into my home.'

'Absolutely not,' said Ginny, promptly. *You're mine, Sweetie. No stepmother for you.*

'And you know we have three children.'

'Mm.'

'I don't want mine to mix with yours.'

Ginny took another long pull on her cigarette, and glanced across at a row of snapshots of Tom and Daisy and Luke.

'Again, agreed.' *An onlie, Sweetie. With all the advantages that brings.* 'Although I suppose Nick might want—'

'Tough.'

Ginny waited before replying, 'True. I agree. With you.'

'And you don't want our money,' said Seraph, in a tone hovering between a statement and a question.

Ginny decided it might now be useful to admit one of the things she most hated admitting.

'I don't need it,' she said, trying to sound nonchalant. 'Nick never guessed, because it's a common enough surname, but my family owns the Cooper's supermarkets.'

'*What?*' Seraph had never met a millionairess before.

Ginny shrugged.

'Convenient,' said Seraph. 'So no contact between me and it, or between my children and it. No cash. If Nick and I stay together, those will be the rules.'

'I accept the rules . . . I hope you stay together.' *And you're not an it, Sweetie.*

'I said *if*, and I don't care what you hope.' Seraph stood up. 'With those things clear, we have nothing further to say to each other. You might as well go.'

Ginny stubbed out her fag, and also rose, slightly awkwardly, from her rickety chair.

'I didn't mean to drag him through all this. Or you either.'

'Ha!'

'I didn't . . . can you forgive me?'

Seraph looked at her.

'What? Forgive *you*? I thought you wanted my forgiveness for Nick?'

'That too.'

'No,' said Seraph, 'I don't forgive you.'

Disha had been looking forward to Ginny's return to reception, and was riveted to see that she was now close to tears.

'You okay? Need a Kleenex?' She plucked one from the box beneath the reception desk, and passed it to Ginny.

'Thanks,' said Ginny. 'Allergies.' It was true. She'd always known she was allergic to wives.

Outside in the square, Ginny zipped up her black leather biker's jacket, bowed her head against the cold wind, and contemplated failure. She felt shivery now, as well as sick. Perhaps she was going down with something. Or perhaps it was just that her visit had gone all wrong. She'd hoped for absolution from guilt, and hadn't got it. 'I don't forgive you.' She'd hoped to effect a reconciliation between Seraph and Nick, but if there was to be a reconciliation, she wouldn't be able to kid herself it had anything to do with her. And Seraph had laughed at her. Seraph had said, 'An independent single mother, free and self-sufficient.' Ha bloody ha! Ginny now panicked there'd be no way she'd be able to cope with Sweetie. She just wasn't cut out for motherhood. She'd need help. She'd need someone. But who? How dare Adam have got caught up in his bloody search for enlightenment? How dare he have left her to face the darkness alone? She started sobbing. *Sorry, Sweetie, sorry, sorry, sorry.*

Lots of people gave her curious glances, and one or two made as if to speak to her, but Ginny ploughed on through the Christmas crowds, regardless. Beyond the Christmas tree, with its erratically blinking lights, she found a bench, filthy with pigeon droppings, and sat down. Disha's Kleenex was by now a soggy mess, and she dropped it, another piece of litter added to the fast-food wrappers and the soda cans. Ginny felt as busted as the tree lights, as blasted as the ground, and she wanted to be fixed, spruced-up, comforted. She wanted someone to wrap their arms around her and whisper 'Hush!' She *thought* she wanted that someone to be Adam. The old ache was so familiar it never even ocurred to her she might have got fed up with missing him. But she did remind herself he'd never been very hot on comfort. She never had wept in his arms and wondered what it would have been like. He was a tall man, lanky, thin. If he were here now and had his arms around her, there'd be no spare flesh, just the hardness of ribs and muscles... Did she want that, or softness? He'd smelled of dope and incense and dusty herbs. Was that what she needed, or rather a hint of some flowery scent, coffee, lipstick and powder? His shirts and T-shirts and jerseys had been wool or cotton. Sometimes only the slip and rustle of silk would do.

Any of the drunks or junkies hanging round the square could have told Ginny she wanted her mother. But she didn't ask them. She just sat on her bench and cried for Adam, for herself and for Sweetie: *Sorry, Sweetie, sorry, sorry, sorry.*

20

As soon as Ginny had left her office, Seraph snatched up her phone and called Nick.

'It's me,' she said.

'Darling—'

'Did you put her up to it?'

'What? Are you—'

'I sent her away.'

'Who?'

'Ginny.'

'Ginny?'

'Yes.'

'What?'

'She came to visit me here – to plead for you.'

There was a long silence. Nick felt filled with dread.

'That was nothing to do with me. I didn't ask her to. I would've told her not to.'

'Sensible. It didn't work.'

'No. I—'

Seraph slammed the phone down before Nick could finish his sentence, then she sat and seethed for a while, before deciding to flee to the sanctuary of Café Beso. In reception Disha was pretending to be engrossed in an article in *Nova!* about silk-tipped nail extensions, but really she was keeping a look out for Seraph.

'All right?' she asked, too brightly, as her quarry passed.

'Yes. I won't be gone long.'

'Bookshop research?'

'That's it.'

'Borders on Oxford Street?'

'Mm-hmm.'

'I'll tell anyone who asks.'

The crowds thronging the pavements and impeding her way, made Seraph feel more furious than ever. She started to calm down the moment she pushed against the giant lipstick kiss on Café Beso's glass swing door. The air inside was humid, coffee-laden and comforting.

'Hi,' called Avi, from behind the counter. 'Where's Amy?'

'I haven't seen her today. Sick, maybe?'

'Yes? Hadar has flu, too.'

Seraph remembered Fiona mentioning the beginning of an epidemic.

'It's going round.' Seraph had by now reached the counter, where Avi and Hadar had placed a menorah in readiness for Hanukkah. She stood and caressed the *torta espresso à la Espagnol* with her eyes.

'Want a slice?'

'Yeah. But I won't. My diet.'

Avi laughed.

'You don't need to diet . . . so it's just the *caffè con leche*?'

'Yes.'

'Medium, with skim?'

'That's it.'

Avi turned to fiddle with the daunting coffee machine.

'We'll be off in the new year,' he said.

'Off?'

'We've booked the flights for the next leg of our trip.'

'Oh Avi! We'll miss you,' Seraph spoke with genuine warmth.

'Ditto. But we can't wait. New York here we come.'

'New York?'

'Yes, then westwards across the States.'

'I'm jealous.'

'You could do it.'

'Right. With three kids along for the ride.' And possibly a husband. Although possibly not.

'They'd love it.'

'It'd be hell.'

Avi grinned and plonked her coffee down on the counter.

'Sure about the cake?' he asked.

Seraph took her coffee to a free stool beneath a reproduction of *Le baiser de l'hotel de ville*, Robert Doisneau's casual, elegant photo of lovers kissing in Paris. But at the last minute she changed her mind, she couldn't face looking at an image of young love today, so she crossed to the opposite side of the café, where there was a sweet, sentimental poster of a small boy kissing a small girl. She slowly sipped her coffee, and tried to think about her situation in a systematic way. What was it Fiona had said last night? 'I don't know what Pete would have done if I'd agreed to have him back and asked him to abandon Bianca.' Could she offer Nick an ultimatum: me, or Ginny's baby? I'll come back, if you abandon all idea of building a relationship with this child, or, you build a relationship with the child and I walk out. But she quickly realized it wouldn't work. Whoever heard of an ultimatum that did?

'Marry me, or else.'

'Okay, or else.'

Or , 'Okay, I'll marry you' followed by years of resentment, deadly as cyanide.

Seraph was staring down into the milky surface of her coffee, wishing she could see the answers to her problems in its whirls and swirls, when she became aware of a body sliding onto the seat beside her.

'Hi,' said a familiar voice.

Seraph jumped.

'Jude! I was miles away.' She was sure she'd blushed, and beneath her clothes her skin was rising in goosebumps. *Stop this.* She told herself. *Stop this.*

'I could see that. Everything okay?'

'Yeah. And you?'

'Yeah.'

Jude didn't look okay, he looked tired, and his expression was even more brooding than usual. Seraph suppressed an urge to reach out and smooth a hand across his hair. She reminded herself he was sleeping with Amy, and that she had enough on her plate without any extra complications.

She took a breath, in preparation for asking him if Amy had flu, when he cut her off.

'Seen Eddie about your budget?' he asked.

'No. He keeps trying to pin me down, and I keep putting him off. Although it's getting harder. You?'

'I was in with him this morning.'

'And?'

'Terrible. Do you understand write down?'

'No.' Both Seraph and Jude were aware that write down was

something to do with the way the books they'd published depreciated in value as they sat gathering dust on the warehouse shelves, but neither of them had a clue how it was calculated, or what a write-down figure meant.

'Me neither. But mine's a joke. Or so Eddie said. And my bottom line's a disgrace.'

'Why? What is it?'

'Eddie didn't say. But not enough.'

'I shouldn't worry. Mine's bound to be worse.'

'That's true.' Jude's tone was teasing.

Seraph pulled a face.

'And don't forget you're an overhead,' Jude added.

'What?'

'An overhead. You, me, all of us. That was part of Eddie's little pep talk too.'

'Blimey.'

'Yeah.'

They sipped their coffees.

'So, how was it you got into this game?' asked Jude, after a moment.

'What game?'

'Publishing.'

'Dunno.' Seraph didn't like to admit that soon after she'd moved in with Nick, her ex-boyfriend's flatmate's boyfriend had wangled her a job as an assistant in the production department at a tiny company specializing in tax books, where he was a copy-editor.

'Who was it,' said Jude, off on a tangent, 'who talked about having his first literary orgasm when he discovered T. S. Eliot at fourteen?'

'No idea.'

'No, I can't remember either. But you remember that moment, don't you? When you first read something that made you jerk and gasp?'

'Um . . .'

'When I started work I wanted to publish books which did that. Books which would be read for a thousand years.'

Seraph took a couple of sips of coffee to hide her confusion, Jude was being embarrassingly sincere – this was almost as bad as listening to Cassie praying to the Great Mother.

'Really?' she said. 'Well, perhaps *www.God*?'

'What?'

'Or one of your others.'

'What *are* you talking about?'

'You know. The one you presented last week.'

'*Heaven.com*?'

'I knew it was something like that. Perhaps that'll be read for a thousand years.'

A split second later they turned to each other and spoke in unison.

'Fuck!'

They'd remembered that at that very moment they were supposed to be at the weekly acquisitions meeting.

'Shall we go back?' asked Seraph.

'You got anything to present?'

'That anti-bloating diet we didn't get round to last week.'

Jude raised one eyebrow.

'Let's stay,' he said.

Seraph didn't need much persuading.

'So,' she said, '*Heaven.com*'

'You couldn't even remember the title!'

'Okay. But if not that, then maybe —' she searched around for any book published by Jude which might still be in print in ten years time, let alone a thousand – 'Something by Shee-Chee Chen? *China Fun*? It won all those prizes.'

'Ah, Shee-Chee,' said Jude. 'Yeah. She's got a chance.'

Seraph wondered at the sadness of his tone and wanted to erase it. 'Anyway,' she said, reassuringly, 'think of me. Want to know what's in my in-tray at the moment?'

'Hit me with it.'

'A guide to depilatory techniques for hirsute women.'

'You're joking?'

'I'm not. It's by Iris Basham, an ageing beautician.'

'Iris?'mused Jude. 'Goddess of rainbows.'

'Really?'

'Yup.'

'Then I should introduce her to another of my authors, although I don't suppose she'd approve of depilation. But perhaps she would, she's got some funny ideas. Cassie Jones. Remember *Rainbow Power*?'

Jude laughed. 'Dye your hair indigo because there's too much greyness in the world?'

Seraph laughed too, as much at his pleasure as at his joke.

'That's it. And now she wants to do a sort of bible for this pagan, mish-mash feminist cult she belongs to.'

'A cult?'

'Mm. Members worship the Great Mother. They claim she's already been worshipped for four thousand years, but God managed to get her sidelined.'

Jude shrugged.

'You never know,' he said, 'if she's already survived that long what's another thousand years? What's-her-name's book could inspire generations of . . .'

'Scholars?'

'The weak-minded.'

Seraph did a double take. It was one thing for her to think the books she worked on were barmy, quite another for other people to agree.

'Oh, I'm sorry,' said Jude. 'I didn't mean . . .'

'I told her it wasn't one for us,' said Seraph in a slightly aggrieved tone. 'More something for a small, specialist press.'

'Oh I don't know,' said Jude, backtracking, 'It might sell. Even very well – all that wise-women stuff often does, doesn't it?'

'Mm.'

'Has she sent in a proposal yet?'

'Not yet. But apparently it's nearly written.'

Jude drained the remains of his espresso.

'I'd go for it,' he said. 'It's bad enough offending the garden-variety mother. You wouldn't want to risk it with one who'd been worshipped for four thousand years. Especially if she'd spent most of that time sulking on the sidelines.'

Seraph laughed.

'Cassie would be pleased. And I owe her, in a way.'

Fortunately Jude didn't ask for details.

'I can think of worse reasons to publish.'

'I suppose so. And if it doesn't sell it'll be no more worthless once it's written down than anything else.'

'True enough.'

'But don't tell Eddie I said so.'
'As if!'

If Disha hadn't known about Seraph's mysterious run-in with Ginny, and believed, along with the rest of Bladder, that Jude was having a fling with Amy, then their joint failure to show up for the weekly acquisitions meeting would have caused her to engage in some serious speculation. As it was the possibility was worth a second thought, but not a third one.

'Eddie's on the warpath,' she warned them the minute Seraph and Jude walked into reception.

Jude laughed.

'Oh God!' said Seraph.

'I shouldn't worry, Seraph.' This was Benedicta, who happened to be passing. 'We scarcely noticed you weren't there. It was *you* we missed.' She smiled at Jude as she spoke, and opened the door into a ground-floor meeting room. Jude immediately peeled away and disappeared up the stairs, in the opposite direction.

Once Seraph was back at her desk she phoned Eddie and left a grovelling message of apology on his voicemail. Then she sat and bit her nails for a bit. Her chat with Jude had temporarily shoved all thoughts of Nick and Ginny out of her head, but for once she wasn't thinking about her colleague's sex appeal, rather about his ambition. Jude wanted to publish books which would be read for a thousand years. She, on the other hand, wanted to publish any book which Eddie would let her get away with publishing, and which might help her meet her fictitious budget. She sighed, and thought about the two books she'd mentioned to Jude: *Hair Today* and *Ta Biblia*. Despite the lack of enthusiasm she'd shown to Cassie, she knew if she pushed hard enough in the acquisitions meeting *Ta Biblia* would make it through to publication – would be carried to term, as it were. And now she rather thought she would push hard enough. The other evening she'd dismissed *Ta Biblia* so summarily because she was annoyed with Cassie, but she was no longer really cross. And Jude might only have been trying to be polite, but he was right, *Ta Biblia* would probably sell. And if it didn't, so what? Most books were stillborn. On top of everything else, Cassie had been both kind and useful. Why shouldn't Seraph help her fulfill her desire to serve the Great Mother? What was the downside? Only the acceptable risk that Cassie might start lecturing her on how the Great Mother worked in mysterious ways.

Iris Basham's *Hair Today* was a different story. Seraph could never push for that, Eddie would think she'd completely lost her marbles, let alone her commercial judgement. She poked around on her desk, looking for one of Bladder's standard, pre-printed rejection cards, but she'd run out, so she left her office and went to the stationery cupboard to fetch a batch – they were the only stationery items whose use was still unrestricted. The wording on the cards was unequivocal:

> Thank you for submitting your manuscript to Bladder & Scrotum. It has been carefully evaluated by our readers and found to be unsuitable for our lists. Good luck with submitting it elsewhere.

As she wrote Iris Basham's address on the back, she suddenly remembered who it was that Iris's voice reminded her of – Vera Thompson, her long-dead grandmother's next-door neighbour. Vera Thompson had been a purveyor of home-made fudge, lemon curd, and other sweet delights. Her hair had been rinsed blue, she'd smelled of lavender, and she'd left puffs of talcum powder wherever she went. Seraph pounded one fist into the palm of her other hand, then ripped the standard rejection card in two. She hadn't changed her mind about *Hair Today*, but she knew she couldn't avoid writing a more personal note to Iris. Personal but unequivocal. The risk that Cassie might lecture her on the Great Mother was acceptable. The risk that Iris might misread words of faint praise was not. Seraph could just imagine the resulting chat if she did, it would be an instance, an example, of a conversation familiar to editors everywhere.

Author: It was generous of you to call my treatment *exhaustive*.

Editor: Er . . . (but *exhaustive* means *dreary*).

Author: And I fully understand why you called it *a little heavy handed*. I'm re-writing to take account of your comments.

Editor: Er . . . (and *heavy handed* means *unreadable*).

Author: It was so kind of you to mention it was *too special* for your list.

Editor: Er . . . (*it won't sell*).

Author: So I'll send you the revised proposal as soon as it's finished.

Editor: Great. Fine. Do that.

Nick had never quite got out of his mind Ginny's suggestion that he might dazzle his way back into Seraph's good books, and he thought now might be the time to see if she was right. With things between his wife and himself at such a low ebb – non-existent, really – it seemed obvious bribery couldn't do any harm. Even if it did no good, taking a chance on a trip to Tiffany & Co. was surely better than doing nothing?

Tiffany's was full of milling people, but the atmosphere was hushed. Here the normal clatter of commerce was deadened by thick carpeting and fur coats. Nick had never seen so many fur coats, all the female customers seemed to sport them. He'd always thought of skins as forbidden, and being surrounded by these totem objects added to his sense that he was in a place of mystery, a temple. Security guards and sales assistants took the place of priests, customers took the place of worshippers, and the jewels were unquestionably divine. He gazed around in awed stupefaction, and caught an assistant's eye. She was a beautifully groomed woman of mature years, who smiled and graciously inclined her head. Nick walked towards her, as confidently as he could.

The assistant got his measure at once – yet another man shopping for will-you-ever-forgive-me rocks.

'These are very classic,' she said, indicating a collection of necklaces, gold chains set with single diamonds at intervals along their varying lengths, 'and they cater to a range of budgets.'

Nick pointed.

'How much is that one?'

The assistant named a sum.

Nick gulped.

'Do you do bracelets?'

'Of course.' The assistant showed him a selection of the

cheaper ones. They were way more expensive than Nick had been expecting.

'What about brooches?'

The assistant was unfailingly polite and patient, and very skilful. After forty minutes or so she guided Nick back to the necklaces she'd first shown him. By now he thought the price seemed more than reasonable, so he didn't even go for the shortest chain, but one a few diamonds longer.

'An excellent choice,' said the assistant as she relieved him of his credit card. 'Wrapping won't take a moment.' Of course it wouldn't. This necklace was so popular with adulterers that, at Christmas, Tiffany's kept a supply ready wrapped.

As Nick was signing away a couple of months' mortgage, or a term's school fees, Seraph was anticipating another evening of lovely solitude. Cassie was out again, at Natasha's. Seraph had already phoned home to check on the children, who were fine, made herself a sandwich and poured herself a glass of Merlot. She'd taken her supper through to the sitting room, where she was perched on Cassie's sofa, wincing at the taste of the wine, it was from yesterday's bottle and had gone vinegary – Cassie, being teetotal, didn't own a vacu-vin. She sighed, and reached for her mobile to call Fiona. Once again Dominic answered the phone, and immediately passed her over to his wife, who put down the tapestry she'd been working on. Tonight Dominic didn't even wait for Fiona to shoo him away.

'I'll be in the study,' he mouthed as he headed out of the sitting room.

'Well?' said Fiona.

'She came to see me!' said Seraph.

'The flooze?'

'Yes. Ginny.'

'Oh Gaaawd!' Fiona remembered her own confrontation with Donna. 'So what did you do?'

'I told her to piss off, basically.'

'All you could do.'

'Yes.'

'So what now?'

'Dunno.' Seraph paused. 'But I've been thinking. Do you remember what you said last night?'

'About what?'

'About not knowing what Pete would have done if you'd agreed to have him back and asked him to abandon Bianca?'

'I remember.'

'Well, what if I tried the same trick?'

'What trick?'

'You know, told Nick it was me or the child. An ultimatum.'

Fiona was silent.

'I do know they aren't generally a good idea,' Seraph said, defensively, 'but . . .'

'You're right about that.'

'About them not being a good idea?'

'Yes.'

'Resentment?'

'Mm.'

'But what about *my* resentment?'

'I didn't mean to suggest it wasn't important.'

'I know that. Do you think, if we stayed together, I could possibly resist bringing this up every time we had a row?'

'I don't know.'

'Nor do I . . . it would take superhuman effort.'

Both women were silent for a moment, and Seraph took a sip of her wine. She made a disgusted sound down the phone.

'What's the matter?' asked Fiona.

'Nothing. It's just my wine's revolting.'

'Oh.'

'Anyway,' said Seraph, slightly changing the subject, 'why d'you think he told me?'

Fiona was distracted by thinking how much she'd like a glass of wine.

'Told you what?'

'About the affair. The baby.'

'Lots of reasons.'

'He'd have kept it secret if he could.'

'I don't know—'

'Of course he would've!' Seraph spoke urgently and loudly, Fiona held the phone an inch or two away from her ear. 'You surely don't believe he told me because he thinks there should be absolute honesty between us? No secrets? Transparency? Trust? . . . No! I bet he only confessed because he knew he could never keep a child secret from me . . .'

Seraph trailed into silence. Fiona cleared her throat.

'W-e-ell,' she began. 'Love—'

'Oh love!' spat Seraph. 'He *says* he loves me, but who's cutting off his options?'

'What?'

'You said yourself you cut off Pete's options.'

'True.'

'But apparently Ginny's made it plain she's not interested in a relationship, a sexual one, with Nick, only in this bloody child.'

Fiona knew that now was not the time to argue that no child is a bloody child.

'So?' She probed again, hoping not to set off another tirade.

'So at the moment she's the one cutting off his options. Nick says he loves me and he wants me back. But that's meaningless if Ginny's refusing to have him. If she's dumped him. Chucked him.'

'I don't see—'

'Oh, come on! If things were different and she were begging him to leave me, and set up home with her . . .'

'Like Donna.'

'Yes, then he might do it. He probably would.'

'Like Pete. But if I'd wanted him to stay, I'm sure he would've.'

'Then what about Bianca?'

'I don't know. It didn't happen.'

'Yeah. Back where we started. But can't you see that when he says he loves me, I'm left wondering whether he means it?'

Fiona rubbed the tip of her nose with the back of her hand.

'What?' she said. 'You think he wants you back because he figures if his mistress doesn't want him, being with the wife is better than being on his own?'

'Precisely. It's fine for him to blather on about loving me, but I could only know it was true if Ginny wanted him, and he chose me over her.'

There was a short silence.

'Well, from what you've said that isn't going to happen,' said Fiona.

'I know.'

'So?'

'So I need to come up with a test, but I just can't think what.'

After she'd hung up, Fiona went through to the study where Dominic was sitting at the desk writing a letter to his godson, who was trekking in Thailand. She slid onto her second husband's lap, curved one arm about his shoulders and placed her mouth against his ear.

'I'm so grateful,' she murmured.

'For what?'

'For you.'

Dominic turned his head, and their eyes met.

'Ditto. But don't be.'

Fiona laughed.

'You neither,' she said.

21

As soon as Seraph entered her office she saw the note Amy had scrawled in huge letters and left lying on her keyboard.

!!!!! AMY XXX.

Seraph didn't bother to take off her coat, she simply dumped her briefcase on her chair, and picked up the phone.

'So?' she asked, when Amy answered.

'Wait there,' said Amy. 'I'm on my way down.'

When Amy walked through Seraph's door she was fizzing in a way quite uncharacteristic of those recovering from twenty-four hour flu.

'Guess what?' she said.

'What?'

'We've got engaged!'

Seraph gasped.

'Wow!' she managed to say through teeth clenched in what she knew to be despicable envy. 'That was quick.'

'I suppose so.' Amy paused. 'In some ways.'

'Love at first sight. The clap of thunder. Lucky you.'

Amy laughed.

'Love at first sight?'

'More or less.'

'Who do you think I'm engaged to?'

Seraph failed to answer her question, so she repeated it.

'Who do you think I'm engaged to?'

'W-e-ell . . .'

'Not *Jude*, surely?'

Seraph flushed.

'You did! You thought I meant Jude!'

'Yes,' said Seraph, 'I thought you meant Jude.'

Amy gave her a knowing, playful glance.

'God no! Guess again!'

Seraph spread her hands, and shrugged.

'*Dave*.'

Seraph gasped, again. 'You're engaged to *Dave*?'

Amy flung her arms wide, and tipped back her head.

'Yes,' she said. 'Isn't it wonderful?'

Seraph laughed, and, belatedly, stepped forward to hug her friend.

'Yes,' she said into Amy's hair. 'Wonderful. Marvellous. Fantastic. Congratulations.'

They pulled apart and looked at each other.

'Congratulations,' repeated Seraph.

'Thanks. I'm so happy.'

'I can see that.' Seraph longed to ask how Amy had leapt from sleeping with Jude, to agreeing to marry Dave, in under a week. But a direct question seemed inappropriate.

'So it wasn't flu,' she said. 'Did he propose yesterday?'

'No. Tuesday evening . . . yesterday we went shopping for a ring. Of course, I wasn't going to wear one, but I thought there'd be no harm in looking, and we just happened to find the prefect thing. It'll be ready next week.'

'What's it li—'

'A square cut emerald, set in diamonds.' Jumped in Amy, whose eyes were shining.

'Sounds gorgeous.' Seraph glanced at her own sapphire and diamond flower. Hadn't she read of a place in New York where wives who felt they'd been short changed could take their engagement rings for an upgrade – swop their three carat whoppers for four. Perhaps if she stayed with Nick . . .

'Does everyone know?' she asked.

'We did a lot of phoning around yesterday. Our families know – they're delighted. Even Dave's parents, and you know what I think of them. And them of me. Next I'm going to tell Disha.'

Seraph laughed.

'The World Service,' she spoke affectionately.

'Uh-huh. So soon everyone here'll be filled in.'

The two women looked at each other.

'Everyone?' asked Seraph.

Amy folded her arms, and lowered her eyes.

'Do you mean, have I told Jude?'

'W-e-ell . . .'

'We've been avoiding each other all week. But I suppose I should say something. After all, it's thanks to him Dave and me are back together.'

'Avoiding each other?'

Amy unfolded her arms, looked up, and laughed.

'Oh Seraph, it was a disaster. Me and Jude, I mean. He's far too handsome for his own good. Makes him arrogant. He just lay back like some Hollywood mogul, and expected me to – well, you know. All he needed was the fat Cuban cigar.'

Seraph nodded, knowingly, although she'd have liked fuller details.

'And his conversation's pretty boring, too.'

'Is it?' Seraph's head jerked up in surprise.

'Well, perhaps not all the time. Perhaps he just didn't know what to say to me. All he could talk about was books.'

'Ah,' said Seraph, remembering her own embarrassment at Jude's sincerity in Café Beso the day before. 'And not self-help books, either?'

Amy laughed, but ignored the question.

'It was after I'd – you know – that I decided Dave was the one for me. He's everything Jude isn't – and I just knew in my guts he was the one. I'd known it for ages, but somehow I just couldn't admit it to myself. Anyway, as soon as I decently could I left Jude's place and headed out to Hitchin. Dave didn't muck around, or play any silly games. And we both decided, since everything felt so right, we might as well make it permanent. There just wasn't any point in hanging around any longer.'

After Amy had finished speaking they were both silent for a long minute.

'I'm so happy for you,' said Seraph, at last.

'Thanks.' Amy rubbed her ring finger, then shot Seraph a shrewd glance. 'But what about you?' she asked, carefully. 'Disha told me about some woman coming in yesterday. Was she who I think she might have been?'

Seraph looked out of the window, to the Christmas tree in the square. Its lights had now completely died. She looked back to Amy.

'Yes,' she said. 'She was.'

'Want to talk about it?'

'Not today.'

'Why not? Because I just got engaged? However dreary your news is, you simply can't depress me at the moment. So shoot, if you want to.'

Both women were standing. Now Seraph sat down, pointed towards the folding picnic chair, and watched Amy unfold it. 'I would have told you ages ago,' she began, 'but your thing with Jude made me shy.'

Amy laughed.

'You surely weren't jealous were you?' she said, teasingly.

'Jealous! No!'

'Oh, come on. Everybody fancies him. Now at least I've told you what you have to do to get him out of your system.'

'If he were ever in it. So what would that be?'

'Sleep with him, of course.'

Now it was Seraph's turn to laugh.

'Oh God!' she said. 'I suppose I was pretty dim to let him come between us.'

'Yes,' said Amy, 'you were. But now?'

'Okay,' said Seraph after a beat. 'You know, of course, that Nick's been having an affair?'

Amy nodded, then, in a low, even tone, Seraph told her everything. The rows, near-rows, proto-rows and misunderstandings. The mistress. The pregnancy. The misery. The whole shebang.

'So that's just about it,' she said at the end of her long, sorry tale.

'It's more than enough.'

'Yeah.'

'So what're you going to do?'

Seraph shrugged.

'What d'you think I should do?'

Amy pursed her lips.

'Dave and I both slept with other people whilst we were apart,' she said, 'and we're not going to let . . .'

'That's different.'

'I know.'

'There's just so much to think about.'

Amy hadn't devoured so many of Seraph's self-help books for nothing.

'You have to be selfish,' she urged her. 'Whatever you do, it has to be what's best for you.'

'And the kids.'

'Isn't it the same?'

'Probably.'

'The past is dead and gone. You need to put this behind you and move on.'

'Yes. But where to?'

'I don't know. Only you can answer that.'

'Well that certainly helps.'

Seraph pulled a face at Amy, and in reply Amy stuck her tongue out at Seraph. Childish, but the gestures of friends reconciled.

When Amy knocked on his door, Jude was sipping coffee from his *China Fun* mug while checking page proofs for *Bamboo*.

'Oh. It's you,' he said, very gracelessly.

'Yes.'

'So? What is it?'

'I came to tell you – I thought I should, although perhaps you might think I needn't have bothered. There's no real reason—'

'You've come to tell me what?' cut in Jude, sharply. She was pregnant? Although not by him. She had Aids? But even if neither of them had intended to, they'd practised safeish sex. Herpes? What?

Amy took a deep breath.

'I've got engaged. To Dave. My long-time boyfriend. We split up for a bit and . . . and . . . and . . .'

There was a moment of stunned silence. Then Jude cleared his throat. 'Congratulations.'

'Thanks – I just thought you might want to know. I . . .'

'So what were you doing?' asked Jude, in a mild tone. 'Using me to double check you were sure about someone else?'

Amy turned bright red.

'Of course not,' she said. 'No! Not at all—'

Jude held up his hand and smiled.

'It doesn't matter,' he said. 'I don't mind – much – and I'm really sorry about – you know – I'm really pleased for you.'

Amy smiled back.

'Thanks,' she said. 'I'm sorry, too.' Then she gave him a sly, sideways glance. 'And you?' she said. 'What were you using me for?'

Jude blushed.

'Nothing.'

Amy looked him full in the eye.

'Oh, come on.'

Jude made a rueful noise, halfway between a sniff and a laugh.

'Oh, okay,' he said. 'But keep it to yourself.' Then he told her about the way Shee-Chee had him in her thrall, and how he wished she didn't. Of course he didn't say he'd hoped sex with a desperate, undemanding woman would boost his ego and help obliterate Shee-Chee's memory, but Amy wasn't stupid.

'Poor you!' she said at the end, very tartly. But then she relented. She was too happy to be truly furious with him, and the main emotion she felt was astonishment that Jude and Shee-Chee had been able to keep their liaison secret in a world so obsessed by gossip. 'The past is dead and gone,' she said, for the second time that morning. 'Don't cling to it. Don't grasp after it. Let go of your anger. Relinquish, and move on.'

Jude looked at her.

'You sound like a self-help book,' he said.

Amy laughed.

'Have you ever read one?'

'No.'

'You should. They're great. I'm addicted.'

'Mm.'

'Anyway. About you and Shee-Chee —' Amy's glance fell on the *China Fun* mug, emblazoned with Shee-Chee's face – 'you could throw that away for a start.'

'This?' Jude held up the mug.

'Yes.'

'Why?'

'What's the point of surrounding yourself with little reminders?'

'You're right.' Jude tipped back his head and downed what remained of the coffee, then held out the mug to Amy. 'You have it!'

'I don't want it,' she said. 'Smash it!' She nodded towards his metal wastepaper bin. 'Sling it in there!'

Jude felt a little foolish, but he pulled back his arm, and flung the mug forcefully into the bin. He scored a direct hit, and the mug smashed against the side with a satisfying clatter.

'Feeling better?' asked Amy.

Jude grinned.

'Thanks,' he said. 'It does feel better to have told someone.'

He stood up, and after the briefest hesitation on both their parts, they simultaneously moved towards each other, and hugged.

'I'm glad we did that,' said Amy, smiling up at her ex-almost-lover.

'Me too.'

Once Amy had gone Jude shoved aside the *Bamboo* proofs. Almost every other book he'd ever worked on had slipped back in the production schedules at some point during publication, so why should Shee-Chee's be any different? And *Bamboo* was nowhere near as good as *China Fun*. It was just a fraction away from being too special for his list. Instead of slaving over Shee-Chee's exhaustive moralizing and her heavy-handed plot, he'd make a start on some catalogue copy Benedicta kept pestering him to produce.

22

Disha was not only an excellent conduit for Amy's news, she also quickly organized her a party. After work that evening the entire Bladder staff de-camped to the newly opened Z'Bar, to celebrate. None of them except Disha and Jude had yet tried Z'Bar. It was very small, very dark, very smoky, and painfully trendy. A pool dotted with floating candles and floating flower heads was set into the floor just inside the door, to help ensure good Feng Shui. A row of niches ran along the wall opposite the bar, each one containing a serene, gilded statue of the Buddha, a candle, and an incense holder filled with smouldering incense. The low wooden tables were decorated with terracotta bowls which also contained floating candles. Seraph was lucky enough to bag one of these tables, and was quickly joined by Gill, Edo and Benedicta, after a while Lucian turned up, too.

Z'Bar was way too noisy to encourage normal conversation, but Gill and Edo were bravely shouting to each other above the din, engrossed in the niceties of South African slang. Meanwhile Lucian and Benedicta were being ostentatiously lovey-dovey – the French sculptress had moved back to Paris a few days before. Seraph nursed her white wine in silence, and watched Jude, at the bar, hollering into the ear of a tall, tawny haired beauty who might well have been a model. Seraph couldn't help but wish them ill, and she was pleased to see the model looked a little bored – Jude was probably trying to interest her in literary orgasms. This jealous reverie was interrupted when a waitress bent down and bellowed in Seraph's ear.

'Excuse me!' she yelled. 'Are these yours?'

All the waitresses here were drop-dead gorgeous, waitresses-in-waiting for something better to come along. This one now looked pointedly at Seraph's feet. Seraph followed her gaze. She'd been to the local street market in her lunch break, and a potted chrysanthemum and three grocery bags, overflowing with vegetables, lay in a higgledy pile on the floor by her chair.

'Yes.'

'Can you move them? They're getting in people's way.'

Seraph knew she was the only person in Z'Bar encumbered by bags of vegetables and a potted plant, but refused to be intimidated by that fact. She leant down, picked up the chrysanthemum, and placed it on the table in front of her, then shoved at her grocery bags with her foot, so they shifted a millimetre or two. That would have to do – there was no other available floor space, it was all taken up by expensively shod feet. She smiled up at the waitress, who scowled, but stepped aside, just as Amy eeled her way over through the crush.

'Here,' she yelled, shoving a bowl of Japanese rice crackers and a tumbler of vodka, in Seraph's general direction. 'Take these.'

'Thanks.'

'I've got to go.'

'Back to Dave.' Disha had phoned him, but he'd not been able to make it to Z'Bar from Hitchin.

'Yeah. He's arranged for us to go over to his parents' tonight.' Amy pulled a face.

'Now, now.' Seraph wagged her finger.

Amy smiled.

'Am I obviously sloshed?' she asked 'Everyone's been buying me drinks.'

'You seem fine.'

'Good,' she paused. 'Eddie's giving me a lift to the station any minute.'

'Yes? He's probably pissed too.'

Amy looked stricken. She'd taken to heart years of drink-driving campaigns.

'I hope not.' She took a handful of the rice crackers she'd so recently thrust upon Seraph and nibbled on a couple. 'I just wanted to check you were okay, before I headed off.'

'Don't worry about me. I'm fine.'

'Sure?'

'Yes. Thanks for listening this morning. I didn't want to mar your day.'

'You didn't.' And nor had Jude, with his tale of woe.

Eddie weaved over to them. He looked shattered, but he flung his arm round Amy jovially enough.

'Ready?' he asked.

'Ready,' she said. 'But are you okay to drive?'

'Oi! Since when were you my wife?'

'That's not fair . . .'

'Don't worry. I've been on mineral water all evening. Boring, isn't it?'

After Amy and Eddie had left, Seraph gulped down the remains of her wine, and started on her second-hand vodka. She too would have to leave soon, as she'd promised to cook Cassie a thank-you meal tonight – and over dinner she'd announce she'd be delighted to see sample material from *Ta Biblia*. The vegetables were for a vegan casserole, and the chrysanthemum was for her hostess, too. Seraph had spent ages choosing the colour, in the end going for a deep bronze, a compromise between red, yellow, orange and brown. She'd chosen a chrysanthemum because she'd had a vague notion it was an Eastern symbol of long life and happiness. But now it occurred to her that perhaps she'd got it wrong, and the chrysanthemum symbolized death? One way or the other, Cassie would know . . . and she surely had happy beliefs about the afterlife, to cushion her from distress should the chrysanthemum mean death? No doubt they were given extensive coverage in *Ta Biblia*.

Seraph smiled to herself as she imagined Cassie in an afterlife just like this one, but greyer and more shadowy, and filled with ghostly vegan feasts. Then she finished Amy's vodka in a long, smooth gulp, before leaning back in her chair, trying to summon the energy to get up and go. But it was hard. She was washed by ripples from other people's conversations, lapped by smoky incense, and woozy from the drink. She turned her head and fixed her gaze on the candle flickering beneath the heavy lidded, placid eyes of the nearest Buddha. Her mind drifted. And drifted. And drifted . . . until it was a blank. A nothing. A void.

For the moment Seraph was just being, just existing. But if she'd been capable of remembering all the guides to meditation she'd published over the years, she might have allowed herself a flicker of pride at the fact that she'd entered a light, meditative trance so easily. The books made it sound so hard. All of them contained variations on a fairly daunting set of instructions which Seraph would, under other circumstances, have been able to quote by heart:

The ideal environment for meditation is safe, quiet, warm and comfortable. Minimize potential distractions by unplugging the phone, and asking other people not to disturb you. If you choose to use music in the background, make sure it is calming and melodic, without lyrics to vie for your attention. You may burn incense if you wish. Concentrating on a lighted candle may help free your mind from the ceaseless background chatter of consciousness. A candle flame has the added advantage of helping to define a sacred space about you.

If you are a newcomer to meditation, either sit in a comfortable chair, with your back properly supported and both feet planted on the ground, or lie on your back on the floor. Keep you body open – do not cross your arms or legs. This way you will be most receptive to the glorious future, which we embrace so joyfully during meditation.

The importance of the breath cannot be over emphasized. Controlled breathing is the first step towards relaxing the mind. Breath deeply and slowly, through your nose. Focus on your breath, and make sure to use your lungs in their entirety. This means inhaling into the lower tips of your lungs, and exhaling fully, from the lower tips, up through your chest. If it helps, make a tape of your voice guiding you through breathing: inhale, 2, 3, 4; exhale 2, 3, 4; inhale 2, 3, 4; exhale 2, 3, 4, and so on and on, into a trance.

No author had ever recommended readers attempt to meditate while sitting in a noisy, smoky, crowded bar, immediately after consuming a glass of wine, followed by a double vodka. But despite these irregularities, an observer would soon have noticed that Seraph, oblivious to her own behaviour, was taking long, slow inhalations through her nose. If this observer had been interested in rhythm, he or she would soon have established that after each inhalation, Seraph's whole chest rose for a count of five, and then slowly subsided to the count of five. Inhale 2, 3, 4. Exhale 2, 3, 4. Inhale 2, 3, 4. Exhale 2, 3, 4. Inhale 2, 3, 4. Exhale 2, 3, 4 . . .

A good-looking young man sporting designer stubble and wooden-framed spectacles eyed Seraph warily, before tapping her on the shoulder.

'Excuse me? Are these yours?' He held up an onion and an aubergine.

'What?' Seraph swayed and spoke groggily.

'These. They were on the floor, and I noticed you had some shopping bags.'

'That's an onion?'

'Yes. And this is an aubergine.' The young man spoke slowly, patiently, and glanced at his female companion, a glam goth with long black hair extensions.

'You want to know if they're mine?'

Wooden spectacles and glam goth exchanged a knowing look. 'Yes.'

Seraph felt the first prickings of self-consciousness, and tried to pull herself together.

'I think they are,' she said. 'I think they're mine.'

Glam goth leaned over.

'Tell you what. Why doesn't Lysander just drop them back in that shopping bag, while you make up your mind?'

'Good idea,' said Lysander, and did as his friend had suggested, then the two of them turned away, back to their drinks and their fags.

For Seraph, it was a bizarre re-entry from the world of nothing, of absence, of emptiness to this world of things and happenings. She slumped motionless in her chair for several minutes. Then she suddenly gasped and jolted upright. The reason? She'd just embraced her glorious future, or it had reared up to crush her in a bear-hug. Either way, she'd suddenly realized she knew precisely what she was going to do about her marriage and her children. Her career. Her life. She had a plan. It had been delivered to her whole, complete and perfect from nowhere at all. Or from somewhere deep inside herself. Or as a gift from the Great Mother. Or something. Seraph was delighted. It was a brilliant plan. A map to guide her as she entered unknown territory – a map whose scale was 1:1 with her own life. She threw back her head and laughed aloud. Lysander and glam goth turned to stare at her.

'It's all right,' she said. 'I'm going – You can have my chair.'

23

The key to Seraph's new map didn't include a symbol for closed doors, but here she was, first thing on Friday morning, hovering outside Eddie's office, and facing a door which was firmly shut. Her conviction that she was following the right route began to waver. If Amy had been sitting at her desk, she might have asked for a second opinion. But Amy hadn't yet made it in from Hitchin. Seraph told herself nerves were only to be expected, and it would be madness to allow them to knock her off course. It wasn't a very convincing spiel, nevertheless she took a deep breath, and rapped on the door. Eddie called for her to come in. He was at his desk, on the phone. As she entered he cupped his hands over the mouthpiece.

'What is it?'

'It's—'

'Sorry? What was that? Projections for third quarter figures?' Eddie spoke into the telephone.

'It's just—'

'But I sent them over to Jerry yesterday – well?' The *well* was to Seraph.

'It's about my continued employment here at Bladder.'

Eddie's head jerked.

'Listen,' he said to his interlocutor, 'something's come up. I'll call you back.' He banged the receiver down, and gave Seraph his full attention.

'What?' he said.

'I've come in to resign. It's not that . . .' Seraph intended to
tell him it wasn't that she was unhappy at Bladder, or dissatisfied,
or frustrated. She intended to tell him it was creative burn out,
in the fairly confident expectation he wouldn't ask her what she
meant by that.

'What?' said Eddie again. 'You're resigning?' He reached for
his mug of coffee, and took a sip.

'Yes.' Seraph steeled herself to meet all Eddie's objections.
She was sure he wouldn't simply let her walk out the door. But
he was less crestfallen than she'd anticipated, and simply looked
at her levelly, over the top of his mug.

'Are you sure?'

'Positive. It's because . . .'

Eddie waved a hand, vaguely.

'Oh. Because.' He paused. 'Are you sure you're sure?'

Seraph wondered whether to be peeved by his lack of curiosity
about why she wanted out, or grateful that it would probably
make life more peaceful for her. Gratitude won.

'Yes, I am.'

'Where are you going?'

'Nowhere.'

'Nowhere?'

'I'm just quitting. I've nothing lined up.'

'Is this some sort of temporary delirium?'

Seraph glanced down at Eddie's shabby carpet. Was it some
sort of temporary delirium?

'I don't think so,' she said. 'It's because . . .'

'You don't *think* so?'

'It's not.'

'Good.' Eddie put down his coffee, carefully positioning it on a bound proof of *'Ere We Go*, a collection of sporting anecdotes he'd commissioned from one of his journalist friends for far too much money. 'I ask because I'm not going to try to persuade you to stay. I accept your resignation – it's nothing personal, I'm not unhappy with your performance. Particularly. I'm not dissatisfied with the direction in which you've taken the list – your growth of the men's health area I regard as a coup. It's just that—'

'Just that what?' Seraph had bristled on *particularly*, and her tone was sharp.

Eddie squirmed in his seat.

'Um,' he said.

'What?'

'I probably shouldn't tell you this – keep it to yourself – but it's just that our profitability's taken a bit of a knock this year.'

'The bottom line?'

'Yes. It's down. Way down. Confidential, of course, but the bankers are on at me. We have to make economies.'

'The stationery?'

'More than the stationery.' Eddie shifted uncomfortably, and twisted his hands. 'Nobody knows this yet, not even Amy, but they've recommended a headcount squeeze.'

'A headcount squeeze?' It sounded like something Iris Basham would provide.

Eddie slammed his palm down onto his desk, making all his papers dance. Coffee slopped onto *'Ere We Go*.

'Fuck it!' he said. 'I have to make redundancies. That's why I need to know if you're sure. Because I wasn't going to have got rid of you – but if you do want to go, someone else's job is saved.'

'Great!' said Seraph, but not bitterly. 'So now I'm morally obliged to resign to save someone else.'

'Edo, actually,' said Eddie. 'He was on the list, but if you go, I'll cross him off – Look, if you change your mind before you leave this office, I'm happy to keep employing you. But if you want to go, I'm equally happy to let you. It's economics, pure and simple. If you quit, I mean quit, quit, if it's not some sort of bargaining ploy—'

'What about Amy?'

'She's too cheap to bother cutting. And my PA's essential.'

Seraph looked at him. They both sighed.

'I quit quit,' said Seraph, determinedly. 'I'm not bargaining.'

Eddie grunted, but said nothing.

'So you're not going to replace me?'

'No chance in the current economic climate.'

'Then who'll look after my list? And all the authors?'

'Dunno,' said Eddie. 'Gill? Edo? Since he's been spared I might as well use him. Benedicta, perhaps?'

'*Benedicta?*'

Eddie hesitated a moment.

'You're right,' he agreed. 'Not Benedicta. But don't worry, I'll find someone. The list will be fine. And the authors.'

Seraph didn't share Eddie's confidence, but she couldn't discuss her worries with anyone, because she was now stuck in a double limbo land – the limbo land of the already resigned but not yet disappeared, and the limbo land of those in the know, but not allowed to tell. It was a difficult day. The news that she'd quit spread round the office like wildfire, together with a rumour that she was moving to Compass Press, where she'd been offered an editorial directorship. Seraph said nothing to encourage the rumour, but nor did she say anything to scotch it, since she didn't want to answer the questions which would result if she did. She felt compelled to avoid Amy, because she didn't want to be wheedled into divulging full details of her plan before talking to Nick. Every time she passed Edo on the stairs she blushed scarlet. But even difficult days come to an end, and soon enough she was on the tube, heading north to Athens Road.

Seraph stepped into her own home for the first time in almost a week and was momentarily disorientated by an unfamiliar smell, reminiscent of Greek holidays and retsina. Then she remembered the huge Christmas tree in the sitting room – it was pine she could smell.

'I'm home,' she called as soon as she was satisfied she was in the right house. There were wild yells from the kitchen. Tom and Daisy exploded into the hall, and flung themselves at her, both of them were carrying sheets of paper. After the initial flurry of kisses and hugs, Tom thrust his into her hands.

'Look, Mum,' he said, jumping up and down with excitement, 'a Martian. From art. We could choose what we did. I did a Martian.'

Seraph took Tom's Martian, all green glitter and pipe-cleaner antennae and held it away from her for a better view.

'This is lovely. We'll put it on the kitchen wall,' she handed it back to Tom and gave him a kiss, then turned to Daisy. 'And what's this?' Daisy's sheet was creased and grubby.

'The hundred board,' she said proudly. She had written all the numbers from one to one hundred in a grid.

'Clever girl.' Seraph kissed Daisy. 'This can go on the wall, too . . . where's Luke?' The question was directed at both her children.

'In the kitchen,' they replied together.

Seraph wriggled out of her coat and hung it up, then held out a hand to each child.

'Let's go and find him,' she said.

In the kitchen Luke was sitting on the floor by the toy box, eating Fruity-Os with furious determination, and Kate was leaning against one of the counters looking grumpy.

'Hi love,' said Seraph, to Luke.

'Hi,' said Kate, to Seraph.

Luke ignored Seraph, and Seraph ignored Kate. Instead of greeting the woman who'd done her job all week, she crossed the room, knelt on the floor by her youngest child, and gave him a kiss.

'Don't worry, Luckie-boo, I'm not going to take the Fruity-Os from you.'

Kate was exhausted, absolutely shattered. Her work load this week had been quite ridiculous. With Seraph absent, and Nick mostly so, she'd virtually been a full-time mum. And to *three* kids! Meanwhile, Richard and Sandra had been nag, nag, nagging her to resign. Perhaps it was time to listen to them. She'd willingly, *willingly*, put her own life on hold to help Seraph through her crisis . . . and now Seraph couldn't even be bothered to say hello! Let alone thanks. Kate came to a snap decision.

'Seraph,' she said, coldly, 'can I have a word'

Seraph was trying to give Luke a butterfly kiss, and he was crossly resisting.

'Can't it wait?'

'A word in the sitting room.'

Seraph glanced up. 'In the sitting room?'

'Yes, it's about . . .'

'Oh God!' Seraph stood up, she was beginning to smile, even though she knew she shouldn't. 'I can guess. It's about your continued employment here at —' she nearly said Bladder, but checked herself in time – 'I mean, your employment with us.'

Kate was puzzled and upset by Seraph's reaction. She hadn't expected her announcement to be met with relief.

'Yes,' she snapped. 'Actually it is.' *And good riddance!* she thought.

24

'Well she's removed one obstacle,' observed Seraph, who was sitting at the kitchen table with a glass of wine.

'Who has?' asked Nick. He'd just returned to the kitchen after a brief foray upstairs. 'The children are all asleep, by the way.'

'Good. Kate has.'

'Kate has what? Apart from resigned.'

'Removed an obstacle. What's that you're hiding behind your back?'

Ever since Nick had arrived home husband and wife had been treating each other with an exaggerated, awkward politeness. But now Seraph's tone was uninhibited, interested. Nick took a step towards her.

'Ta-ra-ra-ra!!!!' He trilled, and, with a showman's flourish, made a box appear. A significant box. Seraph had never been in the presence of Tiffany packaging before, but she'd have recognized it anywhere. Was there any woman in the world unfamiliar with that particularly seductive shade of turquoise? Nick, the adulterer, thrust the box at his wronged wife.

'Open it!'

Seraph pursed her lips and imagined pulling at the bow of white silk ribbon, she could almost feel its satin slide between her fingers.

'Go on!'

She'd prise off the lid, and inside would be a soft pouch, and inside that pouch . . .

'No thanks,' she said.

Nick looked crestfallen, but Seraph pretended not to notice.

'Shall we order Chinese?' She nodded at the Tiffany box. 'I'll think about that afterwards.'

Nick said nothing. Seraph got up.

'Right. Chinese. I'll go and phone the Hot Wok.'

Over at her flat, Ginny couldn't face food. Today had been her last day at S&M, and Tony and Jean had invited her out for a valedictory drink, but she'd turned them down – and not only because she'd guessed they wanted to pump her for gossip. The shivery, sick feeling she'd first experienced after her disastrous encounter with Seraph had got steadily worse over the past couple of days, and now she felt truly terrible. She'd taken a couple of paracetamol – her books assured that it was safe in pregnancy – and was already in bed, still fully dressed, because undressing had seemed such an effort. Despite clothes and the duvet, she couldn't keep warm. *It's that virus,* she muttered to Sweetie, *the one that was doing the rounds in the office.* She felt so grotty she didn't even want a fag, and her head thumped so badly she didn't properly notice she had tummy ache. *Or not tummy ache, Sweetie, not exactly. More of a muscle ache.* More of a cramping pain. A period pain – but she didn't think of that.

Seraph couldn't remember how she'd lived before home delivery. She ordered spring rolls, Singapore noodles, chicken with cashew nuts and string beans in chilli and garlic sauce. Back in the kitchen she put the Tiffany box on top of the fridge, next to the baby monitor, then, in near silence, she and Nick shoved the rubbish littering the table to one side. When the food came, it was packed in foil containers and neat white cartons decorated with red dragons. Together they laid these out, opened the packets of chopsticks provided by the restaurant, poured wine, and then sat down to eat.

'So?' said Nick, serving himself from the container of shiny, slippery noodles.

'So,' said Seraph, through a mouthful of spring roll.

'Well?' Nick kept his gaze on the chopsticks in his hand. He knew if he looked away he'd drop his food.

Seraph used her own chopsticks to pick up a cashew, and chewed on it. When she'd swallowed, she looked directly at her husband, and pointed her empty chopsticks at him.

'What do you want, Nick?'

'What?'

'What do you want? It's an easy enough question.'

Nick put down his chopsticks, and picked up his glass.

'You know what I want. To be with you, and the kids and—'

'So you say. But you haven't gone about showing me it's true in a very sensible way.'

'I know, but—'

'What if I'd chucked you out, and Ginny had been willing to take you on?'

Nick shrugged.

'What if?'

'Would you then have been begging me to have you back?'

'Of course.'

'So you say.'

'Oh come on, Seraph, you know I—'

Seraph laughed.

'You love me? Just words, Nick.'

'No.'

'Yes. I've been thinking I ought to set you a little test. Words won't do. It has to be action.'

Nick stared down at his noodles, they looked like a pile of innards, as if someone had taken the guts from a bunch of animals and just dumped them on his plate.

'Okay,' he said, 'a test. So what do I have to do?'

It seemed to Nick that Seraph ignored his question.

'Kate wasn't the only one who resigned today,' she said, 'I did, too. And Eddie accepted my resignation.'

'What?'

'You heard.'

'You resigned?'

'I did.'

Nick thought she'd regret her action in under a week, and couldn't see what it had to do with their marriage.

'Fine,' he said. 'Anything you want.'

'Gee, thanks.'

'I'm sorry, I didn't mean . . .'

'It's okay. I just decided we can't go back to what we had before, and we can't stay where we are right now.'

Agreed, thought Nick, *but where's this going?*

'So you quit?' he asked.

'Yes. And what's more I want you to go in on Monday and quit too.'

Nick's whole body jerked.

'What? Are you serious? You want me to quit S&M?'

'Why not?'

'A million reasons. The mortgage. School fees.' Nick raised his hands in a helpless gesture.

'Money?'

'Sure.'

'I'll get to that in a moment,' said Seraph. 'I want us to make a clean break. Start afresh and build something new. Together.'

Nick swallowed, and tried to make his tone placating.

'I can understand that. But if I weren't at S&M what would I do instead?'

'Tons of things!'

'But I enjoy my job.' Nick thought of his office, with its door, of his company car, of his trips to Europe. He knew an office door was no reason to stay in a job, but still . . .

'So?' said Seraph. 'Think of quitting as making a sacrifice for a greater end.'

'But—'

'Are you honestly telling me you burn to sell household cleaning products?'

'The product's not the point.'

'Then what is?'

'Challenge. Status. Intellectual stimulation. Interacting with other people. The salary.'

'We can get by without the salary.'

'Balls!'

'And me and the kids can provide challenge, stimulation and interaction.'

Nick just looked at her, and Seraph shrugged.

'Okay,' she said. 'But it wasn't what you wanted from life, was it?'

'What wasn't?'

'Marketing. Remember your poems? Remember *Acting Up?* The screenplays?'

'Yes. But the poems were twenty years ago. Everyone has crazy ambitions.'

'But *Antidote?* That's not years ago. That's work in progress.'

Nick pulled a face. 'This is mad,' he said.

'What's mad about being a writer?'

'Right. Or a composer, a painter, a pop star, a footballer.'

'People become all those things. Are you saying never try?'

'Of course not, it's just—'

'Good. So, I ask you again, do you burn, do you yearn, to sell household cleaning products?'

Nick prodded his noodles with one of his chopsticks.

'Okay,' he said, 'suppose I quit. Do you think I could become a screenwriter just like that?' He clicked his fingers in front of Seraph's face.

'Don't you want to?'

Nick was silent.

'You see.' Seraph pressed her point. 'You would if you could.'

Nick kneaded his eyes.

'I'm pushing forty, don't forget,' he said, patiently. 'And do you think we could afford our lifestyle if I didn't sell your despised household cleaning products?'

'I don't despise them,' said Seraph, truthfully. She could imagine life without laundry powder and washing machines all too well. 'And just forget about money for the moment.'

'Yeah, why not?'

'Please, I—'

'And what message would being jobless send to the kids?'

'That there's more to life than wage slavery. You're pushing forty. So am I. Halfway through our lives. I've quit. Join me. Let's spend a few months thinking about what we want to do with the time we have left.'

'The time we have left? Christ! We're not in the grave—'

'Yet.'

Ginny was desperate for a pee, but could scarcely drag herself to the bathroom. In the end it was either get up, or wet the bed, so she got up. Her room swirled around her in a mad, dizzy whirl, and she staggered as if she were drunk. By now her stomach ache was so insistent she couldn't help but pay it attention, both with her body, clenched teeth, a sheen of sweat, and, all at once, with her mind. She'd just about reached the bathroom when she felt the ice of recognition. *Jesus! Sweetie, is this normal?* No, mum-not-to-be, it certainly wasn't. When Ginny got to the loo, she found blood in her knickers, and also a lump of clear jelly-like material.

Seraph lifted her hands from her lap and folded them across her chest.

'Now I'll tell you how I plan to deal with the money,' she said, firmly. 'We'll sell the house—'

'What?'

'And move to something smaller in the country. We'll move to the real country, not suburbia, just as I've always wanted to.'

Seraph would get trees and fields. Nick would get time for pen and ink. They'd each get the other, and the children. That was the essence of her plan, plus a bit of jiggery-pokery to deal with Ginny and her baby. And if Nick refused? If he called her bluff? Then he'd find out she wasn't playing at negotiation. She was for real. The independent single woman. The self-sufficient divorcee. She wasn't so old she couldn't take on new roles. Even with three automatic anti-freedom-units in tow.

'If this is just about escaping London,' began Nick, 'then—'

'We'll make a ton of money on this place.' Seraph cut in. According to local estate agents Athens Road was 'desirable, sought after, close to shops, schools and all local amenities'.

'What if we didn't? What if we couldn't sell?'

'We will, and then we won't buy, at first. We'll rent. I'm sure we'll make enough to rent a *palace* a couple of hours up the M1, or somewhere.'

'Renting,' said Nick. 'There you go, your built-in opt-out clause.'

'It's not that, but you have to be realistic. We'll obviously take time to settle in to a new area, to check things out, see how we like it. It makes sense to rent until we're sure we know what we want. Until we're comfortable in our new surroundings.'

Nick ran his hands thorough his hair.

'Moving's hell,' he said. 'Sheer hell.'

'But sometimes better than the alternatives. And think! We'll have no mortgage. There'll be a village school, so no school fees. Kate would have been a responsibility – helping her find a new job, and such. But, like I said, she's removed herself as an obstacle.'

'Yes,' agreed Nick, 'but we'll have to replace her.'

'Why? We won't be working, so we won't need a nanny.'

'That would mean your not working *long-term*.'

'Not just me. *Us*.'

Nick ignored that. He looked aghast.

'Resigning from Bladder's one thing, but not working at all – you'd go mad. The kids would have you climbing the walls. At least during school holidays. And Luke's still at home most of the time.'

'I said *we* won't be working. Anyway, even Luke'll be at school soon enough. And if I'm on my own I'll just have to get used to looking after my own children. Millions of women do it.'

'If you're on your own?'

Seraph looked at Nick, and Nick looked at one of the cartons of Chinese food. He stared so hard he saw its decorative dragon start to move in long, sinuous curves. He didn't speak until it had slid right off the box, and onto the table.

'Okay,' he said, addressing the dragon, 'and just look at them.'

'Look at who?'

'Stay-at-home mums.'

'You don't know any.'

'No, but I bet they're all fat and wear flowery dresses.'

'For God's sake, Nick!'

'It's true. And even if we slashed expenditure, there'd still be gas, electricity, clothes, shoes, food—'

'Stop this! If we could get by, you'd quit, wouldn't you?'

'Perhaps,' said Nick. 'Perhaps if we could get by, I'd quit. But the point is, we couldn't get by. And you couldn't just uproot the kids like that. Tom and Daisy love St Bernard's. Luke seems happy enough. All their friends live round here.'

'They'd adapt. They'd have us around so much more. That would have to be worth something.'

'Perhaps. But isn't relocation meant to be one of the worst things you can do to children?'

'Yes, but probably not as bad as their parent's getting divorced.'

Once again Seraph looked at Nick, and Nick looked at a twisting, looping dragon.

'So,' he sighed, 'you really are threatening me.'

'It's not a threat. It's a solution.'

'I don't see—'

'I'm giving you a second chance. I'm giving us a second chance. Us and our family.'

'But Seraph—'

'A chance for us to think about our lives and how we want to live them.'

'I know. But—'

'A chance for us to redefine our marriage.'

Nick picked up a string bean in his chopsticks, and moved it towards his mouth, then changed his mind, and put it down again.

'So what's the idea?' he asked. 'We quit, sell up, move to the country and all live happily ever after?'

'More or less.'

'It's just a stock fantasy, Seraph, like travelling the world or moving to the South of France, or something.' Nick was trying hard, but he couldn't help a note of irritation creeping into his voice.

'A stock fantasy? A cliché?' Seraph's voice was also rising. 'I know a couple who are travelling around the world.'

'So?'

'So stock fantasies can be real.'

'Who is it then?'

'Avi and Hadar.'

'Who?'

'They work at Café Beso, round the corner from the office.'

'Baristas? Yeah, right, and how old are they? Twenty?'

'That's not the point – anyway, if we're talking about stock situations this one's hard to beat – man has affair with younger woman—'

'She wasn't—' began Nick, intending to point out that Ginny was not that much younger than Seraph. Luckily Seraph cut him off.

'Who gets pregnant. You're the one living in a cliché – although I grant you're not doing the really obvious, corny thing, and walking out on me and the kids.'

'Exactly,' said Nick, eagerly. 'Because I—'

'Because you love me? Or because Ginny won't have you? See, we've come full circle and I haven't even got to that part yet.'

'What part?'

'How my plan deals with Ginny and her baby. How my stock fantasy butts up against your stock betrayal. Of course, I've thought about that too.'

After Ginny had found the telltale scarlet in her knickers, she'd spent a frantic few minutes trying to contact a doctor. There was nobody in her GP's office, but a recorded message told her to call an overnight cover service. Which she did. It was engaged. When she got through, a secretary took her details and told her someone would ring back. Ginny hunched by her phone, white with pain and other things. Twenty minutes later an overworked locum was taking her case history.

'So,' he said accusingly, 'you haven't actually seen your GP yet?'

'I told you. I did a home test.' Ginny whispered.

'A home test?' The locum sighed. Women got confused about dates all the time. Women misread test results. This one was probably bothering him with her period. 'To order a scan I need an official result.'

'I calculated I'm about eight or nine weeks pregnant.'

'And now there's a bit of spotting?'

'And something like jelly.'

'Jelly?' The locum's tone changed. Jellybabies weren't just sweeties. Real babies were made of jelly too – at least when they were still the size of their candy counterparts. Jelly meant the woman on the other end of the line had probably been pregnant, and now she wasn't. Bye, bye, baby. 'Do you have health insurance?'

'Yes.'

'Then we'll get you a scan. That'll confirm whether you're actually pregnant. Or were. *If* you are, it'll also let us see what's happening. Is Holy Family okay for you?' Holy Family was a local private hospital originally, but no longer, linked to a convent.

Ginny couldn't answer. She'd begun to cry.

Nick felt sick.

'Go on then,' he said. 'How exactly does your plan deal with Ginny?'

Seraph's tone became crisp, and businesslike, even legalistic. 'I'm not asking you to renounce the child,' she said. 'I'd like to, but I'm not. However, like I told you before, I'm quite clear I never, ever want to meet it, see it, talk to it, buy it a birthday present, or anything else. I don't want the children meeting it, either, although I know we'll have to tell them about it.'

There were many things Nick had tried to avoid thinking about recently, one of them was how Tom, Daisy and Luke would react to the news of their new half-sibling.

'No we won't,' he said. 'Not necessarily.'

'A little brother or sister? Come *on*. And I suppose when they're older they might ask to meet it.'

'But—'

'Be quiet. In short, what I'm saying is I don't want to be reminded of it. Or of Ginny. Or of this whole episode. If we move to the country it puts *space* between me and my children, and Ginny . . .'

'Space? Ginny's no threat to—'

'. . . and her child. When you want to see it, you can catch a train and disappear for the day. Out of sight, out of mind. And no danger of my accidentally bumping into it, or her, while I'm playing with our lot in the park.'

Nick took a deep breath. Was this what Seraph's plan was all about? Was it about fleeing a child? His child. Or a woman?

'You surely wouldn't let her hound you out?'

Seraph looked at him scornfully.

'She couldn't. I'd see her in Antarctica before I thought about moving an inch because of her. No, if I wanted to stay, I'd stay, but I don't. And if we moved out, that would just happen to – clarify things – about your access visits. *Distance.* It's an incidental advantage, a sort of by-product.'

Nick tried once more to pick up a string bean. Once more he changed his mind before he got it to his mouth.

'Okay,' he said. 'Suppose I did quit. Suppose we did move. What then? What would we do in the country?'

'Nothing, for a bit. That's what I keep trying to tell you. With house prices the way they are the money we made on this place would easily fund six months off work for both of us – and that's allowing for buying somewhere else at some point.'

'Six months off?'

'Time for us to be together as a couple, and as a family. Time for you and me to sort things out, to talk, to dream, to plan, to—'

Nick held up one hand.

'Okay,' he said. 'But what happens if we quit and the house won't sell.'

Seraph shook her head, to quiet him.

'Time for us to play with the kids, read to them, muck around. Go on outings, picnics. All that family stuff.'

'We do all that now.'

'Not much. Not often . . . Six months off. And if, at the end of it, things couldn't be sorted, then at least we'd know we'd given it our best shot.'

They were both silent, considering things not being sorted.

'Okay,' said Nick, after a few moments. 'Let's suppose I quit. We sell the house in ten days and make a packet. Suppose we rent a cottage with a big garden, by a lake, in the middle of woods miles from anywhere. We spend six months or so just chilling with each other and the kids. What happens at the end of that six months?'

'I just said. We have to face the possibility we'll decide to split.'

'I didn't mean that,' said Nick. 'I meant what happens about getting back to normal? Getting back into the job market, and stuff. How would we explain the gap in our CVs?'

'We'd say we'd taken a sabbatical, if we needed to say anything at all. Career breaks are nothing these days. But we might decide to start our own business, or go freelance, or to retrain as teachers.'

'*Teachers*?'

'It's just an example. I meant something socially useful.'

'Yeah,' said Nick. 'Bags I get to be a brain surgeon.'

'Nick,' said Seraph, 'our marriage has got stuck. It has to change, or it'll die. *We* have to change. I'm giving you the chance to show me—'

'I know,' said Nick, quickly holding up his hands. 'I know. I'm sorry. Really. But your whole plan's . . . fuzzy round the edges. And that's being polite.' He ran his hands through his hair again, and left it sticking up all over his head in strangely sculptured tufts. 'You're absolutely serious about this, aren't you?' he went on, 'you're convinced we have to make this change?'

'We certainly need to do something. And like I said, I want deeds, not words, from you.'

'Buying a gift from Tiffany didn't count?' Nick wasn't sure whether he meant this seriously, or not.

They both glanced towards the box on the fridge. Seraph

smiled, but said nothing. Her smile encouraged Nick to risk a small joke – a small joke which was *clearly* a joke.

'How about two weeks in the Caribbean without the kids?'

Seraph shook her head.

Nick gazed at his noodles, and his stomach churned. He stood up, carried his plate over to the bin, and tipped the cold food into it. Noodles slid downwards in a greasy, gelatinous mess.

'Do I get to think about this?' he asked as he watched them go.

Seraph waited before replying, 'Do you need to?'

On the NHS scans were office hours only, but in the private sector the service was twenty-four hours a day, seven days a week. Ginny was lucky it was late, because the waiting area in the obstetrics department at Holy Family was deserted. If she'd come in during the middle of the day, she'd have found herself surrounded by obviously pregnant woman, their bellies swollen to various degrees. Revolting to anyone – but especially to a woman in her condition. At this hour there was only her and a nurse. The nurse smeared her tummy with some cold, wet glop, then applied an ultrasound device to the flesh. A magic wand. Except medicine isn't magic, and nurses can't work miracles. Abracadabra, walamazoo, I shall make your baby live, psheww. No chance. This nurse sat at her screen, switched it on, and moved the ultrasound device back and forth for a minute or two. Then she looked at Ginny.

'I'm sorry,' she said. 'I'm very sorry.'

Holy Family wasn't short of beds, and Ginny was kept in overnight. This wasn't just a cynical exercise in economics. She was hysterical. And also single. The medical authorities felt they couldn't send her home to an empty flat, and anyway she needed a D & C in the morning, to scrape away the retained products of conception. The procedure was done under a general anaesthetic. When she woke up, Ginny's womb was squeaky clean, but something had gone wrong with her vision; the world had been drained of colour and everywhere were shades of grey. Once again, Ginny longed for encircling arms. The warmth and comfort of yielding, scented flesh. Clothes which rustled as she pressed her cheek into their softness. Someone whispering 'Hush!' It didn't matter there weren't any drunks or junkies about the place – this time Ginny didn't need to be told who she needed. She didn't need much at all. At Holy Family the sheets were fine linen, each room had its own DVD player and the catering had been contracted out to the Ritz Carlton. Naturally Ginny had a bedside phone. And, okay, a phone cord wasn't an umbilical cord. It couldn't reconnect her to her dead baby – but it could help reconnect her to the world of the living. Ginny picked up the receiver and made a call.

It was still early on Saturday morning. Audrey had not yet dressed. When the phone rang she was sitting in her silk dressing gown, holding a diamond bracelet up to her bedroom window, admiring the way the thin ribbon of ice froze light into rainbows, and remembering. She was a woman on the brink of old age. Whatever these bits of stone had once meant to her, they now meant memory. A memory of beauty where beauty had passed. A memory of power to a woman now powerless. They glittered of the days when she'd been able to flirt and tease. She loved these diamonds because they sparkled of what it was like to be young – and also because she had nothing else to love. Nothing and nobody. Her husband had spurned her. Her daughter had spurned her. What could a woman do, under such circumstances, but find herself a love object which would never, ever turn its face away? Of course, she could have opted for a dog. But dogs die. Diamonds didn't. They were indomitable.

Audrey continued to hold the bracelet aloft as, with her free hand, she reached across her dressing table for the phone.

'Hello,' she drawled, in her ageing, but still honeyed, voice.

'Oh mum,' sobbed Ginny, 'oh mum.'

It was Sunday afternoon, and the Jamiesons had just returned from lunch at their local burger joint. Already chaos had descended.

'It's mine!' Tom was yelling, of a cheap plastic monster which had been given away with his Kidz Eatz Megabox. Or perhaps not his Megabox, but Daisy's. Or Luke's.

'No! It's mine!' Daisy was pulling Tom's hair, and trying to wrestle the toy from his grasp.

Luke was lying on the kitchen floor, pounding his feet and fists against the red lino.

'Luke want it! Luke want it!'

'I can hear the phone,' Nick shouted to Seraph above the din. 'I'll just go answer it.'

After Seraph had asked Nick if he needed to think about starting afresh in the country, the two of them had talked into the small hours. A deep talk, and meaningful. Later, in bed, they'd screwed. The missionary position – and neither of them had fantasized about someone they shouldn't. Things were definitely on the up – but that didn't stop Seraph now shooting her husband a murderous look.

'I'll go,' she said, sweetly. 'You deal with this lot.'

A moment later she was back.

'It's for you,' she said, looking her husband straight in the eye. 'It's Ginny's mother.'

'Her *mother*?'

'That's what she said. She said it was urgent. That Ginny's staying with her. I didn't ask any questions.'

Alerted by their parents' voices, and their body language, the children all shut up, and stared from their own mother to their father – who'd blanched. Now he silently left the room. By the time he returned, they'd forgotten their dispute about the Kidz Eatz monster, and were sitting quietly round the table, collaborating on a craft project. They scarcely glanced up as Nick walked up to Seraph and put his arms around her, for his comfort, not for hers.

'She lost it,' he said.

Seraph held her husband in her arms. *Go on!* whispered a voice in her head. *Smoke! Stunt the runt! Poison it with alcohol! Help yourself to heroin and kill it off! Eat a Listeria sandwich, while you're at it!*

'Oh! God!' she moaned aloud 'Oh God! Oh God!'

EPILOGUE

Seraph's and Nick's six months of productive idleness was nearly up. As Seraph had intended, Nick had used the time to recommit himself to writing, although *what* he'd decided to write had taken her by surprise – he'd chucked in *Antidote* in order to focus on a practical guide to downshifting, or downsizing, or living simply – he was still establishing his terminology – but, anyway, a bible for those disillusioned with the fast lane. Seraph herself had not yet decided what she was going to do with the next phase of her life, and the future was much on her mind as she sat on a train making stop–start progress up to London from her new base in Wiltshire. That morning she'd joked to Nick that she was off on mission impossible: 'Your mission today, should you choose to accept it . . .', Not that she felt she'd had any choice, the duty had been imposed on her twice over, first by Cassie, then by Jude. 'I like him enormously,' Cassie had said during the course of an anguished phone conversation, 'but he is a man, and I just don't feel he gets what I'm trying to do.' Her doubts were justified. 'I just don't get any of this stuff,' Jude had said when it was his turn on the other end of the phone. Seraph had murmured reassurances, and promised each of them she'd be there when Cassie committed the recently completed manuscript of *Ta Biblia* to her new editor's tender care.

After Eddie had announced he'd settled on Jude as her replacement, Seraph had thought nothing about publishing could astonish her. Jude had felt much the same way. So had everybody else at Bladder. The only person who'd pretended it was a good idea was Eddie, who'd justified himself with a metaphor: editors were taxi meters, he'd explained, clicking up costs every minute they were at work. So it made sense to achieve economies of scale by doubling up lists – fiction and self-help, children's books and biography, cookery and dictionaries and so on and so forth. 'Of course I'm looking around,' Jude had confided to Seraph, during the same conversation he'd admitted he didn't get the books he'd been instructed to publish.

'I don't blame you,' she'd replied.

'And what about you? What're your plans?'

'Still ill-defined. I want to do something worthwhile.'

'Worthwhile?' Jude had asked. 'Personally I always thought you'd make a great agent.'

At the time, Seraph had laughed, but she'd immediately seen the sense of Jude's suggestion, and she was balancing pros and cons as her train crawled towards London. To agent or not to agent? That was Seraph's question. She knew the ground, and she could use all her publishing contacts. On the other hand, she'd quit because she'd wanted – and still wanted – a fresh start. Did hopping over the fence from editor to agent count? Or was it chickening out? But if so, chickening out of what, precisely? But then again, she'd pick up two authors without even trying: Cassie and Nick. Yes, and she'd at once get pigeon-holed as someone who dealt only in New Age and self-help. Did she want that?

Questions such as this occupied her all the way to Bladder. As she stepped through the door she saw Amy and Disha chatting at the reception desk. Both women looked up as she entered – both did double-takes. Disha, who was in the middle of painting her nails bright green, whistled.

'Clock the rocks!' she said.

Seraph blushed.

'You mean my necklace? Nick gave it to me last Christmas.'

'Blimey. Whatever happened to soap on a rope?'

'I know it's a bit dressy,' said Seraph, 'but I don't get much chance to wear it.'

'You can wear it for my wedding,' said Amy, who knew the history of the necklace.

'You should ask to borrow it,' suggested Disha. 'Something borrowed . . .'

Seraph laughed.

'How're the plans going?' she asked, meaning Amy's wedding plans.

Amy looked gloomy.

'Oh g-a-w-d! The dress is proving a nightmare. Can you spare the time to come up and look through a few bridal magazines with me?'

Today Amy was in a livid blue, one of the colours of putrefaction. Seraph's head filled with an image of her friend floating down the aisle, not so much giant meringue as giant puffball fungus. She laughed again. Amy thought she was scoffing at the idea of bridal magazines.

'I know you think they're crap,' she said huffily, 'but a girl's gotta do what a girl's gotta do.'

'True,' said Disha. 'But Seraph's wanted. Cassie's already gone on up,' she spread her vibrant emerald nails for the other two to inspect. 'Spring Fever. Like it? I'm going to try to find a leaf design for a bindi.'

Jude openly called his new area of responsibility the self-hinder list, and privately called the books on it non-book books, as opposed to the book books of his fiction list. He didn't usually tolerate having non-book books in his office, but as a sop to Cassie, he'd scattered a few across his small meeting table, on which the newly delivered manuscript of *Ta Biblia* was also prominently displayed. The script was surprisingly thin, Seraph looked at it, and at the books, all of which she'd commissioned, and her thoughts returned to her earlier question: to agent or not to agent?

'Hi,' said Jude, cutting into her mini reverie.

He was still sex on a stick. Seraph was plunged straight back into a more arresting debate: to Jude or not to Jude?

Not to Jude. Not in the past. Not now. Not ever. Seraph gave herself a quick talking to. Temptation, she argued, was inevitable. Probably. Temptation didn't signify, it was what you did with it that mattered – unless you happened to be the Pope, which she, self-evidently, wasn't.

'Hi,' she replied.

'Seraph you look positively blooming,' said Cassie, who was sitting by the table, on a spindly sofa which she'd overwhelmed in yards of flesh and mauve crêpe de Chine.

'Thanks. You too.'

'But I was just saying *he's* looking a little peaky.' Both women looked at Jude, who blushed.

'Next time I'll bring you a bottle of lithosomatic liquor.' Cassie promised him 'Jadeite as a general pick me up.'

Jude tried to return Cassie's smile. He failed.

⸺

Half an hour later editor, ex-editor and author were deep in discussion of *Ta Biblia's* section on hymns to Astarte. These had been written by Daughters living in places like Hendon and High Barnet – places within easy reach of Cassie's house in Golders Green,

'Listen to this,' commanded Cassie, holding up a manuscript page. 'It's by Natasha Crewe.'

'That Hecate woman?' asked Jude.

Cassie frowned.

'Yes,' said Seraph.

'It's one of my favourites. A paean of self-praise.' Cassie cleared her throat. 'Beyond the veil of love and death,' she intoned in a sing-song voice. Jude and Seraph composed their faces into listening expressions, which became more and more frozen as Cassie read.

'I am Astarte.
I am queen of the three worlds, such is clear.
Earthly. Heavenly. Subterranean.
I rule the seasons of the year.
I am the lady of love and childhood.
I like to keep my Daughters near.
Those who fear me need not fear.
Those who hate me I shall pierce with my warrior spear.
Hail my Daughters!
Some among you will penetrate the mystery of my veil.

Some will not.
I accept the tribute of all those who choose
With me to sail.
I accept your love.
Accept my wrath in gratitude.'

The word *gratitude* faded to a silence which extended several seconds too long.

'But that's—' began Jude, looking stricken.

'Absolutely delightful,' said Seraph, very firmly.

'Veil and sail?' asked Jude. 'Veil and sail?'

Cassie missed his incredulity.

'It *is* clever, isn't it,' she cooed. 'Natasha's is an elevated soul, she has an elevated sensibility. The feeling behind this hymn is very intense.'

'Granted,' said Jude. 'I respect that. Of course I do. And I suppose she didn't try to rhyme Astarte with party.'

Cassie looked puzzled.

'Why would she?'

Seraph cleared her throat. Jude ignored her intervention.

'But,' he continued, as if to himself, 'wasn't one of those goddesses a Renaissance symbol of the defence of knowledge and intellectual development? Isis, was it?'

Cassie looked at him, blankly.

'I expect so, dear,' she said. 'Now if you don't mind I want to talk about the cover. Have you had any ideas?'

Jude looked at Seraph, imploringly, but she gave a tiny shrug.

'A fully opened sunflower?' he hazarded. 'I'd thought perhaps a fully opened sunflower?'

'You had?' Cassie was astonished. 'Is that some sort of Bladder trademark?' Luckily, she didn't wait for an answer. 'I don't like to be stroppy, but in this case I really can't see the relevance.'

They got through the meeting somehow, and by early afternoon Seraph was travelling back to Wiltshire. Now she was established in arcadia she liked to claim London was a clammy hand throttling the south-east, and she was happy to leave it behind. One of the advantages of becoming an agent would be that she could do it from anywhere. If she did it. She still wasn't sure. Before she'd bidden goodbye to Cassie, she'd casually slipped in a question about her plans now that *Ta Biblia* was finished, and Cassie had explained she was keen to start work on a guide to the pagan year, just as the two of them had discussed the previous winter. Seraph had been in on the genesis of the idea, and the prospect of selling it to a publisher was certainly appealing . . . or sickening, depending which way she looked at it.

The cottage Nick and Seraph had rented was eerily quiet when she let herself in.

'Hello?' she called, at the top of her lungs, as she entered the kitchen through the back door.

'Down in a sec,' Nick yelled from upstairs – he was in their bedroom, which doubled as his work space. A few minutes later he came into the kitchen brandishing a sheaf of paper – his day's output.

'Hi, love,' he said, giving his wife a quick peck on the cheek. 'Can I read this to you later? It's on sound financial planning prior to chucking the rat race.'

Seraph laughed.

'Just like we did. Where are the kids?'

'Tom went over to Tom L's after school, and Daisy and Luke are with Grace.' Tom L, Tom Lockhart, was their Tom's new best friend. The two boys spent hours playing mysterious games in Tom L's very large garden. Grace was a local widow, who had four adult children. Only one, her younger son, had so far produced grandchildren – and he lived in New York. Grace borrowed children the way some people borrowed cups of sugar.

'Good,' said Seraph. 'And of course I'd love to hear what you've written – but I warn you, I might have an ulterior motive.'

'It sounds a splendid idea,' said Nick, when his wife had finished filling him in on her thoughts about becoming an agent, 'but I'm not paying you a percentage.'

Seraph put her hands on her hips and mock glowered at him.

'You might not get the chance. Even if I do become an agent – if I do – I might not handle self-help.'

Nick laughed, and dropped his papers onto the kitchen table – the same one they'd had in Athens Road, and as messy as ever.

'Pretty flowers,' said Seraph, nodding at the jam jar in the middle, it was filled with cow parsley and buttercups.

'Daisy picked them.' As he spoke, Nick reached into the fridge for a couple of cans of beer.

'A bit early, isn't it?' chided Seraph.

In reply, Nick opened a can and held it out to her.

Seraph was easily persuaded. She reached across to take the beer, and as she did so, her fingers brushed Nick's. The two of them met and held each others' eyes.

'Did I mention that's a great necklace?' asked Nick.

Seraph smiled, not so much at her husband's mild teasing, but at the expression in his eyes. She saw a flintiness in Nick's gaze, and sensed it in her own. It was the flintiness of soldiers, standing shoulder to shoulder as they fought back the enemy. It was the flintiness of an adult love, with deep roots. She raised her can and tilted it towards him.

'A toast,' she said. 'Today's the day. So seize it.'

ACKNOWLEDGEMENTS

Thanks to Teresa Chris, Imogen Taylor, Liz Davis, Andrea Castañeda and Alex Milne.

I worked as an editor on self-help books for a number of years, and I am indebted to that genre, and to the authors working within it, especially to Dr Michael Apple.

I got the idea for lingerie in the colours of the body from a book called *Better Sex* by Glenn Wilson and Chris McLaughlin, published by Bloomsbury in the UK. I used an excellent book called *Having Your Baby: A Guide for African American Women* by Hilda Hutcherson, published by Ballantine Books in New York as a source for most of the information in Dr L.L.O Case's fictitious books. The lists approach mentioned in connection with *Baby Manual* did NOT come from Hilda Hutcherson's informative and sensible book, which seems to me to have relevance far beyond African American women. The advice on breast examination came from *The Royal Society of Medicine Encyclopedia of Family Health* by Dr Robert Youngson, published by Bloomsbury in the UK. I apologize if traces of other self-help books remain unacknowledged and would be delighted to put right any omissions which were brought to my attention. I browsed a range of books for ideas for the kinds of thing Cassie might say to Seraph about coping with the discovery that Nick had been unfaithful. The leaflet supplied with Ginny's home-pregnancy test is based on real leaflets supplied with popular brands. Various men's magazines also supplied ideas.

In addition to self-help books, I also used, or misused, the following two books: *The Forest for the Trees: An Editor's Advice to Writers* by Betsy Lerner, published by Penguin Putnam in New York – for information on the way editors talk to writers; and *The Routledge Companion to Literary Myths, Heroes and Archetypes* edited by Pierre Brunel, published by Routledge in the UK – for ideas about the (made up) Daughters of Astarte's (inaccurately presented) story.